THE
SUMMER
PARTY

REBECCA HEATH studied science at university,
worked in hospitality and teaching, but she always
carved out time to write. She lives in Adelaide,
Australia, halfway between the city and the sea
with her husband, three children and a much-
loved border collie. She spent her childhood
summers at a remote beach not unlike where the
novel is set. This is her debut adult novel.

THE
SUMMER
PARTY

REBECCA HEATH

An Aries Book

First published in the UK in 2023 by Head of Zeus,
part of Bloomsbury Publishing Plc

9 7 5 3 1 2 4 6 8

A catalogue record for this book is available from the British Library.

ISBN (PB): 9781804541005
ISBN (ANZTPB): 9781804540992
ISBN (E): 9781804540978

Cover design: Emma Rogers

Printed and bound in Great Britain by
CPI Group (UK) Ltd, Croydon CR0 4YY

Head of Zeus
First Floor East
5–8 Hardwick Street
London EC1R 4RG

WWW.HEADOFZEUS.COM

For my Sisters – Fiona and Kirsty

Thank you for always being there. Beach summers and heartbreaking farewells alike.

29 JANUARY 2000

The heavy beat of the music thrums through the girl's body in time with the pounding of her heart. She's alone for a moment in the crowded party, but then she sees him across the room and nothing else matters. He's leaning against the mantel, all languid grace, and he's talking to someone else, but when he catches her eye, he winks. And an actual shiver races down her spine.

He's going to meet her later, outside, under the vine-clad arch by the fountain at the foot of the garden. A place for privacy. A place for lovers. Her body warms at the memory of the promises in his lips and his expert hands.

There are butterflies, too.

She hasn't done anything like this before, but she trusts him not to hurt her, physically at least. She has no illusions about what a boy like him will do to her heart. But with her third glass of the delicious punch almost empty, she can't bring herself to care. Because he's chosen *her*.

The hours pass in a blur of music and dancing and more punch, and trying not to pinch herself to be certain this is actually her life. When she finally winds her way through the garden to the rendezvous, she stumbles twice. Intoxication and nerves make her knees tremble.

The twinkling fairy lights mark the paths as if someone has caught the earlier fireworks in tiny glass spheres. White and yellow flowers bloom in perfect stars, their tropical scent heady in the warm night air. She wonders, as the lights spin around her, whether she should have been sipping water these last few hours.

No. Courage was needed, and it's not like she's out of control. A few missing minutes, but nothing important. She takes a breath, fights nausea. No regrets.

There's a boy already there in the shadows. He lifts his head. Clearly, he's been waiting for her. Her heart trips in its beat. 'You?'

He moves closer, more assured than she would guess. 'Were you expecting someone else?'

Her lips part to answer, but he's right in front of her now and lowering his head towards hers. 'You look so beautiful,' he whispers.

His intention is clear but there's plenty of time for her to back away. She doesn't.

One kiss won't hurt even if he's not... She lets his mouth claim hers. And the butterflies in her belly roar into dragons. She never expected this. Not with him.

He makes a sound of encouragement and she arches closer. His hands slip from her shoulders to her waist, to the curve of her hip. Heat skitters from the contact, and she kisses him deeper. His fingertips find skin left bare by the summer dress. Her breath catches. The faint sounds of the distant party are lost in their heavy breathing and the ricochet of her pulse in her ears. Thoughts of interruption are fanciful; they are truly alone here.

She could scream, and no one would come.

He pulls back a little. She feels the absence of his touch like an unexpected pain, and it's all she can do not to whimper.

His hand brushes her hair back from her face and he stares into her eyes.

Don't speak, she thinks. *Don't ruin it.*

The angry scrape of footsteps approaching on the concrete path overrides the distant music.

The boy's eyes widen. Suddenly, he's leaving, ducking away from the footsteps, in the opposite direction to the lights and the rest of the party. The girl hesitates to follow; after all, he didn't ask her to go with him, and she isn't sure where the edge of the cliff lies.

Someone stops just the other side of the archway. The girl is completely hidden unless she moves.

The music volume jumps, now so loud the bass is a vibration rather than a sound. The girl strains to listen through the foliage, catching a grumble of voices. Two, she thinks, but they're low and tense and she doesn't recognise them. Not definitely. The night's drinking and what she's done in the dark is catching up with her. Tears sting her eyes. She just wants them to leave.

There's a cry. Or maybe a scream. The gut-twisting sound of someone in pain.

The girl's body tenses, ready to move, to go to them and offer assistance. But before she can take a single step, there's a new voice. This one is maybe familiar, she thinks, but her whirling brain can't be sure. She leans towards it. The tone holds anger rather than concern. The scream must have been her imagination.

Her whole body is burning. So much for privacy.

Then there's only the sounds of the party drifting on the breeze.

Wait, was that a splash?

She delays a bit longer, hoping whoever is close by will have left. Hoping to avoid questions about what she's doing there. She tries to count to twenty but loses track at thirteen. It's enough. When she steps out from the archway, there's no one in sight.

SHOE FOUND WASHED UP BENEATH JETTY 'MAY CONTAIN HUMAN REMAINS'

A beachcomber walking beneath the jetty in the bay by Queen's Point, two hours out of Adelaide on South Australia's Yorke Peninsula, has found a shoe containing suspected human bones, police have said.

Officers were alerted to the discovery by a local man at about 5.30 p.m. on Thursday and moved quickly to investigate and cordon off the area. However, they reported finding nothing else in the water. The shoe in question was found caught between two chunks of driftwood and there was no sign of a body.

A police spokesperson said the shoe's contents 'do appear to be human remains'. They have been taken to a forensic mortuary for examination.

Police refuse to speculate on the owner of the remains or where the rest of the body might be and have ruled out it belonging to any bodies already in the morgue. However, with no one in the town having reported a foot missing, talk around the area assumes it most likely belongs to someone passing through, or that it must have drifted in on the current from further up the coast.

1

PRESENT DAY

It began with Harry Whitlam buying Lucy a creaming soda, and the flip in her belly when their fingertips touched. But, if she's honest, she probably fell in love with all three of the Whitlams that summer.

Lucy Ross takes one hand off the steering wheel and brushes the pocket of her handbag, feeling for a telltale bulge in the fabric. There is none. The article she printed from the news website took only a single sheet of paper. Even folded, it's too thin to betray its location.

When she saw the headline a week ago, her first instinct was to talk to Nan about it, then the grief hit her afresh. Nan's been gone for months.

Probably for the best. Talking with Nan about Queen's Point and Lucy's summer there never ended well. On one of her last visits, Lucy had mentioned the Whitlams after seeing in the retirement home's sign-in book that Nan had a visitor from the small town in rural South Australia where she used to live. Curious, Lucy asked whether Nan had any news of Anabelle, unquestionably the safest Whitlam.

Nan's features had darkened. Although she remained in the corner of her room at Seaview Retirement Lodge, ironically named considering its complete lack of ocean views, her unfocused eyes put her far away.

'Keep away from them kids,' she'd growled. 'It was a mistake to let you run wild with them.'

'They're not that bad, are they?' Lucy didn't comment on their being closer to middle age these days; correcting Nan in such a manner tended to upset her.

Nan had shaken her head. 'Bad things happen around them. I should never...' Her voice trailed off, her attention caught by a bird on the windowsill.

Impossible for Lucy not to think of the Whitlams now as her little car crests the hill, the last in the long drive from Adelaide, and she slows to enter the town of Queen's Point, the very place she'd once – according to Nan – run wild for a summer.

Her blood fizzes as memories jostle for prominence. Good memories, mostly. It was right to come back. The article was the prod she'd needed to finally make the two-hour trek and clean up her grandparents' cottage, a task she'd put off for the years Nan had been living close to Lucy and the months since her passing.

All that and the thing that happened at work.

Unwilling to let her mind linger on that, Lucy instead speaks to her companion. 'Well, Hades, what do you think?'

She glances in the rear-view mirror, meeting his contemplative deep-brown gaze. Unavoidably, really, since his head takes up most of the view. Hades, a jet-black short-haired mountain of a dog, with drool weeping from his impressive jowls, only tilts his head thoughtfully in response.

Her gaze catches the side of her face and faint surprise registers – not for the first time – at the crinkle of lines creasing from the corner of her brown eyes behind the rim of the sunglasses. At thirty-five, she's not young any more, and her skincare routine is longer and more futile than teenage Lucy could have imagined.

She slows the car to a crawl to take in the view. The sight in front of her is so apparently unchanged that if she squints it could be nineteen years ago and her younger self could be glaring in the passenger seat as Mum drove her towards her summer in purgatory. This was what she'd taken to calling the need to stay with Nan for the holidays. When leaving her that day, Mum grabbed Lucy, pulled her close, and squeezed her in a long hug. In Lucy's head, that moment marks the last hug of her childhood. After that summer, she was different.

The small town huddles around the curve of the coast, like arms outstretched, poised to embrace the rickety old wooden jetty that sticks out into the sea. The ancient structure is as weather-beaten now as it was back then. The wind whips and froths the water around its footings and her mind returns to the newspaper article and the shoe found in the shallows.

May contain human remains.

A few surfers are out in the distance, although the good waves are mostly around the point, the beach there a part of what's made this small Australian town so sought-after. There are gorgeous shacks along the beachfront and a hodgepodge of weatherboard and brick houses in the town proper, with Main Street curling along a block back from the shore. All of it watched over in benevolence by the enormous house on the hill.

No matter where you stand in town, if you look up you can see it. A glimpse of the wrought-iron fence, a hint of grey-tiled roof, or the gleaming white circular turret that could have been straight from a children's book. One where the princess is trapped by an evil witch. From here Lucy can see all of it, perched atop the cliff, its multi-storey, white-painted expanse contrasting with the green, manicured gardens. The sweeping verandas wrap around the ground floor and its many windows reflect the dark blue of the sea.

The Whitlam house.

Beep!

The blare of a car horn startles Lucy from her reverie. In case the horn isn't enough, the driver of the car behind her flashes their headlights, bright in the gloom.

She lifts her hand in apology and accelerates up to the speed limit.

Driving through the town proper, she realises her first impression – that nothing has changed – isn't true. Although it's hardly crowded, thanks to the icy wind coming off the water and the threat of rain, there are still more people around than used to be here at the height of summer tourist season. Trendy cafés have replaced empty shops. Chic gift stores and slick surf shops sit where once there was only an old second-hand clothing store and maybe a chemist. And on the corner, across from the pub that's been renovated into a gorgeous hotel, sits the glass-fronted, elegantly lit 'Whitlam Homewares'.

She's been into the store in the city, but knows she won't be able to resist a visit to the flagship store. Not least because they built it on the site of the old cinema, home of where it all began.

As she heads towards the point, she has to resist telling Hades about the places they pass.

There's the shortcut down to the beach. The surf club

might look official, but the guards did more sunbathing than beach patrol. We're almost to Nan's place.

And always ahead, like the road is leading her there, the Whitlam house.

It looms in her line of sight, right until the road curves with the coast at the foot of the hill.

Nan's cottage looks almost the same. The cheerful yellow stucco walls with blue trim were already faded that summer. Pop hadn't been up to repairs for a long time before he died, his illness making the physical work he'd loved impossible. She figures Nan hadn't wanted to have someone else in to do it. The paint is no worse now, like the sun and the salt from the sea could only leach so much colour before it gave up.

The property management company Lucy has engaged have done their job, leaving the garden merely overgrown rather than wild. The air of abandonment suggests the occupiers having ducked out, rather than never returning.

She gets out to open the gates and Hades stirs, wanting to stretch his long legs.

'Almost,' Lucy promises.

The large gate squeaks a protest but opens, another plus for the management people she rang a few days ago to say she was coming. She drives in and closes the gate. Since the smaller gate next to the letter box is shut, she lets Hades out and does a quick walk of the perimeter to stretch her travel-cramped legs. Her feet sink into the waterlogged grass in places, the squelch drowned out by the gusting wind. It seems to whistle through the bare tree branches like a plaintive cry.

With no obvious openings in the dilapidated fence, she leaves Hades to explore, and returns to the front of the cottage. She climbs the steps to the front porch with heavy legs. Here, Nan's absence is raw, rather than the ache she's grown used to. Mum's passing more than a decade ago meant caring for Nan towards the end fell to Lucy, as does sorting out her estate.

Entering the cottage this way feels odd. When Nan was alive, only strangers used the formal entrance, but this was the only key Nan had when she moved into the home. Now Lucy's copy and hers dangle together on the keyring, the jingle betraying Lucy's shaking hands. She tucks a few strands of hair that have come loose from her ponytail behind her ear and sets herself to face what's inside.

The key slides easily into the lock. She turns it, and the front door opens.

2

PRESENT DAY

The window over the kitchen sink rattles. Lucy realises she's spent who knows how long staring out of it, lost in memories. Nan always claimed this window was a better gauge of a storm coming than any weather forecaster. Outside, the tree branches shake and there's a faint rumbling from the fireplace. She shivers. It must have dropped five degrees since she arrived.

Remembering Hades is out there, she peers through the window, the view distorted by the ancient glass. Although he was sniffing something earlier, there's no black blob that could be him. It's the same when she hurries outside. But the small gate hangs open. She fights off a stab of panic.

'Hades,' she calls, grabbing her heavy waterproof coat. 'Hades?'

But there's no familiar shape loping into view, no movement in the bushes or beyond. She stops at the gate and shrugs into the jacket. Scanning desperately along the narrow road, she tries to think like a hulking dog in a strange place. What might have drawn him from the garden?

'Hades?' The wind whips the shout from her mouth, but she calls again as she crosses the road. 'Hades!'

There's no sign of him. Bloody foolish animal. Why wander from the only place likely to provide his special dog kibble?

Even as she thinks the question, the answer lodges hard in her gut. All the feeding him, walking him, patting him doesn't really matter. He's not hers. Never will be. Hades barely shifted from her husband Brian's side when he was alive, and claimed his pillow when he died, dragging it from their bed with an expression that suggested Lucy would lose her arm if she argued.

'Idiot.' But she means herself as much as him. 'Damn fool.'

They had the funeral outside so Hades could attend. The funeral people thought they were crazy, but it was Brian's wish and Lucy saw Jasmine bury her head in Hades' fur after speaking about her dad. Maybe Lucy should have encouraged Jasmine to take the dog. Now the thought of having to tell Brian's twenty-six-year-old daughter that she's managed to lose Hades forces her forward.

'Hades?'

She veers away from the looming gates of the Whitlam property, impassable despite Hades' long legs, and heads for the distant water. The trail she remembers is now barely a path at all. The sand has shifted, and bushes have grown, reclaiming the narrow way. These dunes have always been a bit wild. Queen's Point had a thing for leaving coastal dunes intact before anyone worried about protecting the environment. Probably more to do with the Whitlams owning so much of the land than an active choice, if the fancy shacks teetering at the edge of the water further along are any indication.

Even with the wind stirring the sand and the dark clouds overhead, the sight of the white and green rolling expanse and the blue beyond hits her somewhere deep in the chest. God, she loved it here.

She stumbles in the wet, rocky sand, but keeps going.

Hades will be by the sea. He loves the water. She slips again, as a fat drop of rain hits her cheek. Then comes another. And then it's like the heavens rupture.

Blinking, she tugs the hood of her coat tighter around her face. The jacket, which she'd ridiculed as a walking sleeping bag when Brian bought it, proves its worth. She's almost completely dry, head to calves. A minute later, the rain stops as quickly as it began. The end of her nose is numb, and probably red to match. She hunches further into her coat.

She sees the water at last, but no dog. Where in summer the blue of the water provided a window to the sand below, this winter blue churns until it flows thick with grit. A wave rolls in and crashes into the sand. She can almost hear Anabelle's voice in memory: 'Come on in, the water's always warm in Queen's Point.'

It seemed believable then, beneath the blazing summer sun, but she doubts the dark, foaming ocean would be anything but icy.

Her mouth opens to call for Hades again when she sees it. A massive tarp, its bright blue absurdly unnatural in the gloom. Remnants of a crime scene?

May contain human remains.

The line from the article echoes in her head.

Whatever it is lies a good distance away up the hill. In her search for Hades, she's gone further than she meant to. Once, there was a fence here, running down almost to the water. 'Keep Out' signs divided the Whitlams' private beach from the public.

She remembers Mae, the oldest of the three siblings, once muttering, *No one should be able to own the point.* Seems someone has listened.

Would the bright colour of the tarp have interested Hades? Can dogs see blue?

It draws Lucy, pulling her that way, all the while making the knot in her belly tighten more. Could this have been the location of the rest of the body?

The ground near the tarp is ripped open like a wound, the clay of the earth visible where sand, rock and shrub have fallen away. Here, the tang of salt from the sea is stronger. The winter smells of rotting damp seaweed a new note, jarring her memories of the warmth of the sun.

She takes another step. 'Hades?'

The ground gives way.

Her foot slips and air gushes from her lungs. 'Help!'

The cry is snatched on the wind. There's no one around to hear it. She grabs at a bush, and clings on as sand and pebbles fall to the beach several yards below. It holds and she scrambles away from the edge. A nearby gull calls its displeasure at the disturbance, before wheeling away. As she catches her breath, she dares a glance down, taking in the jut of rocks poking up from stretches of sand.

But for the shrub she'd have fallen. She'd have been stranded, possibly with a limb broken, maybe worse. Alone with nothing but that ominous tarp, and without any phone signal. And with no one waiting for her at home or otherwise.

Brian.

She misses him afresh, with a yearning as breath-snatching as the fall. The pain of his absence accompanied by the usual guilt.

She edges back. Her ankle, sore from the slip, protests every step. Her hand stings, the palm red raw from taking her weight. She returns the way she came, heading back towards the road. Her feet slip often now, the near fall making her uncertain. There's no sign of Hades, no sign of anyone. Despite the town's growth, it's still isolated out here.

The perfect place to do away with someone.

As she finally reaches the road, a drop of rain catches her cheek and slides down beneath the collar of her jacket, chilling skin warm from worry and exertion. Where the hell is Hades?

Her phone vibrates. Reception at last, and it looks like she's missed some calls. The number is 'private'.

She taps to answer. 'Lucy Ross speaking.'

3

PRESENT DAY

'Lost anything?' asks a masculine voice on the other end of the call. 'Say, an overgrown dog with a nose for rubbish? I found a mutt investigating a bin off the beach road. Figured I'd try the number on his tag.'

'Thanks. Yes, Hades is mine.' Lucy's throat thickens. The wave of relief has her clutching the phone hard. 'I'm happy to come and get him. Where did you say you are?'

'Look, he seems pretty comfy in my ute. Let me bring him to you.'

'I'm staying at the cottage at the end of Beach Road.'

There's a long pause. 'The Antonello place?'

There's something about the way he says her maiden name. Something knowing. But it's been nineteen years since she's been here and she's probably imagining things. 'Yes.'

'I'll be there soon, Lucy Ross.'

He disconnects and she hurries towards the cottage, replaying his last words and overanalysing every inflection.

He must not have been too far away, because the ute pulls to a stop out the front as she reaches the yard. She peers into the cab of the dusty black vehicle, wanting warning as to the man's identity.

He gets out, whistling for Hades to follow.

Her breath solidifies like a lump of concrete somewhere behind her ribs.

She remembers *him*.

The fact that he's wearing sunglasses, has gone through puberty, and nineteen years passing can't change Jake Parker enough that she wouldn't. She hopes her sunglasses hide her jolt of recognition.

He's taller than she would have imagined he'd become, and the excess weight he carried has turned into broad shoulders. His once pale hair has darkened to a messy, dirty blond and where acne dotted his face, there's now a pleasing stubble.

He rounds the front of the ute, Hades trotting obediently alongside, and stops a few feet away. A mocking smile curves his lips. 'Yours?' he asks.

'Yes.' She reaches out a hand. 'Come here, Hades. There's a good boy.' Of course. *Of course*. Hades sits instead, so close to Jake he's practically on his foot. 'Hades,' she says, a little more insistently. 'Come.'

He doesn't budge, doesn't act like he's her dog at all. She fears she's going to have to grab him by the collar when Jake mutters, 'Go on, then.'

And Hades lopes past her and into the yard without breaking stride.

'Thanks for finding him,' she says as she makes sure the gate is secure.

'All part of the job,' he replies. When she frowns, he adds, 'Sergeant Jake Parker at your service.'

Her eyebrows lift. 'Police officer, huh? Didn't you want to be an acrobat?'

'Nah,' he says. 'That was just to impress the ladies.' He shakes his head. 'Only a teenager could get it so wrong.' His tone is light, but his shoulders relax a little as he makes the joke.

Did he really think she wouldn't recognise him, or worse, pretend not to?

'Been in town long?' he asks.

'We drove down today to pack up Nan's place.'

As she says the word *drove*, his gaze flickers to her neat hatchback. He takes in the small size, probably wondering how such a dog even managed to get in there. But then he seems to notice the badge shining on the front and even with the sunglasses his surprise is obvious.

Yep, and I paid for it myself, and the two-storey townhouse in an exclusive beachside suburb in Adelaide. She's not the poor friend of the Whitlams any more. Although, she remembers with a cramp of her chest, neither is she senior partner. The role that was supposed to be the endgame of all the late hours, the missed social events and the strive for excellence that has consumed her adult life. She'd been so close she practically had the nameplate engraved, until she stuffed it all up.

'You and... Mr Ross?' Jake's asking.

'Me and Hades,' she replies.

Jake leans back on the side of the ute, the movement showing the lean, hard length of his body, so different from the short, soft boy she once knew. Is the change simply late puberty? Part of his job?

'Finished looking?' he asks.

'It's been a long time, there's a lot to catch up,' she counters. 'How is country policing? You must have more important things to do than return lost dogs, considering everything that's been happening.'

He doesn't reply for so long that she considers scarpering inside, locking the door and forgetting she ever saw him. Her attempted dig for information wasn't exactly subtle.

'You're asking about the shoe.' He says it slowly.

Of course she was. Since the day she found the article she's been checking the media obsessively, looking for more information. And here she has a cop, a local, who has to know more than the brief lines she's practically memorised.

May contain human remains.

'Let me guess,' she says. 'You can't tell me anything. Not even the type of shoe?' The type would narrow the possible owners. Runners or business brogues. Slip-on, podiatry approved, or platform. 'Because you're a professional.' Her police knowledge might be limited to TV shows, but even she knows that much. 'Anyway, thanks for the help with Hades. I'll make sure I latch the gate properly next time.'

'You might want to check the fences too.'

She nods. 'I will. Thanks again.'

She's walking towards the house when his voice stops her.

'Interesting,' he drawls. 'You haven't asked me if we've identified the shoe's owner.'

She turns back. 'Maybe I just don't care all that much.' But her curiosity is obvious. 'You couldn't tell me, even if you did know.'

He nods. 'I'm surprised you didn't ask, that's all.'

And just like that she remembers how annoying she always found Jake Parker. 'I really should get back inside. Lots to do.'

But he's not listening to her dismissal. His lifts his sunglasses to read a message on his watch. Barely a heartbeat passes, but when he looks at her again everything's changed. His eyes, blue like the summer ocean she remembers, are serious and the shit-stirring of a minute ago is forgotten.

'Bad news?' she asks.

He runs a hand through his hair, messing it further. 'Not good.' He hesitates. 'There's been a roll over. Spring Gully Road has claimed another victim.'

'Official police communication?'

He shakes his head. 'Old Tuck, whose property is out that way, thought I'd want to know.'

There's a weariness to him as he pulls out his phone and types a reply, and she wonders if it will be his job to tell the family, wonders how many times he's had to do such a thing.

She can easily picture the road in question, steep and curvy with edges lost to gravel, and potholes that could swallow a tyre. 'It's a terrible road. I can't believe they haven't done something about it.'

His eyebrows lift. 'Really? A road used by locals, not on the way to any tourist hotspots, in a stable government seat?'

'Fair enough.'

He sighs. 'It'll have been a lost tourist, probably. No local would try going that way after the rain we've had recently.'

She thinks of the open ground covered by the tarp and the way the earth was washed away, and nods agreement.

'How long are you here for?' he asks.

It could be an innocent question. They are old… *somethings*, if not friends.

'I have a month off work, but I don't expect the task to take that long.' And hopefully, she can convince her boss that two weeks is plenty of time to *go somewhere and get your pretty head straight*, as she'd ordered in her gruff manner. She could have simply fired Lucy after what happened, but she didn't, instead suggesting they would reassess after a break. And although seeing her dream role taken by the annoying David Bremner, head-hunted from their fiercest competitors, hurt, Lucy won't forget that she probably deserved so much worse.

Jake takes a step around towards the driver's side. 'We should catch up. Let me buy you a drink.'

She nods immediately. He might be persuaded to tell her more about the investigation.

His mouth curves. 'I'll message you.'

She frowns, about to ask how, and then realises that, thanks to Hades, he has her number from the tag.

Then he slides into his car and drives away, leaving her standing at the gate staring after him. All the questions she should have asked are left caught on the tip of her tongue.

Lucy

Lucy had known the small coastal town of Queen's Point was lame when Mum practically imprisoned her at Nan's place, but arriving at the cinema that first night took things to a whole new level. One theatre, one movie, and the 'new release' was something she'd seen a month ago.

If only Mum had listened to her pleas that she could be trusted. A friend needing their stomach pumped after a New Year's party and Mum was seeing flashing red and blue lights whenever she looked at her only child.

'But you hate that place,' Lucy argued. 'And my grandmother.'

Nan had not approved of Lucy's father. Something made more maddening for Lucy's mother when he'd done the bolt before Lucy was even born. Too stubborn to go back home, Lucy's mum had raised her baby alone. It meant Lucy had only met her grandparents a few times and she'd never visited Queen's Point even though it wasn't far from their home in Adelaide. Located about fifteen minutes beyond Ardrossan and not far from Maitland, they must have almost passed it on their occasional drives to this part of the coast.

Mum just sighed. 'I need these night shifts, and with Joan from next door away, I can't leave you. Besides, there's not

24

enough to do there to get into trouble.' She seemed to have forgotten that she'd found trouble there herself.

About an hour into the drive, Lucy gave up pointing out she was sixteen not six, and glared out of the window instead. An attitude she'd maintained through the awkward family lunch, Mum leaving, Nan showing her the poky room where she'd be staying, and then a long, boring afternoon. The offer to go to the movies where Nan volunteered had given her hope. Hope Lucy now knew to be tragically misplaced.

Nan, however, seemed oblivious to Lucy's bad mood. 'I've seen this one,' she said in the lull between the ticket counter opening and the first customer at the tiny snacks counter. Her practical grey bun bobbed as she spoke, as though to emphasise each word. 'You'll love it.'

And with Nan's brown eyes, the same colour Lucy had inherited, sparkling with excitement, Lucy couldn't bring herself to say that she'd already seen it too.

'It looks totally great,' she said.

'Hurry up.' Nan was gesturing to the other red-and-white striped apron. 'Put it on.'

Lucy blinked. She had to work for this? To watch a movie she'd already seen?

But she slipped the offensive garment over her head and listened to a lecture on how to operate the ancient cash register. At least no one important would see her looking like a candy cane.

There were more people than she expected, given the size of the town. She soon got the hang of grabbing drinks, scanning snacks and ringing up the different sized popcorn buckets.

The first bell to indicate the movie's start had already

sounded when a large group spilled through the doors on a cloud of excited chatter. There had to be a dozen kids.

Another bell dinged and the sign for the theatre flashed. 'Last warning,' crackled a deep voice over the speaker system.

'The counter is closing.' Nan's voice cut across the small space, freezing the group.

As if to underline the point, the dinging of the warning bell got more insistent.

Lucy eyed the hurriedly assembled line of kids and a knot formed in her gut. She shot Nan a pleading look. 'I'll serve them, I don't mind.'

'Only one more,' Nan said firmly.

A boy moved through the small crowd, tall and with a mop of glossy, longish pop-star hair. He grabbed snacks from yielding hands as he passed. A Mars bar from one, a packet of Twisties from another. They were too bewitched by his lazy half-smile and flash of dimple to refuse. He dumped the lot next to the till. The smile widened, and the full force of it sucked air from Lucy's lungs.

'If you are only serving one,' he said, 'serve me. I'll take the lot.'

His low, intimate voice did funny things to Lucy's insides. She felt her eyes widen at the sheer number of snacks in front of him, but she bit back a comment. Mostly because she seemed to have lost the ability to form words, let alone sentences.

The practice she'd gained serving didn't help when beneath his amused grey gaze her hands fumbled the simplest tasks. She snuck glances at him. Yes, those eyes *were* grey, like the winter sky reflected in the sea. Busy relaying the drink orders, he didn't seem to notice the effect he had on her. That, or he was used to turning girls into idiots.

With the last order rung up, she was about to read off the eye-watering total when she realised he was looking at her. Really looking at her. His head tilted and he tucked a few strands of dark wavy hair behind his ear as those eyes studied her in a way that no one ever had before.

He nodded slowly. 'Creaming soda?' he asked.

'Huh?'

His lips twitched. 'You look like a creaming soda kind of girl to me. Put one for yourself on the order. It's the least I can do.'

'Yeah,' she said. 'Soda good.'

He paid without flinching at the total, winked, and turned to hand out the loot before sauntering towards the movie entrance.

As Lucy stared after him, she suddenly thought of all the things she should have said, like *thank you*, and asking his name.

One of the girls peeled off from the group. With blonde curls framing her heart-shaped face and the kind of curves that had Lucy puffing out her own comparatively flat chest, the girl strolled to the counter like she owned the place.

Somehow, Lucy managed not to lift her hand to her own dull, straight hair, the colour of washed-out driftwood.

'You must be new around here,' said the girl. 'I'm Anabelle Whitlam.'

Whitlam. Lucy recognised the name. Didn't Nan work for them, up at the big house on the hill? Inwardly, she squirmed. That made Nan their help.

But Anabelle was still talking. 'That oaf who bought the drinks is my brother, Harry. I also have an older sister called Mae. She's too mature to sit with us kids.' Her cheery tone took the sting from her sister's defection. 'So, do you want to?'

Lucy realised Anabelle was looking at her in a way that expected a response. Did she want to... what?

A heartbeat before it became uncomfortable, Anabelle added, 'I'm sure your grandmother won't mind.'

Somewhere in all that must have been an invitation. Lucy glanced at Nan. 'Can I?'

Anabelle smiled charmingly. 'I'll look after her, Mrs Antonello.'

Nan handed Lucy a ticket. 'I'll meet you afterwards in the foyer.'

Lucy was three steps away from the counter when she realised she was still wearing the apron. 'One second,' she said. She half strangled herself removing it. Then she was walking next to Anabelle and they were joining the group.

Harry Whitlam, as she now knew he was called, was impossible to miss with his height and that hair, and the way most of the girls and half the boys hung off his every word.

Anabelle made more introductions as they entered the darkened theatre, but the names and faces blurred. With Anabelle's arm linked possessively through hers – *Everyone, this is my new friend Lucy* – Lucy knew the important names.

Maybe this summer wouldn't be quite so lame after all.

4

PRESENT DAY

Back inside Nan's cottage, Lucy takes off her coat. The layer of dust is only light, thanks to the property manager, but everything has an air of having settled into place.

Nan was a tidy woman, even with her decreasing mobility, but she'd amassed a lifetime of clutter. Mementos of long-ago holidays, a mish-mash of unmatched cushions, piles of books and carefully placed framed photos. So much stuff.

Swallowing is hard. Where does Lucy even start?

At the beginning.

She can practically hear Nan's no-nonsense retort. She always said Lucy tended towards the dramatic. The memory gets her moving at last.

There's a skip coming on Monday, so before then she'll make decisions on the large pieces of furniture. Then she'll attack what she can handle alone, like the contents of the kitchen and the master bedroom. The desk and its lifetime of receipts and papers can wait for when it all feels a little less daunting.

Hades settles in front of the empty fireplace with a snort, and the sight of it gives Lucy purpose. Before any of that, she needs to make sure they're comfortable. Make up a bed, find wood, check the gas and hot water. Then she'll face the real work.

She brings in supplies from the car, depositing her laptop and some food basics on the table, and Hades' bag of kibble on the floor. The store of mostly dry wood in the shed and the apparently functional kitchen means she's soon picking up her case from by the door. There's no question as to which room to stay in. Fresh linen in one hand and case in the other, she passes the master, with its quilted blanket and ancient dresser still full of Nan's personal things, and heads for the back of the cottage.

The small sunroom where she slept as a teenager is much the same as when she left it, relatively bare, but for a bed, a hanging rail for clothes and a small set of drawers. She sinks on to the bed, letting the linen fall across the drawers.

As a sixteen-year-old, she hid her diary in the bottom, larger drawer, under some old brown photo albums. Unable to resist, she shifts the sheet aside and pulls the handle. It groans protest, the warped wood catching before the drawer comes out completely, sending the contents tumbling. Everything inside is the same as she remembers, except there's no diary. *That* she made sure to take home.

She shoves everything back for now. If she starts reminiscing she'll never stop.

Something glints golden on the small rug next to the bed, catching what little light there is in the dull room. Something that was in the drawer?

Goosebumps rise on the back of her neck as she leans over to pick it up. A ring. Three tiny diamonds set into a gold band. She rolls it between her fingers, the metal heavy enough to suggest this is no cheap costume item. There's detail on the inside, an engraving of a vine, perhaps?

It must be Nan's. But what was it doing in this drawer?

After sliding the ring on to her middle finger, Lucy returns to the bed. The mattress sags and the ancient springs complain but the give of it under her kind of feels like home. The bedding on it still smells like Nan's all-natural washing liquid, although it's mingled with less appealing fragrances. She'll need to strip it, but for now she eases back on to the stack of pillows and plays with the ring.

Inevitably, her gaze finds the small window.

Through it, as the wind catches the tree branches, she sees a patch of white. A tiny piece of the Whitlam house. A moment later it's obscured by leaves, but she knows that if she keeps looking, she'll see it again.

Nan caught Lucy staring out here often enough, usually with a click of her tongue and a reminder that the grass isn't always greener, or some such platitude. But they both knew just how good they had it up at the big house.

Lucy is still staring out of the small pane of glass when her eyes close and she falls asleep.

Lucy startles awake at the click of Hades' paws on the hallway linoleum. She blinks, trying to gather her wits as he sits by the bed. It's dark. The poor dog is probably starving, no wonder he came to find her.

'Sorry,' she mutters. Afternoon naps aren't part of the daily routine at Potts Consulting, the international finance firm where she works, and it's not a habit she plans to get into because she'll be back on board soon. She's worked too hard to let one mistake ruin everything.

I might not have a choice.

She heaves herself upright, fumbles through her case and changes into cargo pants, wincing as every movement makes her ankle throb where she twisted it in the dunes. Maybe she should have iced it but now it's probably too late. Upon reaching the lounge, she switches on the tall lamp in the corner. She's tried and failed in her townhouse, with all kinds of light fittings, to recreate the soft yellow light that spills to every corner from that single globe.

'Fire before food,' she tells Hades.

A low growl comes from deep in his throat as she kneels to arrange kindling. He stiffens, the hackles rising on the back of his thick neck.

'You okay, boy? You hear something?'

A moment later, the front gate whines.

Her hand finds the dog's head with a pat. 'Good boy.'

As if inspired by her praise, he lumbers to his feet and leads the way to the door. They get there a heartbeat before the polite knock.

She holds Hades' collar, suddenly aware of how isolated Nan's cottage is, way out here on the edge of town. And she's unable to avoid thinking of the article, and the meeting with Jake earlier. Someone found a shoe not far from here.

May contain human remains.

This is ridiculous; she's lived by herself much of her adult life, having moved out when she got into university, and having been alone again in the year since Brian's death. Deliberately relaxing her tight shoulders, she takes a breath and cracks open the door.

The sight of the woman standing there slams into Lucy.

Definitely not her remains in the shoe.

Neither of them speaks for long seconds. Lucy, because her mouth seems to have stopped working. And the woman because...

Crap. She doesn't even recognise me.

Lucy's suddenly sixteen again and awkward as hell, like that first day they met. The woman – girl then – coming out of the bathroom of all things, wrapped only in a towel, her long blonde hair wet on her bare shoulders. The black-and-white expanse of the room behind her bigger than Lucy's bedroom back home.

'Always pleased to meet one of Ana-banana's friends,' she'd said, making sure the plush towel was secure. 'Excuse me if I don't hold out my hand.'

'Of course, yeah,' Lucy had mumbled, realising she was probably, mortifyingly, staring.

'Ugh, why'd you call me that?' Anabelle had cried. 'Big sisters are the absolute worst.' She'd shared this fact in such a way that Lucy had felt the appropriate envy for their bond. Casual bathroom interruptions. Nicknames. All of it so foreign for an only child like Lucy.

A sudden lunge from Hades gets him free of Lucy's lax grip. He jumps so that his massive muddy paws come to rest on Mae Whitlam's designer-jacket-clad chest. She arches back to avoid his slobbering tongue.

Then she laughs, throaty and genuine. She eases Hades to the ground and hunkers down to scratch his ears, then looks up. 'Why Lucy Antonello, you haven't changed a bit.'

Lucy doesn't lift her hand to her perfectly blow-dried, if a little flattened, hair. Where once she was mousy brown, there are now artful streaks of ash in the blonde, created at great expense by one of Adelaide's most exclusive hairdressers. Next to the loose, windswept knot of Mae's hair with tendrils honey-golden around her face, combined with her fashionably relaxed-fit, light denim rolled up at the cuffs, Lucy is the city woman trying too hard.

Mae chuckles. 'Yes, the hair is different, but you're still Lucy.'

The glow Lucy feels at her recognition, of Mae Whitlam remembering her, is silly. She's a grown-up; more than that, she's a successful businesswoman. But it's there.

'It's Ross now,' she says. 'Lucy Ross.' She gestures at the dog, who's practically on Mae's lap. 'Sorry about Hades.'

'Hades?' Mae takes in the black fur and bulk, along with the lolling tongue and gentle eyes. 'He's rather friendly for the king of the underworld.' Her smile widens. 'I was wrong, before. Something has changed. You clearly have better taste in males these days than back when you hung out with my brother.'

Lucy chuckles along with Mae as she stands, and bites down on using the opening to ask after Harry. Whether he's in town, or even in the country for that matter. His socials haven't revealed anything the last few days.

With the promise of a treat, Lucy instead coaxes Hades back inside.

She turns from giving it to him to find Mae has followed her through the door and closed it behind her. She stands at ease in the dusty living room, unaffected by the reek of mould and too many years of deep-fried food. Mae has always had that knack, so effortlessly wealthy she doesn't need it to define her.

'Your jacket,' Lucy says, noticing the marks Hades has left behind. 'I'm sorry.'

Mae waves it away. 'I'm sure it'll wipe right off. Anyway, I'm sorry to disturb you so late, but there haven't been any lights on down here for a while. I figured I should check it out.'

'I thought it was time to pack up the place.'

Mae's eyes fill with sympathy. 'I was sorry to hear about Judy. Your grandmother was much loved.'

'I appreciate you thinking of her.'

On behalf of the Whitlam family, Mae had sent a card and a generous donation to the cancer research facility named in the newspaper notice. She'd written something lovely about Nan's years of long service and sent her apologies for not attending.

'And you said you were Lucy Ross now. Is your partner here with you?' Ever polite, Mae keeps her gaze on Lucy, not gawking around the living area.

'Brian's not here.' Explaining should be easier by now, but Lucy's learned after more than a year that the words might get smoother but their truth hurts no less. 'He passed away last March. Heart attack.'

'Oh, I'm sorry,' Mae says. 'You've had a shitty time.'

'He was a good man,' Lucy replies simply, despite there being nothing simple about it. 'Hades was Brian's dog, named for his colour and predicted size. He's six now and a mature gentleman usually, although today he's acting more like a puppy.' Lucy can hear the brittle edge in her voice but can't stop. 'As well as jumping on you, he let himself out of the front gate this afternoon.'

Mae chuckles. 'He's had quite the adventure.'

As though realising he's become the topic of conversation, Hades stretches, belches and begins nosing at the bag of speciality dog food that Brian always ordered in bulk because it's all he can eat.

'I was about to feed him,' Lucy explains as his efforts grow more insistent.

Mae takes it as her cue to leave. 'I should let you get back to your evening.' She moves towards the door. 'Sorry to have intruded.'

'I appreciate you keeping an eye on the place.' Lucy opens the door for her.

'Not a problem.'

With Lucy's hand on the old wooden doorknob, the ring she's still wearing catches the lamplight. Three tiny diamond sparkles nestled in soft gold.

Mae stares for a beat too long. 'That's so pretty.'

'One of Nan's.' She tucks her hand under the crook of her elbow, embarrassed to be caught being so sentimental.

'Actually…' Mae hesitates, tilts her head. 'I'm having an informal gathering up at the house tomorrow night. Dad and Anabelle are coming to spend a few weeks at home, and I thought it merited a celebration of sorts.' She smiles. 'No pressure if you're already busy.'

Lucy thinks of all she needs to do. 'I'd love to come.'

'Wonderful.'

The temperature's dropped in the few minutes they've been inside and Lucy shivers, wishing she had a jacket, then winces at the marks Hades has left on Mae's. 'Sorry again. If your jacket needs to be dry-cleaned, please send me the bill.'

Mae waves away the offer with the ease of the wealthy. 'Forget about it. I'll see you tomorrow night.'

'See you then.'

It's not until the gate has squeaked again to underline her departure and Lucy's lost her shape in the shadows that she realises she didn't turn on the lamp until Hades heard Mae's approach. What light did she see from up on the hill?

5

PRESENT DAY

Going up to the house for a drink is a polite necessity. One drink, some conversation and then back to Nan's place. Because Lucy is in town to get the house packed up, not get caught up with the Whitlams.

Nor in the mystery of the shoe under the jetty.

She's annoyed enough that she lost half her night after Mae's visit scrolling on her phone for more information on the jetty find. There was no official mention of what she has convinced herself is a rough grave site she saw near the point. It's in the comments of various articles though, local speculation that gets removed by some moderator as fast as it appears.

Stepping up on to the Whitlam house's front porch provides immediate relief from the biting wind and Lucy smooths her hair into place as she approaches the door, trying not to hobble as the long day hasn't allowed her twisted ankle any resting time. Her choice of attire was limited, not having planned for a cocktail event, but the little black dress is classic and designer if not likely to wow anyone. A hint of the old nerves flutter in her belly, but she's not a poor teenager any more. The huge door swings open before she can ring the bell.

Efficient staff, or the small camera above the door frame?

'May I take your coat?' asks the young woman.

'Thank you.'

She hands it to another waiting staff member to hang. 'Please, follow me.'

Lucy imagines she hears a faint whir as she passes under another discreet camera in the wide hallway, but it's unlikely, considering the sounds of conversation and tasteful jazz music spilling from the open entertaining area further along.

The host steps out into the hallway. 'Lucy,' Mae cries, taking her hands before kissing each cheek. She's elegant in a long, dark olive strapless dress, her hair shining golden and artfully loose on her shoulders. 'So glad you could make it. The guests of honour will be a little late as the pilot needed to wait for the weather to clear.'

Lucy makes the connection to the helicopter she heard fly over a little while earlier. But of course they'd have such private transport and their own private helipad. Heaven knows the grounds are large enough.

'No problem,' Lucy says. She trails Mae towards the party but slows by the canvas of the three siblings hanging in the hallway. Didn't this beach snapshot used to be hidden upstairs in favour of more formal posed portraits?

'A sentimental touch,' Mae explains. 'It completely clashes with the rest of the décor but I couldn't help myself.' Mae's right in that the faded candid shot with the tilted horizon is at odds with the rest of the tasteful art, but somehow it works.

They enter the huge entertaining space with its domed ceiling and, at Mae's direction, Lucy takes a champagne flute from the tray of a passing waiter. The bubbles tingle on her lips as she takes a sip from the vessel that is real, heavy crystal. Expensive and elegant, matching the surrounds, and she'd expect no less. After all, this is the home of a brand synonymous worldwide with luxury. Instinctively, Lucy knows the décor has changed from all those years ago, recognising Mae's exquisite taste. It's no single vase, artfully placed cushion, or high-end collector's sculpture but every calculated detail.

'I hope you managed to keep that adorable dog from getting lost today,' Mae says with a smile.

'I took him for a long walk this morning to wear him out. Unless he's learned to unlock doors, he should be safe inside tonight.' And then, because it's filled her thoughts since she saw it, she adds, 'We went all the way around the point, past the boathouse to the cliffs and the surf beach on the other side.'

She studies Mae's face for a reaction but there's nothing at all to suggest that just down the hill there was something found. Something that on the local gossip pages they've decided is the rest of the body belonging to the shoe from under the jetty.

Mae's face remains a mask of polite interest. 'Did you manage to make much progress on sorting Judy's things?' Her gaze flicks down to Lucy's hand but she's not wearing the ring.

'Not as much as I would have liked,' Lucy admits.

'It's a mammoth task, I'm sure. If you need any help at all, let me know.'

'I will, thank you.'

Mae's so serene. Could what Lucy saw at the point be unrelated to the shoe under the jetty?

A woman approaches them, tottering a little on her heels. Roughly their age, but the thick eyeliner ages her and her top is hooked up in her bra strap. Lucy debates whether it's more embarrassing to subtly tell her so she can fix it, or leave it be.

She rudely steps in front of Lucy, making the decision an easy one.

'Mae,' she says. 'So good to see you.' She leans in for an embrace but Mae avoids the contact.

Mae's eyebrows lift. 'You are?'

Lucy's stomach knots for the woman deemed unmemorable as she stumbles through an explanation.

'Interesting,' Mae murmurs.

'Not as interesting as the shoe,' the woman begins. 'I heard—'

'I don't think this is the place for such gossip.' Mae cuts her off, eyes narrow, tone deadly.

The woman's mouth is still hanging open when Mae steps around her and touches Lucy's elbow, turning them towards another guest and effectively leaving the woman behind.

Lucy gets the message too. *No shoe speculation with Mae.*

'Lucy, I must introduce you to Rachael Touré,' Mae says. The woman they're standing in front of is tall, dark-skinned and striking, with close-cropped black hair. Her plum lipstick matches her jumpsuit.

'Rachael is our new mayor,' Mae explains. 'Elected in a landslide a few months ago, much to almost everyone's delight. She's worked all over the world for aid organisations but is now focused on writing her memoir after her family came here as refugees. And, Rachael, Lucy spent a summer here as a teenager. She stayed with her grandmother, Judy Antonello.'

Rachael's smile shows straight white teeth. 'Pleased to meet you, and I am so sorry for your loss. Judy was a wonderful member of the community. When were you here?'

'I think it was around 2000,' Lucy says, as if the date isn't imprinted on her brain.

'She practically became part of our family,' Mae says. 'She and Anabelle were so close.'

Lucy feels a pang at the words. So close and then cut off like she didn't exist.

Rachael's smile widens. 'I was studying interstate back then, but I think I came home briefly that summer. We probably met.'

Lucy nods, although she's certain she'd remember someone so stunning.

'Lucy works for one of those big consulting firms with offices in Adelaide, Sydney and internationally,' Mae says.

'How did you know that?' Lucy asks.

Mae waves the question away. 'I must have seen it on your socials.'

Lucy nods; it's possible but it doesn't make sense. If Mae was so caught up on Lucy's life she wouldn't have asked about Brian the day before, unless she went home and read up.

Rachael frowns. 'I've probably worked with you – government departments are always calling in outsiders.'

'Maybe.' The mere thought of work knots Lucy's stomach. It's a break, she reminds herself. If they were going to fire her, they would have done so already.

'And you're coming to the show?' Rachael asks.

'I was getting to that,' Mae says. She unearths an embossed invitation and presses it into Lucy's hands. 'A little something Harry has developed over the years. It's in a couple of weeks. Say you'll come.'

'A little something?' Rachael laughs. 'Only one of the most significant art prizes in the country.'

'If I'm still in town, I will,' Lucy promises.

The consummate hostess, Mae angles her body to include a nearby young man, who straightens at her attention. 'Lucy, have you met Dante?' she asks. 'He's a backpacker doing some work for me while he's in town. He intended to only pass through but lucky for me, he's stayed.'

'It's as good a place as any,' he says. But he watches Mae with an intensity that suggests he's here for more than just the scenery.

'If you two are okay, I've spotted someone else Rachael needs to meet,' Mae says. She doesn't wait for an answer, leading the taller woman towards a business type standing with up-and-coming actress Claire Hamilton. A man Lucy recognises as an important lobbyist. It says something about Mae's influence that they'd have come all the way from the city.

Lucy's not sure whether she's being babysat by Dante or the other way round. He's tall and lean, with short dark hair that curls at the ends. The long dark lashes framing brown eyes and the angular planes of his face make him look like he's stepped off the pages of a fashion magazine and the fitted black T-shirt and black jeans do nothing to dispel the idea. When he looks at Lucy it's hard to look away, despite her being almost old enough to be his mother.

'Lucy, was it?' he drawls.

'Yes. Great to meet you.' She catches herself – that sounded like a teenager. 'Have you been here long?' she manages in a more even tone.

'Four months in the country, some weeks in Queen's Point.'

He has a faint inflection she can't place. 'Is that a Spanish accent?'

She'd always planned to travel more but with work there was never enough time. She'd needed to work through her uni holidays to afford rent then couldn't refuse a junior position at a mid-sized firm straight out of her degree. She had a plan for success and it allowed for no deviations. Brian coaxed her one Christmas to join him skiing in Japan where he had family, but their planned European adventure never happened.

Dante shakes his head but there's a hint of a smile. 'Italian. I'm from Venice.'

'Venice.' She repeats the name of the canal city with a sigh. 'You've been?'

'Wanted to.'

He smiles fully at that, revealing a dimple and a slight gap between his front teeth, and she's again acutely aware of just how young and good-looking he is. 'Like anything, my home is at once better and worse than you might imagine. The pictures and travel shows can't possibly tell you the heart of the city. The wonder within its streets and waterways.' He pauses and sips his beer. 'The darkness below the surface.'

He's probably talking about poverty, or even the daily grind, but Lucy can't help literally picturing something lurking within the canals, and again she thinks of the find beneath the jetty. She shivers.

'Are you cold?' he asks.

Of course, despite his youth, he's the type to notice. 'I'm fine,' she says. 'Did you have any reason for coming here in particular? It's not exactly a backpacker's hotspot.'

'I'm an Aussie by heritage,' he explains, adopting an exaggerated imitation of a broad ocker accent. 'Although I grew up overseas thanks to my mother's work, I was born in Sydney, and my grandmother lives in Perth. I started my trip there and I'm making my way across the country.'

It's only as Mae apologetically beckons him to her that Lucy realises he never really answered her question.

She sips her drink, trying to look busy, swaying a little to the ballad coming from a stunning baby grand piano in front of the far windows.

While she hasn't asked about Harry, she's wondered. Whether Mae *not* mentioning him in the details about the event was an oversight or meant he wasn't in town. She'd said *Dad and Anabelle*. But neither of them is yet present.

She scans the guests, and her gaze clashes with familiar, smirking blue eyes. Jake Parker. She heads for him, weaving through the other guests, unable to miss the contrast of his navy slacks and blue shirt from the jeans he'd been wearing yesterday. He's scrubbed up well.

'I've been busy,' he says the moment she reaches him. 'That crash Old Tuck messaged me about has become complicated. No ID on the woman in the vehicle means a truckload of work for me.'

'O-kay. And?'

His lips twitch. 'It's the reason I haven't messaged you about catching up.'

'It was only yesterday,' she says.

'Anyway, I figured I'd see you tonight..' He reaches out a hand and snatches a glass from the tray of a passing waiter. He holds it out. 'A drink, as promised.'

She holds up the one from Mae, barely touched. 'Too late.'

'Ah, but when that's done, I'll be ready.'

'And *that* will be lukewarm.'

He places the glass on a table with a sigh. 'I can see you have high standards.'

Just then, Mae sweeps past and deposits Dante with them, giving Jake a meaningful look before moving on. Lucy would have sworn some silent communication passed between them but she couldn't read it.

'Manage to get home all right the other week, did you?' Jake asks, before Dante can speak.

Dante's eyes narrow. 'Fine.'

'Well, if you ever need help again...' Jake's offer trails off as Dante gives a polite nod, glances at Mae's back, and then quickly exits the conversation and the room.

'What was all that about?' Lucy asks.

Jake shrugs. 'The kid managed to get his ute bogged. Right in one of those pockets near the cliffs without phone reception. Found him there wandering about.'

'And?'

'I helped.' He grins and has another sip of beer.

It could have been a friendly country cop offering the stranger assistance, but Lucy couldn't miss the hostility. Was it the natural jostling for dominance between two good-looking men, or something more?

'Must you have reminded him of it?' she asks. 'He was obviously embarrassed.'

Jake adopts an exaggeratedly wounded expression. 'You misjudge me. I just want him to know he's not alone out there.'

Again, Lucy's sure there's something more beneath his

words. 'Have you tried any of the canapés?' she asks, to change the subject.

'They're not bad,' he says. 'But a bit lightweight for my taste. I like salmon and capers as much as the next bloke, but give me a brisket slider or a bite of pork belly any day.'

Lucy's about to agree on his choice when a waitress enters carrying a tray with miniature burger buns. 'Mae must have read your mind.'

'Nah, she's always had pretty good taste.'

Lucy's suddenly aware that while she's been away, both Mae and Jake have stayed. They likely have history. She thinks of that look between them, of Jake knowing Lucy would be here. They definitely have some kind of bond.

Oblivious to her thoughts, Jake gets them some food. They eat in silence, Lucy trying to think of something to say.

She's watching Mae work the room, her gaze catching on the pendant nestled above the plunging neckline of her dress. The thumbnail stone is unlike any diamond she's seen before. With its asymmetrical shape and yellow tinge, it could be a costume piece. But there's something about it.

'The Stieglitz diamond,' Jake murmurs, following her gaze.

Lucy nods as though she knows what that is. Exotic, exclusive, typical of Mae and worn with the easy elegance most people would wear something from a market.

She pulls out her phone to give her hands something to do.

'If you're wanting to make a call, you'll have to head back down the hill.' Jake points to where the bars indicating signal on her phone should be. 'There's no reception here. Must be the curve of the point blocking the tower.'

Mae, who's been doing the rounds of the guests, catches the end of Jake's comment. She smiles. 'It's frustrating. I had to get a satellite put in to allow me to get any work done for the business from home. I can give you the passcode if you need.'

'I'm fine,' Lucy says, ignoring Jake's amused expression. 'But thanks.'

Mae nods and moves on to the next guest.

In her hurry to put her phone away, Lucy knocks the stem of her crystal glass and it tips. The liquid soaks into her black silk dress, spreading before her eyes. She closes them, fighting the flashback from the past. Another party, another spill.

'Napkin?' Jake asks. He's holding out a neatly folded white cloth.

She grabs the material and flees.

Judy

'Stop dawdling,' Judy admonished her granddaughter. 'You'll catch flies.' She tried to ignore the long and dramatic sigh she received in response, although it made her jaw clench.

These few weeks were about doing her daughter, Kate, a favour. Trying to make up for the years of distance between them. Estranged all this time, all over that feckless boy she'd run off with.

Judy and Doug had been right about him, of course they had, but Kate had her father's stubbornness, and being right didn't give Judy back the years she'd already lost to get to know the awkward child who'd come to stay. And Doug was gone now and it was too late for some things to ever be made whole. He'd let her reach out to Kate in the end so at least he'd gotten to say goodbye to his daughter. Judy, however, still had time for more than parting gestures and she had a few scores to settle.

But at this rate she'd never get home. Seriously, what was with teenagers these days? Lucy was practically dragging her feet as they walked back to the car with the shopping. It wasn't like she'd given the girl the heavy things.

She'd only suggested the trip to stop Lucy moping about the cottage, all bored and whiny. Back in Judy's day she'd have loved the long idle summer hours to read or knit, the latter something her aching hands didn't allow her to do any more.

Gosh, youth was wasted on the young.

Judy unlocked the car and loaded the bags, only to glance back and see Lucy still staring off into space halfway across the car park. How she reminded her of Kate at that age. Same pretty light brown hair and open face. Same spending half her time off in a daydream. Judy strode back to stand in front of her, hands on hips, and waited for the girl to notice.

'I know what you're doing,' Judy said.

Lucy straightened, and frowned, red flushing her cheeks. 'You do?'

'You've been moping around since you got here. I understand it's not as exciting as the big smoke but it's not all bad if you give it a chance.'

Lucy looked a little abashed. 'I'll try.'

Judy held out a hand for one of the bags. Might as well help and get this done sooner. Lucy went to pass it over, but it slipped from her fingers.

'The eggs,' Judy cried, looking down at the mess spreading at their feet. The contents were halfway to scrambled.

Lucy dropped to one knee. 'I'm sorry.'

Judy waved her apology away. 'Never you mind, it was an accident. Clean up what you can, we don't want to take the mess in the car. I'll go back in and get some more. Can't make a quiche without eggs.'

She pointed out the large skip at the back of the building and left Lucy extricating the few other items from the bag and picking up what she could of the broken eggs.

It didn't take long to duck back inside and get another half dozen eggs. She was back at the car before Lucy was finished at the large bin.

Judy wrinkled her nose; that thing reeked all the way across the car park.

Suddenly, Lucy was running towards Judy, her features pinched, like the hounds of hell were chasing her.

'What's wrong?' Judy asked.

But before Lucy could answer, the burly figure of a man came out from behind the bin. Grey jeans, khaki shirt and a grey straggly beard on a sagging jaw. Eyes sunken in dark sockets. Dried flecks of something around his mouth. He took a step towards them, his hand raised. 'You keep the fuck away from me—' Staggering into the side of the bin cut him off.

Judy stepped in front of her granddaughter. 'You watch that mouth, Teddy Parker,' she called, clear and calm. 'No one wants any trouble.'

Like he'd been pricked by a pin, all the bluster deflated. 'I was sleeping.'

'You ought to go home and sleep,' said Judy. 'Go home to that boy of yours.'

She waited, her arms crossed, staring him down, until he shuffled off around the corner.

'Is he homeless or something?' asked Lucy in a small voice.

Judy sighed. 'He used to work at the supermarket until someone complained about his drinking. He's doing it pretty tough right now.' Sensing Lucy was more upset by the encounter than she'd probably want to let on, Nan pulled out two of the new KitKat chunky bars from the bag with the unbroken eggs. 'I thought you might like to try one.'

'Thanks,' said Lucy, taking one. 'I love these.'

They'd only appeared in the shops that week, but Judy

sometimes forgot Queen's Point was often a little slower to get new trends than the rest of Australia.

Lucy was already halfway through her chocolate bar as she pulled open the passenger door. She slid into the car and spoke with her mouth full. 'What happened to the car? It's all scratched on the back door.'

'Nothing,' Judy said quickly.

'But that damage looks fresh.'

'It's not,' Judy lied, making sure her tone invited no further discussion.

JANUARY 2000
NINETEEN DAYS BEFORE THE PARTY

Lucy

Lucy had analysed Anabelle's parting 'I'll see you around' approximately one million times in the few days since the movie. There was an unspoken promise there, she was sure of it.

Despite Nan's cottage sharing a fence with the sprawling Whitlam property, they might as well have lived on a different planet. And she didn't want a repeat of the incident where she'd been accosted by rags-man behind the supermarket. Nan had said he was doing it tough or something but he'd been terrifying. She'd only gone to the supermarket in the hopes of bumping into Anabelle Whitlam, or even better, Harry.

The beach, however, might be different.

After doing every chore she could think of, she approached Nan. 'Can I go down to the beach?' she blurted.

It wasn't the brilliant, persuasive argument she'd planned, and she thought that maybe Nan hadn't heard as she sat frowning over some papers at her desk.

'Can I please—' she tried again.

'Go,' Nan snapped without looking up. 'Be back for lunch.'

Lucy stood there for a few more seconds. It couldn't be this easy, could it? Without meaning to pry, she read upside down the heading at the top of the official-looking letter. *The Royal Hospital.*

'Are you sick?' she asked.

Nan looked up then and her frown softened to a weary smile. 'Sick of all this paperwork is all. It's nothing for you to worry about. Have fun and be safe. Don't forget sunscreen. And take a bottle of water. Oh, and there are sometimes dangerous currents, so be careful.'

That was more the response Lucy had expected.

She shoved her things in a backpack and slipped her department-store sunglasses on. 'I'll be back for lunch,' she promised.

As she crossed the small road, heading for the paths she'd noticed in the dunes, she considered whether Nan might be lying. That was definitely a hospital letter and it clearly had her worried. Something tightened in her chest at the thought of Nan being unwell. Her grandfather had passed away before she'd met him. She was just getting to know Nan; she didn't want her to disappear already.

She worried about it until the path down through the dunes opened up to a white, sandy beach and turquoise sea backdrop. But at the sight of Anabelle Whitlam, lounging on a towel, all thought of her grandmother vanished.

Lucy hesitated.

Maybe this was a mistake.

The younger girl was curvy and confident in a white fifties style bikini, laughing at something someone out of sight was saying. Her head was thrown back and her blonde curls glinted golden. She was way too cool to want to hang out with Lucy in her plain navy one-piece from last summer. Even her own friends in her group from school didn't, not really. She was only ever included as an afterthought.

Anabelle lifted her head just as Lucy was about to flee. Her smile widened. 'Hey, it's that girl from the cinema.'

Her companion stepped into view. Harry Whitlam. Surfboard in hand, he must have come straight from the ocean. He wore black board shorts and a devilish grin, and his longish hair dripped water on to his tanned chest.

Lucy just about swallowed her tongue.

He pushed a hand through his hair. 'Hey, girl from the cinema.'

'Lucy,' said Anabelle. 'It's Lucy, right?'

Lucy managed a nod. She hoped the thrill of being remembered wasn't written on her face. *Desperate*, her group at school would call it.

'Don't just stand there, come and join us. Like, unless you're meeting someone else?' Anabelle's question appeared only perfunctory, because if you could be with the Whitlams why would you bother elsewhere?

Lucy tried not to stare at either sibling as she spread out her towel, nerves making her hands clumsy. However, she didn't need to worry about conversation because Anabelle chatted easily about the movie they'd seen, admitting she'd had nightmares, and Harry interrupted to tease her about it, and Lucy could have sat and listened to the two of them all day.

Then, as though to counter Harry's 'baby' teasing, Anabelle explained how they went to boarding school in Sydney and reminisced about staying at her friend from school's house at the beginning of the holidays and borrowing one of their BMWs and the two girls getting pulled over by the New South

Wales police and having to charm their way out of the cop calling their parents because they were both fifteen.

It seemed all Lucy had to do was look interested – something she didn't have to try – and smile.

Lunchtime and needing to go back to the cottage arrived far too soon. 'I could come back after,' Lucy suggested.

'Nah, we'll probably be gone,' Harry said. 'We have to get back before Mother gets home.' He frowned meaningfully at his sister.

Lucy looked between the two, trying not to be disappointed.

Anabelle glared at Harry and tossed her hair. 'Whatever.' She took Lucy's hand and in that moment they could have been the only two on the beach. 'Meet me here tomorrow and I'll show you up to the house. You'll love it. Oh, and I noticed that your sunglasses are scratched. I have an old pair of Versaces that would be gorge on you.'

Someone cooler might have played hard to get, but Lucy couldn't get the words out fast enough. 'I'd love to.'

6

PRESENT DAY

The Whitlams' hallway is deserted and thankfully there's no queue for the bathroom. Lucy ducks in, catching a glimpse of her strained features before locking the door and leaning against the cool marble of the wall. So much for turning herself into someone who belongs in a home like this.

She assesses the damage of the spilt champagne. Not as bad as she feared. She uses the napkin to mop it up and soon it's simply a darker shadow. How juvenile to have fled like that. Hopefully, she can return to the party before anyone other than Jake notices she's gone.

Her steps echo in the empty hallway, the blinking red light on a small camera the only witness to her pausing to square her shoulders. Despite being alone, something trickles cold and unpleasant at the back of her neck. A wrongness. Something not isolated to this part of the house, but rather underlying everything. Like blood spilt off the jetty diffusing out into the ocean.

She looks up, catches sight of another camera. That's probably it. She's not used to this kind of surveillance. Her cheeks flame at the thought of someone watching her mad dash of earlier.

'Excuse me, are you lost?'

Lucy turns towards the passage that leads to the grand staircase.

Anabelle is standing two steps up and there's a chill in her eyes that has Lucy's stomach tight, but then she smiles. 'Lucy,' she says, closing the distance between them.

They embrace politely. Anabelle smells like baby shampoo and contentment and the scent of it suits her no less than when she was fifteen and stole her mum's expensive perfume.

Letting go of Anabelle is like letting go of everything Lucy's life should be. Anabelle glows, and the part of Lucy that's been hardened by her corporate climb should envy her but she can't, not with Anabelle smiling warmly now.

Lucy's nerves about seeing Anabelle again after all this time abate with that smile, despite the aloofness from Anabelle in the years since they parted. The letters and emails with no reply, the catch-ups that never happened. And through it all, that final night. It was such a whirlwind of silly teenage dramas. Better to leave it all in the past.

Anabelle holds Lucy at arm's length. 'You're stunning,' she says. 'All grown up.'

It's not as though every trip to the hairdresser, every workout and every missed chocolate brownie has been for this moment, but pathetically Lucy flushes with pleasure. 'Not really.' And then, 'I just spilled champagne on my dress.'

Anabelle peers at the spot and shakes her head. 'Can't see a thing. Mae said you were in town to pack up Judy's place. How are you?'

Lucy's been asked that exact question a million times since Brian and then Nan passed away, but when Anabelle asks it, she's not looking away, already thinking of what she's going to say next, but looking right at Lucy.

She wants to know.

'Okay,' Lucy says. 'Being in the cottage is harder than I thought it would be, but I'm making progress.'

Anabelle squeezes her hand gently. 'I'm here if you need anything.'

It should be empty, such an offer from someone Lucy hasn't seen for so long, but it comforts. 'Thanks. And how have you been? You have a family now?' It comes out as a question, although Lucy's followed too much of Anabelle's social media to pretend not to know. 'How was the trip?'

'Helicopters are not my favourite form of travel, but we're here now. I can't wait for you to meet everyone. They'll be down in a moment.' Anabelle sighs. 'I'll have to make the rounds in there, but we should catch up properly one evening, after the little ones are sorted for the night.'

'I'd love to. When?' The old Lucy wouldn't have pushed, but she suspects that if she doesn't arrange a time now, nothing will come of it.

Anabelle's smile strains a fraction but she nods. 'Soon. What about Jan's?'

Memories of the delicious ice-cream parlour make Lucy's mouth water, but she would have picked Anabelle to prefer something more sophisticated. 'That would be great.'

Lucy gives Anabelle her number and she promises to message, and then their moment alone is gone. Further down the hallway, a door opens with a soft swish, revealing a discreet elevator, a new feature since Lucy last visited, and a man steps out from inside.

From Lucy's online stalking – she's not proud – she recognises him as Anabelle's husband. An Indian man rumoured to be related to royalty. In the flesh he's handsome and charming and he looks at Anabelle adoringly. He's holding a baby wrapped in a soft cloth, only a little of its dark-haired head visible. 'I think she wants you,' he says.

Anabelle takes the tiny bundle and presses her face to it before letting the little body rest against her shoulder.

'This is Lucy,' she says to him. 'And this is my husband, Manan.'

'Nice to meet you,' they say at the same time.

Then Mr Whitlam arrives from another stairway with Anabelle's two older children, one holding each hand. The children are all scrubbed, pink-cheeked and in their pyjamas. They hide behind the adults, peeking out with shy smiles.

'If it isn't Lucy Antonello,' observes Mr Whitlam. He lets the children's hands go to perform a formal peck that doesn't touch Lucy's cheek. He's wearing a cravat and waistcoat, as she remembers he did to the party on the last night of the summer, but appears tanned and fit. She read online that he's been a visiting professor at a number of universities across Europe, and it seems the lifestyle has suited him.

Although they left the party together that last night of summer, Lucy wasn't surprised to see Mr and Mrs Whitlam drift apart in the years that followed. At least, according to their online presence. Her in Paris when he was in Italy. Her sharing stunning photos of New York when he lived in Spain. He always seemed more interested in his work, and his students, and Lucy might have been only sixteen, but she picked up on the tension.

'Nice to see you, Mr Whitlam,' she says.

'Please, call me Grant,' he says stiffly. 'Your grandmother was a fine employee, and we are sorry for your loss.'

'Thank you.'

Lucy trails them into the party, and edges back as the small crowd presses closer to greet the guests of honour. There's much fussing over the children before Manan quickly herds them out to be put to bed with the assistance of two young staff.

Fresh glass of bubbly in hand, Lucy makes herself circulate. She shares an amusing work anecdote with Mayor Rachael, hoping her bravado that she'll even have a job to go back to isn't all over her face, before an older man called Karl corners her about Nan's roses. He's the property manager she has to thank for maintaining Nan's place. He does the work, although reveals that Mae owns the business.

'Mae?' she queries.

Karl nods.

Lucy glances across at her, wondering how many of the town businesses she's involved in. It's only when another man, Bob, joins them and introduces himself that Lucy realises she's met them as a couple before, in the blur of Nan's funeral. 'Thank you for coming to Nan's service.'

'We wouldn't have missed it,' Bob says. 'She was a good friend.'

The men stand side by side in that way that betrays their intimacy. Nan once referred to her friend Karl as a confirmed bachelor. Looking at the way he is with Bob makes Lucy glad nineteen years has changed some things.

She wanders outside. A few of the more daring guests are taking advantage of the heated infinity pool, where steam rises off the surface, distorting the pretty lights. Lucy doesn't feel at all inclined to join them, not least because none of the Whitlams have made a move to the water.

After about an hour of socialising, Lucy's feeling quite pleased with herself. She's on the edge of a group listening to

Manan tell the story of meeting Anabelle on a private beach near Barcelona.

'And just like that, her gaze met mine and I was a goner,' he finishes.

As Lucy chuckles along with the others, she struggles to hide a yawn. It's been a long day, her ankle is aching and there are enough people there that she shouldn't be missed. She scans for Mae to say her farewell.

'You're leaving,' says someone behind her.

Lucy turns, knowing instinctively that it's Jake. 'It's late.'

He studies her over the top of his beer. It's the same level as when they parted earlier and she's irritated that he's interested her enough to notice.

'Are you okay?' he asks.

Lucy blinks at the impossible question. 'Is anyone?'

She wants to bite down on the words but it's too late, they're out there. Her tone was far too serious, too intense. She's given too much away.

But he seems to take her question at face value. 'Probably not.'

She places her half-empty glass on a table and he does the same with his beer.

'Let's go,' he says. He walks next to her as she approaches where Mae, Anabelle and Mr Whitlam stand with a few others.

'Thanks for having me,' Lucy says as they make the appropriate dismayed noises that she's leaving.

Jake adds his own farewells and stays at her side as she retrieves her coat and slides the invitation to the art show in the pocket.

'No jacket?' she asks.

He shakes his head. 'It's not that cold.'

'Whatever.' She slips her arms in hers, enjoying the warmth. She lost the need to wear less than she's comfortable in around the same time she found grey strands in her hair. 'Don't come crying to me when your lips turn blue.'

'I'm glad you're so concerned about my lips.'

'I'm not.'

They step outside and the wind is biting. She fights a smug smile when he shoves his hands in his pockets and shivers.

'Where are you parked?' she asks.

He hooks a thumb over his shoulder. 'That way, but I'll see you to the cottage first. Your grandmother would kill me if I let you walk home alone.'

If he wants to play Mr Chivalrous, Lucy's not going to fight him on it. Not when a shoe with human remains was found so close. Although you wouldn't know it from the light-hearted atmosphere at the party they've just left. It's like Mae bewitched the entire room not to talk about it, but she isn't here now.

'Do you know any more about the shoe?' she asks. 'Should I be scared to walk home alone?'

He hesitates, then sighs. 'We're old friends and besides, by my estimation it was released to the media…' He glances at his watch. 'About an hour ago. It was a woman's high-heel silver sandal. The bones were caught in the upper strap.'

Unlikely it was a drifter, then. And who goes near the water in high heels? Jetty or boat, even sand is tricky. She shivers, her brain going to foul play.

'Not glass, then?' she asks. 'Probably rules out Cinderella.'

He laughs easily, despite the macabre conversation. 'Probably.'

She's still thinking about the shoe possibilities when they reach the heavy, ornate gates a few minutes later.

'It's interesting,' he says.

Lucy had begun to think they were going to walk the rest of the way in silence. 'What?'

'Them all coming back. Now, of all times.'

'Do you know something else?' She stops and turns to look up at him, but he's not giving anything else away. 'Anyway, I came back.'

'You did,' he agrees.

Then he's walking again, and she has to hurry to keep up with him, struggling not to show the pain from her tender ankle. The article Lucy saw played a part in her coming back now, but the Whitlams couldn't all be that curious, could they?

'It could be a coincidence,' Lucy says as they approach the cottage. 'Neither Mrs Whitlam nor Harry are here.'

He stops by the small gate. 'You would know.'

She steps inside and closes the gate between them. 'I'm good from here. Thanks for walking me,' she says. Although it's not like she asked him.

He nods, already turning away. 'Night.'

Then he's striding back up the hill towards the Whitlam house and he doesn't look back. Lucy knows because she stands there, one hand on the latch, and watches him until he disappears from sight.

Two cars passing from the party gets her moving. She doesn't want to be there when Jake's ute comes by. With the gate secure, she hurries to the porch, glad of the small light that allows her to slide the key in the lock.

There's a scrape from the side of the house. A figure leans

against the wall in a spot shadowed by the edge of the porch and the dense foliage of an ancient wattle tree. She tugs her keys free and lifts them in front of her as a weapon, even as she asks, 'Jake?'

The man steps into the light. 'Not Jake,' he drawls, making goosebumps appear on her skin. 'Sorry to disappoint you.'

7

PRESENT DAY

Lucy's heartbeat stutters at the sight of Harry Whitlam. With his brown hair curling at his shoulders, and wearing a black short-sleeved shirt and tight black jeans, he's all liquid darkness. He saunters closer like a shadow, dark and somehow intangible.

'Harry,' she manages.

His full lips curve. 'Lucy Antonello.'

She should correct him, she is – *was* – a married woman, but then his hands are folding over hers and it is so damn hard to think around him. He tugs her closer, leans down and brushes a feather-light kiss across one cheek and then the other.

'It's so good to see you.'

She sucks in a breath. *Idiot*. She should have realised he was there, should have caught that familiar scent of Harry. His cologne of wood notes and exotic spices mixed with paint, and always a hint of whatever it is that's used to clean brushes. She can walk past it in a hardware store and go weak.

Automatically, she glances down at his fingers, still entwined with hers, and there on his nails are tiny flecks of olive paint. He's never far away from his work, it's the only thing consistent in his life. Except his family, and her, maybe. But their meetings are hardly regular.

'I didn't expect you,' she says.

His smile widens. 'I like to do the unexpected, you know that.' And he's still holding her hands. 'I've missed you,' he murmurs. 'I was right to come here, I needed this, I needed you.'

And somehow, he's saying it with lips that are a whisper from hers and she could so easily close the distance between them and succumb to that mouth.

She doesn't.

This man is like a drug she can't quit, but she's stronger now. Despite her every nerve ending wanting to be closer, begging for that human contact after having been so alone since Brian died, she pulls away.

Harry frowns. 'Are you okay?'

The growl of a car coming from the house up on the hill reminds her that they're on Nan's front porch where anyone could see them.

'It's cold,' she says. 'We should go in if you want to talk.'

Say no, she begs mentally.

But, instead, he looks out into the darkness, where it's begun to drizzle, with faint confusion. 'I hadn't noticed the weather turn,' he says as he trails her inside.

It's been freezing all day, his thin shirt is completely inappropriate no matter the hour, but having just felt the warmth of his skin, she understands he doesn't feel cold.

Hades lumbers to his feet at the sight of them in the doorway. He only gives Harry small interest, more focused on heading outside, and Lucy's hope that Brian's dog will somehow save her from her weakness for Harry Whitlam goes with him.

She takes off her jacket and Harry hangs it up for her, anticipating her movements in that way he has.

She knows more about Harry's career from gossip sites than from anything he's shared with her. From prodigy, to international boy wonder, to genuine star of the art world. The dating of models, the affairs, and the scandals that have followed him haven't exactly hurt his profile. She's only seen him a few times in person since that summer, a handful of intoxicating hook-ups. It would be melodramatic to say he's ruined her life.

But not entirely untrue.

By any logic, seeing Harry standing in Nan's living room should fill her body with fear and loathing, but as usual, when he looks at her it creates an entirely different kind of tension.

'Hey,' he says, reaching out to draw her close before she can offer a drink or think of some other chore to move herself away. 'You were limping.'

'It's nothing,' she says, not surprised he noticed.

'Come here.'

She doesn't resist him.

She can't. The heat of him and the way his touch sends thrills beneath her skin. And she is single. There is literally no reason not to meet his lips with hers when he slowly, inexorably lowers his head.

It's a good kiss.

A cynical part of her knows practice is part of his expertise, but even trying to think about how many other mouths he's kissed doesn't help. Because it's all him and he's been this tender, this demanding, this liquefying since that very first time. Guilt battles with heat.

Brian.

She tries to think her dead husband's name and knows she'll hate herself later, but she's powerless to pull away. Not least because of the months it's been since anyone held her.

A moan escapes her as Harry moves to kiss her jaw and then her neck. He must be able to feel the hammer of her pulse in her throat because he kisses it thoroughly, until she thinks maybe his hands exploring her hips, and hers gripping his shoulders, are all that's keeping her upright.

'Why weren't you up at the house?' She gasps out the question, desperate to stop what his hands are doing while just as desperate not to stop what his hands are doing.

It works to break the mood. He steps away and his ragged breathing suggests she's not the only one affected.

He drops on to the edge of the couch and rests his head on his hands, his dark hair falling forward to hide his face. 'I couldn't do it.'

'Do what?'

'Pretend.' He lifts his head, and those beautiful eyes with their thick, sooty lashes are brimming with pain. 'I couldn't make nice with the public, say the right things, smile and fucking simper when she's bloody lying there on a cold table in the morgue.'

Lucy's heart is thumping hard and she sinks next to him on the couch in case her knees give way. 'Who?'

The body and the shoe.

Instinct tells her that right here are the answers she wanted. Right now, he can give them to her. And she gets a strange, sick feeling that once she knows, it will change everything.

But he's dropped his head again and he's not answering.

'Who is it, Harry?' She touches his trembling shoulder, feels his body heat through the thin fabric of his shirt. 'Tell me.'

He takes a couple more breaths. Breaths that sound a lot like sobs but it's impossible to tell when she can't see his face.

Finally, he stands. Strides to the door and opens it. Looks back at her with hollow, haunted eyes. He laughs, a bitter, choked sound.

'Mother, of course.'

Lucy

'OMG Anabelle, did you think of knocking!' came a cry as the oldest Whitlam held a fluffy white towel over her slender body.

Lucy covered her eyes and felt her cheeks go hot.

Anabelle smirked. 'That's Mae's bathroom. Her room is across the hall.'

'Where I was headed,' came a voice from behind them. Then a door slammed.

Anabelle continued the tour as though they hadn't just seen her sister wearing only a towel. She'd already taken them through an actual servants' entrance – Lucy tried not to think whether that included Nan – and then through so many secret stairs and passages Lucy was pretty much lost.

'That bedroom used to be mine.' Anabelle waved at an open door. Inside was nondescript, creams and browns. Nice, but it could have belonged to anyone rich enough to have such a huge space and that many cushions.

Anabelle's face wrinkled in distaste as though she heard Lucy's thoughts. 'Boring, huh? It used to be like a rainbow with every wall a different colour, but Mother had it repainted as soon as I moved out.'

She kept walking.

'This is our lounge,' Anabelle said at the door to a room decked out with a huge TV, speakers everywhere, an air hockey table and a pinball machine.

'How many videos do you have?' Lucy asked, staring at the cabinets full of colour across the room.

'They're DVDs.'

Anabelle was dismissive and Lucy managed not to gasp or say that she only knew one other person who even had a DVD player.

There were double doors at the end of the hallway and beyond that it turned a sharp left. Where Lucy had glimpsed stiff, posed family portraits downstairs, here there was a single canvas showing three young Whitlams building a sandcastle together. The slight blur put their happy faces in motion.

Next to it, dark wood double-doors shone with a soft sheen, the kind impossible not to want to touch, and Lucy found her fingertips on the smooth, warm timbers. One of the doors sighed open. Hand still outstretched, Lucy braced to be told off. Maybe for Anabelle to snap and march her off the premises.

Before Anabelle could say anything, a soft sound floated out from inside the room.

Inside were walls of books, deep chairs perfect for reading and two huge desks. Sunlight streamed in the long narrow windows, falling on two people. A seated woman, her brow furrowed in concentration, her dark, glossy hair falling forward over her shoulder, and a man crouched at her side. His hand rested on the printed document in front of her and his words were soft, intimate and urgent. She wasn't looking at the page but rather at his mouth only a few inches from her own, her face a picture of unwavering devotion.

Anabelle leaned past Lucy and gently, silently pulled the large door closed.

Lucy didn't want to ask about the woman, a woman way too young to be Anabelle's mother. But Anabelle was unconcerned.

'That was my dad,' she said. 'He teaches all over the world and has a few graduate students.' Lucy must have looked blank because Anabelle added, 'Lost languages, translating classic literature. Greek mythology. That kind of thing. The girl with him, Vanessa, is nearly through her doctorate, I think. They all tend to worship the ground he walks on. She's staying in one of the guest rooms for a few weeks because waiting until the term begins is too long.' Anabelle's eye-roll showed what she thought of not wanting to enjoy holidays.

Lucy nodded agreement.

They moved on to Anabelle's room. A space that was even better than Lucy could have imagined, complete with a secret door and hidden tower room.

'This bedroom is the kind of place girls dream of having. It's totally perfect. You are so lucky,' Lucy gushed.

'No, duh,' Anabelle agreed.

But there was an edge to her voice. Thanks to the reflection in the nearby window, Lucy could sneak a glimpse at her friend's face. On it was complete desolation.

Lucy spun, opening her mouth to ask what was wrong, but Anabelle appeared as bright and cheerful as ever. 'Are you okay?' Lucy had to make sure.

'Better than,' replied Anabelle immediately.

Lucy figured it must have been a trick of the light.

But Anabelle soon jumped up. 'This is boring. We should

go down to the beach. Harry's probably there. We'll get snacks.'

Still shaken by what she thought she'd seen, Lucy didn't argue. And when Anabelle rummaged on her dresser and threw her some gold-rimmed black designer sunglasses, she forgot about anything but mumbling her thanks.

This time they went a different way through the lower floor, towards the kitchen.

'What's through there?' Lucy asked, pointing towards a building beyond the pool.

'The pool house,' Anabelle said. 'It sounds fancier than it is. Mostly it's for storing the pool gear. We used it as our clubroom when we pretended to solve mysteries back when we were kids. Mother keeps saying it needs an overhaul, but she says that about most of the house.'

They'd reached the kitchen but there was someone already in there. The woman had the appearance of someone who'd walked out of a sitcom and on to the wrong set. With her sleek black and crimson suit, and her blonde hair straight and shining, she should have been in a penthouse office, not a home.

So, this was what someone who had a housekeeper looked like.

The thought came into Lucy's head alongside a sudden yearning so intense that it snatched her breath. She wanted this. This house, this family, this life. She wanted to be Mrs Whitlam with a desire stronger than she'd felt for anyone or anything before.

'My mother,' Anabelle said, quickly changing direction and steering Lucy outside.

'Lovely to chat, darling,' called Mrs Whitlam drily.

Anabelle rolled her eyes.

Lucy looked back though, trying to offer a polite smile to Mrs Whitlam, but she was gone.

Later that night, as she tried to get to sleep in the small bed in Nan's sunroom, Lucy fantasised she was actually up in the house on the hill, but not as a guest this time. She lived there, maybe even had Anabelle's old room, and Mae treated her like a sister.

When Lucy told her friends she had to go away for the rest of the summer, they hadn't really cared. Someone said she'd have to teach the country kids how to party. Someone else that she'd know more about the latest trends. And someone else that the boys would find her exotic.

But having met the Whitlams, she understood how wrong they'd been. Now Lucy understood what worldly actually looked like.

She was almost asleep when her door creaked open.

'Lucy?' came the soft question from the doorway.

Her heavy eyes begged for sleep, but there was something in Nan's tone. 'Hmm?' she managed.

'Be careful.'

'What?' Lucy mumbled.

Nan didn't say anything for a while – was she going to stand there all night? – and Lucy tried to return to thinking about Harry and the gorgeous house.

'Those kids aren't always what they seem.' Nan's words came as if from far away.

No, they're better, Lucy thought as sleep claimed her.

8

PRESENT DAY

Lucy arrives early to meet Anabelle for their promised catch-up two days later. She parks at the far end of Main Street and wanders back towards Jan's. The pain from her ankle is only a dull ache despite the day of work and she wants to check out the town.

She was sure Anabelle would cancel after what Harry said, but after three unanswered messages, Anabelle had replied as though nothing had happened. So far, there's been no link in the media between the shoe under the jetty and Brooke Whitlam.

One of the first places Lucy looked was Brooke Whitlam's socials. She has – had? – just the one account that she started maybe seven years ago and has barely posted on since. Although she accepted Lucy's friend request, she's never replied to any of her messages or comments.

Lucy's comment about Paris being on her bucket list on a photo of the Eiffel Tower at night was only one among many that didn't receive any personal response. The yearly birthday greetings were never reciprocated.

And the most recent message, sent by Lucy a week ago to each of the Whitlams including Brooke, suggesting they could have coffee while she was in Queen's Point, hadn't even been read.

Now Lucy wonders whether Brooke Whitlam had even been alive when it was sent.

The last post from Brooke Whitlam was six months earlier from Mauritius showing a stunning beach retreat and, like all the others, was just of scenery.

Nothing to say Brooke Whitlam's been at Queen's Point.

Nothing to say she hasn't.

Lucy's jacket wards off the chill from the sea, but the evening sky is clear. The changes in the town she noticed as she drove through on Friday reveal more trendy shops and high-end stores, but still the bleak darkness of a few vacant shopfronts. The flagship Whitlam Homewares store in the old cinema building is closed, but she lingers outside. The illuminated front windows could be in any cosmopolitan city and she presses close, trying to match the luxurious displays with the bones of the cinema foyer.

All this, while her brain screams reminders that Mrs Whitlam is dead.

By the time she arrives at Jan's, situated on the enviable corner of the main street and the beachfront, she's a few minutes late. Anabelle is waiting in the shelter of the front canopy, checking the time on her phone with a frown.

'Sorry I'm late,' Lucy says, remembering with a pang all the times she's tried to reach out to Anabelle over the years without hearing back.

'It's fine,' Anabelle replies in a way that doesn't erase Lucy's misgivings. She leans in for a polite air kiss. Tonight, her expensive, uniquely Anabelle scent is mixed with something sickly sour.

She must notice Lucy keeping her distance because she explains, 'My youngest, Skylar, is at a real spit-up stage. I swear, I could shower three times and still smell bad.'

Lucy chuckles sympathetically, unsure whether the unease in her chest is revulsion or envy. She never wanted to be trapped with a child but, even describing something gross, Anabelle's face lights up when she mentions hers.

'She's gorgeous,' Lucy says on cue.

Anabelle smiles and she leads them inside.

As Lucy follows, she mentally replays every nuance in Anabelle's interactions, looking for a sign she's grieving her mother. There was none. Could Harry have lied?

Caught in her thoughts, Lucy only notices the difference to Jan's when she's stepping over the threshold. It's always been old-fashioned but now it's deliberately so, with a new fit-out reminiscent of a 1950s American diner. There are intimate booths in the back half of the place as well as brighter, more family friendly seating at the front. A look at the leatherbound menu confirms the casual milkshake spot has grown up.

'Wow,' Lucy says, unable to hide her surprise.

Anabelle offers a tight smile. 'A bit different to when we were kids.'

She nods, but as she scans the menu, she takes in the presence of a group of teens at one of the bigger tables near the front, joking around as they slurp shakes. Some things haven't changed.

'It all looks delicious.'

Anabelle leans across and flicks to the last page, her

perfectly manicured nails pointing to an item in the middle. 'You have to have this, surely.'

'A delicate dark chocolate macaron, filled with a scoop of Jan's signature blood orange and chocolate ice cream, with whipped cream and candied orange.' Lucy's mouth waters as she reads it aloud.

'You ordered the choc-orange milkshake every time we came in here,' Anabelle says.

Lucy wouldn't have guessed Anabelle would remember such detail, nor mention it if she did. She snaps the menu closed. 'That's me decided. What are you having?' She stands and nods towards the counter. 'It's my shout.'

'Eton Mess, thanks.'

Lucy relaxes at not having to point out how many milkshakes she owes Anabelle, not having to beg to prove she's not the poor kid any more. As she places the order, she's still thinking about what Harry said. Should she mention it?

Anabelle puts her phone away as Lucy returns. 'Manan just letting me know the kids are all settled. He's very hands-on.'

'That must be nice.' Lucy's managing to maintain her end of the conversation but a new troubling thought occurs to her – is it odd if she doesn't ask after Anabelle's mother?

'It lets me get out occasionally,' Anabelle continues. 'But I've found I like being home with my family more than I could have imagined. One of our properties has a few acres and there we keep chickens and maintain an extensive vegetable garden. Getting the eggs, cooking with produce I've grown, it's fulfilling in a way I never expected.' She chuckles. 'Listen to me, I sound like some hippy. Tell me about you. I heard you lost your husband?'

Lucy squirms, thinking of the two sisters talking about her. 'Brian was a wonderful man,' she says. 'But he wouldn't want me to sit around feeling sorry for myself.' He'd told her to find someone else one day, but she's sure he didn't mean someone like Harry. 'Work keeps me busy and I try to keep tabs on his daughter. She's a doctor and probably a bit old for me to help her with her bedtime routine.'

Anabelle leans forward. 'You didn't want children of your own?'

'It's never been the right time,' Lucy says lightly. It's hard not to think that Anabelle would know all this if she'd responded to any of Lucy's attempts to stay more in touch. Clearly she hasn't been following Lucy online the way Lucy has been with her.

Anabelle changes the subject as the food is delivered. 'Did you make much progress at the cottage today?'

Lucy stifles a groan at how little difference she's made. 'I need to get the big items out of the way before I can go through all Nan's personal items and paperwork.'

She takes a bite of the macaron shell and it melts in her mouth.

Anabelle is already halfway through her dessert and there's a dab of cream on her lip when she pauses and frowns. 'How will you manage all that by yourself?'

'I don't know.' Lucy rubs at her side. 'I strained something trying to move one of the buffet pieces today. I'll probably have to look into getting some help. Simply taking the small boxes to the charity store in town will take dozens of trips in my tiny car. They're keen for whatever I can donate, but don't have anyone to collect it.'

'I know.' Anabelle leans forward, her face alight, and for a second she's teenage Anabelle full of an exciting idea, not this aloof virtual stranger. 'What about Dante?'

'The backpacker working for Mae?'

She's nodding. 'I'm sure she could spare him for an afternoon. It's the least we can do after Judy's long service to our family.'

Lucy bites back pointing out that she can afford to pay someone. This is kindness, not charity; sometimes her past makes it hard to tell the difference. 'I'd appreciate it. But only if he's not needed at the house.'

'How's tomorrow? And I'll have him drive down in one of the utes for the bigger items.'

'I'm sure I'll have plenty for him to do.'

'Excellent,' she says.

A comfortable silence settles while they make short work of the delicious desserts.

Lucy's so relaxed she's about to ask Anabelle why she didn't write back all those years ago, when a sudden cold draught slices through her, then a nearby chair clatters to the floor.

'You can't come in here!'

In unison, they turn their heads towards the doorway. Jan stands there, hands on hips, her heavily wrinkled face creased in consternation. The door is open, explaining the chill, and she's trying physically to block a woman with a microphone and a man, carrying what looks like a news camera, from coming inside.

'We only want to ask a few questions,' says the woman, pushing forward.

The man waves the camera in Jan's face. 'It's in the public interest.'

Jan steps back at the onslaught, colliding with the

overturned chair and sending it screeching back across the floor. She winces but plants her feet and crosses her arms. 'I'll call the police.'

A solid young man comes from the kitchen at a run to stand at Jan's side; the likeness between them is obvious. 'Don't worry, Gran. I've already called them.'

The microphone woman, dressed in a smart burgundy skirt and jacket, ignores the argument and scans the small café. Her gaze lands on Lucy and Anabelle's little booth.

'There she is.'

The man swings the camera up to rest on his shoulder and points it their way.

Lucy's stomach lurches but it's not her they're focused on.

'Ms Whitlam,' calls the woman. 'Is it true that your mother's body was found near the cliffs at Queen's Point?'

Anabelle blanches. But it's not surprise in her expression. It's anger. At the woman? The interruption? Any of it would be enough, Lucy guesses.

Anabelle grabs a menu to cover her face.

'We understand it was her shoe found beneath the jetty a few weeks ago. Can you reveal for us the cause of death? How are the rest of the family feeling? Is Harry in town?'

The journalist has managed to get closer to deliver her barrage of questions, although Jan and her grandson are still trying to block their path.

'I told you to leave,' Jan repeats.

There's an electricity in the air. Murmurs of shock and curiosity. Even the teenagers are paying attention at the news of a body being found.

With a jolt, Lucy's brain starts to work again. She allows

her hair to fall forward over her face and she uses her huge jacket to shelter them both.

Anabelle's smile is grateful. 'I need to get out of here,' she says. 'I am so sorry about this.' Again, there's no hint of grief in her; rather, she could be apologising for spilling a glass of water at a posh afternoon tea.

Sirens sound in the distance.

'There must be a kitchen exit,' Lucy says.

Anabelle nods and they stand together, the coat providing a shield. They fall easily into step and it strikes Lucy as reminiscent of that time they used a towel to shelter from the summer storm and ran laughing and breathless to get under cover.

There's no laughter as they move towards the bar and the kitchen beyond.

Jan has guessed their intention and followed, leaving her grandson to run interference. There's the sound of a scuffle and 'This camera's worth more than your front teeth, son'.

'This way,' Jan says. 'I tried to stop them.'

'And I appreciate it,' Anabelle replies.

Then they're following Jan, moving through the swinging door and into the kitchen and the journalist's questions are cut off as it closes behind them. They're led through a room of gleaming steel surfaces to a lane outside.

Anabelle appears unflustered. 'The dessert was delicious as always,' she says to Jan.

'It was,' Lucy chimes in.

Jan waves away the compliment. 'Thank you.' She ducks back inside.

Anabelle glances both ways down the narrow lane,

wrinkling her nose at the stench from a nearby bin. 'I should go.'

Lucy nods. 'Do you want this?' She holds out her jacket.

'No, but thanks. Don't be a stranger.'

Then she pulls her hood over her head and strides into the darkness, rounding the corner and disappearing from sight.

9

PRESENT DAY

Staying at Nan's cottage with its lumpy mattress, boxy television, and a microwave the only nod to convenience, Lucy should long for her modern townhouse with its half-dozen streaming services, proximity to any cuisine she could desire and luxury fittings the way she yearned for the Whitlams' lifestyle as a teen. But she doesn't miss any of it. Except maybe the coffee machine. And it's this that has her at Jan's before she's properly awake the next morning, having walked all the way from the cottage to get Hades exercised at the same time.

She can't face going through any more of Nan's things without some decent caffeine. That and wanting to hear what the town is saying about Brooke Whitlam. She'd fallen asleep the night before scrolling on her phone, trying to find out what the media are reporting. The answer being 'not much'. No wonder the journalist was trying to get something out of Anabelle.

There's already a queue at the café – well, of two people – and they're talking quite openly about the discovery.

'I heard she slipped and fell into the water,' says the elderly gentleman.

The woman with him shakes her head. 'Not at all. My

neighbour heard it was a gunshot.' She makes a small hand gesture imitating a gun, absurdly animated as she does so.

The man's voice drops, but not much. 'Could it have been one of the family? There is a lot of money up there to argue over.'

'No.' The woman is certain. 'They were all so close. Such a happy family.'

Lucy coughs to cover her snort of disbelief. That's not how she remembers it.

The woman frowns then continues, 'It was definitely a robbery gone wrong.'

Although this is the kind of gossip Lucy came looking for, hearing it makes her stomach turn. She's glad when they take their conversation outside, but the relief is short-lived as Jan recognises her. 'Oh dear, have you recovered from last night?'

'Yes, thanks. Can I please have a long black to go?'

Jan calls the order to her grandson and shakes her head sadly as she holds out the machine for Lucy to tap her card. 'It's so terrible of the media to be harassing that poor girl when the news must be fresh. That poor family, losing their beloved mother.'

Lucy mumbles something that sounds like agreement. Better than airing her observation that Anabelle didn't seem sad.

'I do wonder how it happened though,' she says. 'You know, how someone like Brooke died? She always had everything under control.' Jan leans across the counter, lowering her voice. 'Did Anabelle share anything with you? You know, last night. Any details? I didn't even realise Brooke was back in town.'

'She didn't, sorry.'

Thankfully, Lucy's coffee is ready. Jan picks it up from where her grandson has placed it on the counter, but she isn't in any hurry to hand it over. 'Are you two close?' she asks. 'I know that Grant is up at the house but I haven't seen anything of young Harry. I'd expect him to come home for the funeral. They will hold one, don't you think? But I guess it depends on when the forensic people release her body.'

The longer Jan's inquisition goes on, the more Nan's instant coffee doesn't look so bad. Lucy could grab the cup out of her hand and make a run for it, but then she'd have to avoid this place the rest of the time she's here.

'Is that your dog outside?' comes a familiar voice from behind Lucy.

Lucy shoots Jake a grateful look. 'It is, and he's probably fretting.' She smiles apologetically at Jan. 'I should take my coffee before Hades scares away any of your customers. He's a big softie, but you wouldn't know it to look at him.'

Disappointment on her face, Jan finally hands over the coffee. But then she sees Jake and brightens. 'Sergeant Parker. What can I get for you? Lots going on at the station, I bet.'

Feeling a flare of sympathy for the grilling Jake is about to receive, Lucy escapes out to where Hades is waiting. By the time she's managed to untie him, Jake is outside, takeaway coffee in hand.

'How did you manage that?' she asks.

He waggles his eyebrows. 'I have my ways.' But then he adds, 'The young lad saw me coming and made up my order, so it was ready by the time I reached the counter. Then I pleaded important police business.'

He's in worn jeans and a leather jacket, hair messy and stubble on his jaw.

'You don't look dressed for work.'

'I have a few things to do before I go in, but she believed me.' He shrugs. 'Want some company?' he asks as he gives Hades' ears a thorough scratch.

'We're heading back to the cottage from here,' she warns him.

'I figured.'

He falls into step beside her as she turns Hades towards the beach. She could have driven but the dull ache in her ankle isn't enough for her to ignore the dog's big, brown, pleading eyes, begging to get out on the beach. Hades' pace picks up as he spies the whirling gulls, gliding and flapping over the water.

Happiness surges through Lucy at the crunch of sand beneath her feet. 'This new walkway is fancy,' she says. 'I remember when you had to walk on the road, battling cars, or on the sand to get into town from Nan's place.'

He chuckles. 'I reckon it's about five years old and then some, but you're right. It makes for an easier walk.'

'It attracts a swankier crowd than in the old days.' Lucy gestures to the handful of expensive SUVs and sports cars parked along the beachfront.

Jake shakes his head. 'Hard to tell whether the rich and famous found us and insisted the town shape up or they came after we did. Either way, it's the surf around the point that keeps them coming back.'

'The Whitlams' isn't the only posh house for miles any more.'

'But it's still the best.'

Lucy's trying to work out how to turn the conversation to Brooke Whitlam when he's just bailed on the same conversation with Jan, when he continues, 'Are you okay after last night? You were gone by the time I got here. Bloody reporters.'

'I'm fine.' Thankfully, neither Lucy's name nor face made it into the media. Her boss would be less than thrilled with such an association. 'You can't really blame them,' she adds.

His grunt says otherwise.

'It's probably the most exciting thing ever to happen around here. And on that topic, shouldn't you be working the case, hunting leads, hounding the forensic team for answers?'

His laugh is a pleasing rumble. 'Crime drama fan, are you?'

'I've seen my share.'

They walk a bit further, his body providing a welcome shield from the biting wind. 'They've got others working the case.'

'Because you knew the victim? Surely that will happen with anything and anyone around here. You can't be excluded from every case. What's the point in having a police force here at all, if they're going to bring in strangers? What about your local connections? Local knowledge?'

He lets her run out of breath before responding. 'There are reasons.'

It still rings as unfair to Lucy. And what are the reasons? 'Aren't you mad?'

'I just want to do my job as well as I can and do the right thing by this community.'

It's hard to argue with that but she's tempted. In the TV shows it's these kinds of cases that make careers, but maybe that's not important to him and she doesn't know him well enough to ask.

They reach a point where the dunes lower a little and the

Whitlam house lies ahead in the distance, on the top of the cliffs. A shaft of sunlight breaks through the clouds, lighting it up.

'It's beautiful.'

Jake tilts his head, considering. 'Only on the outside. I wouldn't swap places with any of them.'

'I guess so. No one wants to have their mother die, and there's already gossip.'

He shakes his head. 'Even without all that. There's something to be said for striking out on your own path and making an honest wage. Like you.'

'Me?'

'Nice car, nice clothes, a confidence you didn't have before. You've made it,' he says.

This kind of acknowledgement is what she's worked towards. It's never enough just to be successful, she wants to exude it the way the Whitlams do... The way Brooke Whitlam did. Maybe it's knowing how close she's come to throwing everything she's achieved away that has Lucy feeling defensive. 'I'd say they all work pretty hard.'

'Do you even know what Anabelle Whitlam does?'

There's a smirk around his mouth. He's guessed she was thinking about Harry and preparing to argue the value of art. Lucy tries to recall what she knows about grown-up Anabelle. She had a fashion label for a while that she modelled herself, but once the world confirmed her taste and beauty in a way her mother never had, she must have got bored. Mostly she posts about her family.

'Parenting is important,' Lucy says.

His laugh is disarming rather than mocking. 'Their wealth, and the expectations that go with that, has chained them, as much as given them opportunities.' He shrugs. 'I'm just saying I don't envy them.'

'Any more.' Lucy can't help the reference to the past. Jake was as enamoured by Harry as she was.

'We all have to grow up sometime.'

Lucy tries to read his face. Is that a dig about her and Harry? Jake doesn't know the half of it. She falls silent.

They continue to walk towards the cottage, with Hades slowing to sniff particularly interesting grass tufts, and she notices Jake glance up at the Whitlam house more than once.

'You know, Anabelle's turret is visible from most of the town,' Lucy says.

Jake frowns. 'Oh, you're talking about the tall thing at the side of the house.'

'You were looking at it.'

She thinks he's about to deny it, but then he sighs. 'Anabelle's?'

It's as much of an admission as she's going to get. 'Her bedroom is in that part of the house. Well, it used to be when we were teenagers.'

'I didn't know that was big enough to be a bedroom. I thought it was some kind of observation tower.'

'It's bigger than you'd think. Plenty of room for a bed and cupboard and a huge desk, as well as a seat across one full side to read and look over the ocean.'

'She doesn't strike me as ever being a reader.'

Lucy ignores the sarcasm. 'It was the coolest thing. To get up there, you have to go deep into the second floor then up this old staircase. Well, you had to when we were kids. I haven't seen any lights at night since I've been here. It might not even be used any more. And there's a secret room beyond a door that looks like a cupboard. It's storybook stuff.' It hurts Lucy that she doesn't know Anabelle now the way she once did, their relationship a sort of summer fling as intense as teenage friendships can be, but then almost nothing since.

'You spent a lot of time at the house back then,' he says.

'It was so different from my place with my mum in the city or Nan's poky cottage. They were all so welcoming.'

'All of them?'

The spectre of Harry Whitlam appears between them and Lucy wishes she'd never mentioned it.

But Jake simply gives the house one last look and then turns his back on it. 'I should probably get to work,' he says. 'These landmark cases won't solve themselves to bring me fame and glory.'

Lucy can't help a chuckle. 'I'm here for advice if you need it.'

'I won't forget.' He drops a hand to Hades' head, grins and heads back towards town.

Lucy walks on, keeping her gaze firmly on the Whitlam house, because she's spent far too much of the last few days staring after Jake Parker.

JANUARY 2000
SEVENTEEN DAYS BEFORE THE PARTY

Anabelle

Anabelle breathed in, her brain arguing with the anxiety constricting her chest. There *was* enough oxygen. She *wouldn't* faint. Another breath. Deliberate tensing and then relaxing of every muscle. Some stupid calming technique she'd read about in a magazine while getting her hair done.

No therapy for her – what if someone found out? They couldn't have anyone questioning the Whitlam name.

I can breathe.

If she said it to herself often enough, she might believe it, might overrule the feeling of an invisible fist tightening around her body. Squeezing the air from her. Squeezing the life from her.

I can breathe.

Being home, under this roof, sleeping in the room she'd called her own since she'd convinced Dad to let her move up to the turret room was the problem. And there were weeks until school went back.

She'd stayed with her friend Hannah Dowd for the first week of the holidays, but her family were off skiing in the Alps and wouldn't be back until term started. Besides, Dad preferred them all to summer at home. Together. He argued that they spent so much time at boarding school he might not recognise them if they didn't come home. He missed them.

And Mother didn't refute this, although Anabelle couldn't imagine her feeling the same. More likely she'd hate the town wondering why the Whitlam children were absent.

Anabelle's chest tightened again and her nails bit into her palms. *Don't think of Mother.*

Easier to achieve that at school. Even at Hannah's. Her friend would have been shocked by the envy snaking through Anabelle over family dinners. Meals where Mrs Dowd smiled and laughed and didn't say a word about what was on Hannah's plate.

She'd heard Mrs Dowd's teasing reminder for them to take fruit with the chocolate when they grabbed snacks. Thanked her for the ice cream brought as a treat after dinner. Witnessed the softening in Mrs Dowd's eyes as she commented wistfully 'You're beautiful' in response to Hannah's moan about getting fat.

When Hannah complained about her mum, Anabelle had commiserated, but inside she'd wanted to scream.

Now, standing in front of the mirror in only her underwear, she twisted, studying the exposed skin. Mentally, she measured the curves and valleys and compared them with her friend.

Not much difference.

But no one called her beautiful. No one who counted. Boys saw nothing but boobs, and her dad saw the little blonde-curled toddler who'd sat on his knee for bedtime stories.

She scowled at her reflection. Fifteen and ugly.

Put on a few pounds over term time, Anabelly? She heard again Mother's greeting on her first day at home, felt again the pinch of her manicured nails in her arm as she turned her this way and that. *No one likes a fatty.*

The soft creak of the stair outside her room had her scrambling to cover up before the door handle turned. Cold sweat formed slick on her spine as her whole body contracted. Disobedient arms refused to slide into the shift dress, and it got stuck on her head as she tried to force it over her body.

But the door only opened a crack.

'You okay, Ana-banana?'

Mae. And using her old nickname. Three words, with all the love of a big sister hug, without her even entering the room.

'I'm fly,' she managed. 'I'll be down soon.'

'You'd better be,' Mae said. 'I need you to teach me some of that slang. When did I get so old?'

'Fly is like the term "cool" was for ancient people,' Anabelle teased.

'Hey.' Mae's voice softened. 'Everything is better when you're home.'

The door clicked shut.

Anabelle glanced towards the mirror again, but thanks to Mae it was just a mirror now. It showed nothing more than flesh. Not heart or worth. Somehow her sister had a way of knowing what Anabelle needed to hear.

She hurried to dress, her reluctance at going down for dinner with its inevitable battles pushed aside by Mae's request for her company. She didn't envy her sister the longer university holidays and hadn't missed the arguments with Mother about Mae studying overseas.

Mae wouldn't have to face their mother alone this time.

10

PRESENT DAY

Dante arrives at the cottage the next day five minutes before the agreed time, striding up to where Lucy's stacking bags full of clothes on the porch. He absent-mindedly pats the head of an appreciative Hades and says, 'Where do you want me?'

He's wearing a black singlet, worn jeans and a charming smile, and the heterosexual woman in Lucy thinks a number of things that the woman-probably-old-enough-to-be-his-mother doesn't say.

'Thanks for coming.' She gestures to the ute he's parked out on the road. 'If you don't mind, I need to get these bags into town.'

'Leave it to me.'

After directing him for the first few minutes, it's clear he's picked up Lucy's Post-it note system and she can focus on cleaning out the overflowing bookshelf. Having him moving in and out of the cottage around her helps her not to linger over the memories each book inspires. Until she picks up a tattered old hard cover of *Pride and Prejudice*. It was hers and Nan's favourite.

She opens it.

An old photo falls out. It's faded and worn but the woman

in it looks like a younger version of Nan, only with finer features. Could it be Nan's mother?

The ring on the woman's finger catches her eye. She holds the picture close and squints then retrieves the ring from where she'd left it next to her bed. It's hard to tell thanks to the old picture's quality but it could well be the one Lucy found. That doesn't explain, though, why Nan never wore it.

She slips the ring on to her finger to remind herself to look out for it in any old pictures, then returns to the task. The photo and the book, along with a few other well-read treasures, get put on the keep pile, then she sets about boxing up the rest.

'That's my room,' she calls when she sees Dante coming out of the small sunroom a couple of hours later. 'There's nothing in there ready to be moved yet, but the twin sets of drawers in the other room can go in the skip. They're rotted through and no good to anyone.'

'No worries, mate.'

His attempt at an Aussie accent is terrible but she laughs anyway, her fingertips finding and twisting Nan's ring in place. Going through Nan's things has her on an emotional knife edge and it's better to laugh than break down in a mess of tears in front of a virtual stranger.

The clinical detachment she's always been able to call upon for work seems to have deserted her along with that promotion that everyone agreed would be hers, until it wasn't. Until it couldn't be thanks to what she did, and instead she was shunted out of the way to take leave and get herself together. She closes her eyes.

Don't think about work.

If only she'd called in sick that day. But something like it would have happened eventually.

A hand touches her shoulder.

She jumps, eyes flying open. 'Shit.'

It's Dante – of course it is – and he's frowning. 'Are you okay? You've been standing there for, I don't know, a while, and your face it was all sad.'

The smooth tones of his voice remind her of someone, but she's never met anyone with quite that delicious accent. 'I'm fine,' she lies.

'It must be difficult,' he says. 'All of this with your grandmother's things. You are allowed to be emotional at this time. I remember when I lost my grandfather I felt as though nothing would ever be the same.' The rawness in his voice suggests he really does know how she feels.

'Were you close?'

He nods. 'We lived with him when I was a small boy. He was the man I wanted to be when I grew up.'

'I am sorry for your loss too.'

'Thank you, Lucy.'

He moves away, but that little bit of human understanding has allowed her to pull herself together and she faces the linen press with fresh determination.

A bit later she catches Dante back in the sunroom, trying to pack up some of the small boxes she's mentally labelled 'things to go through at a later date'.

He startles and quickly puts the biggest of the boxes down.

'None of that is ready,' Lucy explains.

'Sorry. I thought you said to take them.'

His efficiency means he's caught up to everything she needed him to do. He's taken all the bags of clothing and linen donations to town, moved the selected bigger items to the skip and shifted two old armchairs that were going mouldy in the shed to the back of his ute after chatting to the woman at the store in town and discovering she's into reupholstery.

'Would you like a cold drink before you deliver those chairs?' she offers.

'That would be awesome,' he says. 'Water, please.' He trails her to the kitchen where she pours them both drinks from the jug in the fridge.

As they stand side by side in the cramped space, glasses in hand, she's aware of his lean body and the way the singlet is now sticking to his skin with sweat, despite the cool air. It shows every defined muscle. She takes a breath and his masculine scent is an assault that has her gulping the icy cold liquid. He's ridiculously pretty, and the way he watches her as he drains the water makes her think he knows the effect he has.

She lifts her glass again and clings to it, trying not to look inappropriately at this kid who is far too attractive for his own good. 'I needed this,' she says.

'Yeah,' he drawls. From those full lips, the word is somehow more than it should be. Suggestive. 'You knew the Whitlams from, like, ages ago, didn't you?'

It takes a second for her brain to catch up with the question. 'I stayed in Queen's Point for a summer. You probably weren't even alive then.'

Is he going to ask about Mrs Whitlam? He must be curious. Part of her is surprised that he didn't leave when the news broke identifying the body.

He ignores her comment on his age and passes his empty glass from hand to hand. 'Do you have siblings?'

'No. I'm an only child.'

'Me too.' He's looking across the room but it's like he can see through the walls up to the white house on the hill. 'What were they like as teenagers? The Whitlams?'

'Close. They had everything – looks, charm, anything money could buy. And they had each other.'

'Tell me about each of them.'

Where should she begin? 'Mae did the big sister thing, looking after the other two. I remember thinking I'd never met anyone so grown up but without being old.' Lucy tries not to think about how teenage her would categorise the woman she's become but it would probably start with *elderly*. 'And Harry could charm anyone. I could tell back then he'd succeed as an artist. He always had "it", whatever that is – a magic about him and his work. He could put feeling on canvas like no one else. And when Anabelle walked into a room, she brought sunshine. She had this spark of joy and it was infectious.' Lucy catches herself and stops, hoping she doesn't sound too lame or whatever the word is these days.

But Dante's expression is full of wonder. 'It sounds like the perfect life.' His voice is vulnerable, the polished façade slipping for a moment. 'So lucky.'

'That's what I thought,' Lucy admits. 'But maybe it wasn't quite as perfect as it seemed.' She waves her hand towards the grave site of Brooke Whitlam that lies somewhere beyond the dunes. 'Someone had it in for her.'

He's staring at the hand she waved, the one wearing Nan's ring. He doesn't look at her face again until she slides it behind her, out of sight.

'You must have been special.'

Lucy's head tilts in question.

'For you to have interested all three so much.'

Questions spring to her lips. What have they been saying? But she doesn't ask.

He arches like a cat stretching, and amusement twists the cool curve of his mouth because it's impossible not to look. 'Back to work.'

He reaches past her to place the glass down, the move bringing his arm across her so she can feel the heat of him. She breathes in his aftershave, something sandalwood and sweet, like the knock-off of an expensive brand.

There's laughter in his eyes now and she gets the distinct impression she's being played.

The question is, why?

11

PRESENT DAY

Next morning, Lucy walks with Hades into town for her coffee from Jan's. It's not that she's looking for Jake, but minutes after her coffee is finished she's still standing outside in the drizzle, waiting.

Dante's help clearing so much of the furniture means her excuses for avoiding the huge drawers of paperwork and old photographs are fast running out. After the uncomfortable moments with him in the kitchen, she'd searched online for him over a glass of wine in front of the fire the night before. Without a last name, she didn't get far. She reasoned Jake had seemed suspicious of him too, but as she typed his first name into various social platforms it felt a bit too much like stalking a one-night stand after a hook-up. But she can't help wondering if there's more to him, and to his arrival in such a small town in the middle of nowhere.

Back at the cottage, without seeing Jake, with a pot of tea brewing, she forgoes the desk for the larger expanse of the table, squares her shoulders and begins Nan's paperwork.

It's boring and slow, but she makes herself skim-read through each of the papers to decide whether to keep or bin it. After all, these were the things that Nan thought important enough to hang on to. The paperwork around her move to the home and her estate are familiar and easy to sort out, but when Lucy goes back further in time it becomes more difficult. There are some bank statements filed in date order but some are missing.

Ditching all the department store receipts and utility bills older than the most recent one halves the contents of one drawer and moves Lucy into the medical paperwork. With her grandfather being so sick before he passed away, there's a huge stack. She knew he'd battled cancer, but seeing the pages and pages of medical documents makes her eyes prickle. Such a shitty thing for anyone to go through, and it seems his condition involved experimental treatments along with the more usual suspects like radiation therapy and chemotherapy.

Expensive and likely rough on both her grandparents.

Her vision blurs with tears and she finds herself staring out of the tiny kitchen window. If only she could somehow go back in time to that summer and tell Nan how sad she is for what they went through.

'Sorry, Nan,' she whispers.

However, she finds herself smiling again at the next item. The walking stick receipt. God, Nan hated that thing. Her doctor insisted she get it if she wanted to be able to stay independent, and she detested it even more because it helped.

Next in the file is a series of correspondence with a law firm, but it's not the one Lucy's dealt with in handling Nan's estate.

The language on the documents is annoyingly general, referencing a meeting and a possible legal action, but not much else. Nor is there any suggestion of how the matter ended up.

What could have made Nan go outside the firm she'd used her whole life?

Lucy does a quick search on her phone for 'MacArthur and Sons, Lawyers' and discovers they have an office in Adelaide. Queen's Point isn't a large town, but it only takes her a minute on her phone to find five different law firms that are closer, and four of them are more than twenty-five years old.

Why would Nan have gone all that way to seek legal counsel?

Mum always complained about Nan's insistence that everything she wanted or needed could be found locally. The specialists required to treat her grandfather's cancer were a rare exception.

Them and this law firm.

And she'd never mentioned it, not in all their painful conversations about her estate. Before the memories of those final conversations can overwhelm her, Lucy calls the number on the website.

As a woman answers, 'Good afternoon, MacArthur and Sons, Anya speaking. How may I help you?', Lucy's hit with a memory from that long-ago summer.

Nan going out all day for an appointment in the city. Coming home so distracted she didn't mind that Lucy returned late from being with the Whitlams. The trouble she'd expected to get into not coming.

'Can I help you?' the woman asks again.

Lucy clears her throat. 'My name is Lucy Ross, and I've been going through my grandmother's things since she passed away. Judy Antonello. I've found some paperwork connecting her with your firm. Is there anyone I can speak to about this matter?' Her attempt at sounding professional comes out garbled.

There's a faint rustle, the click of computer keys and then the woman speaks again. 'I'm sorry, but we can't give out information like that over the phone. If you can provide evidence that you are the executor of Mrs Antonello's estate, we may be able to help more.'

'I am.'

'Would you like to make an appointment with Mr MacArthur? We have a cancellation next Thursday at eleven.'

It's a long drive to Adelaide but Lucy's curious now. 'That would be great.'

Anya takes Lucy's details and reminds her that their fees are listed in detail on the website and will need to be paid up front. She's still talking when Lucy hears the squeak of the front gate and Hades rushes to the door.

'Thank you,' Lucy says, finishing the call.

She opens the door, while trying to hold on to Hades.

'Hi,' Anabelle says brightly, backing away from Hades' reach. 'Have I caught you at a bad time?'

She looks like she's stepped out of a country living catalogue, complete with riding boots and a tweed jacket, and the combination suggests the kind of money where trends are something the wearer creates rather than follows.

Lucy fights the urge to sniff whether the hoodie and leggings she's been wearing to clean and exercise Hades smell. The subtle placement of brand names is no match for probable body odour.

'I was on the phone,' she explains.

'Can I come in?'

'Why?' Lucy blurts the question, still off balance from the mysterious legal stuff, aware of the mess behind her on the table.

Anabelle pouts. 'No real reason, it's just a bit intense up at the house. Look, if you're too busy…'

And with that Lucy's reminded that this poor woman has lost her mother. So much for being an old friend and mentally bemoaning the distance between them. But she can't forget the paperwork on the table. It's not only the law firm documents, more that Nan was the Whitlams' housekeeper and Lucy wouldn't want her boss catching sight of her private accounts after her death.

'I should probably walk Hades,' Lucy says, grabbing the lead and pocketing the key. 'We could chat and walk.'

Something like disappointment flashes across Anabelle's face as she peers over Lucy's shoulder. 'I'd probably pref—'

'Great.' Lucy closes the door.

With Hades leading the way, they cross towards the beach.

Anabelle looks back at the cottage. 'I see what you were talking about at the café. It must be a lot of work.'

For a second, Lucy thinks she's assessing her progress, but Anabelle wouldn't know what it looked like before. As a teenager, the thought of inviting one of the Whitlams inside Nan's tiny, dated cottage would have mortified Lucy. And Anabelle wouldn't have ever visited Nan.

'It's harder than I thought,' Lucy admits. 'But I owe her this much.'

'Of course,' Anabelle agrees as they reach the sand.

They head towards the old boathouse in silence, Lucy waiting for Anabelle to be ready to talk and Hades sniffing happily.

As they round the point, away from the protection of the bay, the surf is pounding. The perfect waves have attracted a few hardy souls despite the chill of the spray of salt off the water. Wetsuit clad, with boards light years advanced from the simple ones Lucy remembers using as a teenager, they paddle out beyond the break and then come in on the wave, harnessing the power of the ocean.

One falls and Lucy winces. She looks away, gaze snagging on the boathouse. From this side it's obvious it's had a makeover, with a new level added above the yacht storage. Modern and sleek, with floor-to-ceiling windows.

Is that a series of canvases on easels she can see? Has Harry upgraded to working out there? Up in that space he'd be practically floating above the waves.

Before Lucy can ask, Anabelle speaks. 'Sorry about the drama at the café the other night.'

'Forget it.'

'If only I could. It's all a complete nightmare.' Something in her voice reminds Lucy of dramatic teenage Anabelle, but then she lifts her head and she's a weary mother.

'How is everyone holding up?' Lucy asks. It's more polite than what she really wants to know – like who did it, but they're not close enough any more for Lucy to ask such a thing.

Anabelle exhales in a long sigh. 'Honestly, the questions coming from all directions are ludicrous. We are all as much in the dark about what happened as anyone else. While we've all got our own lives now and aren't living in each other's pockets, the whole thing has come as a dreadful shock.' Her voice wavers, and it's the first hint of grief Lucy's seen. 'I feel hollow inside, not to mention confused about how to process her having been buried nearby.'

Lucy feels a rush at her guess being confirmed as she follows Anabelle's gaze towards the gash in the ground, but it's hidden by the boathouse.

'You don't know when she went missing?'

Anabelle shakes her head. 'We didn't communicate much. She was largely estranged from the family. There were letters, emails and of course instructions for the estate.'

'You never saw her?'

Anabelle's eyes flash but her tone is light. 'Perhaps we weren't as close as I would have liked, but she was my mother, my flesh and blood, and now she's gone.'

Lucy's hit with a sudden memory. Brooke Whitlam sneering at her youngest child. Powerful, sophisticated and incredibly vicious.

Lucy drags her gaze to the surfers in the water. Is this the point where she should express sorrow for Anabelle's loss?

'It's sad,' Lucy says, when it seems she has to say something.

'It is. I had to break it to the kids that now they'll never meet their grandmother.'

'Never meet?' Lucy tries to recall how old they are and where Anabelle was living when she had her first child. 'She didn't come to you when they were born or in the years since? What about birthdays? Christmases?'

Anabelle wraps her arms around her waist. 'She planned to. We emailed about it. She'd become a bit of a nomad, cutting off most of her business interests the day she left Queen's Point and leaving all that to Mae.' She turns abruptly and starts to head back before Lucy can wonder how busy anyone is that they can't meet their only grandchildren. 'They've confiscated my computer, looking for evidence. As if I keep anything older than a month. Nobody does.'

I do, Lucy thinks. She's a bit of a hoarder, a keeper of every letter and document, a trait she's beginning to think might be hereditary after going through Nan's things.

Then it sinks in what Anabelle said. 'Wait, why have they taken your computer? Does that mean you're a suspect?'

Anabelle's eyes flash. 'How can you ask such a thing? I thought we were friends.'

'We are,' Lucy says quickly. 'Is it like routine? Have they taken everyone's devices?'

But Anabelle's already moving on. She's leading them back to the cottage at a rate that has Lucy out of breath and her ankle twinging again.

'I just wish they'd stop bothering all of us and look for whoever did this. It's obviously some lunatic.'

'I'm sure they're doing their best.'

'Anyway, enough about me.' Anabelle smiles, her mood instantly more upbeat. 'I noticed I interrupted you doing paperwork in the cottage. Was it work? I remember you're in something business?'

'I'm a financial management consultant.' She ignores the little voice in her head questioning whether she can say that with any truth right now. 'But no, that was Nan's and there's more where that came from.'

'Dad and Mae are the executors of Mum's estate.' Her nose wrinkles in distaste. 'Not that they can do much until the police finish poking around.'

It's a strange way to describe looking for her mother's killer. Lucy can't imagine what it must be like for them all. Losing first Brian, and then Nan over the last eighteen months has been hard enough, without having to face a terrible question of how they died.

'Will all of you stay in town until their investigation is complete?' Lucy asks.

'Yes, I think we're stuck here,' Anabelle says. 'At least we can catch up with old friends, but it's hardly a holiday with the police wanting to talk to one of us every five minutes.' Her smile doesn't reach her eyes. 'There's also the small detail of the missing ring.'

'What ring?' Lucy asks. But a sudden contraction of her belly is making a guess. Impossible for it to be the same. After all, it's in the photo of Nan's mother.

Anabelle's gaze meets Lucy's. 'Mum's favourite ring was missing from the body. It's quite distinctive.'

'How so?' Lucy's glad her voice comes out steady when the ring in her pocket might as well be burning into her skin. She's been wearing it for the last few days, only taking it off this morning when she'd been about to use bleach to clean the toilet as a way to avoid the paperwork.

'It belonged to my maternal grandmother, Rose,' Anabelle explains. 'The namesake rose is wrapped around the band, which is studded with small diamonds.' She smiles as though she can hear the heavy thud of Lucy's heart. 'There's a small thorn, of course. My grandmother handed it down to Mum.'

Lucy nods, hoping her face portrays polite interest. Is it Lucy's great-grandmother's or Brooke Whitlam's? After all, the photo is old and blurry.

As Anabelle changes the subject to how the whole situation has aged her poor father, Lucy tries to think how the ring could have got to her grandmother's cottage if it is Brooke Whitlam's.

Could it have been a gift for long service that Brooke Whitlam never mentioned to her family? If it's not the one from the photo, could her grandmother have stolen it?

Neither seems likely.

'I should go,' Anabelle says when they reach the gate and Lucy shows no sign of inviting her in.

Lucy blinks, nods. Is it obvious she hasn't been listening?

'Ah, yes. Thanks for coming by.'

Hand on the gate, Lucy agrees they should catch up again. But all of it's on autopilot, and Lucy gets the sinking feeling that Anabelle's missing nothing.

A sudden thought nearly has her gasping aloud.

Is this why Anabelle came to the cottage?

Mae caught a glimpse of the ring that first night. Dante seemed to be staring at it too. Would she have sent Anabelle here to find out for sure?

If required.

For some reason, Lucy has no doubt that Mae would do whatever it takes to find out whether she has Brooke Whitlam's ring. It takes every shred of Lucy's self-control to keep her hands loose at her sides and to maintain a relaxed smile.

As Anabelle waves a final goodbye, she doesn't appear to have a care in the world. In fact, there's something in her confident stride that says 'mission accomplished'.

Inside, door closed, Lucy takes the ring out of her pocket with trembling hands.

Light catches the small diamonds that Anabelle described. A rose branch wraps around the dull gold band, and on the inside, like it would prick the wearer's finger, is a tiny thorn.

This might be a dead woman's ring.

JANUARY 2000
SIXTEEN DAYS BEFORE THE PARTY

Lucy

Anabelle lay back on her towel, her bronzed curves glistening with sun oil. Next to her, Lucy felt the shiny white sunblock Nan had insisted she wear lathered on like an impenetrable second skin. At least she had the cool sunglasses Anabelle had given her. Two girls had gushed over them in town the day before.

It could have been boring hanging out at the beach if not for the company. With Harry and Anabelle, things were never dull.

'Tell her about Andre,' Anabelle said as Harry appeared at the foot of her towel, fresh from the water.

Lucy couldn't help herself. 'Who's Andre?'

A smirk played on Harry's full lips, but he didn't say a word.

Anabelle sat up and glared at her brother. 'Tell.'

He hesitated, and then collapsed on to the towel, flipping his wet hair out of his eyes. Water droplets sprayed, making Anabelle squeal.

He studied Lucy.

She straightened, then, deciding she looked too keen, leaned back, pretending not to care.

'So, this guy, Andre, turned up in advanced music theory

class at the start of last term,' Harry began in a conspiratorial tone. 'He introduced himself to the newish teacher, explaining he was a French exchange student. An admin stuff-up meant his name didn't show up on the class roll, an error that happens sometimes at a school as big as St David's.

'The teacher, Ms Ousley, had always wanted to visit France. She'd get distracted talking to Andre about his home. About his daily life, the food, his school. After a week, she talked him into giving a presentation to the class, complete with photos from home and an apple tart made from his grand-mère's special recipe.

'After a few weeks, the music teachers swapped units and Mr Residovic took over. He asked about Andre, and Ms Ousley explained the class list error. Together they went to the school office, and then when that failed to give them an answer, they met with the teacher in charge of all exchange students.'

Harry paused, a lazy smile on his lips as he allowed the tension to build.

Although determined to play it cool, Lucy found herself up on her elbows.

His eyes crinkled at the corners. 'They discovered Andre didn't exist.'

'It was Harry,' Anabelle interrupted. 'And the whole class knew the whole time.'

Harry's chuckle seemed to vibrate through Lucy's body. 'I had a free period in that line. We'd spent a few weeks in France in the middle of the year so I had the pictures and your nan found me the recipe. I didn't tell her what it was for.'

Part of Lucy was thrilled that Nan had played a part in the prank. 'Did you get in trouble?'

Her gaze met his and her cheeks heated. Why had she asked something so pedestrian?

But then he wasn't looking away, and the flush of embarrassment became something else, pooling low in her belly.

'I'm always trouble.'

Anabelle kept talking, oblivious to Lucy's dry mouth and pounding heart and the sudden certainty that Harry was trying to tell her something private.

A little while later, it was just the two of them.

Harry stretched his hands above his head, the languid movement making his T-shirt ride up a little. It exposed a flat, tanned expanse of stomach.

Lucy felt her cheeks flush when the twinkle in his grey gaze suggested he'd caught her looking.

A smile played at the corners of his mouth. 'You should come and see it sometime.'

She racked her brain. What had he been talking about? 'The garden shed?'

'It's more of a retreat,' Harry corrected. 'Marcelo has helped me restore the place. It used to be a greenhouse. It's full of natural light all times of the day for my work.'

'Your work?'

'I paint,' he explained.

Of course, he was an artist. She should have known.

'It's a hangout too. I bought an old fridge from the junk shop in town so there's snacks, and Jake and I found a couch. It was left by someone on the side of the road but it's in pretty good condition.'

'Jake' was Jake Parker, a boy she'd seen with Harry a few times. He had the advantage of being able to use his dad's old ute sometimes. Harry's convertible sports car was stylish but relatively impractical. She couldn't help imagining the short and dumpy Jake offering to help Harry in that clinger way he had. And Marcelo was the maintenance guy since Lucy's pop had passed away.

'We could have some fun together,' he said. 'Just the two of us.'

'Totally,' she agreed. Then wished the word back. Maybe she should have played it cool. But cool around Harry didn't seem to be something she could do. Although she could practically hear her mum's lecture about being alone with boys in sheds, she ignored it.

Being around Harry did something to her insides, made her breathless and put a silly smile on her face. He wasn't simply gorgeous but also smart and exotic, and he came from a world she craved more with every glimpse she caught of it. He talked about art and feelings and things boys she knew couldn't imagine.

He was everything she'd ever wanted.

12

PRESENT DAY

Lucy should probably take the ring straight to the police. It would be the reasonable action of any law-abiding citizen.

But she doesn't.

Instead, she drives to the private home of an officer who has specifically told her he's not on the case in question. And she waits until the evening, when he'll be off duty.

The 'thank you for rescuing Hades' basket of wine and cheeses on the car seat next to her is pretty flimsy as far as excuses go, but she's hoping he won't question it. She thought she saw Dante in the deli section of the supermarket when she was choosing between roasted peppers and sundried tomatoes, but when she went to the end of the aisle he wasn't there.

As she turns into the long driveway of the old farm on the other side of town, she exhales relief that Jake's ute is there. Considering the terrible thing that happened there not long after that summer in 2000, it wouldn't have surprised her if he'd sold the family home, but from the fresh paint and new-looking sheds and a burgeoning vineyard, it seems he chose to do the place up instead.

He saunters out to meet her, wearing grey trackies and a navy T-shirt that fits just right. His hair is damp and he looks like he just stepped out of the shower. She's suddenly glad she showered and changed into clean jeans and a flowing, feminine black top.

'Evening, Mrs Ross,' he calls. 'I was just thinking about you.'

She lets Hades out of the car and grabs the hamper. 'Is that a good thing?'

He ignores the question. 'What do you have there?'

'A thank-you gift. For finding Hades the other day.' She shoves it at him, giving him no choice but to take the large box.

His sceptical expression fades as he has a quick look through it. 'I can only take this on one condition.'

'That is?'

'You come inside and have a glass of this Pinot Noir.'

Despite being what she hoped he'd say, she hesitates. 'Will Hades be all right?'

'The house yard is fenced out the back, or he's welcome by the fire.'

'Inside, I think.'

He whistles and Hades comes. Then he leads them into the old stone-fronted homestead. There's a small foyer and then a hallway and an open-plan room beyond.

'You've done a lot of work on the place,' Lucy says, impressed by the updated white kitchen, flecked stone benchtops and polished timber floors. A blazing fire crackles at the far end of the room and there's a black leather sofa in front of it.

His lips twitch. 'I don't remember you visiting.'

'It all looks pretty new to me.'

'Just teasing. Yes, it's been a bit of a project over the last five years. The vineyard is a hobby thanks to a favourable response from the council on redeveloping the place. I wanted to make the house fresh, but I razed all the old sheds to the ground.' A shadow crosses his face, but he makes no other reference to his father and his family tragedy.

She hadn't heard about the suicide in the wool shed at the Parker place until years afterwards, but isn't sure she would have known how to reach out to him if she had been told. As a teenager herself she had no wisdom, no idea how to comfort.

Now it's clearly not something he wants to talk about.

Hades has already found the warmth of the fire by the time they sit on the soft leather couch, cheese and crackers arranged on a platter on a small table in front of them.

Jake holds his wine glass so the deep red liquid shimmers, takes a sip, and considers. 'Nice drop.'

Lucy sips hers, thinking how to steer the conversation. 'Why were you thinking about me earlier?'

He places the glass on the table and his expression turns serious. 'You'll need to make sure you stay in town for a few days. And we'll need your Adelaide address.'

'We? As in the police?' Her stomach does a sickening loop. 'Why?'

'You didn't hear this from me, okay?'

'Not a word.'

'The investigative team is waiting on forensics to confirm the dates, but Brooke Whitlam's death is not recent. No one around here has seen her for nineteen years. If I were to hazard a guess from the questions I'm being asked, and all I'm not being told, I reckon her date of death will be put around the end of January 2000.'

Lucy's breathing is loud in her ears. 'What?'

'This didn't happen recently.' He says it like he's breaking bad news. 'They have no legitimate sightings of her after the summer party.'

'Ever?'

'Not one.'

'But she has a social media account. She posts on it.'

He shrugs. 'Faked, most likely. There are no pictures of her face.'

'Who would do such a thing?'

'Excellent question and one I'm sure they'll have the best tech people looking into, but tracing anything online is difficult if the person knows what they're doing. It's unlikely the family could be fooled, however.'

'You're saying they all knew?'

'I'm not saying anything. Anyway, the decay of the body is consistent with that night being the last time she was seen alive.'

'You've seen it.'

His nod is matter-of-fact. 'I was one of the first on the scene after that backpacker you're so fond of reported it in, and no, I didn't recognise her.'

'Dante found her?'

'As part of his work on the Whitlam property, he was doing maintenance down on the hillside. He found something that had clearly been long buried and was revealed by rain washing away the top layers of rock and soil near the beach. Although it was impossible to tell what was wrapped in there, he was apparently alarmed by the shape and what he could see. According to him, he was concerned enough, given the find under the jetty, to immediately alert authorities.'

'How could the bones have stayed in the shoe all those years?'

'The plastic kept most of the skeleton together. I'm guessing it was only dislodged from the burial site a short time before it was found.'

Lucy tastes acid at the back of her throat and is unable to stop herself picturing what was in the plastic. How does a body's remains look after all that time? But she resists asking the question, not sure she really wants to know.

He's still talking. 'Whoever made those posts, it wasn't her, unless she learned to type from beyond the grave.'

It's like his words shake the world, and when he finishes the pieces have settled in a different place. Brooke Whitlam has been dead for nineteen years. Lucy saw her on what was possibly the last night she was alive.

And she might have her ring.

'Am I a suspect? Is that why you wanted to talk to me? You weren't supposed to share any details about the case, but you're telling me all this. Is it some kind of warning?'

As though she hasn't fired questions at him, he continues, 'What was your reason for returning to Queen's Point now after such a long absence?'

'You know why,' Lucy says.

She can feel the irritation coming off him in waves, despite the lack of any obvious sign. 'Why choose now to pack up Judy's estate? She's been gone for months.' Each word is said slowly, as though to a toddler.

'As the only child of an only child, the task of going through everything falls to me alone. The truth is that I simply needed time before I could face it.'

There's a flicker of something on his face – sympathy? But it's gone as fast as it appeared. 'But then you could? What changed?'

'Nothing,' she says. 'Just time.' Even as she says it, she

sees again the boardroom table, the one as familiar to her as her own at home. More so, if she's honest. She sees the faces blurry around it, their expressions changing from concern to anger. She pushes the memory aside, blinks to focus on Jake's face. 'Why do you care anyway? I'm here. You can drag me to the station for questioning if you want. Oh, that's right, you're not on this case.'

'Don't make this difficult,' he says. 'I'm on your side.'

'What do you want me to say? That I saw the article about the shoe under the jetty? I did, but so what? It's not like I'm here because of a guilty conscience. I assumed the victim was a drifter or something, but reading about the town stirred my memories, got me moving. And I had holiday leave saved, so I came. Is that what you wanted to hear?'

He shakes his head. 'This isn't about what I want. There's a dead woman and they're going to find out what happened whether you help them or not. You might not understand this, but the town matters to me. I'm responsible for everyone feeling safe when they walk the streets. That can hardly happen if there's a murderer walking free.'

She bristles at the hint of arrogance in his tone.

'Well, I didn't kill her.' Although even as she says it, she's aware that a murderer isn't likely to confess. And worse, of the ring in her pocket.

She needs to think about the ramifications of all this because the Whitlams' party was one of her first experiences with alcohol. And the truth is her memories are blurry.

'It's obviously some lunatic or something.' She finds herself echoing Anabelle.

Anabelle.

Does she know? She must, and yet only hours ago she was

talking as though her mother has been alive all these years. It's one thing for Lucy to be fooled by social media posts with scenery and the occasional non-distinct angle of a woman who roughly matches Brooke Whitlam. But Jake's right, her family couldn't be tricked. Could they?

Lucy thinks of Anabelle on the beach, her voice wavering. So clearly at the end of her tether. No, she can't have known, no one is that good an actress.

By now, there must have been police searches beyond the grave site. Like up at the house. It must have been investigated. Stripped of anything that could be a clue. It didn't look disturbed the other night at the cocktail party but then Mae had a whole warehouse of furniture and decorative pieces, and staff to clean up.

'It can't be someone we know,' Lucy whispers.

'I guess the Queen's Point killer has a certain ring to it,' Jake says. 'But it's unlikely.'

'How can you joke about such a thing?'

For a moment, his eyes show pure melancholy. 'Believe me, this is serious.'

'And you can't really talk about it, I know. Yet here we are. Everyone at the party should be questioned.'

'I'm sure they will be.'

A memory hits Lucy of taking a shortcut through the Whitlam gardens one afternoon and seeing an argument. 'What happened to the gardener?'

Jake frowns. 'Your grandfather?'

'No, after him. Even before he died, he was too sick to do the heavy groundskeeping and other odd jobs that Brooke Whitlam required. They had someone else.' Lucy has to strain to remember his name, although she can picture his face. 'He was handsome for an older guy. Very fit. Some exotic name, I think. Maybe they were having an affair and she broke it off and he killed her in a fit of rage.'

'And then faked her being alive since, managing to fool that entire family? Next you're going to suggest she committed suicide but ran her business and social media from beyond the grave.'

Her social media. Lucy flushes. Oh no, those messages sent to her over the years. She'd tried to keep in touch like with all the Whitlams but had never dreamed she could have been communicating with a killer instead. Who was reading them?

'Anabelle said she'd handed over her business interests to Mae. She said they were all estranged.'

He nods. 'That's their story. Mae stepped in to run the business and then they only communicated with her sporadically via letters at first and then email. Civil conversations about the family and the estate. And before you ask, no, they didn't keep any of them. But it's the reason they've given that no one ever reported her missing.'

It sounds far-fetched, and Lucy guesses the detectives won't think it's any more likely than Jake. Everything points to someone in the family knowing, or all of them.

'It's hard to believe that we were there at the party the last time she was seen alive.'

'I know.' He stands and crosses to the fire. 'There was that argument by the fountain. I've been trying to think back but it's so long ago. Do you remember anything that might help?'

Tell him about the ring.

Lucy ignores the voice in her head. 'I don't know.'

'Try, it's important.' His words are clipped, tone frustrated.

'You of all people know I was drinking that night. Besides,

you walked right near whoever was there, you must have seen something.'

'I didn't, not really. Maybe there was someone on the seat around the far side of the fountain, but I was head down, staring ahead.'

'If it was Brooke Whitlam, she wasn't dead.'

'How can you be sure?'

'I think someone else came after you left.' Lucy drops her head in her hands. 'It's all so foggy, but I think she argued with more than one person. Maybe there was a splash, but it could have been the fountain. Anyway, you were there at the end of the night, you must have heard her.'

After what had happened between them, Lucy had been aware of Jake standing across the grass.

He rubs at the back of his neck and admits, 'I wasn't really listening.'

'After we'd gone our separate ways, they had that late fireworks display.' She remembers looking up, surrounded by the crowd and thinking the show in the sky above was nothing compared to the feelings from Jake's touch. 'Then the fireworks had just finished when Brooke Whitlam appeared at the top of the stairs on the deck. She was framed by the lights inside and there was no one else around her.'

Jake nods agreement.

'She had that suitcase,' Lucy continues. 'It was small, more like an overnight bag. I don't know what she said at first, I was too far away, but the silence rippled over the crowd like a wave. Maybe she didn't need to speak.' Lucy remembers she'd been the kind of woman who commanded attention. 'She was wearing a light long coat, obviously expensive. It swirled in the sea breeze. Her hair swung as she turned to eye the gathered crowd.' Lucy's throat aches a little with the knowledge she's just described the last time she'd ever see Brooke Whitlam.

Jake takes over. 'Then she said "Goodbye".'

A simple word but said with the kind of conviction that carried. 'Yeah, then she added something about being done with the town and everyone in it.'

Jake sighs. 'That's what I remember too.'

'Whatever, well, happened to her…' – Lucy waves rather than say aloud that she was killed – 'must have happened after that. She drove away. I didn't see inside the vehicle but remember watching the tail lights of one of their BMWs disappear as I headed for Nan's place. The party was kind of over at that point.'

'She didn't get very far, considering where the body was found.'

'Maybe she went separately from Mr Whitlam and a stranger attacked her in the car. They buried her close by.' This prospect is unsettling but at least it clears everyone Lucy knew back then.

'Maybe,' he agrees.

But he doesn't sound like he means it and Lucy takes a big gulp of the wine.

Then there's the matter of the ring. If it isn't Nan's, then could Lucy have taken it from Mrs Whitlam in one of those hazy parts of the evening? Impossible. Surely she would remember such a thing. Her mind skitters away from the idea but she needs to know the truth, about how the ring came to be at Nan's cottage and what happened after Brooke Whitlam left the party.

She needs to know for sure if there's any way she has blood on her hands.

13

PRESENT DAY

Jake was right about the investigators talking to everyone. With needing to speak to so many people who were at the party, the police take until Friday to get to summoning Lucy. As she crosses the car park towards the small, low-slung building that houses the town's tiny police station, she thinks of Jake working there each day and the pride in his voice when he spoke about his job. She couldn't help noticing his ute wasn't one of the few vehicles out the front. She recognised the reporter from Jan's having a smoke in the shelter of a van, but she didn't seem particularly interested in Lucy.

If she could hear the hammer of Lucy's heart and feel the clamminess of her palms, the reporter might wonder whether Lucy has something to hide, but the composure that failed her so spectacularly at work now allows her to maintain an air of relaxed confidence.

The media are concentrating on the family, stirring up every dirty scandal from Harry's past, the life of fame and excess, splashing the huge money of the Whitlam Homewares franchise as though that's motive too, ignoring that Mae created the whole thing herself. They've questioned everything from Mr Whitlam's publishing record as a professor to

Anabelle's sexuality. No wonder none of the family have been seen out of their house.

Beep!

Lucy jumps at the sound of a horn. Looking up, she stares right through the windscreen of a Whitlam ute and into Dante's dark eyes. He's stopped the vehicle only an arm's reach from her. So close that she could brush the bonnet with her fingertips if she didn't have her hands up to her chest, where her heart is pounding in fright. Where the hell did he come from?

She smiles apologetically. 'Sorry,' she calls. 'I should have been watching where I was going.'

'No worries,' he says.

She hurries on to the footpath, but she's sure she looked before she crossed the road.

Inside, the station is not much to look at, although to be fair those who work here are probably not looking to win design awards. Yellowing walls that could use a coat of paint and the kind of bland office décor that is cheap but serviceable.

It's not hard to picture Jake strolling in, coffee in hand, that frown of concentration he has when he's thinking about something. Walking with the easy confidence of a man who's good at what he does. How must it feel for him to have others come in and take over?

He said he understood but Lucy would bet he wants answers. No matter what he says about following procedure and keeping his distance.

She gives her name to a young officer on the desk and is shown into a small room. It's less intimidating than she's pictured for an interrogation scene, with its worn carpet and wilting plant next to a plain table. Maybe she's seen too many TV shows. She refuses the offer of a drink, the mental reminder that she's just there to answer a few questions not enough to erase the fear that she'll spill any liquid because of her nerves.

However, despite the turmoil going on inside her – *I'm being questioned about Brooke Whitlam's death!* – her negotiations experience continues to serve her well. Her hands hold steady, and when she catches a glimpse of her reflection in a darkened window, her expression is polite and helpful. Concerned citizen, rather than guilty party.

'The detective will be with you in a few minutes.'

'Thank you,' Lucy says.

She's alone for less than five minutes – she knows this from her constant checking of her phone for the time – when a man strides in, and the room shrinks.

'Detective Antonio Georgiades,' he says. His grey hair is cropped short against a square head that matches his blocky, Lego man's body. His black suit is surprisingly well fitting. As he introduces himself, he cracks his knuckles absent-mindedly, each crunch an audible punctuation to his words, but when he holds out a hand to shake Lucy's, his fingers are more pianist than thug.

'Lucy Ross,' she says, although she's sure he knows that already.

The young officer from earlier scurries in and places two glasses of water on the table and scurries out again.

There are no niceties about the weather. His smile shows neat but oddly small teeth and then he begins. 'Tell me about the last time you saw Brooke Whitlam.'

Lucy describes what she can remember of her movements and Brooke Whitlam. Most of it is the same as what she told

Jake on his couch but without the emotion of what happened between them colouring the explanation.

Although she recalls it as the exclamation mark end of her summer in Queen's Point, a time that changed the direction of her life, when she summarises the evening, it's not a lot. As hostess that night, Brooke Whitlam was everywhere and nowhere, and Lucy was more interested in Harry. And then, of course, Jake. She explains how she witnessed the Whitlam matriarch's dramatic exit from the party and then how straight afterwards, with the mood dampened and the hour late, her grandmother took her home. 'I saw the tail lights of one of their BMWs as we walked. I presumed it was Mr and Mrs Whitlam after she'd announced she was leaving.'

She tries to convey that she's relaxed about being there using all the techniques she's collected on personal development days. Open posture, holding eye contact, smiling.

Smiling? He'll think you're happy she's dead.

She loses the smile.

'I never saw her again,' she finishes.

He consults some notes. 'Is it all right if we go back over a few things?'

'Of course.'

'There was an altercation at the beginning of the night. You mentioned it briefly, but I want to be sure of the timeline.'

Her stomach churns in remembered embarrassment. 'Yes, Mrs Whitlam didn't approve of the dress Anabelle was wearing, so she changed.' It sounds so simple in retrospect, although felt anything but at the time.

'This was early though?'

'Yes. It was still light.' That moment seems like a different event and Lucy hasn't thought much about it since. More important things happened later, for her at least. And obviously now Mrs Whitlam too.

'Thank you,' he says, and he looks down again. 'Your statement that you spent time with Jake Parker that evening has been confirmed by others who were present. Did you see Mrs Whitlam at all during that time?'

Again, she strains to hear the voices by the fountain and can't be sure. 'I didn't see her, but she might have been around. I'm sorry.' She feels heat rise in her neck and takes a quick sip of the water. What has Jake told them? She's almost certain he isn't the type to kiss and tell. Anyway, surely the details of their teenage encounter aren't relevant to this investigation.

He nods. 'I understand your grandmother worked as a housekeeper for the Whitlam family?'

'Yes, she had done so, but didn't by the night of the party. She'd retired earlier that week actually. Mr Whitlam invited her to attend as a guest since she'd been with them for so long. Admittedly, the invitation wasn't that special considering most of the town was in attendance.'

He nods again. His face, with patchy stubble lining his jaw and deep grooves in a fleshy forehead, tells Lucy precisely nothing. He asks her to repeat some details of the night. Who she spoke to – Anabelle and Jake, maybe Mae in passing. What she ate and drank – she says the punch was probably laced with alcohol but he doesn't lecture her retrospectively about underage drinking. The questions are all casual but repetitive, and she feels like it's part of his routine to make sure her story is consistent.

The whole thing passes in a blur of trying to remember and feeling like she's not being any help. But somehow the patchy spots in her memory never come up. It's not that she means to hide the truth, but he's most interested in her movements after Brooke Whitlam left the party and they are rather boring.

'Nan told me to collect my things, but I didn't have anything to get from inside. She told me off for not wearing a jacket. Mae was the one who saw people out at the door, thanking us for coming and apologising for her mother being upset. Then we walked down the drive and around to the cottage since Nan couldn't manage any shortcut. Then we went to bed.' As Lucy finishes, she feels like she's repeating herself but he appears no more or less bored than the first time.

'Would you describe the family as close?'

She's reminded of talking to Dante in the kitchen before she knew Brooke Whitlam had been dead so long. It feels a little like betrayal, but anyone will say the same. 'Not to their mother.'

'Were there arguments?'

Lucy struggles to swallow, her throat like one of the sand dunes. 'Some. They were teenagers.'

She's afraid he's going to ask her for details, but he simply says, 'Of course.' Then he changes the subject. 'Would you have said Harry was a good artist back then? I understand he's quite the world-famous talent.'

This is a line of conversation she's more comfortable with, although she's not sure what it has to do with the murder. 'He was already amazing. He'd lose himself painting for hours in the studio he'd set up in an old greenhouse.'

'And yet he had applied for early entry medicine courses.' The detective doesn't seem to expect a response and doesn't give her time to make one. 'Have you had much to do with the Whitlam family since that summer?'

Images cascade through Lucy's brain. Harry at the fancy

bar. Harry at the expensive hotel. Harry in the back of a taxi. In her bed, hot and sweaty, skin on skin.

'Not really. I caught up with Harry a few times for a drink. We're connected through social media but nothing personal.' The detective opens his mouth to speak but she adds, 'Mae sent something for my grandmother's memorial.'

He makes a note. 'Social media, you say. Does that include Brooke Whitlam?'

She has a sudden picture of police storming Nan's cottage and seizing her devices to verify her story. The searches. The electronic record of her fascination with the family and, in the last few days, Brooke Whitlam's death.

'Yes,' she admits, her skin feeling too tight for her body, holding herself from squirming only by sheer will. 'I mean it's not her, obviously I know that now, but I was connected with the account.'

'And recently?'

'I don't understand.'

'Since you've been in town, have you spent any time with them?'

'A little. We are next-door neighbours.'

'When did you notice Brooke Whitlam's absence? Were you given an explanation for it?'

'I didn't notice it as such. The family appeared to have gone in their different directions, so I didn't automatically assume I'd see her. It didn't come up.'

'It didn't come up,' he repeats.

'Anabelle did say something about not having seen her for a long time. I can't think of anything else. We're not close enough to pry into each other's lives.'

'Hmm.' His murmur says exactly nothing. 'What was the atmosphere like at the end of the summer party?'

Lucy hesitates. She thought they were done with the night. 'It was a party,' she says lamely.

'So, there was no tension?' His smile is encouraging.

She tries not to react. 'I don't know,' she says eventually. 'I was sixteen and pretty naive.'

'So, you think there was. Between all the family or particularly Mrs Whitlam and one of the children?'

Her stomach is tight. 'I didn't say that. It was fine.' She remembers Harry dancing with Anabelle, trying to cheer her up after the dress thing. He lifted her in a twirl and she giggled, ignoring their mother's disapproving glare.

It's like he can read Lucy's thoughts. 'Perhaps they were being silly and got carried away and Mrs Whitlam didn't approve.'

'I didn't say that.'

But he's writing another note. 'And you were drunk?'

'Yes.' The word catches, comes out more belligerent than Lucy intended. 'As I said, someone spiked the punch.' She's not sure why she's making excuses for a couple of underage drinks nearly two decades later. It's not her place to ask but she can't help it. 'Do you have a suspect? Am I a suspect? Do I need a lawyer?'

'I'm not in a position to share anything with you. Be assured, however, that we will determine what happened to Brooke Whitlam and those responsible will face justice. You decide whether you need to engage counsel.' He stands, dismissing. 'Thank you for your time.' It's unmistakably her cue to leave. 'Please, if you remember anything that you feel might be relevant, however small, don't hesitate to let us know.'

'Of course,' Lucy says.

But despite the opening, she doesn't rush to get the ring out of her pocket.

Maybe it has nothing to do with Brooke Whitlam's death, and she'd be inviting questions and accusations that would allow the real perpetrator to go free. It's not as though she would have lied if he'd asked her directly.

There's a man in a wheelchair waiting in the small reception area. His head is lowered, his shoulders hunched, and he breathes with the assistance of a small tube attached to a tank in the back of the chair. He doesn't look up as she passes but even in profile, he seems familiar. Faded tan of a former outdoor life, matching sunspots on large but frail hands. A full head of mostly dark hair, silver at the temples.

She's seen him before. Maybe he was a friend of Nan's.

His head jerks up, his dark eyes are narrowed, and she realises that not only has she slowed almost to a standstill, but she's staring at him.

'Terrible weather,' she says quickly.

'Every day is a gift.' Each word is wheezy, and somehow the meaning is the exact opposite of what he's saying.

She should have kept walking.

She pulls her jacket close, nods and hurries out into the bitter wind, her own breath coming easier when she's away from the man with eyes of unfathomable pain. Maybe it's a police station thing, but when she steps out into the rain, she feels rather like she's got away with something.

JANUARY 2000
TWO WEEKS BEFORE THE PARTY

Mae

'What are you looking for?' Mother asked from the doorway.

Mae ignored her. Sometimes, not engaging defused the situation. Mostly, it didn't.

'I asked you a question.'

Mae lifted her head slowly and turned to face her mother properly. 'My passport.'

'Why?'

Mae returned to her rummaging. 'You know why.' Tired of the slow progress, she tipped the contents of the desk drawer out on to her bed. It had been in there only a few days ago, she was sure of it.

Mother sighed. 'You're not still on this silly idea.'

'It's not silly, it's Oxford.' Mae's voice shook. She hated when her body failed to hide her frustration. Why did anger and fear sound so damn similar?

'You won't find it.'

Mae spun back around. 'How can you be so sure?' And then, with realisation, 'You've taken it.'

Mother lifted her hands, palms up. 'I didn't say that, but either way, it doesn't matter. We agreed that your place is here.'

'I'm not going to follow in your footsteps. Dad said—'

Mother cut her off with a step into the room. 'He's not the one paying. I've made my decision and I'll have no more arguments. Don't make this embarrassing.'

Embarrassing? Mae's fingernails bit into her palms as she struggled to keep her tone level. 'You can't stop me going,' she ground out. 'I'm an adult. I want to follow my own dreams.'

'You want to abandon your family.'

That hurt. She'd do anything for Anabelle and Harry and Mother knew it. But didn't she deserve to have her own life too? She was too late to muster a retort, Mother had already walked away.

'You don't even know what family is,' Mae muttered anyway on a gulp of frustrated tears.

Alone in her room, her head whirled doing the sums, trying to work out how far the scholarship would go and then add it to her own meagre savings. At Oxford, there would be food and rent and books to buy. Her stomach sank. She was beginning to think following your dreams wasn't a path for the poor.

And as much as he'd want to help, Dad didn't have any substantial assets of his own. The town might call their home the Whitlam house, but Brooke Thorne had inherited it from her parents and it belonged to her.

If Mae wanted to get out of Queen's Point and away from her mother, she'd need to come up with a solution on her own.

'Hey you, couldn't help but overhear.'

Mae lifted her head, wiping her cheeks as Harry entered the room and gently shut the door behind him. She couldn't manage to speak past the lump in her throat but she didn't need to. His arms came around her and she let her head rest against his chest.

'She can't control you,' he said.

How she wanted to believe that.

The steady beat of his heart calmed her in a way that all the self-talk and deep breaths couldn't, but the situation felt just as hopeless. 'She's never going to let me leave.'

His arms tightened. 'Then we'll have to do something about that.'

14

PRESENT DAY

It's not until later that afternoon that Lucy recognises the other lingering feeling following the police interview. *Relief*. Antonio Georgiades radiated the competence of a man who will get his man. This whole thing will be cleared up soon and she can stop seeing flashes of a woman's hand in water that she's pretty sure is a figment of her imagination.

Because they all saw Mrs Whitlam storm out of the party after the altercation by the fountain. And Lucy was with Nan for the rest of the night.

She's barely made a dent in Nan's piles of paperwork. It's tempting to start a fire using it all and call it done. But she can picture Nan's horrified expression all too easily.

Most of Nan's lectures focused on the wild ways of the Whitlam offspring but she didn't think a lot of Brooke Whitlam either. One time Lucy was waxing lyrical about Brooke Whitlam's style and class and Nan scoffed at her 'misplaced values'. Lucy thought Nan was jealous that she'd never have the wealth they took for granted up on the hill.

She's on her feet, having crossed to look out of the small window in the sunroom that allows a glimpse of the white of the Whitlam house, when it hits her. This inability to settle and concentrate is more than the distraction of the police investigation and the ring that's even now in her pocket. What she's feeling is grief.

She only knew her a few weeks, but Brooke Whitlam shaped Lucy's life.

I believed she had everything, and that she was everything by which anyone would define success.

The wind catches the branches and she sees the house a moment before it's gone again. So many hours spent staring up there, longing to be in that family. But it couldn't have been as perfect as Lucy thought because someone killed Brooke Whitlam.

Don't they say it's always the husband? She pictures Mr Whitlam and can't morph the smiling eyes and gentle voice into a killer.

Maybe she should be afraid, standing here, all alone, so close to the home of a murder victim, and possibly the killer too. As she leans closer to the window, straining to see more, the fear is there, fluttering its wings against her chest, but along with it there is something else – excitement. This terrible situation is by far the most interesting thing that has ever happened to Lucy.

She shakes herself. Time to get out of this tiny cottage.

It only takes a minute to find the lead and then she's heading outside with Hades. Her ankle is almost healed, with only the odd ache late in the day reminding her of her fall. They cross the road and enter the dunes as sand swirls in the wind. As they pick through the sand and clumps of shrub, she keeps Hades on a loose lead.

'Wait up. You can have a run on the sand,' she promises.

There's no doubt who would win in a tug of war, but he responds to her tone, if not the words, and doesn't pull free. At last, they're down on the sand and she scans the horizon. The beach is deserted but there are a few heads out on the water closer to town. Too far away to recognise, they're merely bobbing figures on boards in the grey, choppy expanse.

She unclips the lead and Hades bounds down to the water's edge. The sheer joy of him brings a smile to her lips. She heads away from the people, with Hades running in and out of the crashing waves. Her feet veer further on to the Whitlam property, to where sand dunes become rock and soil. Closer and closer to the unremarkable slash in the earth that she now knows was Brooke Whitlam's resting place for nearly two decades. This is where she wanted to come when she was with Anabelle.

She slows, studying the path up towards the house over the top of the hill. If the body came straight from up there, how did they do it? It would have been treacherous carrying something so large. One person could not have managed it alone.

Murderers?

She moves further up the rising ground towards the cliff path. Her eyes squeeze shut, trying to remember more from that night. Someone drove one of their cars out on the road, she's sure she recognised it. But with the night and the tinted windows, that could have been anyone. She presses her palms into her eyes until stars bloom behind them.

There's nothing.

'Hey, *grande cane*, you lost?'

Her eyes fly open at the sound of a man's voice carried on the wind. That was Italian, and that probably means Dante. It's beginning to feel like he's everywhere she goes.

'He's not lost,' Lucy calls. Her heart's racing, although she wasn't doing anything but walking her dog, as she heads towards the sound. She spots man and dog together.

Dante straightens when he sees her, his hand lingering on the top of Hades' head, and flashes an easy smile. 'I thought maybe he'd escaped,' he explains when she's close enough to see the assorted gardening equipment at his feet. 'Again.' He grins.

'Not this time.' She laughs and hears it ringing on and on in her head until it's like she's laughing at herself. Pathetic middle-aged woman simpering to a man who's still virtually a boy. 'He usually stays close to me or the water. I hadn't realised he'd wandered. I'm sure he would have come when called.' She's not sure at all, but doesn't need to tell Dante. 'I thought we should get a walk in before it rains again.'

'Good idea.' He's moved closer to hear her properly over the swirling wind, his body angled to create intimacy in a way that her own has unconsciously mirrored.

Her gaze meets his but she looks away fast. At least she's not gushing about travel plans like the first time they met, or ogling his muscles like in the kitchen.

'What are you doing out here?' Lucy asks.

He picks up what looks like a giant pair of scissors. Rust speckles the long blades and the wooden handles have the dull sheen of prolonged use. They could be a toy the way he holds them, but they have a look about them like they could do real damage. Instinct reminds her that the beach is basically deserted. Anything could happen and no one would know.

She chases away the thrill of fear.

He's just a kid handyman who's too handsome for his own good. The people she should be worried about live up in the white house at the top of the hill.

'... maintaining the path because there's no fence,' he finishes.

She nods, although she hasn't a clue what he's been saying. 'I should leave you to your work. Get back to the cottage.'

'Of course, you probably want to have a nice hot shower after being out in the cold.'

Is that insinuation in his voice? There's nothing in his expression to say it's anything other than casual but she edges back a step.

He reaches out and catches her hand. His grip is just a little firmer than necessary and her pulse jitters at the touch of his warm fingers. 'Wait.'

He's still holding her hand, looking down at her fingers. Is he looking for the ring? She's been too scared to wear it the last few days, but carries it with her. Suddenly she pictures his fingers tightening, holding her down while he searches for the missing item.

'Do you have your phone?' he asks, returning her to reality.

'Why? There's no reception down here.' She catches herself immediately, wishing she'd not reminded him of that fact.

'I know. Can I?'

She hands over her unlocked phone, which makes him let go of her hand and place the tool on the ground. He presses the screen and hands it back.

'Now you have my number if you need anything.' He pauses a beat that feels suggestive. 'Any more help for your grandmother's cottage.'

'I should be fine.'

'It's no trouble. Perhaps I come tomorrow or Sunday? Let me know.'

'Thank you.'

She clips Hades back on the lead, and heads back towards the cottage. Is that Dante's gaze making her neck prickle? She doesn't look back to check. He was strangely insistent about coming over to help and she doesn't want to encourage him.

Hades is panting, soaked and sandy by the time they finally emerge out on to the road opposite Nan's place. There is a vehicle parked out the front. And Jake is leaning against it, his hair wet, seemingly watching for them. He's off duty in worn jeans and a check shirt that looks like it would be soft to the touch.

'Hey,' he says. 'I thought I saw you two.'

The wet hair, ruddy cheeks and something salty and alive about him click into place. 'Were you out on the water?'

'It's a bunch of oldies who surf or swim every day, rain or shine.' He shivers. 'No matter what the temperature is. I try to join them when I can, be on hand in case one of them gets into trouble.'

It's decent of him and not at all surprising. 'And you thought you'd say hello?'

'Pretty much.' He looks to the cottage. 'How's progress?'

'Slow.'

'Probably not helped by spending the morning at the station?'

For someone not involved, he seems to be keeping up with the investigation in detail. 'It was fine. And, if you're wondering, I didn't tell your colleagues any details about our time together.'

He wipes water drops off his cheek. 'Didn't think you would. Anyway, I should probably leave you to it.'

She swallows. The question that's been bothering her is harder to get out than she could have imagined. 'We're all being questioned from the party. Are you?'

Jake's Adam's apple works in his throat and his eyes shut briefly. 'Are you asking if I'm a suspect because of my dad?'

'Your dad?'

'Teddy Parker, town loser. Killed himself in the family wool shed. You have to remember.'

Lucy does. The scary man behind the supermarket who lost his job because someone complained about his drinking at work. Someone she guesses was probably Brooke Whitlam. 'I remember,' she says gently.

Somehow his attitude and the way he's skirting the edges of this case when he's been pulled off it suggest to Lucy he's already been cleared. It could be that he's above scrutiny because he's an officer, but Detective Georgiades doesn't seem the type to dismiss anyone as a suspect without good reason.

Jake's jaw tightens. 'I was standing with the old police sergeant, Alan Stevens, when Brooke Whitlam made her big exit. He'd attended the party as a guest that night, but a junior officer had paged him to say my dad had been in another fight and he'd pulled me aside.'

Lucy remembers Alan Stevens as being terrifying. 'Another fight?'

Jake sighs. 'After the fight my dad ran for it, didn't he? He'd gone and broken someone's jaw, the dumb bastard, and thought he'd end up behind bars again. Always fucking everything up. Anyway, I spent most of the night in Stevens' car looking for Dad. Stevens had a good heart, for all his gruff exterior, even mentored me when I decided to join the force.'

He's told her more than she asked, but she still feels there's more that he's not sharing. 'As far as alibis go, it's a good one.'

He mock salutes, mouth twisted in a half grin. 'Glad it passes your scrutiny, officer. I'll be sure to let Georgiades know.'

She senses this wasn't at all what he came here for but can't work him out. 'Okay. Thanks for dropping by.'

He's almost to the driver's side and she's inside the gate when he calls. 'Lucy?'

She turns back, her pulse inexplicably jumping at the tone of his voice.

His expression is impossible to read. 'Be careful.'

'What do you mean?' she asks. But her mind races. Did he see her somehow, drawn as she was to the gash in the ground where they found the rest of the body? Or was it her talking to Dante that has him worried? She tries to laugh off his concern. 'I'm okay.'

'Remember, that body got there somehow.'

'Are you suggesting I should be afraid of something that happened nearly two decades ago?'

'I'm saying you should be careful. Think of it as a warning from your friendly neighbourhood police officer.'

'This isn't really my neighbourhood.' She raises her eyebrows. 'And I know how friendly the police around here can be.'

His mouth twitches but there's something serious in his eyes. 'Don't.'

'Don't what?'

'Rewrite history. I'm not stupid enough to think I was who

you expected to meet under the arch that night when I saw he wasn't going to show, but I gave you all the opportunity in the world to pull away.'

This conversation had to happen, but Lucy feels her cheeks get hot. 'I was sober enough to know who I was kissing,' she says quietly. 'You were nice.'

The silence builds. Not in a bad way but like they're both remembering.

Then he breaks the moment. 'Nice? You know how to wound. I thought I was sexy.'

She recognises his attempt to lighten the mood. 'That's probably what I meant.'

He's lifting his hand in farewell when she calls out. 'Hey.'

He waits.

'How about that drink?'

Anabelle

Anabelle didn't intend to go into the kitchen while Mother was out, but she was bored. She'd been reading and then done a few of the workout suggestions from the magazines Mother kept leaving on her bed. That at least was better than the personal trainer she'd been stuck with last holidays.

Maybe Mother had noticed how hard Anabelle was trying, or maybe she'd decided she was a lost cause.

Thanks to the workout, and she'd totally done like most of it, she was hot and sweaty. It was only reasonable that she head to the kitchen for a glass of water, her towel over her shoulder. As she opened the fridge, the cool from inside hit the bare skin of her thighs. Goosebumps rose on her flesh and she found herself staring at the dimpled surface. *Doughy* was the word her mother had used when she commented on how they met in the middle.

'Not losing a cent down there,' her mother had joked when they had those council people around for dinner.

Anabelle had laughed along with everyone else. She could take a joke.

But her throat ached at the memory and her stomach gurgled and she'd feel better after a biscuit. One biscuit wouldn't matter after all the calories she must have burned in that workout. And Mother would never know.

Letting the fridge close, she turned to the pantry. Hand on the door, she paused, listening for anyone coming, but there was only silence.

She pulled at the door and grabbed the nearest packet of chocolate-covered treats. The wrapper tore. That chocolatey smell rose from within. Her mouth watered.

Although cool from the pantry, the chocolate would quickly melt. She lifted it to her mouth, panting now. She darted another look around to make sure she hadn't missed the car's arrival because of the rustle of the packaging.

How she longed to shovel it in. Then another and another. Instead, she opened her mouth and slowly bit into the very edge, letting the corner of it crumble on to her tongue. There, it melted, sweet as a promise.

Her eyes closed.

Slowly, she reminded herself. Every article she'd read on healthy eating said to take your time, to savour each mouthful and this way she'd naturally prevent overeating. She bit again and it tasted just as good. Then again, and again. And then it was gone.

One more wouldn't hurt.

This one she forgot to savour. Could she dare another?

The alternative was to leave the package there with two gone.

Her belly heaved. Mother would know it hadn't been open when she left. And she knew they were Anabelle's favourite. Had scoffed when Anabelle suggested she not buy them.

A woman must be able to resist temptation, she'd replied.

'I'm only fifteen,' Anabelle whispered, having somehow

eaten another while worrying. Now there was no way she could leave this here. In a rush, she shoved the biscuits and a bag of chicken crisps under her towel and scurried towards the door.

'Where are you going?'

Anabelle turned back. Mother stood across the kitchen, her slender figure silhouetted against the afternoon sun, her huge sunglasses hiding her eyes. But Anabelle didn't need to see them to know they'd be narrowed in suspicion.

'N-nowhere,' Anabelle stammered.

'Then you can come and try on this dress I bought you.'

Her stomach lurched. She and Mother most definitely did not have the same taste. Nor did they have the same understanding of the size Anabelle required. Everything Mother came home with was either too small or so big as to make Anabelle wonder if she'd turned into a small planet overnight.

It would end in tears. It always did. And always Anabelle's.

As she scrambled for some way to escape, the food packages under her towel seemed to crackle with every beat of her heart. Any second now and Mother would demand to know what she was hiding. Shame licked at her insides. Why had she taken the stupid biscuits?

Suddenly, there came the sound of heavy steps on the stairs. It could only be Harry. He burst into the hallway, obviously having been at the beach some time from the sand on his legs.

Understanding passed between them with a look.

'Hurry up,' he said. 'You don't want to be late to the volleyball game. Everyone's waiting.'

Mother wouldn't hold her up from exercise, wouldn't have a Whitlam be a no-show at a social event. It might have people thinking things weren't perfect up at the Whitlam house.

'I was about to change after my workout,' said Anabelle. And then she was moving, leaving the kitchen.

Behind her, she heard Mother become distracted by lecturing Harry about the sand. 'You know I cannot stand that stuff on my floors.'

Upstairs, she dumped the food behind the cushions in her secret room. Her heartbeat hadn't steadied by the time she'd stripped out of her workout gear and dressed again. She didn't bother with the biscuits – the way her stomach felt after almost getting caught by Mother, she probably would have brought them straight up again.

She slipped out of her room and down the stairs, not daring to even breathe, and made it outside to where Harry waited without incident.

He grinned, but didn't speak until they were halfway down the treacherous path towards the beach. 'You know there's no game, don't you?'

'I know.'

'I hate her,' he muttered, so low it was almost lost on the breeze and the distant waves.

'Me too.'

15

PRESENT DAY

When Jake doesn't answer Lucy's drink suggestion straight away, it's all she can do not to babble a retraction.

'I don't want to talk about the case,' he says.

'That's not why I asked.' At least, she doesn't think it is. 'But I can't promise it won't come up in conversation. Friendly speculation between friends who have no official capacity, like would be happening all over town.'

He nods slowly. 'I guess that's to be expected, and I am feeling pretty thirsty.'

She changes into jeans and her favourite black cashmere jumper. Her hair is a lost cause after the wind and damp air so she settles for twisting it into a casual knot and then applying lip gloss. It's not like this is a date. She secures Hades in the laundry, but refuses to cave in to the puppy-eyed expression. 'No early dinner, remember what the vet said last check-up.'

He's not placated, and she sighs before throwing him a treat as she locks up.

'That dog,' she says as she gets in the passenger side of Jake's ute. 'He's supposed to be on a weight programme, but he looks at me and all my good intentions seem to disappear.'

'I don't blame you.' He chuckles, and drives them towards

town. He must have put on deodorant while he was waiting, and the cab smells clean and masculine with a hint of the sea.

They talk about pets on the short trip. He lost his border collie two years ago and can't bring himself to get another, and Hades is the only pet she's ever had. 'And he's still Brian's really,' she admits as Jake finds a parking space outside the pub.

It used to be a bit of a dive, but the beer garden is modernised with huge gas heaters keeping the cold at bay and their table overlooks the sea. They both choose locally brewed cider and she doesn't argue when he pays.

'My shout next time,' she says.

'I've seen your car,' he teases. 'Yours can be dinner.'

She has to resist an urge then to tell him the truth about her apparent success, to come clean about what happened at work and the ramifications that might still be coming her way. Doing so would be admitting she's not come as far in the last twenty years as she'd like to think.

It's hard not to talk about the Whitlams, considering they're being whispered about at every table, but she tries. 'What about the Spring Gully Road accident you were called away on the other day? Is that sorted?'

'The car was totalled. And there was a small fire in the wreckage that took some time to extinguish. The woman's ID must have been in her handbag on the floor, where the worst of the flames had their way. We still have no idea who she is.'

'Another mystery.'

'More likely bad luck for some ordinary woman than any great secret. There are no reports of anyone missing but if her family are from interstate or overseas, they might assume she's been too busy to call. And her friends might believe she's visiting family.'

'At least she has you,' Lucy says. She flashes back to the first day in town and looking for Hades in the dunes, when she could have fallen and no one would have known where she was. 'How do you find out who she was?'

He sips his drink. 'You can't expect me to give away all my methods,' he jokes. But then he's serious. 'It's slow work because so many resources are tied up in the Whitlam case. Headlines and public pressure will do that. Unfortunate accidents don't compare with exciting murders. Before you ask, she's getting attention – it's more that some of the forensic processing is backed up. This stuff doesn't happen quite like it does in the movies, not if you'll need the scientific analysis to hold up later. She probably has a family and for them as much as her, I don't want to get this wrong.'

'You're a good man, you know that?' It wasn't something Lucy ever imagined saying to pimply-faced Jake Parker, but she means it.

'Well I never.' He doffs an imaginary hat. 'Thank you, ma'am.'

'Don't let it go to your head.'

His face gentles. 'I won't.'

And their gazes meet and it's not like when Harry looks at her but something stirs, something she thought had died with Brian. She searches for a subject change. She fucked up so badly with Brian; she can't risk it again. But her eyes sting and she has to look away.

Jake touches the back of her hand. 'What did I say?'

'Nothing.'

'You don't need to pretend with me.'

Strangely, she believes that. 'Sometimes I miss them, you know. Nan. Brian. It's been a shitty couple of years.'

He takes her hand. 'I remember Judy well but I don't know much about the rest. Tell me about your husband.'

'You really want to hear?'

He holds his glass up to the light. 'I have a cider to finish. So, yeah, hearing about someone who was important to an old friend of mine sounds like something I'd like.'

It's hard to know where to begin. Thanks to work, she'd never had much time to date, but in the last months of her mum's life she'd found herself at the hospital pharmacy filling scripts often enough to be on smiling terms with the man in charge, and then when she'd fallen apart one day after knocking over a display he'd comforted her. Comfort became a coffee and that became dinner a few months later. He'd never got to meet her mother as she passed away before that first dinner, but he'd been a rock of support through her grieving and supported her putting work first, maybe because he was older and he'd done all that family stuff already.

Nan had adored him. He'd always made time to visit her, even when Lucy was on a big project and couldn't get away.

Lucy takes a shaky breath, sips her cider, and tries to do justice to the man she married. 'He was decent, reliable, hard-working. Honest to a fault. A wonderful father to his daughter, although he said that was a work in progress.' Her throat aches. 'I'm doing a terrible job of this. Making him sound like a bore. He was also adventurous and thoughtful.'

Jake follows her every word.

'He was a bit of a cycling fanatic. Loved to battle the road, hills and distances, the more gruelling the better.'

'Was that something you did together?'

She makes a face. 'No. He had a group who went out on a weekend. They saved up to do the Tour de France companion ride one year. I couldn't imagine anything worse, but he loved the challenge and the feeling of accomplishment.'

'What do you like to do?'

She hesitates. The old answer – work – feels so empty after talking about Brian and she's not sure it's true any more. 'Work keeps me busy. I have a townhouse close to work and I surprised myself with how much I enjoyed decorating it, filling each room with things that I love.' She realises with a pang how many of her choices were influenced by her memories of Brooke Whitlam's style, how much she's bought from the Whitlam Homewares range. 'Hades needs a good walk each day, which has allowed me to feel less guilty about how little I use my gym membership. What about you?'

'Married to my work,' he admits. 'But I try to get out and surf when I can. Being out on the water clears my head. Often it's the circuit breaker I need.'

It shouldn't surprise Lucy. Not with the chiselled cut of his body and the deep tan of his skin, but it's hard to let go of her memories of him as a decidedly less athletic teen.

'And,' he leans forward over his glass, 'I have probably seen every episode of *The Great British Bake Off*.'

'I have never seen one.'

His jaw drops in exaggerated astonishment. 'You haven't lived.'

She laughs and the gloom lifts.

But a couple of hours later, long after Jake left her outside the cottage, her brain can't let go of Jake's parting comment. 'Your husband sounds like one of the good ones. You two must have been very happy.'

'We were,' she says aloud to the empty linen cupboard.

Nearby, Hades lifts his head, wags his tail once and then goes back to sleep.

That doesn't mean Brian and she were without their hard times. The first when they'd been seeing each other for a year. She'd thought he was looking to make things more permanent; he'd sat her down to ask for a break.

It was her second night newly single when she got the message from Harry. So unexpected as to have her thinking it was a prank. But he convinced her it wasn't and they agreed to meet at a bar.

He was waiting when she arrived and when she looked at him her body felt that same thrill as it had at sixteen. No matter how unfair, as Harry stood to greet her, the hurt from Brian's dumping meant she'd been unable to help comparing him with Brian.

Harry unfolded his limbs from the stool he'd chosen at the bar. His dark hair had grown longer, more rock-star-on-tour than suburban hotel bar. His simple T-shirt emphasising a muscular chest. His slow, languid smile making a heart-fluttering combination with his model cheekbones, soot-lashed grey eyes and chiselled jaw. His slightly crooked teeth the detail that made him human, and infinitely more attractive for it.

Against this, Brian's neat physique built on doctor's orders after his first heart scare. His style more functional than top end. His glasses often smeared at the spot he'd pushed them to sit more comfortably on his nose. Nice-looking. A nice man. Or at least she'd thought so until he announced that he needed time to rethink his future.

To rethink Lucy.

Wounded and hurting, she'd fallen into Harry's arms

as though Brian didn't exist. Felt the shame of it when she discovered all the messages from him that she'd missed.

After a day of battling guilt, she'd agreed to meet Brian to discuss their future. He declared he'd made a terrible mistake and their time apart had shown him just how much he needed her in his life. She couldn't help but agree.

When he got down on one knee and proposed there and then, in the middle of the doughnut bar, she couldn't say no.

She never told him about that time with Harry.

Nor when she'd been waylaid by Harry after working late – just a drink that time, but bad enough – the night Brian went to the hospital with the heart attack that would end up killing him.

Not for the first time, thinking about all the ways she screwed up with Brian has Lucy scrolling through her contacts until she finds Jasmine, Brian's daughter. Over the time she had with Brian, their relationship had thawed from frosty to civil, occasionally even pleasant.

Like so many times when he was well, Jasmine had been the subject of one of their last conversations. So many discussions about his efforts to connect with her, so much wishing on Brian's part that Lucy and Jasmine got along better. It wasn't Lucy's fault the girl thought there was room for only one female in her father's life.

Jasmine had ducked out for a coffee, a toilet break, a cry, leaving Brian and Lucy alone in the hospital room.

'Look out for her,' he'd croaked.

'Of course I will,' Lucy had said, squeezing his hand. After everything with Harry, she would have promised him anything. And part of her still stupidly hoped he'd walk out of there.

'I know it's a lot to ask, but she's not as strong as she looks.' His mouth curved. 'Neither are you.'

Now, Jasmine doesn't answer the phone for the longest time and Lucy can picture her staring at the screen, debating ignoring the call. It's not time for the once-every-couple-of-weeks asking about Hades that they maintain.

She's a busy young woman and could well be at work. She pushes herself to be the best, working practically around the clock. That, at least, is something she and Lucy have in common. Well, *had*, maybe.

'I'm listening,' Jasmine says, finally answering.

It always throws Lucy how she doesn't say her name. 'It's Lucy,' she says, although she will have seen it come up on her screen. Likely as 'the wicked stepmother'. 'How are you?'

'Good.'

As usual, she doesn't exactly help the conversation flow. Lucy can practically hear Brian remind her to be the grown-up. 'And how's work?'

'Good.'

Lucy's hand tightens on the phone as she scrambles for something to say. Lately, thoughts of Brooke Whitlam and what happened that night have been all-consuming, but she's certain Jasmine won't want to know about her links to a mysterious death. 'Hades went for a swim today and he's covered the place with sand.'

'Ratbag.' Jasmine's voice softens. 'Dad loved that bundle of trouble.'

'He did.'

For a moment the silence between them is almost companionable. Then Jasmine sighs. 'I should go.'

She doesn't even make up an excuse and Lucy can't blame

her, not really. 'Wait.' Lucy spots the pile of doctor's reports she was going through earlier. 'Do you know anything, ah, about, um…' She's stumbling over the words and she senses Jasmine's impatience. 'Mesothelioma,' Lucy finishes.

'What about it?'

'Anything? Everything? I've discovered some papers and reports in my grandmother's things that suggest that's what my grandfather had.'

Jasmine sighs, still impatient, but maybe less annoyed. It could be sympathy, could just be resignation. 'What about the internet? Surely there's tons of information.'

'I'm sure I've heard you rant about the problems with believing Dr Google.'

'Maybe once or twice.'

That was almost warmth in her tone, Lucy's sure of it. 'I don't need the science, just a bit of understanding for the complete idiot.' Her brain hurts at the thought of trying to trawl to find out what she needs. And besides, Jasmine is right there on the phone and she's a doctor and she's actually having a conversation with Lucy for a change.

There's the sound of a chair scraping. She must be sitting down. 'I'll keep this brief because it's not really my area. There's one main risk factor, or way you can get this type of cancer, and that is exposure to asbestos. You know what that is?'

'A building material they used to use. I've seen it on the news, and they have to get people in hazmat suits in if they find it.'

'That's the stuff. They didn't know about the dangers back in the day. It's made up of tiny fibres that can be breathed in or swallowed, affecting the lungs, heart and abdomen. Once in the lining of say, the lungs, these tiny fibres can damage the cells, causing inflammation, and this over time can cause a malignant tumour. This is the most common and it's called pleural mesothelioma. But the symptoms might not appear until years and years after exposure, beginning with shortness of breath and chest pain. The prognosis is often less than two years. There are treatments but they are generally just giving time.'

'That's awful.'

'Yeah. It's hard on the patient and on those left behind.'

They're both thinking of Brian. 'Thank you,' Lucy says.

'Any time,' she replies.

And for a change, Lucy thinks she probably means it.

After ending the call, Lucy's tempted to head to bed but Hades is restless and wants to go out. She lets him out the front and grabs a couple of the rubbish bags to put out in the skip while she's waiting for him to do his business.

But he runs straight to the front fence and barks.

'What's up, boy?' she asks, but the barking stops as quickly as it started.

Finished with the rubbish, Lucy's about to go back inside when she sees it. There's a glow in her car. The interior light is on. That's strange, she can't remember the last time she was in there. Maybe she didn't close the door properly. That's the most likely explanation.

But her stomach is tight as she walks towards it.

One of Nan's roses on the bush next to the car is broken. The flower has been snapped off at the stem and the petals are scattered on the ground. Drops of colour, like blood at a crime scene.

She checks the back seat, but there's no one in there waiting to leap out, despite the conjurings of her imagination.

The glovebox is open but the change she keeps for ticket machines remains in there, glinting golden from the tiny bulb. And there's more than twenty dollars and some designer sunglasses still in the centre console.

It feels a lot like a warning.

Unsure if she's overreacting, she calls the police.

'Probably teenagers on a dare,' Jake says a little while later after he's had a look around.

Of course it's her luck that he was the one assigned to come out. Hopefully, he doesn't think seeing him was the reason she rang. 'But the money's still there.'

He shrugs. 'Teenagers. Or you didn't close the door properly last time you were in the car. Something like that is easy enough not to notice.'

Maybe he's right, but she still feels uneasy. Nothing she can explain. Nothing that would make her argue with someone who literally does this as their job. 'Maybe Hades and I scared them before they could take anything.'

He grins. 'Most likely.'

He makes a note of the incident, takes some photos and makes her promise to report any other disturbances. There's a moment where she thinks he's going to offer to stick around, but then he gets a call.

She's glad. With no evidence of anything out of place other than a broken flower, easily explained by the passing of a large dog, she's probably lucky he didn't laugh.

However, as he drives off into the night and she heads back inside, she's careful to lock the front door.

16

PRESENT DAY

Thanks to Lucy's chat with Jasmine and then Jake responding to the disturbance, she forgets about the strange feeling she got from Dante when she saw him on the beach. The uneasy feeling that she's seeing him everywhere she goes. That is, until she's tackling some of the smaller boxes of more personal items in the sunroom late on Saturday afternoon.

He'd been so insistent about helping. Almost too insistent. She almost drops the box of glass figurines she's holding.

Mae saw the ring on Lucy's hand. If she thought it was her mother's, she'd want to know more. What if, when Dante continually went into the sunroom the day he spent helping Lucy, it was part of a plan to look for the ring? He did jump when she caught him in there.

Maybe Jake was right to be suspicious. He's probably looked into Dante as much as he can through his police channels, but that's not much. He could lose his job if he tried to access something out of his scope. But he doesn't have the experience she does in internet sleuthing. She's not proud of how much time she's spent reading about the Whitlams online over the years, but the interest – okay, borderline stalking – will pay dividends if she can work out Dante's connection to the family.

Abandoning the sorting of Nan's knick-knacks, she opens her laptop, aware that she hasn't used it since she arrived. The sleek, trusty machine probably hasn't gone so long unused since she took it out of the box. But when she hotspots to her phone, she's not tempted to touch base with her clients or catch up on the group conversation threads from the office. Instead, she begins looking for Dante in earnest.

Lucy quickly learns that Dante is not a common name, but a general search gets her no further than last time. She changes tack, scrolling through friend lists of the various Whitlam family members. She discovers Anabelle has more friends called Chloe and Caitlin than Lucy has friends, but a few hours later, she's sure there are no Dantes among them.

She leans back and tries to think. Alone as she is, she's slipped Nan's ring on to her finger and she turns it round and round as she tries to think harder. He could have strict settings on his personal information, but that wouldn't extend to others' photos. Which means she needs to find him in them.

This progresses even more slowly, and her eyes begin to water. She lifts her head and stretches out her aching shoulders. It's later than she realised, and now the only light comes from the computer screen. The small windows show it's already dark outside. She's spent who knows how long lost down the tunnel of social media and the internet. Looking for Dante, finding possibilities, then looking for a connection to Queen's Point.

She rubs at the knots in her neck. It's only been days since she last spent so long in front of a computer. It's amazing how quickly the body gets out of practice, despite having done such for what feels like a lifetime.

A noise comes from outside.

A flutter at the window. Is it the wings of an insect? Is that what stirred Lucy from the picture of a friend of a friend of Anabelle's holidaying a year ago on the Amalfi Coast, scanning the names for mentions of Dante and the faces for his familiar one?

The sound comes again. A soft tap against the glass.

Hades' ears prick up.

'Probably one of those huge moths they get around here,' Lucy tells him. They used to scare her as a teen, the thought of one of them caught in her hair making her skin crawl.

It has the same effect now and she stands, annoyed at her accelerated heart rate.

Moving around the small cottage, she snaps on lights, pushing back the darkness and her silly imagination. Moths. And the car thing was teenagers or her leaving the door open. Nothing to be afraid of.

She opens the freezer and scans the frozen meals but none appeal. However, it's already past nine. Queen's Point might have progressed, but there's unlikely to be anything open this late in winter. Resigned, she shoves the frozen spinach agnolotti in the microwave, sets it going and fills Hades' dinner bowl with kibble. His tail wags appreciatively.

The Dante problem nags at her. There's something she's not seeing. But what? Was it that last picture by the sea?

No.

Her eyes fly open. Not that picture, but a memory. Of Mr Whitlam's graduate student, Vanessa, relaxing out by the pool in her bathers that summer. The gorgeous skin, dark hair and eyes with naturally long lashes.

Urgent now, she finds Mr Whitlam's accounts and then

scans his friend list. No Vanessa of any sort. What was her last name?

It takes her finding a research paper they published together to learn her maiden name is Ryder. Lucy tries 'Dante Ryder' with no luck, but she's sure they're related. Could they be mother and son?

Vanessa and Mr Whitlam were close. If they'd had an affair resulting in a child, that would explain why Dante had come all this way. And his fascination with the family.

Hades lifts his head and hackles rise on his neck.

This time Lucy didn't hear anything over the whir of the microwave and him eating.

He trots to the back door, leaving his food. She follows more slowly, opens the door, and flicks the switch for the back light – well, the single pathetic globe. As though it's heard her criticise its reach, the globe sputters and fails.

The light spills out from the door but fades quickly. The wind has picked up. Maybe Hades heard another storm approaching, although thunder doesn't usually bother him. A small mercy, since winter in Queen's Point isn't lacking in storms. It must be the way the wind comes off the ocean and moves up and around the point.

Hades growls and Lucy steps out with him. If she wanted to wait for a man to fix her problems, she'd still be stuck inside her first apartment. That time, the noise outside turned out to be a rogue possum.

The light from inside stretches even less distance than Lucy thought. Within a couple of steps Hades is simply a dark blob in the gloom. The torch function on her phone does its best to light the way ahead but it's limited.

The wind bites through her oversized knitted jumper and stretchy leggings. She shivers, wishing she'd grabbed her jacket. Hades heads straight for the side fence, the one that provides a boundary with the furthest reaches of the Whitlam land. No growls now but the fur on his neck stands on end and his tail is up at an unnatural angle.

Small sounds come from the undergrowth nearby, louder than the wind. Scurrying feet and tiny chomping teeth. Rats, maybe? Lucy shudders. They're worse than moths, but better than it could be.

In her head she sees the newspaper article.

May contain human remains.

She's wearing boots. Heavy enough to sink rather than be washed up under the jetty? She chases away the silly thought. Now they're beneath the overhanging branches and the light from her phone is only a weak beam.

Hades lunges forward. He barks. Staccato warnings, teeth showing white in the torchlight. Lucy's frozen in place, but he bounds through and over bushes, snapping twigs and tearing leaves. Her shaking hand struggles to follow him with the beam of light.

There's a louder sound beyond him. Something moving, something bigger than a rat.

She remembers Jake's teasing: 'I guess the Queen's Point killer has a certain ring to it.'

'Hades,' she cries, panic making it a screech. She longs to flee to the cottage but he's Brian's dog, and she could never live with herself if something happened to him. 'Hades!'

There's a clatter up ahead and a yelp as Hades hits the fence dividing the properties. The criss-crossed wire bends but doesn't give beneath his huge weight. He leaps at it again.

Then he's through and Lucy has to climb the fence to follow. She's on Whitlam property now, still a long way from the house but with no Hades in sight.

She tries to keep up with the sounds of him, pushing where she can, dodging and ducking under branches. *Ouch.* Something digs into her arm. *Fuck, that stings.*

'Hades, come here, boy.'

Has he slowed? They're closer to the house now than she thought. Through the branches, a light shines up on the second floor. Of course, someone is home. With all the rumours and gossip, the whole family is probably pretty much hiding up there.

Hades appears through the low bushes, panting but no longer distressed. Whatever he was chasing is gone. There's no other sound but the wind and the first drops of rain.

Even though Hades is back at Lucy's side, she moves a little closer to the huge house, drawn to it as if the flashes of white through the trees are the beckoning hands of a lover.

She's quiet and Hades doesn't make much noise, despite his size. The wind through the garden completely muffles their movements and her torch is off. She stops on the edge of the manicured area, finding Hades' collar to keep him from going any further. There are lights on downstairs too. The blinds are all drawn but a shadowy figure moves in what she thinks must be the living room. It paces back and forth, then comes to stand by the window.

The blind flies up.

Lucy staggers back, behind a tree, dragging Hades with her. When her heart slows enough to peer back around the branch, the room is empty.

That was close, but even if she hadn't moved, surely it was

too dark to see anything. Besides, she's simply a dog owner retrieving her pet.

They head back down the slope, Hades hurrying past her to get back to the cottage and his dinner. It takes a bit more effort to get them back into Nan's yard than it did to get out, and they're negotiating a fence when a rumble splits the night air. It's the sound of a ute, she's sure of it.

But whose?

Jake? One of the vehicles from the Whitlam house? Her head fills with images of Dante and the easy way he hefted the hedge trimmer with its long blades. She practically runs the last few steps to the back door.

Inside, she double-checks the door is locked. Blood drips on the linoleum from a gash on her forearm where she missed dodging a low branch and her ankle is throbbing from pushing herself over uneven surfaces. Nan's first-aid kit is still in the bathroom and she manages to patch up the bleeding.

Then she paces the small cottage, her heart drumming hard, her breathing ragged.

She tells herself nothing has changed.

But still she finds herself on her knees in the darkened hall, making sure she can't be seen from any windows, fumbling with a loose floorboard. Hiding it away will give her the time she needs to find out the truth of where it came from. Her trembling hands make her clumsy until she manages to lever up the corner of the old wood. Then she places the ring, wrapped in an old tea towel of Nan's, into the dark hole.

Only then can she breathe a little easier as her gaze confirms she's left no sign of anything in the hallway being disturbed.

Afterwards, she discovers the pasta has been overheated to a gluggy mess. Her stomach turns at the sight and she dumps it in the bin, eating cereal straight from the box instead while she continues her computer search. She needs answers.

Vanessa's work profile shows her fascination with the classics continued and she's lived and worked in the field in Greece and also Italy, including at a university in Venice. Lucy remembers Dante talking about living in the canal city and excitement flares, but there's nothing online that suggests Vanessa has a son. Rather, she's married with two young girls.

Lucy sits back, deflated. She struggles to focus, unable to shake the uneasy feeling that she's not alone. Twice she gets up and checks everything is locked. They're a decent way out of town; whatever Hades heard was probably a kangaroo or even a stray dog.

Probably.

Or it was someone spying on them.

Harry

Sometimes Harry meant what he said. The compliments, the admiration, the whispered praise. Girls were, in general, more beautiful than they realised. He loved how he could make them light up with a word or two, loved basking in the rush of feeling between them.

Occasionally, he said something just because he could. He murmured a line so cheesy and insincere that hearing it made him want to slam his own face against a wall to shut himself up.

He didn't know why he did it.

Every time he did so, part of him hoped the girl, or boy, he was charming would erupt and turn on him with the violence he deserved. When they inevitably laughed or smiled or even winced, accepting it, he hated whoever he was with – and himself – just that little bit more.

The whole game was too easy.

Only in his studio did anything feel real. There he could lose himself in the paint and the art, and create something that really mattered.

He stepped back to properly consider the canvas he'd been working on half the morning.

Woman asleep.

The working title didn't completely suck but it didn't quite capture his intention. He wanted the audience of the piece to get a sense of her in repose, but also feel her unease. No sweet dreams for this one. His hand tightened on the brush. Why couldn't his body produce what his brain visualised? Why did it refuse to translate everything he felt somewhere between gut and groin on to the canvas?

He bit the inside of his cheek, thinking. Something wasn't right.

He'd been too heavy with the pink, definitely, but he didn't hate all the flesh tones. Maybe he could add some grey, for balance, and some red to twist the expectations. Although twisting expectations wasn't exactly difficult.

Everyone thought they knew him. Knew about the money, felt the charm, and didn't bother wondering if there was more. No one ever saw who he really was because no one bothered to look. Why would they?

Only Anabelle and Mae knew what it was really like to live in the house and have the life that everyone else thought they wanted. Only they saw their mother's true colours.

He reached out and slammed his hand down into the palette, then smeared it across the middle of the canvas in one angry stroke. Breath shuddering in his chest, he brought both hands into the tray of paint, flipping it on to the ground in the process.

He left it there, paint pooling on the floor. Then dragged his wet, sticky palms back and forth until there was more mixed, muddy brown than any particular form on the hand-stretched canvas.

With a shove, the destroyed painting followed the paint on to the floor.

Harry stared at it a moment, then he sank to his knees and sobbed.

JANUARY 2000
ELEVEN DAYS BEFORE THE PARTY

Lucy

'I will be gone all day,' Nan announced at breakfast while Lucy pushed her cornflakes around the bowl.

'Okay.'

'I considered taking you with me. However, it's a long drive and you just got those books from the library.'

The books in question were stacked in a pile on the small chest of drawers next to the bed. Lucy had grabbed a few without looking when dragged to the library.

'A long drive?' Lucy repeated before Nan could ask her about the books, which she had no intention of reading. Lifting her head from the soggy cereal in her bowl, she noticed the neat slacks, pale blue shirt and navy cardigan Nan wore, topped off with dark blue dangly earrings. Not her usual attire.

'Yes,' Nan said briskly. 'I have a meeting in Adelaide.'

'And you won't be back until tonight?' Lucy saw the glimpse of freedom like the sun breaking through the clouds.

'I'll be back by five, sharp. I expect that you'll go no further than the Whitlam house and you won't swim alone.' She peered over the top of her silver-rimmed glasses. 'No one is too old for the buddy system.'

'What's the catch?'

'No catch, but I will expect the chicken casserole I prepared to be hot in the oven and the table set for dinner.' Her features softened. 'You've been a good girl so far and I trust you. Please, don't let me down.'

'I won't,' Lucy promised.

She polished off the rest of the mushy breakfast without tasting a bite.

Knowing she had a whole day to herself meant Lucy arrived at the beach with a spring in her step.

'What's got you in such a good mood?' Anabelle asked, setting out her towel in the best spot for watching the surfers out on the water.

'Nothing, really.' Lucy put hers alongside with a grin. Not even her disappointment that Anabelle was the only Whitlam present could ruin this day of freedom.

Anabelle did her best to dampen things over the next few hours, with a run of complaints about everything from too much sun to the water being too warm and annoyance at the boys showing off on the waves. Then Harry arrived just as Lucy was about to leave.

'Heading off already?' he asked, with a smile that made her stomach flutter.

He'd noticed her packing up her things. Did that mean he was aware of her the same way she was of him?

'Yeah, I reckon I'm done here.' She aimed for casual, rather than admitting the fact her grandmother expected her home.

'It's out of your way, but I've been painting all day. Want to come and see?'

If she hurried, she could still make it back before Nan. She swallowed hard and squeaked, 'Sure.'

As they walked, she tried to read his expression. Maybe he

was bursting to show anyone his work. *Or maybe he wanted to be alone with Lucy.*

As they reached the garden at the top of the cliff, Lucy checked the time again. Four thirty.

'You need to be somewhere?' Harry asked.

'Nope.'

He opened the greenhouse door with a flourish that showed his pride. And she couldn't blame him. It was all the things he'd said and more. The *more* being the painting she didn't need to pretend to admire.

'This is incredible,' she whispered.

His arms slid around her waist, setting her body on fire. 'Do you really think so?' he murmured against her neck.

'Paint for me.' She didn't know where the request came from, nor the breathy tone to her voice, but she longed to see him create. She turned in his arms. 'Show me what you do.'

His eyebrow quirked but his full lips parted in a murmured agreement. 'It can get pretty intense. Are you sure?'

Footsteps clicked on the cobblestone path outside before she could answer.

Lucy froze, stared at Harry. He stood so close she could see the flecks of dark blue in the depths of his grey eyes.

His hand on her shoulder nudged her away from him. 'Quick, over there.' He gestured to an open cupboard door and she found herself bustled behind it before she could muster a protest.

A heartbeat later, the shed door creaked open and a cloud of expensive-smelling perfume drifted into the room. 'I know you have someone here.'

Mrs Whitlam.

Lucy couldn't mistake the voice. Nor the tone. Her cheeks flamed.

'Where is she?' Mrs Whitlam continued. 'Or is she gone already, pushed through some window? Which is it this time?'

This time… Lucy wasn't foolish enough to think she was the first girl Harry had invited over, but hearing it pointed out like that made her press her hands to her face to cool it. How naive of her to think they had a real connection.

Harry chuckled, a low rumble of sound that didn't resemble amusement. 'There's no one here.'

Mrs Whitlam clicked her tongue. 'Any piece of trash who'd come in here with you doesn't matter anyway. What matters is that you've been painting again. If you insist on wasting your time with all this, you'll end up a nobody without a cent. The girls won't be so keen on you then.'

'You said if I kept my grades up, I could…' His voice trailed off as if he'd just remembered Lucy was there.

Lucy's discomfort only increased. She didn't want to listen in on this private conversation. Hated the derision dripping from Mrs Whitlam's words about her son and the pleading note in Harry's voice.

'The paintings are simply not good,' said Mrs Whitlam. 'And the sooner you face that fact, the better. You're no special talent, nothing at all without me. Come up to the house, it's almost time for dinner.'

A few moments later, the door closed.

Lucy didn't move, didn't want to step out from behind the cupboard door and see Harry's face, not after what his mother had said about the art that was obviously so important to him. It took long seconds to muster the nerve to push the peeling paint and expose the room.

Only to find it was empty. Harry had gone.

And Nan would already be home. She skulked into the garden and down the long driveway. Her brain swung between pity for Harry and fear for how mad Nan would be. What if she forbade her from going to the beach again?

Lucy had an excuse of losing her watch ready to go, but when she burst through the door of the old cottage, Nan was sitting at her desk, concentrating on some paperwork. She didn't even notice Lucy was late.

17

PRESENT DAY

'Morning Lucy,' Mae calls, leaning over the cottage fence on Sunday morning. She's clearly on her way back from a run by the look of her attractively rosy cheeks and her brand-name activewear. 'How's your progress?'

'Slow,' Lucy replies as the wind snatches at the plastic bag in her hand and sends it flying.

Mae catches it before it can tumble across the road.

It poured with rain earlier. Lucy got caught out in it twice and had to give up on her hair, tying the damp strands back out of her face in a ponytail. But from the shine on Mae's golden locks and the freshness of her clothes, she's timed her run perfectly.

'Thanks for that,' Lucy says as Mae hands the bag over. 'And for sending Dante down here the other day. It's the personal items that have me mired now.'

'Glad to assist a neighbour.'

There's no hint from her manner that would support Lucy's idea that Dante – Vanessa's son? – had the ulterior motive of searching for her mother's ring when he came to help at the cottage. So much for that theory. A fitful sleep where she heard every creak of the cottage has dampened her certainty about anything, and the morning light wiped the ridiculous notion that there was someone in the yard.

'Well, thanks anyway,' Lucy says, smothering a yawn.

Mae scans the front of the cottage with interest. 'Have you thought about what you'll do with the place when you're finished?'

'Sell it, probably.' It's the logical course of action but the thought of someone else in the place that is so intrinsically linked with Nan bruises Lucy's heartstrings.

'That can't be easy,' Mae says, picking up on her tone. 'This has been part of your family for a long time. Your grandmother was a special woman. Let me tell you, she's been hard to replace at the house.'

'I haven't got down here in years – keeping it would be silly.'

'And the area is doing well with people looking for holiday places,' Mae agrees. 'Listen, if you do decide to sell, get someone local to have a look, someone who knows the market. When you come up with a fair price, talk to me.'

'You?'

Mae shrugs. 'I'd love to have first look.' She raises her hands, palms up. 'No pressure, of course.'

As much as Lucy's admired the Whitlams over the years, part of her baulks at the idea of them owning this too. They have so much land, so much power.

'I'll keep it in mind,' she says.

Mae smiles as though she owns it already. 'I'm hosting a family dinner tonight and I'd love for you to come.' Her manner makes the invite reminiscent of acceptance into the popular circle at high school, but she takes Lucy's silence as hesitation. 'You must come. We'll all be there. Dad, Anabelle... Harry.'

There's emphasis on her brother's name. Lucy hasn't seen Harry since the other night on the porch. She's heard from the gossips in town that he's been down to the police station more than once. Seen the unmarked, but obvious, cars snaking up to the house. Wondered if he's been in the old studio working through all this in the way he always did – on canvas – or if she was right about the boathouse renovation.

Lucy squirms. While it's not like she's ever been subtle about her fascination, it would be nice to think she's grown up a bit. But she's simply delaying the inevitable. What better place to learn more about what happened to Brooke Whitlam and the ring than dinner with the major suspects?

'What time?'

Lucy arrives up at the house a careful ten minutes late, just after seven that evening. She walked along the road, not wanting to risk her mostly healed ankle by taking a shortcut through the garden. The lack of cars parked out the front suggests only family are inside.

Squaring her shoulders and passing the bottle of wine to her other hand, she rings the doorbell. As seconds pass and the chill threatens to become drizzle, she has a sudden, knee-weakening fear she's made a mistake. But then the door swings open.

'Lucy.' Mae grasps Lucy's hands, leans in and brushes the lightest of oriental-scented kisses across her left cheek.

Is it Lucy's imagination or did Mae's gaze linger on her fingers, looking for the ring?

Eyeing Mae's black silken pants, floaty cream halter-neck top and tasteful gold hoops, Lucy's glad she dressed up for the occasion in a classic camel skirt and a long black top with balloon sleeves.

Mae takes the wine – 'You shouldn't have, really' – and clicks for someone to take Lucy's coat. A girl materialises as though waiting for Mae's command.

'Did you walk?' Mae peers past Lucy at the sky. 'Remind me to have someone drive you home.'

'It's not far.'

'Well, you're right on time, we've just moved to the dining room.'

Lucy trails Mae down the hallway, under the watching red eyes of the security cameras, past the large living area where they were for the cocktail party and into the dining room. Inside the intimate space, there's a table set for eight; obviously this is only family and a select few. Whatever it is that's going on here, with the body and the investigation, they all understand it. While part of Lucy feels she's been allowed admission to a very exclusive club, a larger part wonders, *why?*

But then she's too caught up to question. People mill around, clearly mid-conversation. There's a young Indian woman, who Lucy recognises as one of the nannies, holding Anabelle's baby near the door while Anabelle fusses over bedtime instructions. The older daughter is waiting alongside, already in her pyjamas.

There's a warmth in the room unlike any Lucy's felt in this house.

She realises, as Anabelle's middle child is lifted high on Harry's shoulders, squealing his delight, that these Whitlams are closer than ever before.

So often she's read in the news or in books how losing a family member to a violent, terrible end can destroy a family. The grief and the trauma tear the remnants of the family apart. But here, with this family, the loss of Brooke Whitlam has done the exact opposite. It's brought them even closer together.

Does that say more about the deceased or about those she left behind?

By the time Lucy's sat down as directed by her host and accepted a glass of wine, the rest of the chairs have been filled and Anabelle's children have disappeared with the nanny. As well as Mae, Anabelle and her husband, there's the cravat-wearing Mr Whitlam and Dante. The latter's presence a show of hospitality to the foreign visitor or something else? How close is he to Mae?

And, of course, there's Harry.

He said an off-hand hello in greeting when he passed close to Lucy carrying his nephew and she tried to act just as casual. Tried not to stare. His longish hair is more tousled than usual and his jaw dark with stubble. He's in tan chinos and a short-sleeved black shirt. The shirt being the same as the one he was wearing the other night when he surprised her on the porch. When they kissed. Her fingers curl in memory of its silkiness beneath her touch.

But he's seated at the opposite end of the table. The young mayor, Rachael Touré, is at his side, wearing a bright-red trouser suit that is both simple and stunning against her dark skin. Her head leans close to his as she murmurs something that causes his beautiful mouth to curve in a smile.

Lucy looks away, taking a larger than intended sip of the wine, and focuses on Dante. He's next to Mr Whitlam and, thinking of last night's theory, she studies their profiles for a resemblance. Maybe there's a hint? But it's hard to be sure in the soft glow from the tasteful pendant lights above.

All the while, she's listening to Anabelle and Manan share some tale of a missing sock belonging to their son that was found up in Anabelle's childhood secret turret room.

'It's a big house for him to explore,' Lucy says, remembering how as teenagers Anabelle led them through secret passages and down hidden staircases.

Manan agrees with a smile.

Mae lifts her glass, the movement enough to draw attention, and a moment later there's silence. 'Welcome, dear family and friends.' Her gaze moves around the table; when she looks at Lucy, her doubts about belonging disappear. 'Please, let us enjoy each other's company and, while I know it's a hard time on all of us…' She pauses significantly. 'Tonight, let's have no talk of any unpleasantness.'

Lucy nods along with the others.

Mae's smile is a blessing. 'Wonderful.' She raises her voice a little. 'Dinner is served.'

A girl in a neat black skirt and black-and-white shirt enters with the first course. It's something green served in small shot glasses.

'Oh, this looks wonderful,' Rachael exclaims.

'It's a cucumber gazpacho soup, and it's actually sourced from one of our own vegetable—' Mae frowns and stops mid-sentence. 'Excuse me, I think that was the door.'

Lucy didn't hear anything but strains to listen as Mae clicks along the hallway.

There's the sound of the large front door opening and then Mae speaks. 'Jake? What are you doing here?'

'Sorry I'm a few minutes late,' he replies easily. 'I'm sure not letting me know the time was a simple oversight.'

A quick recount of the chairs and putting it with Mae's response, Lucy feels he's not late so much as here uninvited.

A few loaded moments pass and then Mae says, 'Glad you could make it.'

Lucy is certain there's something going on between them.

It could be the bond of two people who stayed around when everyone else left Queen's Point. Or maybe it's the fact that he's a police officer and there's an open investigation into her mother's death. Or just because, as he trails her in, Lucy can see he's smiling. The man is rather convincing in his own way. And he's dressed to impress, wearing a crisp white shirt, sleeves rolled up to the elbows, and perfectly fitted navy trousers.

At a quiet word from Mae, the table is reset in the time it takes Jake to greet everyone. He's seated right next to Lucy, but ignores her raised eyebrows, settling instead for the same relaxed hello as he's given everyone else.

The cold soup is light and bright and the perfect starter. Lucy can't help but wonder if there was panic in the kitchen at the need for an extra serving, but if there was, it doesn't show. Nor in the salad. Fresh greens topped with two delicate mushroom-stuffed salmon balls.

'That tasted delightful,' says Lucy.

Mae inclines her head to accept the compliment. 'Jules Salisbury-Morony flew in this morning to oversee the menu and prep but unfortunately he was required back in Sydney tonight.' She names one of the country's hottest young chefs as though he was the local takeaway owner.

There's a lull before the main, and Lucy finishes her second glass of wine. It melts across her tongue, dry with a little bite. Recognising it as expensive only means she's more aware of how lavishly it's poured.

'No thanks,' Jake murmurs when a young serving girl moves to fill his glass.

She asks again if he'd like a refill a few minutes later, and Mae intercedes with a reprimanding look. 'The girl's new,' she explains apologetically. 'And we're rather proud of that drop. It's from one of our smaller vineyards but it's won a few awards.'

'Of course,' says Jake without sarcasm. 'I understand.'

Lucy's reminded again of the gulf between herself and these people. Her grandmother once worked here, although the reprimands were probably not so pleasant when Brooke Whitlam was in charge.

When Jake catches Lucy's eye, he winks and murmurs, 'It's so hard to find good help these days.'

Having just sipped more wine, it's only through supreme will that she manages not to spray the expensive drink out of her nose.

Jake chuckles too.

It's not until the staff return with the main course, a rack of baby lamb with an herb-Dijon hazelnut crust, that Lucy's able to speak again. In between mouthfuls of the perfectly cooked lamb, with the wine relaxing any shyness, she contributes her thoughts on a bestselling book turned TV series that is coming out soon. Apparently, the historical author is one of Mr Whitlam's favourites. 'I'm looking forward to it,' Lucy agrees. 'But I hope they stay true to the original.'

'It might be better,' Dante argues. 'Change can be good, shake things up.'

Lucy tries to read his expression. Is he talking about more than entertainment?

'I bet it's no *Great British Bake Off*,' Jake whispers, nudging Lucy's shoulder.

And again, she has to struggle to keep her laughter in check.

It's then that she realises Harry is watching her. His grey eyes are stormy and he's so intent on Jake and Lucy that Rachael next to him says something twice before he hears her.

'Sorry,' he says, his tone as dark as his expression. 'I have a lot on my mind.'

It's the closest anyone has come to mentioning the death of the family matriarch since Mae's instruction around unpleasantness. Close enough that a short, shocked pause follows his pronouncement. The whole table seemingly holds their breath until he adds, 'I simply cannot decide whether to hold the upcoming launch of my new pieces in Tokyo or Milan.'

Lucy allows herself to loosen what had become a painful grip on the stem of her wine glass as the others offer their opinions on the merits of each city.

It gives her the chance to look around the room some more. There are subtle changes here at the Whitlam house she didn't notice at drinks the other night. Hints of an awareness of privilege that weren't present in the Whitlam youth. Talk with the mayor of volunteer programmes. Offers of assistance in using one of the greenhouses to propagate local flora. And on the mantel, a small thank-you card from a Cambodian orphanage.

Mae conducts most of the dinner conversation like a symphony. There's no fear of veering towards the banned unpleasantness with her in charge, and Lucy starts another glass of wine. She lets the modulated voices, clink of fine tableware, the delicious food and the intoxicating effects of expensive alcohol lull her.

This is where she's always wanted to be.

'Is your work managing without you?' Rachael's question is like a glass cracking.

Lucy straightens. 'I'm simply a cog in the wheel.' It comes out with the right amount of modesty and just the slightest of slurs.

'You're more than that, surely,' Mae says. 'Success simply radiates from you.'

'No one wants to talk about work on a weekend,' Lucy says lightly. She doesn't want to think about it at all.

Mae's gaze is fixed on her. 'But I'm interested in how little Lucy Antonello grew into such a worldly businesswoman.'

Lucy blinks, trying to pick her words, the alcohol not helping. 'The usual. I went to uni, got a degree and then I worked my way up.'

Not usual for any of them, she realises as soon as she says it. And the inequality of it stabs her between her ribs. None of them had to wait tables and work two jobs to attend university while helping to pay their mother's medical bills. Not for a Whitlam to need the favour of their boss when they make a mistake. Not for them to get so close to senior partner and be forced on leave with an assessment coming on her return.

'We might need more detail,' says Anabelle with a laugh.

Every Whitlam gaze is on Lucy. It could be casual conversation, but she knows enough of the game to be aware that their interest has cause. But what? The typical reaction of societal sharks smelling blood in the water, or something more?

Heat climbs in her throat. 'Enough about me,' Lucy blurts. 'Being here with you all has me thinking of the past, and of course those not here.'

She imagines Jake shaking his head in warning – *don't go there* – even as Mae's eyes narrow and Anabelle's lips compress.

'I don't think we really—' begins Mr Whitlam warningly.

Lucy lifts her glass, ignoring him. Too far gone on her rush to stop now, the peril of this better than the alternative. 'To the dearly departed.'

There's a moment of icy silence.

'To Judy,' Jake says loudly.

Lucy's grandmother's name echoes around the table as some of the lines smooth from Mae's face. 'She was a special woman,' Mae says.

Then Manan begins a tale of his childhood housekeeper who was similarly adored as family, like Lucy's grandmother was, and the danger – real or only in Lucy's head – is past. But her heart is still racing like Jake just pulled her out of the way of an oncoming train.

And she isn't sure whether or not she's glad.

18

PRESENT DAY

'Digestifs in the living room by the fire?' Mae suggests when the last dessert bowl is scraped clean of the decadent espresso martini brownies.

'That means after dinner drinks,' Jake mutters in Lucy's ear, his breath tickling her neck.

'I knew that.'

Although there are only a small number of guests, there's a bit of a logjam when Mr Whitlam drops his reading glasses in the doorway and one of the lenses comes out.

'Wait,' Harry mouths, catching Lucy's gaze.

She pretends not to see, glad that annoyance flares on his usually controlled features.

But he's not one to be deterred and although she means to stay near Jake, he's pulled into a conversation with Mayor Rachael upon entering the larger room and Lucy finds herself alone by the fire. Harry joins her and they're momentarily isolated. When he touches her arm she wants to press closer, but she pulls away.

'It isn't how it looks,' he murmurs, the words almost lost in the crackling blaze.

That velvet tone does such annoying things to Lucy's insides. 'What isn't?'

'Rach.'

'Don't mistake me for someone who cares.' At least she sounds more dismissive than she feels. This thing, whatever it is, with her and Harry has gone on too long and she's tired of it. Sick of the games. The good feeling with Harry always ends up something else afterwards. Always.

Besides, the room has become just a little fuzzy since her last drink.

'Please, Lucy,' Harry says. 'It's hard to explain.' His hand lifts, and for a second, she thinks he'll reach for her and damn the audience. But it drops just as fast. 'You need to trust me. Trust in us.'

She laughs then and Harry blinks like he realises that for once he's pushed the charm too far. 'There's never really been an "us". Never.'

He reels back. 'You know I care about you.'

Her heart leaps. How she wants to believe this, but she's not a kid any more and she needs more than a few pretty phrases. 'Then why haven't you come to me to explain? Why wait for this chance meeting?'

He doesn't have an answer and as the silence settles between them Lucy smiles, shaking her head at Jake, who's crossed to join them.

'Share the joke,' he says.

She raises her eyebrows at Harry. 'Go on then.'

His lips thin. 'Forget it.'

He moves to Rachael's side and, as he does, Lucy feels like a few people in the room relax.

There are so many undercurrents at play here, Lucy would be safer in the rip on the far side of the point where surfers have been known to drown. She lifts her glass to her lips and drains it.

Jake stays nearby after that, the safety of his company compared to Harry nearly as soothing as the wine. For a country cop, who Lucy remembers being a painfully awkward teenager, he's surprisingly adept at small talk, something Lucy seems to have lost her knack for. It's being in this house that's doing it. And of course, her hosts. For all their apparent warmth, the Whitlams have a way of othering those not in the family.

'Excuse me,' Lucy says, suddenly needing a breather.

Ever aware, Mae smiles as she moves towards the door. 'You remember your way to the guest bathroom?'

'I can find it.'

But Lucy discovers the one she escaped to at the cocktail party is in use. It must be one of the waiting staff; hopefully Mae doesn't catch them.

She should wait, but she can't resist the excuse to have a look around. Quietly, she climbs the main stairs to the second floor. The place is huge and Anabelle's children are in a different part of the house but she doesn't want to disturb them. She passes what appears to be an intimate home cinema and then a games room, both in darkness.

A soft light spills from a partly open door a little way along and Lucy moves towards it. Her mouth opens in a silent gasp. She blinks to make sure it's not the wine playing tricks. There's a large bed and next to it an empty wheelchair. Is this the reason for the addition of the elevator? She stares and the piles of pillows and bedding resolve to include a man.

He's asleep.

There's a whir. The source of the sound is a small oxygen tank that's assisting him to breathe. It's the man from the police station, she thinks, but the figure is almost lost in the huge bed. His skin is grey, and he wheezes for air and eyelids flutter as he dreams.

'Marcelo.' Recognition snatches his name from Lucy in a gulp of sound. Her head is spinning as she's trying to understand what she's seeing. It's the old gardener, the one whose name she was trying to recall when talking to Jake.

Footsteps approach up the stairs.

Sprung.

There's no time to escape – even a sprint won't get her out of sight, and she's not familiar enough with the secret passages not to lose her way. Desperately, she eases the door closed a moment before the figure appears.

It's not Mae who's found her, rather it's Mr Whitlam.

His face is unreadable. This man was barely a peripheral figure when Lucy spent time in this house and knew his children, and so many years have passed since then.

'You found our guest,' he says.

He must have known the door was open. 'I didn't mean to pry.'

'I hope you didn't wake him. Marcelo has been my dear friend for a very long time and he is not at all well.'

There's something in the way he says *friend*, in the shape of the other man's name on his lips. Lucy rethinks everything she knew of the relationships in this house nineteen years ago. Vanessa *was* simply a student, Dante is not some sordid love child of theirs. Mr Whitlam's eye might have strayed, but it was not to her.

'What were you looking for up here?' he asks.

She means to say 'bathroom', but his steady gaze and cultured tones won't allow the lie. 'I don't know,' she admits.

He glances towards Marcelo's door. 'Then maybe you shouldn't be looking. Because you might not like what you find, and we value our privacy.'

He's broader of shoulder than she realised, and in good shape for his age.

It's always the husband.

Her banter with Jake the other day repeats in her head. She forces herself to relax. His whole family are downstairs, not to mention a police officer and the mayor. But there are no cameras up here, in stark contrast to the floor below.

'Is that some kind of threat?' she asks.

He chuckles. 'Of course not, Lucy. You're practically part of the family.'

She's already gone too far tonight, but she can't stop herself. 'That didn't help your wife.'

Surprise widens his eyes.

Part of her is glad to show a bit of something unexpected, but sweat dampens her palms. 'You should be organising a memorial, not having fancy dinner parties.'

'Don't make the mistake of thinking you have any idea what is happening here.' His tone is such that they could be discussing the weather.

'I don't.'

He closes the distance between them and she thinks for a moment about running. But she's a guest here. No one is going to hurt anyone.

His arm slips over her shoulder. 'No one is going to hurt you.'

It's like he's heard her thoughts, but his arm is heavy and his fingers grip her upper arm.

'Of course,' she manages. There's a moment where all the self-defence she's done swirls through her brain. She has the element of surprise. For now. But he knows this house and she's got lost in here before.

'And you've had a rather emotional few days,' he continues, the force of his grip turning Lucy and leading her back towards the stairs.

'I have,' she agrees. 'I'm sorry. No one knows what to do in a situation like this. The waiting must be unbearable.' She hears the conciliation in her voice and flashes back to being sixteen and saying and doing whatever she needed to so these people would like her.

'Your understanding means so much.' There's approval in his tone now. 'To all of us.' He doesn't let her go until they reach the others. There, Lucy is quickly caught up in an animated debate about Japanese versus Scottish whiskies. When she admits she wouldn't know the difference, one of the staff is sent to the climate-controlled cellar to retrieve what Mae describes as 'a decent example of each'.

A little while later, the waitress who was told off earlier appears at the door. Her expression is a question that Mae answers with the smallest of head shakes. There won't be the offer of more food or drinks.

Dante stands. 'I think I'll head out to bed. Thank you for a wonderful me—'

The sound of the doorbell and the loud rap of a fist on the front door cuts off his sentence.

Lucy's heart jumps. She straightens, instinct wanting to see who it is demanding attention so late at night. But this isn't her house and not her place to answer. Nor is it Mr Whitlam's; he hasn't lived here for years.

All eyes go to Mae.

Her smile is apologetic. 'Excuse me a moment.'

Someone must have turned off the music ready for the general farewells. In the silence left behind, it's impossible to miss Mae opening the door.

'I heard it's supposed to rain again tomorrow.' Anabelle's attempt to cover the event at the front door falls flat and no one answers. Her face is pale, and her knuckles show white where they grip the whisky glass.

No one meets anyone's gaze.

But they all listen.

'Apologies for the late hour, Ms Whitlam,' a man says.

Lucy recognises that voice, the slow deliberate tone she last heard in the police station. Detective Antonio Georgiades.

There's a collective intake of breath.

She's not the only one who knows who it is. They're all wondering what's brought the police to this house so late at night on a Sunday, what it is that can't wait until morning.

Only Jake appears completely relaxed, but he gives nothing away.

By the front door, Mae says something polite but too low to be properly heard, perhaps aware of her audience by the flickering fire.

There's a sudden draught of cold air and Lucy imagines the door opening wider.

The detective speaks again. 'Is your brother here?'

Harry doesn't even flinch. He doesn't run for freedom. Rather, he takes his time to finish the amber liquid in his glass, seeming to savour each drop, as Mae answers in the affirmative and footsteps approach along the hallway.

Rachael's hand curls around his bicep protectively, but he seems oblivious to her touch. He stares down at the flames until the police enter.

Thanks to the crime dramas Lucy's so fond of, she's prepared for a dramatic announcement, but it's all rather orderly. Mae and the police reach the doorway and Harry stands. He crosses to them, the slightest drag in his step the only hint of anything amiss. There's a female officer with Detective Georgiades but no backup needed.

Lucy's itching to ask Jake if he knew that this was happening tonight, but she doesn't dare break the silence. If she'd had less wine, maybe she would feel like this wasn't happening on the other side of the glass. Maybe she'd muster a protest in Harry's defence. But she says nothing. Simply remains in position – tableau of guests after a dinner party – and watches the show along with the others.

The detective speaks to Harry in low tones, then he is placed in handcuffs. It's that quiet click that makes this real.

Harry Whitlam is being arrested for his mother's murder.

A soft moan escapes Lucy, but the sound is drowned out by Anabelle's cry. 'Mae, you can't let them do this!'

Mae's face is tight. 'These people must be allowed to do their job. It won't be long, and he'll be back home.' She turns to Harry. 'You are innocent. You'll be released before you know it.'

He nods, but when he lifts his head, his eyes are blank.

She speaks quietly to the detective, and then they're gone.

Mae sweeps those who aren't family out of the house. Before Lucy knows it, she's out on the porch. Jake's vehicle is already gone, and with it any opportunity to interrogate him. Lucy refuses Mae's offer of Dante to walk her back to the cottage, instead managing a weak, 'If there's anything I can do, please call.'

Again, Mae is disturbingly polite. 'Thank you for coming. I really must get back inside.'

'Of course.'

And then the door is closed, leaving only the family and Mayor Rachael in the house, and Lucy's picking her way down the drive towards the cottage, still trying to understand what happened there tonight.

Hours later, as moonlight seeps into the tiny bedroom at the cottage and Hades snores softly on the floor nearby, Lucy still can't sleep. There's something nagging about the evening, something beyond the dramatic end. Yes, images of Harry, the police, and the click of the handcuffs replay like some bad movie in her head, but there's something else.

The evening was exactly how she imagined an intimate dinner at the Whitlam house would be. More precisely, it was the way sixteen-year-old Lucy would have imagined it.

Before the police arrived, it was all so… fancy. Fancy food, fancy setting, fancy people. It is almost as though the whole event was orchestrated. And Lucy's left wondering, who for?

JANUARY 2000
TEN DAYS BEFORE THE PARTY

Lucy

Lucy heard the trill of the phone as she was leaving. Heard Nan lumbering to answer. Lucy knew, given the time, who it would be, but still sighed when Nan called, 'It's for you.'

The bi-weekly calls from Mum that had at first seemed too few now felt intrusively frequent as Lucy dragged herself back inside. What could she say that Mum could possibly understand?

Mum, with her bone-aching shift work and grind from day to day, couldn't imagine the life Lucy was seeing up close. She didn't want to try to explain the wonder of long summer days up at the Whitlam house.

'Hi,' she mumbled.

'Is something wrong?' Mum asked.

Only that I'm wasting my time. 'No, I'm fine. Did you want something?'

'Just to say hello.'

'Hello.'

There was a long silence. 'I'm good,' Mum said. 'Thanks for asking. Work's a killer though. Only a little over a week until I come and pick you up. I can't wait to see you.'

'Yeah,' Lucy mumbled. But her mind was elsewhere. How was it so soon? At least she'd be around for the big party up at the Whitlam house. She finished the call on autopilot and then headed for the beach. She had the strangest sensation that time was running out.

Despite her mum's call making her a few minutes late, Lucy arrived where she'd planned to meet Anabelle to no sign of the other girl. Some kids from town had set up towels and a volleyball game near the water, but Lucy didn't want to join them. Meeting Anabelle apart from the others made her special.

Besides, even from this distance she could tell that Harry wasn't with them.

A burst of laughter drew her attention. One of the boys had flipped over on to his hands and managed several 'steps' before collapsing into the sand in an embarrassing heap. He surfaced to applause from the others.

Jake Parker. Ever the comedian, she should have guessed it would be him. Part of her wanted to tell the short, acne-riddled boy that the others were laughing at him, not with him. But then she'd have to actually talk to him.

Like she'd called his name instead of thought it, he turned to look at her. He grinned and she looked away before he could do anything else, like call out or, worse, come over to ask what she was doing loitering by the fence.

With a last glance up the steep path – there was definitely no sign of Anabelle – she strode towards the point like she had somewhere important to be. She headed for the old white-and-blue-painted boathouse perched just around the tip of the point. There, a small jetty often moored one of the Whitlams' boats. Today, the silver dinghy rocked gently against its ropes, rather than one of the bigger craft.

Lucy shook her head. Imagine having so much money, it wasn't whether you took a boat out, but which one.

The door stood ajar. Lucy ducked inside into the cool, damp, dark space. She'd have a breather and then hopefully Anabelle would arrive. She hitched her bag higher on her shoulder and considered the shadowy outline of what she guessed was a yacht.

She sniffed.

There was something out of place in the air. Something faint among the heavy, musty scents of sea and wood and wet sand. She breathed in deep. *Smoke.* She was sure of it.

Her stomach tightened.

What to do? If there was a fire extinguisher in here somewhere, she could try to put it out. Although she'd only ever seen one in use when some idiot kid had sprayed the boys' toilets with one at school. Maybe she'd be better going to get help.

Imagine if she were the one to stop a fire destroying the Whitlams' boats. 'I knew there was something special about Lucy Antonello,' they'd chorus as they invited her to stay with them for the rest of the summer.

The scrape of shoe on concrete came from her left.

She spun, blinked and her eyes adjusted to see a small orange glow flare for a moment, before a voice spoke. 'What's a pretty girl like you doing in a place like this?'

That voice. Smooth, like the very best chocolate. Her heart raced. 'Harry?'

He stepped forward into the light, close enough to touch. Wearing swim shorts and a tight white T-shirt, with his hair all mussed from an earlier swim, Harry actually took her breath away. Or maybe it was the smoke.

She coughed and he moved to put out the cigarette, tossing the dead butt into a small jar.

'It's a disgusting habit,' he said as he stood and brushed the sand from his hands. 'I should quit.' His mouth curved in a way that made her feel like he was sharing a secret. 'I'd hate to make you want to keep your distance from me.'

'I don't.' The admission was immediate.

A couple of years ago, Lucy's mum had lost one of her best friends to lung cancer. A quick and vicious illness that left the friend bedridden and pain-filled. Witnessing its effects on a once strong and vibrant woman had made it easy for Lucy to find it repulsive. But Harry was different.

He stepped closer and took her hands as he looked into her eyes.

Part of her recoiled at the hint of smoke on his breath, but she didn't move away.

'That's good,' he murmured. 'Because then I couldn't do this.' He brushed a strand of hair off her face, the touch of his fingers on her cheek sending hot sparks through her body.

He was going to kiss her.

He had to.

And she wouldn't care that he tasted like smoke because he'd taste like Harry.

His hands moved, sliding to her wrists and tugging her closer, even as he edged her back so she felt the hard side of the boat against her shoulders. He lowered his head as she swayed towards him.

'You are captivating,' he whispered.

Then his mouth claimed hers. Gently at first, and then his tongue teased her lips apart and slipped inside. He was like a match and his touch lit her whole body. Everything in her was focused on him and the feel of his mouth.

Far too quickly, he eased away. 'I should let you go.'

She nodded and at a slight nudge from him, she made it back outside. Anabelle arrived as she reached the fence, but her mind was still back in the shed with Harry.

He'd really kissed her.

Distracted, she settled next to Anabelle on the sand.

A little while later, seeing Anabelle looking away from the others towards the point and hearing her sigh, 'I can't stand volleyball, why are we even doing this?', Lucy grabbed her chance.

'I know, talk about juvenile. There must be something better we can do. Didn't you say we should go out on the water sometime?' Lucy couldn't help mentioning boats. She couldn't stop thinking about what had happened with Harry.

'Yes.' Anabelle clapped her hands together. 'I'll see when Dad can drag himself away from his stupid books.' Her nose scrunched. 'Ugh, Vanessa will probably want to come. But it should be fun.'

'And Harry?' Lucy asked before she could stop herself. Quickly adding, 'And, like, Mae and everyone?' She waved at the volleyball game that he'd joined, pretending she'd never meant to single Harry out.

'Not Harry, he hates being out on the water. Turns positively green.'

She should have known that about him, but when they were alone all her thoughts and the questions she meant to ask seemed to vanish. 'So, he doesn't use the boats at all?'

Anabelle laughed. 'I wouldn't say that. Harry likes to give girls private tours of the old boathouse. If you know what I mean.'

Lucy did. All too well. She could still feel his hands on her wrists, even glanced down to check there was no mark from the burn of his touch where he'd gripped them. His eyes had been filled with such intensity when he stared down at her in that intimate, shadowy darkness that it hurt to think of it. An ache that could only be helped by being alone with him again.

But as Anabelle's words sunk in, Lucy's blood chilled. Had she surprised him waiting to meet another girl?

She dismissed the fear as soon as she thought it. He'd been alone, and she knew Harry better than anyone.

19

PRESENT DAY

Lucy lies awake half the night after the dinner party, scrolling online for details about Harry's arrest. The Whitlam family's money and power aren't enough to keep something like this quiet. There are too many journalists in town and too much interest in the case. It's made headlines right across Australia and internationally.

According to the internet, Brooke Whitlam most likely died from a blow to the head, around the end of January 2000. The summer party is mentioned as the last place she was seen.

After her shower, Lucy catches the wavery reflection of herself in the mirror. Could the man who's kissed every inch of that skin have killed? Despite the headlines, Lucy's gut insists *not Harry*.

Not the man who's smiled at her sleepily after a night in bed. Not the man who once couriered her macarons from a café in Melbourne because they'd talked about liking them while catching their breath after sex.

Such a man couldn't bludgeon his mother to death and bury her without a qualm.

The police must have evidence. She remembers the way his mother spoke to him about his art, the rage in his eyes when he talked about her wanting to destroy his dreams. Enough to drive him to kill? Could it have been an accident?

Lucy's seen enough news reports to know that people have died for less, but wondering whether one of the Whitlams was the culprit is quite a different thing to it being so. It's hard to even think of Harry locked up at the station.

Before she can stop herself, she fires off messages to Mae and Anabelle, hoping they're okay, and offering her neighbourly assistance.

She tries not to think of the ring hidden away and what it might mean for all of this. She stares at her phone screen where it lies next to the bathroom sink and tries not to think about what kind of person is so desperate she's bothering the family of someone arrested overnight.

There's no reply.

Lucy is queueing for coffee a couple of hours later at Jan's, having walked into town with Hades. On her way in she would have sworn she heard the rattle of one of the Whitlam utes approaching behind her, but the vehicle never appeared.

Two middle-aged women in front of her are talking about the case.

'It's terrible for that poor boy,' says one.

'They must be devastated,' the other agrees. 'I thought they were the perfect family.'

Again with the perfect family. It seems someone has worked very hard to rewrite history, because surely no one who knew them back then could think such a thing. Could Lucy have been the only one who saw what they were like together behind closed doors?

There's a ding on Jan's phone. She reads a message and then switches on the small TV behind her.

'That's our police station,' someone says behind Lucy, pointing at the screen.

'Turn it up,' adds someone else.

There's a crush of people moving closer to see the screen behind the counter and Lucy ends up in prime position as the reporter from the other night speaks directly into the camera.

'We're live here in Queen's Point outside the station, where we understand international artist and playboy Harry Whitlam is about to be released after being detained overnight in relation to the death of his mother some nineteen years ago.'

The camera pans out to show the doors and Lucy can feel the tension of the people around her as they wait. She glances over her shoulder as someone's elbow connects with her ribs. The old lady responsible doesn't seem to have noticed inflicting the blow.

Behind the woman, in a booth in the far corner of the café, is Jake.

How long has he been there? Lucy meets his gaze questioningly.

He shrugs.

The reporter is talking again. 'We understand there is some forensic evidence linking Harry to the body. However, a solid alibi has come forward. It's unclear whether this release is bail or the police dropping charges. We can't be sure that formal charges were even laid.'

The camera zooms out fast and uneven, making Lucy's stomach revolt. But there's no movement at the station doors.

She edges out from the crowd by the counter, turning over this new information. Someone was with Harry? All night?

There's a prickle of resentment as Lucy realises that if he'd come to meet her like he promised, he would have been with her.

The small crowd quickly swallows where Lucy was standing. After checking on Hades through the window, she sits opposite Jake, able to see just a sliver of the screen from there.

'Did you know he'd be arrested?' she asks. 'Last night, when you invited yourself for dinner?'

'Nice to bump into you, too. And not officially.'

Interesting that he doesn't deny that Mae didn't ask him to be there, nor does he reveal what he might have known unofficially.

It makes her wonder if he knows about Marcelo being in the house and his closeness with Mr Whitlam. Marcelo has already been interviewed by the police, so maybe their relationship is public knowledge. An affair would be motive, even though it's hard to imagine Marcelo having the strength to hurt anyone seeing him now. Back then he was lean and fit, and he did have that argument with Brooke Whitlam.

Lucy's about to press Jake further when there's a cry from those watching the TV.

'There he is.'

She turns back to see a glimpse of Harry, still in the same clothes as last night, being hurried away. The media swarm around him like flies to a carcass, held off by what must be his legal team.

Jake snorts. 'Wonder they could get a word out of him. The guy is completely fucked.'

'He's what?' Lucy frowns. This is a guy Jake used to follow around, but now there's only derision.

'He's wasted. In withdrawal. Somewhere between very high and whatever you are when you're in desperate need of your next hit.'

'Harry?'

'Harry,' he echoes. 'Who bloody else?'

'He likes a drink, sure, but that's not what you're talking about, is it?'

When Jake looks at Lucy, there is something like pity in his eyes. 'That's not what I'm talking about.'

She slumps back in the seat. She's an utter fool. So many of her experiences with Harry click into place. Of course. Harry is on drugs. The most expensive kind, she's guessing. She's seen eyes like his across the boardroom table at work. The colleagues who rise too fast for their own good. It's the money and the pressure, and the desperate need for escape, and that would pretty much describe Harry's life.

'I don't get it,' Jake says, still watching the screen.

'What?'

'The appeal of a pretty boy who shows no sign of growing up.'

Did he really want to do this? She sneaks a glance, takes in the set of his jaw. No, he doesn't want to hear about the allure of the artist inseparable from the man, the desire to be a muse, the way he makes a woman feel inspiring and how bloody hot that is.

When she looks over again, the news has shifted to something else and then Jake's standing to leave.

She touches his hand. 'Do you know who it is?'

Even if he does know who the alibi is, he's not going to tell her and the fact that she's asking makes her pathetic, but she can't help herself. There were so many girls, women too, around that summer. Who has come forward and why are they such a good alibi that he's already been released?

'You're so goddam sure he's innocent, aren't you? Why?' he asks, lip curling. 'Because he's good in bed?'

'Don't be crass.'

He leans close and lowers his voice. 'What event do you think inspired his early collection?'

'What do you mean? What collection?'

He stares at her long and hard. Then he's shaking his head and leaving. Although she's obviously pissed him off, the annoyance doesn't extend to Hades, who he stops to pat on the way past. Lucy's tempted to follow him out there but what the hell would she say?

By the time Lucy gets to order, she's the only one in the small café.

'I never thought it was Harry,' Jan says as she makes the coffee. As if he's been locked up for months, not spent a single night in custody.

'Why?'

She smiles fondly. 'He's a good boy, always has been. Respectful and charming, especially around his mother. I hope the police widen their search, beyond the town. Brooke Whitlam was revered around these parts.'

Lucy doesn't argue but it's not at all how she remembers things. Nan wasn't alone complaining about Brooke Whitlam.

Jan hands over the drink.

'Thanks,' Lucy says.

She heads back out into the cold and unties Hades from where he patiently waited, before beginning the long walk back towards the cottage.

The whole time her mind is swinging between two questions.

Why does no one seem to remember Brooke Whitlam's real character?

What collection was Jake talking about?

Lucy

'What's all this?' Lucy asked. They were in the turret room, escaping the afternoon heat.

Anabelle snatched the large box from Lucy's grip. 'Nothing.'

Lucy cradled her hand against her body. A red mark showed on the webbing between thumb and forefinger. Should she apologise?

Before she could decide, Anabelle sighed. 'Look, sorry about your hand, but you need to remember this is my room. There's private stuff in here.'

'Sorry,' Lucy said in a small voice.

Anabelle lifted the lid of the box and pulled out some high heels and a couple of wigs. 'It's mostly mementos from the stage shows I've done at school.'

She could tell from Anabelle's tone that this was safer territory. 'I didn't know you were into theatre,' Lucy said. 'I helped with lighting for ours last year.' She eyed the wig quality. As inexperienced as she was, she could tell these were expensive. 'What have you performed in?'

'So many,' Anabelle said, warming even more. 'I've been Matilda, Liesl and this one was from playing Cosette in *Les Mis*.' She held up the blonde wig. 'We decided this would work better than trying to straighten my curls.'

At Anabelle's nod, Lucy reached out and felt the soft strands of fake hair. 'It's so pretty.'

'You try it.'

'Really?' Lucy asked. 'I'd hate to wreck it.'

'You won't because I'll help.' Enthusiasm hummed in Anabelle's voice. 'Come on, I bet you'll look like some kind of princess.'

Not wanting to piss her friend off again, Lucy twisted her hair into a rough bun and pinned it in place.

Then Anabelle eased on the wig. She studied the result, a frown on her face. When Lucy turned to see her reflection, Anabelle held her chin in place, tugging at a few mousy strands of Lucy's hair that had escaped. 'Mae will have pins,' she said. 'Wait here.'

Lucy should have stayed where ordered. Or at worst, strolled over to the window to admire the view of the town. But the box was right there. And what could be in it that had Anabelle so mad?

Listening for Anabelle's return, she flipped open the lid. Inside, sequinned dresses caught the light and a short black wig had become tangled in some beaded costume jewellery. Why the fuss? But something crackled as she moved a gold tiara. She glanced towards the door then lifted the accessory, ready to drop it at the slightest hint of her friend returning. Beneath the tiara lay... rubbish. Chocolate biscuit packets, crisps packets, sweet wrappers. They filled more than half the box.

What on earth?

'Thanks.' Anabelle's call of gratitude carried from the depths of the house to where Lucy sat, stunned and confused.

She moved quickly, returning the box and herself to how it

had been when Anabelle left the room. Just in time, because the door flew open and Anabelle came in. 'Victory,' she said, waving the pins.

Lucy sat as instructed while Anabelle fixed her hair into place and put the wig on. She managed to ooh and ah at her reflection, not disagreeing when Anabelle said, 'We could be sisters, now you've got Mother's hair.'

But the whole time she was trying to make sense of why Anabelle would be hiding rubbish in her room.

Later, she was still thinking about the puzzle when her friend waved her off at the door. She was supposed to go straight home, but found herself giving in to temptation and detouring towards the art studio. Even as she slowed her steps to prolong the opportunity to bump into Harry, her heart raced with nerves.

'Hey,' she practised under her breath. It wasn't much as sparkling conversation went, but it was a start.

The trees cast long shadows across the gardens, and she kept her path in their shelter. There were risks to surprising Harry. Like him being caught up in his art and not noticing she existed, or, much worse, caught up in someone else.

A warm, sea-soaked breeze stirred the branches overhead. She glanced back up at the house but there were no signs of life. Ahead, the studio's windows showed it to be deserted. She could have been all alone on the property. Could pretend it was her house.

'Not good enough.'

The assessment could have come from Lucy's brain, but instead it was Mrs Whitlam's voice that split through the summer air. 'How can I be expected to entertain when my garden, my showpiece, that you are paid to maintain, is riddled with weeds?'

'The space will be prepared for the party, Mrs Whitlam. Have no fear,' said the gardener, Marcelo, in his relaxed, accented tones.

'It is you who should be afraid. Of unemployment.'

Lucy ducked further beneath the overhanging branches. She tried to pick where the voices were coming from, but the swirling breeze made it impossible.

There was a moment of quiet but then Marcelo spoke. 'It is a large property and much maintenance is required. There are only so many hours in the day.'

'Work harder then,' snapped Mrs Whitlam.

Lucy winced. She'd seen Marcelo working long hours in the blazing sun, his shirt soaked with sweat. The woman was speaking to him like he spent his days slacking off.

But Marcelo stayed calm. 'You won't find a better worker than me.'

In trying to edge away, Lucy nearly stumbled into them. She froze, unable to miss the proud tension in Marcelo's stance or the anger in Mrs Whitlam's cool features.

'Maybe that's a risk I'm willing to take,' sneered Mrs Whitlam. 'What about you? How much do you need this job? How much do you want this job?'

They stared at each other for a long moment during which Lucy didn't dare breathe.

Then Marcelo exhaled hard, nodded, and allowed his shoulders to soften. 'My apologies, Mrs Whitlam. I'll pay more attention to the weeds.'

'Thank you, Marcelo,' she said, before turning on her heel and striding away.

Lucy watched her go and then waited for Marcelo to pack up the rest of his tools. He didn't once look after his employer.

Relieved that she hadn't been discovered, Lucy ran to the gates and down the hill.

20

PRESENT DAY

As Lucy makes her way along the beach, Hades looks at her reproachfully every few steps – like he's asking why she keeps getting rid of all the decent men around. She makes it to the cottage's front porch as the heavens open.

The rain lashes the steps as she fumbles to unlock the door. Hades bursts inside the second it opens and collapses on the rug in front of the fireplace with what sounds suspiciously like a grumpy sigh.

'It's not like Jake and I are close,' she tells Hades as she gets a fire going. He doesn't lift his head.

'And I think he's innocent as much as I do Harry,' she adds as the flames catch on the kindling and she tries to defrost her numb fingers. 'Anyway, I'm sure he's not telling me everything.'

But someone did kill Brooke Whitlam and Jake did not seem at all convinced by Harry's alibi. Instinct, or he knows something?

Hades' eyes are closed now and he's not paying any attention to Lucy's attempts to explain herself. The whole cottage smells like damp dog. She hopes the smoky aromas from the fire will soon cancel it out. There are still days' worth of sorting to do. She didn't think it would take so much work, although this cottage is the accumulation of Nan's life. Maybe she should be sad that it's not more.

Instead of tackling any of the tasks she's listed above where she's stuck the invite for the art show, an event that will probably be cancelled now, she switches on her laptop. Jake's pointed reference to Harry's first art collection is impossible not to follow up. Despite her interest in Harry over the years, that early period of his success was during her degree, when studying and topping every subject filled her life, the drive for success all-consuming.

She'd been so certain having the success and wealth of Brooke Whitlam would give her the life she wanted.

She starts with Harry's website. As she waits for the page to load, she sips the dregs of her lukewarm coffee and thinks again of Jake's question about why Harry is so damn attractive. He's gorgeous, of course, but it's the fascination. When Harry looks at Lucy, he is so obviously, so genuinely intrigued. He wants to know her deeply, more than that, he *needs* to.

It will be the same for the next woman. But there's something about that attention that's more powerful than the looks, the art, or the money.

The home page of his site has his latest piece, and Lucy's body recoils a little as she takes it in. His work is in no way easy to look at, critics having described it as a blow to the senses. In blues and browns, there's something about the tones of this one that remind Lucy of the rock pools on the far side of the point, although it's not exactly photographic. Unlike some of his works, this piece has none of the faces or human shapes that haunt his last collection.

The spiel beneath the image describes Harry as taking

inspiration from the Australian landscape and contrasting it with the shapes and lines of squalid consumerism and modern disposable culture. All Lucy knows is that he can make people feel with a brush and a canvas.

She goes back through his catalogued works, looking for his earliest paintings, looking for what Jake wanted her to see. The designer of the site has included awards Harry's won and records he's set at auction and, oddly, quotes from some of his more vehement critics. Maybe art only fails when there is no reaction invoked.

She's seen most of these before and she scrolls quickly through each period but, strangely, there's nothing listed before 2005.

A dig around the site tells her that it's been updated in the last few days. Presumably there's something that Harry or his management doesn't want the world to see. It won't keep whatever it is from the police, but perception matters to the Whitlams.

Their move doesn't allow for the fans who have visited this page across several devices. It only takes a minute for Lucy to make sure her phone is offline so it doesn't update and then to access a cached page. It loads a second later. Her stomach rebels. Fingers shaking now, she drags down the page. Image after image assault her senses.

Blood.

Gore.

Pain.

And on this early one, is that a woman's face?

Lucy's eyes close, a defence against seeing any more. Knowing what happened to Brooke Whitlam, the sight of them has her tasting acid. Has her fearing for Harry. If these get out... *When* these get out, it will be hard to convince the public that the teenager who painted them didn't have violent thoughts. She knows him intimately and she is struggling not to doubt.

But thoughts aren't actions.

Like thinking about how she should have handled things better with Jake. Thinking won't help clear the air. She sits back in the chair and closes the web pages. Then she calls Jake.

'I'm sorry,' she says when he answers.

There's a long silence. But he hasn't hung up.

'This whole thing is unsettling with it all so close to home,' she continues. 'It's no excuse but I'm not experienced with being questioned over a murder.'

He makes a small sound, clearing his throat. He's still there, he's listening. And suddenly that matters a lot.

'Please,' she says. 'Let me make it up to you. Don't I owe you a dinner? Say anywhere you like and it's on me. Or if you'd rather stay in, you can come over, eat, and I'll do my very best not to imply you've murdered anyone.'

Her voice peters out. It was a risk, that last bit, trying for banter, and she holds her breath waiting for a response.

'Tomorrow,' he says.

It's abrupt but she'll take it. 'Where?'

'Not out. I am sick of hearing about the Whitlams.'

'Here, then. How's seven?'

Another long pause, and then, 'I'll see you then.'

When Lucy heads into town late the next afternoon to shop for dinner, she begins to understand why Jake didn't want to eat out. The interest in the Whitlam case has exploded since Harry's arrest and subsequent release. It's all anyone seems to be talking about.

At last, she's back at the cottage with bags of ingredients. Unloading is no simple task, however, as Hades keeps getting in the way, trotting from the front door to the back.

'I'll let you out in a second,' she says, using her toe to open the fridge since her hands are full.

A clenched fist bangs on the old, warped window over the sink.

The butter falls from her hand, hitting the floor with a dull thud. Hades growls.

'Lucy?'

The familiar voice carries through the cracks around the window and her body responds, a quickening of her heartbeat, a curling feeling in her belly. *Harry*. She picks up the butter and crosses to the back door.

'You scared the shit out of me,' she says as she opens it, one hand on Hades' collar.

Shadows around Harry's eyes make them moodier than usual and his cheeks are hollow. There's a red sheen in the glassy whites of his eyes. How did she not realise he was on something?

'Can I come in?' he asks, bouncing on the balls of his feet and glancing repeatedly over his shoulder.

She steps back to let him by, and lets Hades outside at the same time. Harry's wearing a hoodie and a cap that's pulled low. Together, they do a fair job of disguising Harry's identity. He's probably being hounded by the media.

For good reason, he was arrested for killing his mother.

No. This is Harry. She knows Harry. He's not a murderer.

But now she's thinking about why the media are so interested. About his arrest, and the fact that the police must have had some evidence. Then there's the paintings. How could a hand that has been feather-light on her thighs be the same that expressed such rage?

He takes off the cap and drags a hand through his hair.

'I wanted to talk to you,' he says. He's pacing around the tiny kitchen, making it shrink further with his inability to stay still. 'More than that, I needed to talk to you.' He turns and his gaze locks with hers.

She's caught by it, unable to think or talk or do anything but nod.

He closes the distance between them in two strides and his hand brushes her cheek. 'God, I knew I could count on you to understand.'

'Understand what?' She finds her voice.

He collapses into a seat, his head in his hands. 'You can't imagine how terrible it's been. I wanted to tell you at dinner and then the police came, and now I probably shouldn't be here. Thanks for the messages. I've been feeling too low to answer anything, but it meant something that you cared enough to check in.' He glances up, long lashes shining with unshed tears. 'I definitely shouldn't be here. But I had to come.'

There was a time she would have melted at the tortured sincerity in his voice, but she's matured. And she's aware that Jake is due to arrive any time.

Putting away the butter helps break the spell. 'Whatever it is, say it, because I'm expecting a guest for dinner.'

His eyes widen and he seems to notice for the first time the black trousers, indigo top and carefully blow-dried hair that aren't usual house-cleaning attire, but he doesn't ask who's coming. 'You're right,' he says. 'I shouldn't linger. Man, my family would kill me if they knew I'd come, and if the press finds me it will be even worse. It's about Rach.'

'The mayor?' As she asks, she's trying to process the casual way that he said his family would kill him.

He nods. 'The other night she was there at dinner because we have a history. It's nothing serious or anything, but we've spent some time together over the years.'

It's not like Lucy thought they were exclusive, but what he's saying sounds painfully like how she'd describe their relationship, such as it is. 'Okay. I don't know what that has to do with me.'

'Nothing, except that she's who I was with the night of the party.' He hesitates. 'When I was supposed to be meeting you.'

It stings.

She always knew he was probably with someone else, but hearing it…

'She's your alibi.' No wonder the family have been keeping her close. Harry can't have killed his mother if he was wrapped up with the mayor.

'Yes. It's not like I wanted to drag her into this mess. She's a good chick. She has a lot to lose getting caught up in a murder investigation. She could easily hang me out to dry.' He sniffs and wipes at his nose. 'You get it, don't you?'

'She seems nice,' she says when it seems like he's waiting for her to agree with him.

'It's just that they have my fingerprints on the plastic used to preserve the body. The same kind that I had imported to protect and ship the canvases I bought. I mean it's obvious, isn't it? Whoever did this terrible thing took the plastic from the studio. It's not like I ever locked it.'

He sounds so sincere, but you wouldn't know from his expression that the body he's referring to belongs to his mother.

'Did you tell them that?'

'More than once. Anyone could have got in there. Your nan cleaned it for me sometimes. You remember the studio being open all the time, don't you?'

She ignores the question. 'My nan?'

'Before she retired. Man, the place went to crap pretty fast after she left. We missed her.' He's slurring his words a little.

With the hidden ring always on the edge of her thoughts, she blurts, 'Did anyone give her a parting gift? Like maybe your mother?'

As she waits for him to answer, she feels like the ring is pulsing in its hiding spot. She stares at Harry so she doesn't scan towards the hall and give anything away.

He blinks, confused. 'Not that I know of, not that night anyway.'

It was a long shot that he'd tell her anything useful in this state. 'Because you were with the mayor,' she says, quickly changing the subject back to the one that brought him here.

His lips curve into a shadow of one of his charming smiles. 'Well, she wasn't the mayor then, but yeah. That's where I was, so you see, I couldn't have hurt Mother.' He stands and moves close enough to take her hands. 'You believe me, don't you?'

Despite having thought as much to herself, she finds herself shrugging slowly. 'I don't know what to believe.'

A rare expression of hurt flits across his face. 'You're angry, aren't you? You're jealous of Rach. You don't need to be.'

She hates most of all that he's partly right. 'You said they had your fingerprints on the plastic.'

'I'm not denying the stuff came from my studio. But someone else must have taken it. They wanted to frame me, probably.'

'Why?' She can hardly believe the question coming out of her mouth. 'It's not like you were famous back then, why would anyone frame a kid?'

He scans her face. 'You really are mad. I am so sorry, Lucy. For having to tell you all this when I already know that just by not showing up, I really let you down that night. I have literally felt bad about it ever since.'

For the first time in this conversation, she truly doesn't believe him. Harry Whitlam is many things but regretful is not one of them.

She tugs free of his hands. 'All the times we've met, and screwed, and talked over the last nineteen years, and you want me to believe you have thought about the night of the party in terms of me for even a second?'

'I have.'

'And you're only mentioning it now?'

'Lucy—'

The faint squeak of the front gate stops whatever he might have said. And as he makes for the back door, his eyes wild, she discovers she's quite relieved not to hear it.

Mae

With Anabelle off somewhere with Lucy, and therefore out of Mother's firing line, Mae went looking for Harry. He'd been down at his art studio more and more lately. While she hoped it was because he'd been inspired, she feared he was struggling being back at the house and was taking it out on canvas.

Although she didn't have any brilliant solution to offer, she figured at least she could let him know he wasn't alone.

And maybe they could both avoid Mother.

The door opened with the faintest of squeaks but Harry didn't look up. Instead of being caught up in his work, he was standing and staring at two finished canvases, not a brush in sight. They were propped on the ground, leaning against an old set of drawers. His expression suggested he was a heartbeat from kicking the material through the frame.

'Don't,' she blurted.

'Why the fuck not?' he muttered without looking up.

She'd been right. Sometimes she could read him better than she could recognise herself in the mirror. 'These are good. Too good to destroy. Don't let anyone tell you otherwise.'

Harry lifted his head. His smile more brittle than charming, and his eyes red-rimmed. 'You don't know that.'

She swallowed hard. 'I do. They are so good, I promise.'
Even as she said it she had to stop herself screaming in
frustration, because his talent shone in every piece he created
but he couldn't believe. And that was all down to one person.
'She doesn't know what she's talking about. She's probably
jealous.'

He shrugged. 'Big sisters are pretty biased, so I've heard.'

Mae shook her head. 'Not this one.'

His head dropped again and he kicked at the ground, the
toe of his shoe brushing the edge of the frame and sending the
piece skidding back. 'Nah, she's bloody right.' He swallowed
hard, his Adam's apple working in his throat. 'It's a fool's
dream.'

Mae crossed to him, wrapped her arms around his waist
from behind and rested her chin on his shoulder, staring down
at the deliberate slashes of colour on canvas. Just the sight of
his creations filled her with wonder. How she wished he could
appreciate that what he had was magic.

'Never say that. She is not right. That woman is all kinds of
wrong and we both know it.'

She felt the slow relaxation of Harry's muscles until he was
soft and sweet in her arms and she got a sudden flash of a
memory. They were kids, maybe seven and nine, and they'd
both snuck out of their bedrooms to run away at the same
time. It had felt really late but was probably only about ten
at night. She'd been creeping through the quiet house when
she saw him creeping too, his backpack in hand. He was so
little, and so stupid to think he'd last five minutes out of the
house alone.

The older sister in her had kicked in then, and she'd turned
the whole thing into a late-night feast. She'd collected his

favourite snacks and made up some story about them going on an adventure, before sending him back to bed.

She hadn't left either.

She'd blamed not wanting to abandon him or Anabelle, but she suspected the real reason was a lot more cowardly than that.

21

PRESENT DAY

Somehow, Lucy manages to welcome Jake into the cottage without revealing the fact that Harry was there only seconds ago.

'Thanks for coming,' she says as she takes his jacket.

'You look really nice.'

The sincerity of the simple compliment doesn't do anything to help her nerves. She takes in his navy shirt and dark jeans and the freshness of his cleanly shaved jaw. 'You too,' she says. 'I really am sorry about yesterday.'

His smile doesn't quite reach his eyes. 'I'm in no position to knock back a home-cooked meal when I've been late at work the last few nights.'

'The Spring Gully crash?'

'Mostly, but there's all the usual town stuff as well.' He holds out a bottle of red wine. 'I didn't know what you were making but I brought this.'

'Thank you. You didn't need to bring anything.'

As she turns away to place the bottle on the counter, she can't help comparing this stilted politeness with the easy conversation they had before.

When she turns back, Jake is still by the front door but

he's not looking at her; rather, he's staring around the room in puzzlement.

'Where's Hades?' he asks.

Her cheeks go hot. He was outside because of Harry and hopefully he hasn't tried to follow their uninvited guest back up to the Whitlam house. However, the idea of Hades having Harry bailed up against a tree isn't entirely unamusing.

'Out the back,' she explains. And, sure enough, he's there at the door, tail wagging.

Hades rushes past her to Jake, who drops to one knee to pat him properly.

Smiling at the male bonding, she moves to the small kitchen area to wash her hands. 'Dinner shouldn't be long, if you'd like to take a seat,' she says with her back to Jake. 'I took a bit longer than I thought at the supermarket and I was late going because I wanted to have the cupboard in Nan's room finished. And—' His hand on her shoulder stops the babble of explanation.

'I'm sorry about yesterday too. This whole thing is pretty full on. You know, I make a pretty handy sous chef.'

'And I'm good at giving orders.'

This time when he smiles, it crinkles the corners of his eyes.

They work well together and half an hour later she serves them each some of the finished pasta, placing the bowls down on the rickety old table before returning to grab cutlery from the drawer. She's acutely aware of just how close to him she has to pass to do anything.

Apparently oblivious to her discomfort, he pours them each a glass of wine from the bottle he brought. 'I should have guessed white,' he says, gesturing to the creamy fettuccine strands.

'This isn't exactly fine dining. We'll probably survive.'

He takes a mouthful of the pasta and his eyes close in a look of pleasure that stirs something low in her belly.

'This is good.'

'I like to cook,' she says simply. She doesn't explain that before getting together with Brian, she existed on takeout and supermarket salads that she often as not ate at her desk. 'And this is hardly gourmet. Quality ingredients can make anything taste good. The supermarket had everything I wanted.'

'And more, I bet.' He chuckles. 'They like to chat.'

'Yes, I remember that from when I was a teenager.' She tastes some pasta, pleased, as the rich flavours of sundried tomato, baby spinach, cream, herbs and freshly cracked pepper melt together in her mouth. 'Although, if anything, it's gotten worse. I guess there wasn't the mystery and scandal of a body to talk about back then.'

'They found plenty of other topics, trust me.'

She remembers then how often it was his father that the gossip flowed about, and concentrates on eating.

His eyebrows lift in that questioning way. 'What are they saying about Brooke Whitlam now? Let me guess. Despite Harry being released, they're sure someone in the Whitlam family did it. This has all the hallmarks of something personal.'

She nods.

He has another mouthful of pasta. 'Or the killer was a stranger passing through town. Maybe a criminal on the run.'

'Are they so predictable?'

But what she's really wondering is, *am I?* Because what he's describing is similar to her own theorising.

He shrugs. 'A fleeing criminal would be long gone. That means they don't need to look at their neighbours or friends and wonder what they're capable of doing. Similarly, if it's someone close to the victim it's then separate from their own lives. The main thing is to make it other. To make them feel safe.'

She's tempted to ask who he thinks is responsible, but they've only just returned to being comfortable around each other. And she doesn't want to reveal accidentally that she knows about what the police have on Harry and who his alibi is.

It's hard enough not to mention the ring and her worries that it belongs to Brooke Whitlam. The words hover unsaid in her mouth, desperate to escape. Like that feeling of wanting to step over the edge when you're close to the top of a very tall cliff.

Instead, she finishes her glass of wine and doesn't argue when Jake pours her another. His glass is noticeably empty.

'Driving,' he says simply. 'But I'll have some more pasta if you're offering.' His expression is so hopeful she has to laugh.

'I was about to.'

'Then I gratefully accept.'

He demolishes another huge serving of pasta while she sips more wine, feeling her muscles relax. The feverish conversation with Harry before Jake arrived feels a different reality to this one.

When he's finished, she stands to clear the table.

'I'll dry,' he volunteers. 'I'd offer to wash but there's something about the food on the plates and the soapy water.' He shudders.

'Right,' she says, filling the sink. 'Scared of food on plates. Another thing to add to my list of things I know about Jake Parker.'

'I wouldn't say scared,' he counters, grabbing a tea towel.

'But if you gave me the choice between that and examining a body…' He shrugs. 'Well, I'm not a kitchen hand.'

She pulls up her sleeves without thinking, exposing the angry red welt across her forearm from her dash through the trees the other night.

He leans closer. 'That looks nasty.'

It still hurts a little. This is her chance to tell him about the other night and the feeling someone was watching her. But she doesn't, afraid he'll think she's some helpless female imagining the worst at every noise in the night. Nor does she want him to know how she lingered near the windows of the Whitlam house, peering in. And of course there's the ring under the loose floorboard in the hall.

'Just a scratch,' she says.

He doesn't push the matter, placing cutlery, plates, bowls and saucepans away as he works, guessing correctly where most of the items go. To be fair, it's not hard in the small kitchen with most of the cupboards now emptied.

When the last dish is put away and the sink sparkling clean, Lucy braces for him to leave. He's eaten and it's getting late, but it's been nice having him there, keeping thoughts of her neighbours at bay.

But he doesn't say any of the expected farewell lines. Instead, he pulls a small tablet out of one of his jacket pockets, the screen coming to life under his touch. 'I know you said you haven't seen any *Great British Bake Off*, but I have here the opportunity you've been waiting for.'

They settle on the couch, her with her wine and him with a cup of tea. They watch together in comfortable silence, only interrupted by him excitedly exclaiming, 'This next bit is so good.' All with the soundtrack of Hades snoring.

'I liked it,' Lucy admits when the credits roll, when she guesses from the earnest kid-like expression on his face that he's about to ask.

'Another?'

Her eyelids are heavy, and her bones feel liquid thanks to the wine and the long day going through Nan's things, but she's not ready for him to leave. 'I'm game if you are.'

'This next one is a beauty,' he says. He presses something on the screen and while he waits for it to load, he glances around the small cottage. It's so bare now compared to when she arrived but some touches, like the rug and the fire, make it still seem like Nan's home.

'You've done a lot to pack up,' he says.

There's a certainty in his voice she recognises. 'You've been here before.'

He hesitates and shoves his hand through his hair, making it all messy in a way that has Lucy itching to smooth it down for him. 'Your grandfather took an interest in my footy team when I was a little tacker. Footy is everything around here and my dad played, was even pretty good before things went to crap for him.' He shakes his head. 'The year we went from skills to small games was the hardest. Other kids had a parent come out to cheer them on. I didn't have anyone.'

She didn't know Jake as a little kid, but she can picture it. Short, cute and so incredibly sad but trying not to show it. 'But my grandfather was there?'

'Yeah. Second game, and mostly every damn one after that until he got too sick. He didn't say much. Mostly told me where I'd messed up, but there was the odd "good game" in there too.'

'And he showed up.'

'Yeah. He didn't make a big deal out of it or anything. I tried to tell him once how much it meant to me. My voice broke trying to get the words out. Reckon I was maybe fourteen.' He swallows hard and stares into the fire. 'He said I might not be the best player, but I was a decent teammate.'

'High praise.'

'Yeah, I thought so.'

'It was you,' Lucy exclaims, making sense of something that's been nagging at her for months.

'What?'

'The visitor from Queen's Point who came to see Nan in the nursing home.'

'Seaview? More like see-no-view.' His nose crinkles. 'She hated that place.' He holds up his hand before she can protest. 'You had to move her, I know you did, but she missed the ocean. I didn't get to see her as often as I should have.'

'But you weren't at the funeral?'

'Sorry. I was on my way when there was a station emergency. One of the joys of the job.'

She takes his hand. It's rough and warm and it feels pretty good in hers. 'I'm glad you had them in your life.'

'Me too. Judy pushed me to join the force. Knew it was my dream. Even had me round for a meal a few times as long as I helped with the washing-up.'

'That explains you knowing where everything went. You achieved your dream then?'

He looks away. 'I guess.'

'How is your progress on the Spring Gully car accident?'

'Slower than I would expect. It's like this woman doesn't want to be identified.'

'What do you mean?'

'It should have been straightforward, but she had no ID and the fire was pretty convenient. There's no missing person's report. All of this can happen, but all together... I don't know. And then there's the forensic testing. A slow enough process on a good week, but it's glacial at the moment. You wouldn't believe the number of staff on leave across the various departments.'

There's something about the way he says 'you wouldn't believe' that suggests he doesn't. That there's too many coincidences.

'It's winter?' Lucy suggests. 'Sick season.'

'Maybe.' But he sounds sceptical. 'And there's the car,' he continues. 'It has plates, is well maintained, even has a service sticker. But details of registration and the owner are nowhere to be found.'

'But you'll get there?'

'I will.'

They've snuggled in close so they can both see the small screen. She breathes in his scent of sea mixed with a hint of the chocolate he just finished from the mixed selection box she'd bought for dessert. There's a tiny crumb in the corner of his lips. Without thinking, she reaches out and brushes it. His eyes darken, his gaze drops to her mouth. There's a question in his hesitation.

As always, between them it's Harry and the Whitlams and whether this is a good idea.

It might not be, but she presses her lips to his anyway. She tastes the chocolate and Jake and appreciates anew how *nice* can be so much more. It can be hot and sweet and urgent, and as he deepens the kiss, she can't help noticing the improvement in his technique over the nineteen years since they last kissed.

And then she can't think about anything but his mouth on hers and his touch.

Right up until the screen slips off their legs, landing on the floor with a clunk.

They break apart. 'It's not cracked,' she says, rescuing it from the rug.

Instead of kissing her again, Jake shifts so that, with her body still languid from his touch, she curves into the crook of his arm. In some ways, it's more intimate than the kissing.

'What is it that you do in the big bad city?' he asks against her hair, making the loose strands tickle her neck.

'Manage portfolios, investments, make people money...' Her voice peters out. Her work is filled with meetings and computer screens and deals that should make it hard to sleep at night and talking about it makes it hard to avoid thoughts of that last, ugly board meeting.

He chuckles. 'I meant, where do you go to eat? Do you cook often? Do you have other family?'

'We're making small talk now?'

He says nothing, waiting patiently for her answer as his hand trails up and down her arm. The silence stretches and she's been to enough therapists to wonder if his refusal to take back the question or respond to her obvious avoidance is a tactic. Has he employed this with suspects, this annoying gap that it's almost impossible not to want to fill?

But the thing is, Lucy has tactics too. And when she angles her face to meet his lips with hers, he doesn't insist on more talking. Nor on starting the episode he was so eager for her to see.

What starts as a distraction becomes more. He takes over, his tongue teasing her mouth open. His hands exploring.

This, this is what she wanted.

She meets each questioning touch with her own. The rush of her blood in her ears not enough to drown her gasping for breath. She presses closer, unable to help herself.

Too soon, he's pulling away.

'I'm going to go home now,' he murmurs against her lips.

'But what about the episode?'

'That is not the reason I'm tempted to stay.'

She kisses him again. 'Then tell me why you haven't moved off the couch?'

He shakes his head. 'I'm thinking detailed descriptions here aren't going to help any with me trying to do the right thing.'

She thinks she could probably convince him, but she likes that he doesn't want to rush.

'Okay.' She stands and pulls him up.

He lingers at the door. 'Thanks for dinner.'

'Any time.'

'I care about you, Lucy Ross.' It's gruff but the tenderness is there. Impossible to miss, even for her. And she believes him. Believes in him, in a way that she never has Harry, for all his bewitching promises.

'Thanks.'

His mouth kicks up at the corner. 'It's part of the profession. Don't let it go to your head.'

She thinks of Brian then, which is odd. One is all rough man, and the other bookish and older, but there's a similarity between them.

'Night, Jake. See you soon?'

He kisses her once more. Hard. 'You will.'

Lucy

'Go ahead and wait by the pool if you want, I'll get us towels.' Anabelle's nose crinkled in thought. 'And maybe snacks. Are you starving? I am. It will be fruit though, all healthy.'

'That sounds great,' said Lucy. 'But can't we use the beach towels?'

Anabelle laughed but Lucy hadn't tried to be funny. 'No, duh, they're sandy.'

'My bad,' Lucy agreed, not sure whether the problem was with getting it in the pool or just having it in proximity, but not wanting to show her ignorance by asking.

She made her way around the side and through the gate into the pool area, only to discover she wasn't alone. She tried not to stare at the feminine vision approaching her from the side of the pool. Skin bronzed and gleaming, curves she'd only seen in a magazine and huge sunglasses hiding most of her face. Model-like, but familiar somehow. Then it registered. It was the girl who'd been in the study the other day. Mr Whitlam's prize student. Vanessa, maybe?

It was odd, the two of them there next to the pool, both strangers at the Whitlam house. But the few years she had on Lucy gave the other girl confidence. 'Nice afternoon for it,' Vanessa said as she passed. 'The water is divine.'

'Great,' was all Lucy managed in response.

The girl squeezed droplets from her hair, flicked the tresses over her shoulder and strode from the pool area with a parting smile.

Lucy was staring after her, wondering how foolish she'd look if she tried the hair toss, when Harry arrived from the opposite direction. His hair was damp and pushed back and he wore only low-slung black board shorts. And Lucy promptly forgot anyone else existed. After too many seconds, she realised she was staring and jerked her gaze away.

'You're waiting for Anabelle,' he drawled. It wasn't a question.

'She's getting towels,' Lucy explained, darting a look at him from under lowered lashes.

His teeth flashed white. 'Can I tell you a secret?'

He was standing closer by then, and the murmured question had warmth pooling inside her. 'Um, yep,' she squeaked.

His breath teased her neck as he leaned close. 'You don't need a towel to get in the water.' He laughed and took a couple of running steps, before launching himself into the deep end with a fluid grace. He surfaced down the far end of the pool a moment later, grin wide. 'You coming in, or not?'

'Totally.'

She couldn't have shucked the lace-edged floral dress she'd worn over her bikini faster. The red lines from her earlier sunburn had faded but she didn't linger on the pool edge, torn between wanting his gaze on her and terror that he wouldn't like what he saw. She jumped, wondering as her body hit the water just how awkward she'd looked. Graceful dolphin or baby elephant? More likely the latter.

Holding her breath underwater until her lungs hurt, she

eventually gave up and had to surface, breaking into the air with great gasping breaths.

Only to meet Harry's gaze.

He had been watching her from his spot on the steps in the shade, his face a mixture of sunshine and shadows. He was still watching her, and thank God she could touch the bottom here because she was struggling to remember how to float.

His eyebrows lifted and he gave her a slow smile. 'Come here,' he said.

She did as he bid her, of course she did.

The water caressed her skin as she swam closer. Every part of her melted. She didn't know where she finished and the water began. His hand reached out and she let him tug her across the final gap, until she floated between his knees, her body almost touching his.

He smiled, and leaned in to close the distance between them.

22

PRESENT DAY

The invite to afternoon tea at the Whitlam house comes while Lucy's delivering another box of old, but functional, kitchen things to the charity shop in town. The two elderly ladies who work there have begun to greet her with an offer of coffee and she's thankful for the ding on her phone that gives her an excuse to escape their well-meaning inquisition.

Not that they're the only reason for her slow progress. There's Jake too. Had they really kissed on Nan's couch in front of the fire?

Over the last few days, she'd sent Anabelle and Mae messages of support, as well as suggestions for getting together, but hadn't received any replies, so the sight of a message from Mae at last has Lucy smiling as she opens it.

'... an intimate afternoon tea for a proper catch-up.'

She taps out her answer before starting the car. 'I'll look forward to it.'

Despite her anticipation, the day flies. She's beginning to see the end of the cottage work and about an hour before she has to head up to the Whitlam house, she logs on and answers her boss's email of polite enquiry.

Yes, I'm fine, thanks. No, I don't need counselling. Yes, I'll be back at work when my leave is up and I look forward to our conversation.

As she types, she tries to ignore the pang in her chest at the prospect of leaving Queen's Point.

Email sent, she opens the search bar. Sometime in the middle of the night it struck her that there might be a photo online of Brooke Whitlam wearing the missing ring. Then she'd know whether it was the one she'd found.

The Whitlam siblings have been busy uploading childhood happy snaps in the last few days. The cynic in Lucy wonders if it's part of some act to appear grief-stricken.

The attention from the media means there are other pictures of Brooke Whitlam too, sourced from various town events that she oversaw. Council meetings, environment meetings, race days and local sporting teams' finals all had her giving a speech or presenting some award.

Lucy doesn't need to retrieve the ring from its hiding place as she scrolls; she'd recognise the distinctive design anywhere.

Like Mae did?

She quickly finds her rhythm. Make any photos full-screen, then zoom in on Brooke Whitlam's hands. None of the family have any suitable pictures, each of them stiffly posed group shots where the five of them look more like models for a sitcom family than real people.

With only a few minutes until she needs to be at the Whitlam house, Lucy finds an article describing Brooke Whitlam's wonderful contributions to Queen's Point. She skips the text, scrolling to the foot of the web page. In the picture, Brooke

Whitlam is holding 'thank you' flowers for her work as judge on a fashion show, September 1998.

Lucy zooms in. Her stomach drops.

She closes her eyes but when she opens them it's still there. Simple gold band, small diamonds, distinctive engraving. The grainy image can't disguise the truth. The ring she found in Nan's cottage is right there on a dead woman's hand.

Her hand covers her mouth; she's going to be sick. How did it get to the cottage? Is it coincidence it looks like the one in the old photograph? And what the hell should she do with that information?

Nothing right now. She's due at the Whitlam house for afternoon tea.

It takes a while for the clack of footsteps to sound from the other side of the big heavy front door of the Whitlam house. So long that Lucy checks the time. She's sure it was four. Dante is up on the roof, working on something up at the cupola windows, she noticed as she approached the house. He seemed to be watching her every step but now he's not looking this way at all. Maybe she should try to get his attention.

Before she can do so, the door opens.

Mae smiles. 'Have you been waiting long? I expected you to come around the back. I was out in the summer room.' Today her hair is sleek and shining in a low ponytail, which with her casual wide-legged ochre pants and white top makes her seem fresh and elegant.

In contrast, Lucy's hair didn't quite dry from the shower and her cargo pants feel decidedly workmanlike. She resists fidgeting and smiles in return. 'I'll know for next time.'

'Come in.'

She leads Lucy down the long hallway, a few turns and then through the kitchen area. It's sparkling clean, the appliances Lucy once admired almost certainly updated and now secreted out of sight in a butler's pantry. Three exquisite glass pendant lights add the expected touch of elegance over the white marble waterfall bench.

'Ajaire Fiok,' Mae says with a wave at the lights. 'She's a brilliant artist. Hand-blows each one to give them the signature one-of-a-kind imperfections. Only makes a few pieces a year. We were lucky to get these as a set.'

Lucy doesn't comment that it's likely more a matter of wealth than luck.

From there, it's out past the pool. It's pristine, of course, despite the icy chill in the air, the clean blue of it reflecting the clouds above.

What Mae referred to as the summer room was once the pool house, and it lies the far side of the water. It's had the renovations Lucy remembers Anabelle, or maybe it was Harry, bemoaning that it needed one afternoon nineteen years ago when they hung out there. Only someone with a pool house could complain that theirs wasn't fancy enough.

Where before it was a simple shelter, now it's the kind of indoor-outdoor living space featured in magazines. Four white brick pillars support the rustic whitewashed overhead beams and huge windows capture the view of the distant water and the faint sunshine. Wooden stacker doors are closed to keep in the heat from the incredible fireplace. The light grey stone column with a styled gas flame is the centrepiece to the whole space. The couches arranged intimately in front of the fire are leather, white of course, and the coffee table wooden. There's a modern outdoor kitchen on one side and bar and dining on the other.

At Mae's direction, Lucy sits on the couch across from her. There's a delicate blue and white floral tea set on the low table between them. Only two cups.

'I thought Anabelle might be joining us.' Lucy can't hide her disappointment. Her old friend's recent distance is like the aloofness between them after that summer. She'd begun to think they were on their way to growing close again but now Anabelle isn't replying to any messages.

Does she have something to hide?

Lucy scraps the thought as Mae explains her sister is caught up taking her children to visit a nearby nautical museum at copper coast town Wallaroo across the other side of the Yorke Peninsula. 'It's important that the young ones get out despite everything going on.'

'Of course.'

'Excuse the mess.' Mae waves to a small pile of papers and her closed laptop. 'Tea? Or, if you'd prefer coffee, I can get some brought out?'

'Tea would be wonderful.'

'Excuse me if I don't attempt a traditional ceremony, I'd never do it justice. This green tea blend is created by a friend of mine in Japan.' She lifts the little ceramic pot by its carved wooden handle and pours into the small gold-rimmed cups. 'Her family have a small tea shop in Maebashi, a couple of hours out of Tokyo. The set is one of theirs too.'

'It's gorgeous.'

'I think so, too. We're investigating how to scale the production to have select pieces included in the stores. Even if it doesn't work out, I've made some good friends.'

Lucy takes the offered steaming cup of fragrant tea.

Mae shares a little more of the challenges and rewards of working with small producers as they slowly sip their tea. And it is as good as she promised. Light and fresh and Lucy feels better to have drunk it, like her insides are thanking her.

'Enough about me,' Mae says. 'Tell me more about what you do with yourself when you're not in Queen's Point?'

Lucy's breath hitches. The pride she used to have in her success feels a lot more like shame after the boardroom disaster. 'I work for a company called Potts Consulting,' Lucy explains. 'We're the people other companies hire at great expense to design a solution for the mistakes their permanent employees have made. I'm in finance.'

'I've heard of them,' Mae says. 'They're the best.'

'It keeps me on my toes.'

'No wonder it's taken you a while to get down here to Judy's cottage. You must be in high demand. Why now?'

Her eyes are interested but there's something in her tone. Sweat forms on Lucy's lower back. Mae couldn't possibly know, could she? Lucy's boss assured her letting what happened get out would be in none of their best interests.

Lucy, what are you doing?

Images flood her brain. Wide, horrified eyes. Mouths falling open in astonishment.

She can taste her last sip of tea climbing up the back of her throat, but when she places the cup on the table her hand is steady. 'I had months of holidays owing.'

Mae smiles and the odd feeling that she knew more than she was letting on passes. Lucy allows herself to relax. The conversation returns to Anabelle and her children and how nice it is for Mae to be able to spend some time with them.

Then she talks about the handyman work Dante has been doing.

'I noticed him up on the roof as I came in,' Lucy says. 'Interesting that he seems to have made himself so at home here.'

Mae sighs, her face a picture of compassion. 'I feel offering the poor young man some work is the least we can do for him after the ordeal he went through with what he found.'

Lucy remembers then that Dante was the one who found Brooke Whitlam's body. She sounds so genuine, but part of Lucy wonders if the family need to keep him close while the investigation plays out. 'There must be a lot to do on a property this size. Particularly one built so long ago, with all the sheds and other buildings surrounding the main house.'

'It would be irresponsible of me to let it get run down.'

'There are all kinds of dangers lurking in old buildings.' Suddenly, Lucy thinks of her grandfather and the terrible illness that shadowed his last days. From what she's read and Jasmine said, it's something he's likely to have been exposed to in his work. And most of his working life was on this estate.

But Mae simply nods. 'Dante is all caught up on the garden upkeep and he offered to do some of the long overdue maintenance on the window security.' She smiles. 'You can't be too careful, even in such a friendly community as ours.'

'Especially so far out of town.' Lucy's not foolish enough to ask directly about Mae's mother, but she's curious. 'Why did you end up staying in Queen's Point?'

Mae shakes her head. 'You say that like it's a bad thing. I've created a business with showrooms in the world's most cosmopolitan cities. I have properties all around the globe but it's always nice to be home.'

'Didn't you win some special scholarship to study in England?'

Lucy always thought Mae had given in to her mother's demands to stay. But Brooke Whitlam was dead. Lucy's not the only one who can't believe that any family can be estranged enough not to recognise that someone else was impersonating Brooke Whitlam. For the first time, she wonders if it was the woman sitting opposite. Did she read Lucy's attempts to connect with the woman she'd admired? Did she see how Lucy gushed that Brooke Whitlam was her inspiration?

'I'm happy with my choices,' Mae says. 'My life here is full and satisfying, and I can travel first class to anywhere in the world, any time I like.'

'Of course,' Lucy agrees. But she remembers the look on Mae's face that night she saw her at the petrol station on the edge of town. Leaving, Lucy realised later, and then changing her mind. If they fought on the subject and Mae killed her mother, the guilt might have been enough to keep her here, watching over the town to keep her secrets, and the body, buried.

Suddenly, Lucy thinks of Jake and how comfortable he and Mae are with each other. It would be important in such a scenario to have the local police onside.

Could the woman sitting opposite Lucy have taken some blunt object and caved in her mother's skull?

Lucy startles at a touch on her hand, nearly knocking the teacup on to the floor. She looks up into Mae's warm gaze, feels the rush that inclusion and friendship from this woman sends through her.

'I asked if you would like more tea,' Mae chides, settling back opposite. 'You were a million miles away.'

Not a million miles, rather I was just down the hill a bit with your mother's body. Lucy feels a surge of guilt through her that she'd been even thinking along such lines.

'More tea would be lovely, thank you.'

'I'm so glad we've had this chance to chat,' Mae says as she takes the cup and lines it up precisely next to her own. 'It has been too long. And you're coming to the little show on the weekend?'

Only Mae could describe one of the most significant art prizes in the country as such. 'Of course.'

'We feel as a family it's important to give back to our community. Mum would have wanted the event to go ahead.'

As Lucy nods agreement, she pictures Brooke Whitlam's snarl of contempt when she talked about Harry's art.

'I'm looking forward to it,' Lucy says. 'Should be a lovely evening.' Despite the investigation surrounding the family, and the whispers, and the fact that Harry, who's the face of the whole thing, she last saw in Nan's kitchen, wild-eyed and practically raving. 'What are those?' Lucy can't resist asking the question since Mae's touched the pile of sealed pages on the couch next to her more than once while they've been talking.

'Death threats.' She says it the way someone else might say *junk mail*.

Lucy's hand lifts to her chest. 'Against you?'

Mae's hand trembles as she finishes refilling their cups. 'No. Not that I don't get the odd scary letter from someone who thinks my colour palette in the latest Whitlams catalogue is in poor taste.' She hesitates in a way that makes Lucy feel like she's sharing a deeply personal confidence. 'These were to Mum.'

Lucy stills. That she did not expect. 'From when?'

'The weeks before she died.'

'And you kept them all this time?'

'Not me,' Mae says. 'During my interview with the police, they enquired whether I knew of anyone who might want to cause Mum harm. I couldn't think of a single one.'

Lucy tries not to choke. 'Of course.'

'But then, when I got home, I remembered these. Mum waved it off at the time as someone annoyed from all the town committees she led. She said she wouldn't be doing her job properly if she didn't ruffle a few feathers. These papers were filed and dated in her desk in the study off her bedroom. None of us had gone through her belongings. We always thought she'd come home, and she was very particular about her things.'

There's no grief in her tone but Lucy's not really surprised. According to their story, they all lost contact years ago.

'I'm making copies before I hand them over to the police,' Mae continues. 'Although the paint and charcoal used was like some of Harry's, it's important to look deeper.'

'Harry's?' Lucy feels like a parrot echoing Mae, but it's all she can do to keep up.

'Yes, but I've engaged a forensic specialist. Preliminary analysis suggests they were most likely written by a female.'

'They can tell that?'

Mae shrugs. 'The word choice used, the style. At the very least, I should be able to create enough doubt to question any link with Harry. And after all, everyone knows Harry was never in want of feminine company. Gosh, I probably shouldn't be telling you any of this, but I consider you practically family.'

'Harry was popular,' Lucy agrees. 'I'd bet there were dozens of girls going in and out of his studio. The mayor, for one.'

'And the paper is the cheap kind from the supermarket.' Mae's nose scrunches. 'Not the special supplies he had for his art.'

Lucy sips her tea, not tasting it. Mae is only sharing this because she trusts Lucy, but she can't be sure Lucy's ring was her mother's. Lucy knows she didn't send any threats, but could Nan have done so?

'I'm sure the police will analyse them thoroughly,' Lucy manages. 'They can do wonders finding DNA these days.'

Mae's eyes narrow slightly. 'The police say it will be difficult on the paper after all this time but we have one envelope, so if the person licked the seal, they might have left some trace behind.'

'Hopefully. This must be so hard on all of you.'

Mae lowers her head a little, as if the burden of it all is weighing her down. 'And,' she continues, 'if, after further analysis, the perpetrator proves not to be female, I've been thinking really hard and there are other people who had issues with Mum.'

'Really?' Lucy asks.

'Like Teddy Parker. Our friend Jake's dad. I hate to say it, but I can't keep anything from the authorities. I'm sure Jake would understand. You remember there was that time he came to the house? You were out here with the other kids in the garden and I remember you were terrified. I don't blame you.'

Lucy mumbles something suitable while remembering how Jake said they were looking for his father the last night Brooke Whitlam was seen alive. Is that what Jake's been hiding? He's not a suspect, but his father is?

Mae touches the top note as though trying to picture who might have written it. 'Teddy Parker held Mum responsible for him losing his job at the supermarket. The man was always drunk, often aggressive. She was right to complain, but I guess a man in his state was unlikely to view anything with rationality, especially the disintegration of his life. He had to blame someone, and no one likes to blame themselves.'

'But he's dead. He...' She hesitates with how to describe it. '... died not long after the party.'

Mae nods sadly. 'Yes, it all makes sense if you think about it. The guilt must have gotten to him.' She seems quite pleased with her theory. 'He killed Mum and then took his own life.'

It's neat and tidy and entirely possible. If not for the fact that the hiding of the body suggests someone with more rationality than Lucy remembers Jake's father possessing.

Lashing out in anger? Sure.

Careful planning and covering up? Not so much.

'I'm sure the detectives will discover the culprit,' Lucy says eventually. Her tea is done, and as nice as it is to be treated by Mae as a confidante, she needs to know if this is the reason Jake's been acting strangely. 'It's getting late. I should probably head back down to feed Hades.'

Mae rises. 'Yes, it's easy to get carried away chatting to old friends. Speaking of old things, I noticed you wearing a ring the other day. It was quite distinctive.'

Lucy should have been prepared for this. 'Probably one of Nan's,' she says quickly.

'I'm probably imagining things but I have to say, it looked a lot like one that's missing from Mum's things.'

Lucy's head spins as the blood rushes from her extremities.

She lifts her hand to her lips, hoping to hide how pale she must be. 'There are lots of similar rings, I'm sure.'

'I'm sure you're right.' Mae leads the way to the front door under the watchful whir of the security cameras in the hall, takes Lucy's hands and kisses both of her cheeks fondly in farewell. 'One more thing,' she says.

Lucy waits.

'As a neighbour, I wanted to warn you about a night-time disturbance we had recently. You are terribly alone down there.'

Heat rises in Lucy's neck, remembering Hades crashing through the fence. 'Thank you,' she says. 'I'll be careful.'

Mae gives her hand one last squeeze before letting go. 'That's good. We wouldn't want anything to happen to you.'

JANUARY 2000
SIX DAYS BEFORE THE PARTY

Judy

Judy raised her hand to knock, then shook herself, reaching out and turning the handle of the small side door instead. This entrance to the grand and sprawling Whitlam house around the far side of the garage, the one known to be the servants' entrance even if not officially named, was unlocked this time of day, as she knew it would be.

Once, she'd thought coming here was a matter of doing good, honest work for a fair wage. Now, stepping over the threshold sent a trickle of shame through her. Because, unlike her parents – God rest them – Brooke Whitlam believed her employees to be lesser, and the attitude was hard to shake.

'Hello?' Judy called. Not loud enough to disturb the family in the main areas of the house, but to give any nearby staff warning of her approach.

One of the seasonal farmworkers had been caught by the boss on an unauthorised smoke break a few weeks earlier and Brooke had fired him immediately.

Judy didn't want to give anyone heart palpitations.

The wet rooms and large laundry were empty of people but several machines ran full loads, creating a familiar rumble that drowned out the click of Judy's low heels across the tiled floor. With the Whitlam children home for the holidays there was much washing to be done, and it was hard to walk past and not check the progress.

But if Judy detoured now, she might not stay her course.

On legs with only a little tremble, she walked quickly through the back hallways where the family rarely ventured, up the stairs. There was worn wood and a chilly draught, so different to the ornate staircase in the main part of the house. Doubts niggled with every step.

Should she have called and set up a time?

No, better this way. She clutched the envelope with its typed letter inside and forced herself towards the closed study doors at the end of the hallway. This suite of rooms, far from the children's bedrooms and the library, was the domain of Brooke Whitlam, the self-appointed queen of Queen's Point. Judy had been called to meet her employer there more than once over the last few years to answer for some perceived failure in performance.

Her Doug had fared even worse. Judy's heart ached at the thought of the man whose relaxed nature had been like fingernails down a blackboard to their boss. He'd have been sacked if his continued employment to retirement wasn't a part of the conditions of Brooke inheriting the house. As Judy's was. Brooke's parents' love for their daughter not so blind as to not make sure their employees would be looked after.

They'd been good people, as had their parents before them, supporting Judy's mother when she found herself widowed and pregnant. Giving her a loan to buy the cottage for little enough in return. The token loaned and then kept and even now in Brooke's possession.

Generations entwined.

But not for much longer.

Judy clutched the letter to her bosom and knocked hard on the door.

It swung open, but it was neither Brooke nor her latest assistant who stood there.

'Judy,' cried Grant Whitlam, apparently unconcerned by her obvious surprise at seeing him in this part of the house. 'Good to see you.' He pressed a warm kiss to her cheek, then frowned at her affectionately. 'But aren't you supposed to be on holidays? I've seen your granddaughter around the place. Lovely girl.'

Judy managed to gather her wits and reply. 'Yes, Lucy is most delightful. I just had some business I needed to take care of.' Judy could feel her smile becoming unnaturally tight. 'May I have a moment to speak with Mrs Whitlam?'

Grant darted a look back over his shoulder. Behind him, the door to the main study was closed and raised voices grumbled from beyond. 'She's busy at the moment. Is it something I can help with?'

Theoretically, he was just as much her employer as his wife, but in reality… 'I don't think—' Judy began.

'Please tell me that isn't what I think it is?' he interrupted, his gaze on the envelope.

Judy held it out. 'If you think it's my official letter of resignation, then you would be correct. It's time, I'm not getting any younger, and with the holidays I have owing I would like this to be considered my notice.'

He took the envelope from her with a sad shake of his head. 'This is most certainly our loss. You'll be missed around here, but of course I wish you every happiness in your retirement. Do you have plans?'

She thought about telling him then, but only for a moment. There were official channels for a reason.

She shrugged, hopefully appearing unflustered. 'Spending time with Lucy for now,' she said lightly. 'And after that, who knows?'

He took her hand and squeezed it. 'Well, don't be a stranger. You'll come to the big party? As a guest of course?'

'That would be nice. Please let me know if Mrs Whitlam has any questions.'

'I will,' he said, but a cry from the study muffled his words. 'We'll be in touch with a final settlement on holidays and sick leave.'

Judy managed to make out Brooke's strident 'You listen to me, you little—', before Grant bustled her out into the hallway.

'Take care,' he said, then he firmly closed the door.

Judy was fighting fit but her advanced age gave her the excuse to make her way rather slowly along the hallway. It meant she lingered there when, a few minutes later, Brooke's office door burst open and Grant's young, attractive student came flying down the hall past Judy, tears streaming down her face.

23

PRESENT DAY

Lucy doesn't get to decide whether or not to tell Jake that his father is being flagged by Mae as a possible suspect because he doesn't answer Lucy's call as she's walking back to the cottage.

Nor does he reply to her message an hour later.

Which means she doesn't have any excuse for avoiding Nan's paperwork, considering the appointment at the law firm is tomorrow.

It's only when she sits at the table that she discovers how little she'd achieved before she got sidetracked by calling the firm, and then by Anabelle's arrival. She's read the first page, which is a receipt, and only flipped through the rest.

What she finds in the fourth page down, stuck as it is by an ancient coffee cup ring mark to the page above it, has her on her feet and pacing the cottage.

Whitlam.

The name leaps out from the flimsy, stained A4 page like a stack of books falling on her head. A legal matter with the family whose matriarch is dead and killed that same summer. She thinks of her grandfather, and his battle with an illness most likely caused in his work at the Whitlam property.

Although she goes through the rest of the pages linked to

the law firm carefully, they tell her nothing beyond hourly rates and scrawled legal jargon. The penmanship is hurried, and time has rendered it impossible to decipher.

'Could she have needed help with the hospital bills?' she asks Hades, but he seemingly has no opinion on the matter, not even raising his head from the rug.

The niggle that first struck her at afternoon tea won't go away.

Could Nan have held them responsible for her grandfather's cancer? Is that why she stole the ring? Could she have sent the threats to Brooke Whitlam?

As Lucy enters the offices of MacArthur and Sons right in the centre of Adelaide, she still hasn't heard from Jake. So much for his promise of seeing her again. It wouldn't be the first time a woman's been ghosted, but why did he bother?

'This way,' says Anya, the same woman Lucy spoke to on the phone. The office is all grey, black and white, with clean lines and sharp edges. Quite the contrast to the traditional stonework and elegant cornices on the outside of the squat building, which has turned out to be only two blocks from Lucy's work.

'Ms Antonello?'

Mr MacArthur is younger than she thought he'd be. Barely older than Lucy, with thinning hair and the soft, pale features of a man who doesn't see a lot of natural light.

'Yes,' she says a fraction too late, giving away her disappointment. 'I'm Lucy Ross. Judy was my grandmother.'

'Calum MacArthur.' He shakes her hand and then sits opposite. 'I can see you were expecting my father.' He seems unconcerned by this and his gaze flicks to his watch. 'Given the hour, he's probably already out on a golf course. He retired two years ago.'

'That's frustrating. I was hoping to talk to him about my grandmother, who was a client of his nineteen years ago.'

'I understand, but hopefully, I can help.'

Lucy shows him the official documents that prove she's the executor of Nan's estate and then the legal paperwork she found. 'I am having some trouble with all the jargon. It seems like she was making a claim against someone.'

She doesn't say the name but 'Whitlam' echoes in her brain.

Calum MacArthur quickly scans the pages. When he lifts his head, his gaze is direct, as are his words. 'You've grasped the general gist of what it says here, which unfortunately doesn't tell me much else.'

'What about your father? Could he help?'

'My father's mind isn't the same as it once was. I did ask him about your grandmother when Anya told me about your enquiry. However, he couldn't recall any specific details. You appreciate, I'm sure, that he's had a lot of meetings over the years.'

'What about the firm's records?'

'Good question. You might have noticed our relatively new décor. There was a leak in the sprinkler system a few years ago that caused a flood. While we escaped anything structural, unfortunately many boxes of records were damaged beyond repair.'

The more he talks, the more Lucy fears she's wasted a trip. 'Is there anything you can tell me?'

He takes a breath and touches his screen, bringing the computer to life. Then he brings up a file he obviously had prepared. 'Judy Antonello met with my father a number of times regarding a personal claim. It appears it was medical in nature and to be made against an employer.' He frowns. 'There's a note that suggests her enquiry was made on someone else's behalf.'

Her grandfather.

It's so obvious now. Nan must have had proof he'd been exposed to asbestos through work on their property.

Lucy leans forward, trying to order her thoughts. 'I understand that you don't have many details from back then, but can you answer a few questions?'

'Of course.'

'Could my grandmother have made a claim for compensation from where my grandfather worked, given that my grandfather was diagnosed with mesothelioma?'

He considers a moment. 'I can't comment on the specifics of that case without more detail, including medical reports, but given the diagnosis is correct, whether there can be legal proceedings is then a matter of the laws in the particular state or territory where the person was exposed. It will also depend on the ability to prove that the exposure occurred at a specific location. I've pursued a number of such matters over my career.' He hesitates and for the first time his face shows signs of real compassion. 'It can be a benefit to the family who are left with medical costs.'

'They were significant.'

He nods. 'These days there are two types of claim, both through the courts and for compensation under a government scheme. However, you're talking nearly two decades ago.'

Lucy's throat aches. 'You can't tell from these documents whether the suit went ahead?'

'Unfortunately, no. But you might be able to discover more through the state's legal records. I'd be happy to have someone do the legwork for you.'

'For a fee,' Lucy finishes.

'Yes.' He doesn't apologise. He's running a business, not a charity.

'Then do so. Thank you.'

He glances again at the time and stands. 'My next appointment is due any moment. If there's nothing further?'

Lucy gathers her pieces of paper, her brain turning over the possibility of Nan suing the Whitlams for what happened to her grandfather, and slowly rises to her feet. 'Is there any way you can tell who in particular Nan was looking to make a claim against?'

He comes around the large desk and plucks one of the pages from her hand. This one has mostly illegible scrawl written underneath the company logo and has not weathered the passing of the years well, with the ink smeared and unidentifiable marks across it.

Calum MacArthur points to the middle, where the white of the paper is most discoloured. 'There,' he says.

Lucy frowns, trying to make sense of what might as well be scribble. 'I don't see it.'

'My father wasn't known for his tidy writing,' says Calum. 'It takes some getting used to but I'm pretty confident the name there is Whitlam.' He squints and leans a little closer. 'Brooke Whitlam.'

Somehow, Lucy makes it out of the offices on wobbly knees, settling the bill and signing off on the agreement to have them complete the investigation they discussed. But she can't get past that name.

Brooke Whitlam.

This wasn't something against the whole family, but one person.

Lucy had thought her grandparents old back then, but he'd have barely been mid-sixties when he died. Looking now from the wrong side of thirty-five, Lucy can appreciate just how young that is.

Nan would have been hurting. Enough to take the ring?

It decides one thing; Lucy must get rid of it. And hope like hell that Nan didn't send the death threats, because she wouldn't have thought twice about licking the envelope.

Could Mae have guessed somehow about Lucy's nan having motive? She didn't seem suspicious of Lucy at afternoon tea, more looking for support. If only Lucy could better remember the argument she overheard by the fountain, but she clings to what she does know. Even if Nan and Brooke Whitlam did argue, Lucy was with Nan when Brooke Whitlam was killed.

Lucy's so caught up in her thoughts that it's only when she's several steps past the man sitting at an outside table at the café on the corner that she comprehends what she's seen.

Mouth falling open in shock, she spins around.

Jake Parker, a black cap pulled low on his head, is about to skulk off in the opposite direction. Their gazes lock and he winces in a way that says he's just realised he can't pretend not to have seen her.

She waits, hands on hips.

He approaches slowly, more like a man heading for the gallows than someone approaching a woman he kissed only days ago.

'What the hell are you doing here?' Lucy asks. 'Did you follow me?'

He holds out his hands as if to show he's unarmed. Rather than putting her at ease, it brings to mind the fact he's familiar with weapons and how little she really knows him.

'Answer the question.'

His hands fall to his sides. 'I came by the cottage to talk to you and saw you heading off.'

'That was hours ago. Have you heard of texting?'

'A car pulled out and followed you. No signage, but possibly one of the Whitlam work vehicles.'

Lucy's mind goes straight to Dante and how she's thought she heard the ute he drove following her when she's been walking. She scans the street for a familiar vehicle or Dante's figure, but nothing stands out.

Jake seems genuinely concerned, but that could be because he's been spotted.

'Supposing for a moment there was a car, and it was actually following me—'

'It was.'

Lucy holds up a hand. 'If all that's true, that doesn't explain why you didn't call. Or even alert me to your presence when I stopped.'

He takes a beat. 'I wanted to be sure before I said anything.'

'And you are now?' But even as she asks, she's painfully aware he wouldn't have spoken to her at all if she hadn't seen him.

'The vehicle tailed you and then lingered until you entered MacArthur's offices.'

She doesn't ask how he knows who she met with. It would be easy enough to find out. If Jake knows, then so does whoever it was who followed her.

If there was someone.

'If you saw all this, then you must have seen the driver?'

He ducks his head and avoids eye contact. 'The windows were tinted. He was wearing a cap.'

She covers her face with her hands. Could Dante have been following her? Why would Jake lie?

Instinct tells Lucy the man who kissed her so ardently the other night is hiding something.

He touches her shoulders gently. 'I'm not trying to make this harder on you.'

Her laugh is bitter. 'Then tell me what is going on.'

'I've been checking out the vehicles for other reasons. That's why I noticed it in particular. Sorry, but I can't tell you any more than that. And as for why I followed and didn't call?' He swallows hard. 'I probably shouldn't be near you at all.'

'Why?'

He doesn't say anything but his gaze flicks to the building she came out from a few minutes earlier.

'Because my grandmother had issues with the Whitlams and she's been linked to the threats?' As the question spills out, she realises she could be giving away information. And to a policeman at that.

He nods. 'You should know that Harry's release says more about the people who don't want him dealing with police than any proof of innocence.'

'What do you mean?'

'You don't get a habit like that, and party with the people he parties with, and not make influential friends.' He winces. 'I can't tell you anything else. Just be careful.'

'I should trust you?'

'You don't know them as well as you think you do.'

Lucy can't help thinking that his warning could apply to

everyone in Queen's Point. Nan included. She makes a point of examining his weak cap disguise. 'It's you I don't know.'

'You know the important stuff.'

'Do I?' Her teeth grind together. 'Fine. You go ahead and keep your distance. Give me a call when the investigation is done. Or not.'

JANUARY 2000
FIVE DAYS BEFORE THE PARTY

Lucy

'Take a jacket.' The order came from Nan, who stood in the kitchen leaning heavily against the sink, the light through the window highlighting her wrinkles.

Having timed her leaving to be a casual one or two minutes late to meet Anabelle, Lucy sighed. 'It's fine out there. Blue sky, the works.'

As she spoke, the wind rattled the ancient glass above the sink.

Nan nodded towards it. 'There's a storm coming, mark my words. And when you get drenched and catch cold, you'll be sorry that you can't go out with your fancy friends.'

'But the weather guy didn't say anything about rain.'

'And if you'd just gone and got the jacket instead of arguing, you'd be halfway to the beach already.'

Lucy hesitated. Could Nan really stop her if she tossed her hair over her shoulder and strode from the cottage? Anabelle would do it, or Mae. But Nan might follow her down to give her a jacket. In front of everyone. Talk about social nightmare. Or worse, she'd call Mum. And then Lucy could be back in Adelaide by nightfall. Now she'd met the Whitlams, she didn't want to leave. Not yet.

'Fine,' she muttered.

As she walked past Nan, she noticed black on Nan's fingertips. 'What's that from?' she asked.

Nan tucked her hands out of sight. 'Must have gotten some charcoal on them when I was cleaning up after young Harry. Don't you worry about that. Make sure you're back for dinner.'

It was only as Lucy was heading out of the door that she wondered why Nan would have been up at the Whitlam house cleaning when she was supposed to have resigned.

Around four hours later, Lucy was reclining on her towel next to Anabelle when the first raindrop landed on the tip of her nose. The thick clouds hung so low overhead, it felt like she could touch them if only she lived up at the Whitlam house. Perhaps leaning out of the tiny window in Anabelle's secret room she could swish her hand in their fluffy depths.

Another drop fell. Then another. Then a cascade of big fat plops landed on towels and sunglasses, drinks and hot skin.

'Rain,' Anabelle squealed.

Lucy managed not to say the 'no shit' that came to mind, instead picturing the jacket she'd stuffed in the bushes across from the cottage.

Anabelle was on her feet and running before Lucy could move. She caught up at the base of the cliff. Thunder rumbled across the sky and Lucy found herself laughing and squealing with her friend.

'Let's go up until it blows over,' Anabelle said. 'I need to grab a book anyway.'

'Okay.'

The path up to the house twisted and turned along the rocky face through bushes and shrubs before it reached the more manicured grounds of the gardens proper. Lucy didn't look forward to the return trip, having lost her footing twice on the way up, but had managed to disguise it from her chattering host.

'He really listened to me, you know? Like he thought I was intelligent. Seriously, when you're blonde and cute that's a rare thing in a guy.' Anabelle paused for Lucy to murmur agreement. 'He looks like the type that would prefer the classics. Is Austen too girly? Should I choose Tolstoy or maybe Nabokov?' She giggled. 'That's hardly subtle, but sometimes guys like that need a big hint.'

Lucy liked to read but hadn't heard of any of those except Jane Austen. However, her friend didn't seem to expect a response.

Anabelle paused when they reached the huge glass doors leading inside. 'I'll only be a second. You can wait out here, or grab a drink from the fridge.' She frowned. 'Avoid Mother though.'

She'd be longer than a second. Just to hike up to her room in the huge house would take minutes. And Anabelle didn't care about keeping others waiting.

Lucy watched her friend head towards the stairs and then went inside, hoping to see Harry or Mae, despite worrying about what Anabelle meant by avoiding her mother.

Both her fears and hopes were wasted as the place was deserted. After a glance around to make sure she was truly alone, Lucy approached the closed white kitchen cabinets. Heart thudding, she tried to recall where Anabelle had gestured. Fingers trembling, she pulled on one of the black handles and peeked inside. Wrong cupboard. Plates stared back at her in neat piles. Sets of eight. All matching.

She pushed gently and the cabinet door closed without a

sound. Emboldened, she opened the next door along. Glasses resting in military straight lines caught the light.

Swallowing her nerves – Anabelle *had* offered – she took a glass and moved to the fridge. Inside was a window to the exotic. Fancy brands she'd never seen at her local supermarket filled the condiments shelf. Fresh vegetables, ripe and swollen, overflowed from the crisper.

After filling her glass from the water bottle, she lingered. As she sipped the water – cooler and fresher than any water she'd had before – she allowed herself to imagine all this was hers. If she was a Whitlam, if she lived there, she could simply reach forward and take one of the shiny red apples and bite into it.

The crunch of the apple's flesh beneath her teeth startled her. Juice ran down her chin as she stared at the piece of fruit that she'd picked up and bitten into without realising. She'd been so caught up in the fantasy that she'd gone and done it. How could she have been so stupid?

'Making yourself at home, I see.' The voice coiled from the doorway leading to the more formal part of the house.

Lucy turned slowly. Mrs Whitlam stood there in a knee-length charcoal dress that could have been a sack, but for the pinches and twists, and the soft fall of fabric that made it effortlessly chic.

'I'm sorry,' she squeaked.

Mrs Whitlam smiled. 'Don't be,' she said. 'You're Lucy, right?'

Lucy nodded.

'You look hungry, dear. I've been saving some chocolate biscuits – would you like one? They're delicious.'

Lucy relaxed. She'd begun to think, with the way Anabelle

and Harry spoke, and the things they didn't say, that their mother was an ogre. That, and how she'd argued with Marcelo and derided Harry's art.

But obviously Lucy had got her all wrong.

'That would be nice, thank you.'

24

PRESENT DAY

A gust of salt-drenched wind greets Lucy as she steps out on to Main Street, heading for coffee after her supermarket visit the next morning. There's nothing in her shopping bag, which she's left in the car, that will be harmed by a few minutes' delay.

She passes the town's only sports store, slowing up as she sees a small crowd gathered near the Whitlam shopfront a little further down. They're jostling each other and murmuring behind their hands. As much as she doesn't want to join a group that reminds her of a pack of stray dogs around a bone, she can't help diverting to see what has them so hungry for blood.

A couple of teenage girls in short uniforms that expose their blue-veined legs snap photos on their phones, even as a young father covers his small son's face as they pass by. The boy evades his father and then stares back over his shoulder, eyes wide until they turn the corner.

Lucy can't see anything much past the bodies of those people standing closest until a little old lady shakes her head and hurries off down the street, and suddenly there's nothing in her way. She gasps, inhaling a gulp of the old woman's cloying perfume.

MURDERERS.

A single, terrible word, painted in dripping red letters. Big enough to read from across the road if there weren't so many looking and whispering and judging in front of it.

'It's a terrible thing,' mutters someone and Lucy can't tell whether they mean the vandalism or the Whitlams themselves. Without any other viable explanation, it's becoming harder to see how they didn't know something about what happened. One of them must have been impersonating Brooke Whitlam online, unless they all took a turn.

It's too early for the shop to be open and only the overnight lights are on inside the store. Mannequins dressed aspirationally, living their fake lives in manicured home sets, are visible through a film of accusatory red paint.

Suddenly, there's the rattle of a lock sliding across the Whitlam shop door.

The crowd turn towards it as one, every mouth slightly ajar like they are all in one of those clown games at the fair, and Lucy can't help looking with them.

Mae strides out on to the street, her head high, the low heels of her suede boots clicking on the concrete. There's a hush and people quickly move aside until she has a clear path to the huge window. She stops in front of the bloody accusation, her hands on her slender hips.

Lucy's the only one who approaches her. 'Mae? Are you okay?'

She turns slowly and then frowns, shock blanking her face like she doesn't even recognise Lucy.

'Mae, it's me.' She touches her arm. 'Can I do anything to help?'

Mae's expression clears but instead of seeming glad to see Lucy, her frown deepens. 'Oh, Lucy.'

'What is it?'

Mae takes a step back. 'I'm sorry. We—' Her voice catches. 'We shouldn't be talking.' Her gaze takes in the graffiti and the crowd. 'I hate this. All of it.'

It's like Lucy's teetering on the edge of some huge chasm. What is going on? 'Talk to me,' she says.

Instead of responding, Mae reaches out and touches the end of the 'R' where the red paint has run almost to the ground, looks down at her scarlet tainted fingertip, sighs and hurries back to the door she came out from without looking at Lucy at all.

Lucy's still standing there staring after her when, a few minutes later, an older man in a Whitlam store uniform comes out, carrying a bucket and scrubbing brushes.

Despite Mae's strange behaviour, Lucy can't help herself, stepping into the man's path before he has to push through those gathered to see the drama.

'Is there anything I can do to help?' she asks.

He jerks to a halt, soapy water sloshing over the top of the bucket. His brows gather in annoyance. 'Move.' And then he raises his voice to encompass the whole crowd. 'Move along please, it's not a bleeding side show.'

He barges through, wielding the bucket ahead of his body like a battering ram.

Lucy doesn't move fast enough and gets a spray of water on her legs for her trouble. The soaking material of her trousers is instantly freezing cold thanks to the wind, the soap making a white ring on the edge of the black fabric.

But he doesn't begin cleaning straight away. He waits. Does he expect the crowd to disperse before he gets to work?

But then Lucy hears the rumble of a vehicle. It stops, and

a door opens then slams. Lucy feels the presence of the driver and knows who it is.

Jake.

A good guess or something more? Her heart flutters at the sight of him getting out of the police car, despite their argument the day before at the lawyers, but his mouth is pressed into a grim line and his focus is on the window.

'Hey,' Lucy says with a peace-offering smile.

He doesn't smile back, instead snapping a picture of the window on his phone.

'But this is obviously related to Brooke Whitlam and you're not on that case,' she says.

He shrugs. 'I'm just here to speak to Mae about an incident. They had to send someone.'

Mae must have lingered by the door because she steps out at the sound of her name. She looks from Jake to Lucy then back, her mouth trembling. 'Please tell her, Jake, because I can't.'

His hands are shoved in the pockets of his jacket but he still manages to make a questioning gesture. 'Are we really doing this?'

A long look passes between Jake and Mae. 'There's no other choice,' Mae says sadly.

He sets his shoulders and doesn't quite meet Lucy's gaze. 'The Whitlam family would like you to know that if you don't leave them alone, they'll get a restraining order.'

'A what?' Lucy asks, although she heard perfectly. It's not only the order, it's the way Mae and Jake relate that suggests the two of them have an even deeper connection than Lucy guessed.

'I'm so sorry,' Mae says.

'But what am I supposed to have done?'

Mae's arms wrap around her waist and she bites on her lip. 'This isn't personal. We have to follow our legal advice and the police are saying you told them about Harry. That he was arrested because of you.'

Lucy's body goes hot then cold. 'What did I tell them?'

But Mae's already gone back inside and Jake is following.

He offers an apologetic glance, disappearing into the Whitlam store behind the woman who's just tearfully accused Lucy of... something. Just him doing his job or is he picking sides?

The cleaner begins his work and the crowd starts to drift away as the red paint drips on to the pavement and the window becomes a soapy mess, obscuring the word. But Lucy stands and watches until the last hint of red is gone.

Jake doesn't come back out and eventually the cleaner goes back inside. Lucy's slow to walk away, with no enthusiasm for the coffee she wanted before. But she knows she'll regret it if she doesn't get one. On the way to the café, she mentally replays her interview with the detective, but the details are blurry.

If the legal people are blaming Lucy for revealing that the three Whitlam children weren't super close to their mother then, surely, they'd have to be mad at the whole town. No one would say anything different. Would they?

Exactly how much power do the Whitlams have around here?

The store would create jobs, and have people wanting to be on their good side, but what else? How closely would they be involved with the police department; with the council, for things like the special clearance Jake got to redevelop his property?

Maybe the Whitlams' reach is broader than anything Lucy had imagined.

Her wandering of the small streets of Queen's Point returns her close to the Whitlam store again ten minutes later, takeaway coffee steaming in its paper cup.

She looks out for Mae or Jake, hoping to find out more about what she's supposed to have said. The detective asked her as much about her grandmother as he did about the Whitlam children.

Harry's arrest can't possibly be her fault.

Thud.

Pain flares deep in Lucy's thigh following the dull noise. She looks down then lunges with her free hand for the road bike she collided with. She catches it, but not before it scrapes an expensive pedal across the pavement.

A man, middle-aged and squeezed into white Lycra like toothpaste into a too-small tube, yells something from the other side of the nearest store window. It's the sporting goods store. No wonder there was a bike left outside.

He hurries towards the entrance, a distorted shape through the glass.

Brian, Lucy thinks. Knowing it's not him even as her body reacts to the misplaced and impossible hope that it is. Her pulse leaping with anticipation, tears welling in her eyes.

Hey, love, you got to be careful with the expensive stuff. Brian's voice, gravelly and tender in her memory, admonishes her clumsiness.

She sways a little, flirts with giving in to the ache. All the aches.

Mum, Brian, Nan.

She's just so tired of keeping it together.

'You okay?' The man in front of Lucy speaks in a higher pitch than Brian, the sandy hair on the top of his head is thinning more, but the concern in his eyes is real.

She tries to pull herself together. Can't have a repeat of the boardroom performance.

She doesn't know what she's talking about.

'I'm fine,' Lucy says. 'But I'm afraid it's scraped.'

'Never you mind,' he says. 'As long as you're not hurt.'

She gulps past the lump in her throat. 'I'm good. Sorry about the bike.' The smile comes more easily this time. God knows she's had enough practice faking normal.

She walks away, pretending she didn't nearly fall apart on the pavement.

Lucy spots Manan when she's nearly back at the car. She waves, but either he doesn't see her or he's on board with the legal advice to keep his distance. He hurries along the street away from the beachfront.

Lucy follows. Maybe he's meeting Anabelle and she'll talk to her.

Maybe you should leave them alone.

The voice in Lucy's head sounds like a weird mixture of Jake and Nan, but either way she's not listening.

It begins to drizzle and Lucy pulls her jacket closer, clutches her coffee and tries not to appear suspicious.

He stops suddenly beside a shining black SUV, and Lucy almost walks into him.

'Oh, hi,' she says when he looks up, trying to act surprised.

Just then the passenger door opens and she sees Anabelle inside, ensconced in the plush leather seats. Her smile is missing the warmth Lucy's come to expect, and her hand tightens on the coffee.

'Lucy,' she says. Lines radiate from around her eyes. Weariness. Worry. Not surprising, considering everything that's going on.

'What are you doing in town?' Lucy asks.

'I needed something from the chemist,' she replies. She jerks her head over her shoulder and on cue there's whimpering from the back seat, from within the baby capsule. She glares at Manan. 'We should have sent for a doctor.'

His jaw tightens. 'I needed to get out of that house.'

Lucy tries to defuse the obvious tension. 'What's wrong with her?' She can't remember the baby's name but her little cheeks are red, and she looks miserable.

Anabelle folds her arms across her chest. 'It's not really a good time to talk.'

'I saw what happened at the store. It's terrible.'

Anabelle's eyes close like she doesn't have it in her to reply.

'We had a bit of a late night,' Manan says diplomatically. 'Teething problems. Better get missy back up to bed.' He checks the straps of the baby's car seat and closes the back door before hurrying around to the driver's side, leaving Lucy standing on the footpath.

'I didn't expect to see you until the art show. Is it still going ahead?' It's the closest Lucy dares come to asking if she should attend.

But Anabelle's 'yes' doesn't resolve anything.

'The baby's not ready for scary movies then.' Lucy can hear the desperation in her voice but can't seem to stop. After Mae's rejection, she wants so badly to connect with Anabelle, to get back the feeling of being part of the Whitlams' inner circle the way she was a few days ago. The way she was that summer, when Anabelle first took Lucy under her wing.

'Remember, Anabelle, that first movie we saw together at the cinema? What was it called?'

'I don't know.'

Then she's pulling the door towards her. 'Sorry, Lucy, but we really should be going.'

The door is closed and the engine starts. They pull away without lowering the window or even waving goodbye. Lucy's left staring after them, still holding her coffee.

'*The Blair Witch Project*,' she murmurs as the car turns the corner and the drizzle becomes rain. It sprays her cheeks and she can't tell if the sting in her eyes is the bitter wind or threatening tears. 'It was *The Blair Witch Project*.'

Anabelle doesn't remember. Doesn't even care. Lucy has spent so long being defined by these people. People who it turns out she barely knows. Wanting to be accepted. Working to the bone to live up to a standard that only exists in Lucy's head.

And they don't even remember.

Lucy heads back towards her car, her steps heavy. It's then that she sees the figure nearly a block ahead, standing under a deserted shop awning. Even from this distance through the rain, she can feel the familiar dark gaze. She recognises him with a visceral jolt through her body.

'Dante?'

The figure turns and walks away, his head down, his long strides easily putting distance between them.

Lucy starts to run, sloshing her coffee. 'Dante? Wait.'

But by the time she gets to the corner, the man is gone.

JANUARY 2000
FOUR DAYS BEFORE THE PARTY

Harry

Harry plucked packets of potato crisps and boxes of crackers from the shelves as he walked along the aisle, tossing them over his shoulder to Jake, who walked behind with a trolley. To give the kid credit, he was more coordinated than he looked, catching each one.

'Reckon that's enough?' asked Jake after a similar trip past the chocolates and sweets.

Harry considered the snack load. 'Nearly.' He jerked his head towards the front of the store. 'You start unloading and I'll grab drinks.'

Jake hesitated, then nodded. Harry hadn't waited for Jake to agree, grabbing some Skittles off the shelf as he passed. People always agreed with Harry.

Except his mother.

Pop. Skittles fell around him like candy rain, bouncing and scattering across the floor. He looked down in surprise at the packet clenched in his fist. Deliberately he relaxed his grip, exhaled, turned on the charm to the manager, who came running at the sight of the mess.

'I am so sorry,' Harry said, offering his best apologetic smile. 'I picked it up and it burst everywhere. I'll pay for it, obviously.'

The older woman, name tag 'Jenny', smiled. 'Don't you worry about that, young Harry. Probably a faulty bag.'

He smiled again and left her to clean up the mess, popping Skittles in his mouth as he went. He pushed thoughts of his mother out of his head as he heaved slabs of soft drink off the bottom shelf. Annoyed that he'd let himself think of her at all, he didn't bother to look at what kind of drink he was getting. It didn't matter. He'd be indulging in something stronger as soon as he got to the bonfire.

'Um, Harry?' The call came from Jake, who was standing at the checkout. He'd put through the rest of the items and was waiting.

How long had Harry been standing there, not thinking about his mother? Probably seconds, but he couldn't be sure. His jaw tightened. Were they looking at him? Laughing at him?

'Impatient, huh? Why don't you go ahead and pay for those?' he called back, taking his time.

The other boy's face blanched. 'I... uh... I didn't bring my wallet.'

Harry smirked. They all knew that not having his wallet on him wasn't the issue. He could actually see drops of sweat forming on the kid's pimply forehead. Jeez, it wasn't that much money. Although maybe Jake would hold his tongue and just bloody wait next time.

'Kidding,' he said lightly. 'I've got it.'

He jogged over, dumped the cartons of soft drink on the counter and waited for the chick to put it through.

Outside, he shoved Jake in the shoulder. Just hard enough to hurt. 'Man, the look on your face.'

Jake stopped and folded his arms. 'Whatever. Not everyone can have the perfect life.'

Perfect? Ha! What did some loser kid from some backward small town even know? This place was everything to Jake but Harry went to school in Sydney, the biggest city in Australia. His family had houses in the most incredible places in the world. Harry had experienced things Jake couldn't begin to understand.

And the kid was naive enough to believe the façade Harry and his family presented to the world.

It was all Harry could do not to punch him in the face. Every muscle tensed and the street around him blurred at the edges of his vision. He breathed in and out.

Jake wasn't worth it.

Hell, the kid was so pathetic he'd probably be grateful. He could show off the shiner and tell everyone it came from Harry Whitlam. But that would mean he'd cared enough to take a swing.

He didn't.

Neither did he tell the fucker how little he knew about anything. Instead, he cleared his throat and let amusement curl his lips, knowing no one would look close enough to see tears stinging his eyes. 'Sucks not to be me.'

Then he walked on without looking to see if Jake followed. He would.

Harry didn't say anything else. Mostly because his brain wanted to give him his own private show on all the ways his life wasn't perfect.

The paintings are simply not good.

Maybe alcohol wouldn't be strong enough tonight. Surely someone would have something more potent. Without something to numb the pain, he didn't know what he'd do. Lately it was getting harder and harder not to snap.

Oblivious, Jake trailed behind, probably assuming Harry's silence was him being enigmatic or some shit. The truth wouldn't fit with the idea of Harry he had in his head, that of happy families and life on easy street.

25

PRESENT DAY

Lucy spends the rest of the day packing and cleaning the cottage in a kind of frenzy. Every time she remembers how she practically begged for Anabelle's attention, shame coils hot in her belly. She thought she'd grown out of her Whitlam obsession, but it seems it's always been there in the background, in her online stalking, and her hook-ups with Harry, just waiting to return.

It's hard to avoid thoughts of the hidden ring, and the potential fallout of Nan's lawsuit. From what Jake said they already know something about the situation, but maybe Lucy should go to them to show she's not hiding anything.

Anything *else*.

Late afternoon has her sitting cross-legged on the floor in Nan's room, going through an old sewing basket. The material has a musty smell and a dampness she can't initially work out, but the bright cat and rainbow prints have her remembering Nan's love of colour, which didn't seem to appear until after the summer Lucy stayed in town. She'd always kind of thought maybe she'd been part of that change.

She's about to put the whole ruined mess in the skip when a clump of paper catches her attention underneath the material.

She dumps what feels like mountains of fabric before she manages to get the soaked and mouldering paper free.

Her stomach flips.

It's impossible to be sure, thanks to the water damage, but this looks a lot like white paper written on with charcoal like Harry used to use.

Like the death threats.

She closes her eyes but when she opens them it's still there. This could be evidence that her grandmother sent those notes.

Throat aching, Lucy gathers all the pages into one damp mess and then dumps them in the fireplace. Hands only shaking a little, she manages to get the fire going and soon the whole thing is nothing but ashes.

It's only then she has a pang of wondering if she should have kept it, but the thought is quickly discarded. It might not even be related to the death threats. Most likely she was simply disposing of rubbish.

By the time Lucy's standing by the open fridge gulping water straight from the jug, her heart still racing from her earlier find, night has fallen. She's wearing only an old T-shirt and leggings, having discarded her warmer layers as she worked and the fire burned. Her stomach gurgles, reminding her that she missed lunch and it's a while past dinner.

She goes to let Hades in at the back door, shivering as the wind takes the opportunity to swirl inside. It's quiet now, but throughout the day the whistling wind has rattled the old windows, interspersed with gusts of heavy rain and hail hammering the glass.

'Hades,' she calls, but he doesn't come. At least he's in sight, sniffing at something under the lavender bush in the back corner of the yard. 'Come on, boy.' She wraps her arms around her waist and sniffs as her nose begins to run from the cold. Yuck, she could use a shower. But more important things first. 'Dinner time.'

Even the two words that usually have him loping towards her don't penetrate his fascination.

She heads out to him. 'What's got you so captivated?'

Using her phone as a torch, she looks into the thick shadows beneath the shrub. But she's too late as Hades finally notices her presence and finishes whatever he's been eating in a few hasty chomps. Then he looks up at Lucy with guilt in his big brown eyes as if to say, *I really had to eat the thing.*

Excellent.

It was probably something disgusting. She makes a mental note not to let him rest his big, slobbery head on her lap while they curl up on the couch later. Inevitably she'll open a book with the intention to read but get caught up in some internet rabbit hole.

Maybe she shouldn't go to the art show. Keep her distance, as Mae so tearfully requested. Finish cleaning up the cottage and get out of Queen's Point.

Back in the kitchen, she gives Hades less dinner than usual. He's been known to overeat to the point of upsetting his stomach. Usually all over the nearest rug. But despite a sniff of the bowl, he doesn't eat any of it.

It's not like him, and Lucy checks twice more to make sure it's untouched as she prepares and forces down a Thai chicken salad from the supermarket. She chases it down with a glass of water, wishing she'd bought some wine.

By the time she's finished, she's pretty sure Hades hasn't eaten a single bit of kibble. He leaves the food and walks to the door in oddly jerky movements, but doesn't go out when she opens it. Instead, he returns to his favourite spot upon Nan's rug. There, he lies down but doesn't settle.

Fifteen minutes later, he's barely moved from his position on the rug in front of the small TV, which Lucy's put on for company. As she finishes cleaning the kitchen, washing everything and putting all the dishes away, her once-a-fortnight message from Jasmine arrives. 'Checking in on my favourite boy.'

Usually, Lucy sends a picture of Hades in response. Sometimes even a selfie with Lucy in it, and an enquiry as to how she's going. Sometimes Jasmine replies. Often, she doesn't.

Lucy finishes wiping down the sink, checking the whole kitchen area is spotless as Nan always liked it left after dinner, before crossing to the dog.

'Hades,' she says, phone in hand, but he doesn't lift his head.

Something isn't right with him.

She sits nearby on the edge of the couch and puts the phone down on the table without replying to Jasmine's message. She can't send a picture with him like this.

His chest rises and falls. Lucy kneels at his side, murmuring his name, and his tail stirs. A half wag at best, but he knows she's there. She runs her hands over the top of his head and scratches the spot he likes best, just behind his ear. A damp patch has formed around where his head rests on the rug. Drool runs from his jaws as he pants a little. Lucy's stomach knots.

'What was it you ate, boy?'

Of course, he doesn't answer. Her attempt to search the

internet for possible causes only creates more worries. There are no good reasons for him to be like this.

She won't sleep tonight if she doesn't get him seen by someone.

It's already dark but not that late. She finds a number for a local emergency vet and calls. The woman says that although they closed a little while earlier, if Lucy can get him there in fifteen minutes the vet will wait for them.

Lucy realises it's Friday night. 'Thank you,' she says.

After disconnecting, she tries to coax Hades up, but he barely lifts his big head. She puts on an old, warm hoodie before clipping on his lead. She waves leftover chicken in front of his nose. 'Who's a hungry dog, then?'

He turns his head away.

This has to be from whatever he found in the bushes. Her brain cycles through possibilities – a dead snake with venom, a diseased rat, a rotting bird carcass. If only she'd been quicker to notice, if only he'd come when she called instead of gulping the rest as fast as he could.

She pulls gently on the lead. 'Hades, we have to go in the car.'

He doesn't respond. There's no way she can lift him, but time is ticking. Her chest is tight. The woman on the phone said once they close, the number gets diverted to a central location on the peninsula and it will be a matter of waiting until their number comes up in a queue.

Lucy tugs a bit harder on the lead. 'Want to come see Brian?' Her voice cracks on his name but Hades lifts his head. 'Yes, Brian,' she lies, hating it. Hating having to get Hades' hopes up, if that's even possible with dogs.

None of this would be happening if Brian was just bloody here.

'Come see Brian,' she repeats, not trying to stop the tears.

Hades hauls himself up on unsteady legs.

She grabs her purse and coaxes Hades out of the door, before locking it behind her. 'We just have to go in the car. Brian will be waiting.'

Maybe it's a coincidence that he's moving now, but she keeps saying her dead husband's name like a prayer as she manages to get Hades into the back seat.

It's not far into town and the vet, and the side door to the building opens before she's even out of the car.

'Mrs Ross?' asks a tall young man in jeans and a T-shirt, who looks barely old enough to be out of high school.

'Lucy,' she says.

'I'm James Tucker, and I'm one of the vets here. Our receptionist said that you have some concerns about your dog?'

She nods, not trusting her voice.

The vet takes over, manoeuvring Hades out of the back of the car and on to a small cart with an ease that makes her battle of earlier feel a bit ridiculous. Lucy's assessment of him as a kid changes as she watches his confident work. She's grateful though, glad to have someone who knows what they're doing in charge.

Inside, the vet gets Hades on to an examination table and studies him under the bright fluorescent lights.

'What do you think is wrong with him?' Lucy asks, trying not to gag at the warring scents of bleach and animal urine.

'It could be lots of things,' James says, running his hands

over Hades. 'Maybe even nothing. You said he ate something he found? Do you have any of it left?'

'It was something in the back yard. He finished it before I could get to him.' There's guilt in her voice.

'Not unusual,' James says without rancour. 'And particularly for a dog this size. Did you leave anything out? Pesticides or other chemicals? Rodent baits?'

'No. I had nothing like that. It's not my place though. We're staying at my grandmother's house, packing up her things.'

'Could she or someone else have accidentally forgotten to put something away before you arrived?'

'No, it's stood empty for ages and if it had been there before, Hades would have found it days ago.' Suddenly, she can see where this is going. 'You think he's been poisoned.'

He smiles gently and in such a way that suggests she won't like what he says next. 'We haven't had any reports of baiting in the area recently but it's possible someone left something for him to find. He's showing all the signs, probably something pesticide-like. We'll induce vomiting and run a few tests as well as keeping him in overnight.'

'That sounds bad. Why would anyone do such a thing?'

'Who knows? People are people.' He shrugs but his attention is on Hades. 'I've always preferred the company of animals myself. But it's possible he's simply found something to eat that doesn't agree with him.'

Lucy's heart is pounding. 'What's the prognosis?'

He looks at her properly then and her fear must show on her face. 'It was good that you brought him in so quickly. There are no guarantees, of course, but he should be okay.'

'Thank you.'

Relief slackens her shoulders but she won't really believe it until Hades is back to his usual self. She fills out her details on some forms and whispers her apologies to Hades at having to leave him there, but he's too lethargic to notice.

A few minutes later, she's back at the cottage, already feeling Hades' absence. It's somehow darker and more isolated without him. She glances up the hill but can't see any of the Whitlam house. Her mobile phone vibrates in her hoodie's pocket as she slides the key in the lock of the front door and turns it. Conscious of the expanse of darkness behind her, she ignores her phone until she's inside with the door locked and chain across.

The vibrating stops briefly and starts again and she fumbles for the phone. 'Private number' reads the display. Jake called her from a private number on that first day with Hades, but she hesitates. He'd use his own phone if he wanted to talk and she doesn't have the energy for telemarketers.

But maybe it's something about the case. Maybe it's important.

She shucks off her shoes and taps the screen. 'Hello?'

Nothing. Only silence.

'Hello?' she repeats as she moves through the small cottage, flipping light switches until every single bulb is blazing and light fills every corner.

There's the sound of breathing. Ragged and loud in her ear.

'Who is this?'

Her hand tightens on the phone. She should hang up, but then whoever it is will know they're getting to her.

The breathing stops.

'This isn't funny.' Her voice rises but the only response is the faintest of rustles. Then, a moment later, the beep of the dial tone.

'Bloody kids,' she mutters.

But she checks the side door to make sure it's locked and scans every window to confirm they're all closed tight.

If only Hades was here. She's taken her share of self-defence classes, but the dog's huge, warm presence is like having a strong, silent man around the house. Better in some ways; he never leaves his towel on the floor or buys the wrong washing powder.

What the vet said about baiting gnaws at Lucy. Getting rid of Hades isolates her at the cottage. She's far away from anyone and anything but the Whitlam house.

Who would want such a thing? Why?

It's not like she's a threat to anyone. Not even considering Nan's lawsuit and Brooke Whitlam's ring. Her mind goes back to the party and standing there in the dark by the fountain. This time, the voices she heard seem louder. It was definitely an argument.

How dare you?

Three words, clear in Lucy's brain. Was it Mae's voice? Memory or imagination? How can she be sure?

She presses her palms hard against her eyes. What does it matter? She can't be sure of that or anything else that night.

No, she needs to think of other things. Hades is in good hands at the vet but he's still vulnerable. Maybe Lucy should let Jasmine know what happened. The scare might encourage Jasmine to spend some time with Hades and Lucy. Is that what Brian would want?

Lucy doesn't know.

How can she decide when he's not bloody around to tell her?

She makes a decision. Not Jasmine, not tonight anyway. If

Lucy texts her what happened, she might call, and for now Lucy doesn't have enough answers. She shivers. The cold has seeped in through her socks. Everything will feel better in slippers.

She's heading to the bedroom when she sees it.

The small water glass – Vegemite glass, Nan called it – rests, upside down and draining on the kitchen sink. Lucy's skin seems to shrink on her body. She cleaned the kitchen carefully straight after dinner.

She did not leave that there.

JANUARY 2000
FOUR DAYS BEFORE THE PARTY

Lucy

Someone threw a log on to the bonfire. Sparks climbed into the night sky and smoke billowed from the pit. Lucy's eyes watered but she kept scanning for Harry. He'd said he was looking forward to hanging out with her and she'd dressed to impress in her shortest denim skirt and a peasant top that was so thin she was shivering.

Maybe he'd be fashionably late. Or maybe he'd left already. She bit her lip at the thought.

'Drink?'

She looked up but it was Jake Parker, holding out a Bacardi Breezer. 'I'm good,' she said, showing off the creaming soda she'd found in a cooler. Harry had bought it just for her, she was sure of it. He remembered their first meeting at the cinema.

Jake sneered. 'Too good to drink, are you?'

As tempting as it was to take the bottle from Jake and drain it to prove him wrong, she just shook her head.

'You know he's like that with all the girls, don't you?'

'Who?' she asked. But she knew, of course she knew.

Jake kicked at some sand, sending it into the fire. 'He's not a nice guy. You're wasting your time.'

'Am not.' Great, she sounded about twelve. 'And what do you care, anyway?'

'I don't.' He shrugged and walked over to where some bikini-clad girls were happy to take the alcohol off his hands.

She didn't know why he'd even bothered to talk to her, and she didn't want to waste time thinking about it. Instead, she turned her back on the blaze and stared out at the ocean, trying to think like Harry. Where would he be?

The dark shadow of the boathouse reared up in the distance, a silhouette in the orange glowing horizon. Her heart kicked up a gear. He'd go there for a smoke and privacy.

But would he be alone?

Maybe she should grab one of those drinks after all; she could use a bit of courage. But she couldn't wait to be alone with him. Lately, being alone with Harry was pretty much all she could think about.

If she could be the second of her friend group to do *it* – not that she believed everything Diana said anyway – and with someone like Harry, it would make this whole summer worthwhile. Never mind the sick feeling in the pit of her stomach.

Without realising she'd made a decision, she found herself far away from the fire. She slowed a little as she reached the darkened building, stopping at the slightly ajar door. Inside was pitch black.

'Harry?'

No answer. Maybe she didn't know him that well after all.

Or he's otherwise occupied. The nagging voice in her head sounded annoyingly like Jake Parker.

'Harry?' she called louder.

Harry stepped into view, wearing tan shorts and a scowl. 'What do you want?'

She moved back. 'Nothing.'

He crossed his arms. 'And yet, you're here, calling my name.'

The slight sickness in her belly had become churning nausea. 'I... You said we should hang out.' God, she couldn't sound more desperate. 'I just thought—'

'Don't,' he growled.

'What?'

'Don't think, and don't come looking for me. Christ, can't a guy be alone in this godforsaken, fucked-up town?'

Stupid tears stung her eyes. 'Sorry.'

He sighed. 'Whatever.' Then his expression softened just a fraction. 'Look, I'll find you later, okay?'

She somehow managed a nod. And then she was turning and running down the sand and away from the boathouse as fast as she could.

She meant to go all the way back to the cottage but Anabelle called out to her.

'Lucy, there you are. Want a drink?'

'Love one,' she replied.

Was it her imagination or did Jake snicker at her from across the fire? He could laugh all he wanted, who cared?

Anabelle tossed her a bottle and she caught it just before it hit the sand.

Her friend grinned. 'Nice.'

Lucy took a long sip, allowing the cool of it to fill her throat and the sweetness to distract her from the memory of Harry's face. A few more sips by the dancing flames with

Anabelle and her friends, and she discovered the whole thing at the boathouse didn't feel quite so monumental.

Harry had probably had a shit day. She could give him space, there were still days before the big end of summer party and she knew the dress Nan had bought her would impress. She sipped and listened and laughed along while playing in her head her favourite fantasy of Harry meeting up with her in Rundle Mall and her friend group dropping literally dead in amazement.

'What are you smiling about?' Anabelle asked.

Lucy blinked. 'Nothing.' She lifted her drink, the second bottle of Breezer. 'A good night with good friends.'

Anabelle echoed her and a cheer went up around the fire.

'A few of us are heading up to the house to get more snacks before the parents get home,' Anabelle said. 'You'll come, right?'

Although not the biggest fan of the trail up the cliff, Lucy was quick to agree. 'Sounds good.'

She followed the others to the foot of the narrow, twisting trail. A heartbeat's hesitation saw those in front already several feet ahead and those behind jostling.

'Hurry up,' called a girl's voice.

Lucy didn't look to see who it was, afraid the world might spin off its axis if she turned too fast. A little way up, she slipped and would have scraped her knee but a hand caught hers from behind and steadied her.

Without letting go of her saviour, she glanced back. Jake was looking at her and for a change he wasn't laughing.

'Thanks,' she muttered.

He let go of her hand. 'Don't worry, I've got your back. It's not the easiest climb in the dark.'

She continued making her way up the trail, but mentally she was shaking her head. Boys really were strange; she was sure someone like him would have let her fall.

Anabelle waited at the top. 'We have to be quiet.' Her order rang out across the dark and silent yard. 'To the kitchen,' she cried.

She broke into a run, and everyone cheered. Lucy joined in with the others, dodging shrubs and trees and going around the water features.

A light switched on ahead.

Lucy froze along with the others. Shushing echoed beneath the trees. Lucy shared a glance with Jake and had to stifle a giggle.

'It's coming from the front door,' Anabelle said, the whites of her eyes bright in the shadows. 'Let's see who it is.'

Like some bad TV robbers, they crept around towards the side of the house in single file, Anabelle in the lead. The ridiculousness of it kept making Lucy want to laugh so she didn't notice the raised voices until they were all crouched by the fence, front door in view.

'I just want to talk,' a man yelled. With his back to them his face was hidden but Lucy recognised him from his stained, bedraggled clothes, could imagine the urine stench of him. The man from the supermarket. Suddenly she didn't feel like giggling at all.

The front door had been open a crack, but it slammed shut.

'Don't just send the help, you fucking coward.' The man pounded on it, fist clenched. 'You goddam bitch, you owe me this.'

The door remained closed.

With a scream, the man launched himself at the door,

pummelling until there were faint streaks on the white paint. His own blood? How crazy must he be to do that?

The merriment of the watching group had vanished.

Someone whispered, 'Hey Jake, isn't that your dad?'

Lucy looked at the boy, who'd stayed close by, but he wasn't looking at any of them. Head lowered, he took off, running into the darkness of the garden.

'Wait,' Lucy called.

He didn't stop.

'Someone should go after him,' Anabelle said.

Lucy thought about the trail and how she would have fallen. 'I will.'

Catching up with him was easier than expected. He turned at her approach, wiping a hand roughly across his face. 'Here to make fun, are you? Jake Parker's stupid, no-good, drunk dad, how funny.'

'Nah, I don't reckon it is.'

Jake's shoulders sagged. 'Why can't he just be normal?'

Lucy sighed. 'I don't know. But if you ask me, no parents are, really.' She hesitated. 'My dad ran off before I was born. At least yours is kind of around.'

Jake kicked the ground. 'Maybe.'

'And my mum is calling me like daily, and if she wasn't stuck in the city she'd probably have turned up at the bonfire to drag me home.'

'That is weird.'

'Parents,' she said, with a shake of her head.

Jake bumped gently against her side. 'Speaking of parents, need some help getting down the trail before Anabelle's parents get home and discover we're all out here pissed?'

'Thanks,' she said. 'That would be nice.'

26

PRESENT DAY

Someone has been inside the cottage.

On trembling legs, Lucy forces herself to approach the water glass to make sure it's not some figment of her imagination. Tiny beads of water drip from it on to the sink. Definitely real. She's sure she didn't leave it out. But is she sure enough to call the police?

As she inspects every room and cupboard of the tiny cottage to make sure she's alone, she imagines how the police would react. Possible baiting, a prank call and a glass don't add up to much. There was her car, but Jake wasn't convinced she hadn't left it open. However, there is an ongoing murder investigation next door.

Stumbling to the floor, she checks for the ring. She lifts the loose flooring, moves the towel and the narrow gold band, with its distinctive swirl, glints back at her. Still there. Only once it's hidden again does she return to the couch and pull out her phone. She hesitates, her finger over Jake's contact.

Before she can call, there's a sharp rap on the door.

Her phone falls from her hand, landing with a dull thud on the rug. With lights blazing and her car in the drive, she can't pretend not to be home. But then again someone with ill intentions is unlikely to knock politely.

She picks up the phone, thankfully not broken, and approaches the door.

If she's slow enough, maybe they'll give up and leave. But as though hearing her thought, they knock again. Then speak. 'It's only me.' Undeniably male.

'Harry?'

'Who else?' he teases as she opens the door.

She frowns at the incongruous smile on his face and then gathers her wits enough to let him in, peering out into the darkness behind him but seeing nothing out of place.

'You seem upset,' he says.

It's hardly brilliant intuition. Her breath is still harsh in her ears and she must look a mess. Tears sting her eyes, ready to fall.

He's waiting for her to explain but she can't. Such terror over a stupid glass. Except it wasn't her. She's sure of it.

He steps closer. His hand goes to her chest. Rests there lightly. 'I can feel your heart racing.'

Like his touch is going to help matters.

'Hades is at the vet.'

His brow creases in confusion. 'The dog?'

'Yes.'

Did he forget she has a dog? It means he probably didn't leave the bait. Or does it?

Someone did. Her head aches with trying to figure it out.

'That's too bad,' Harry says.

'The vet thinks he might have been baited, but he's going to be fine. However, I think someone might have been in the cottage while I was gone.'

He looks around. 'Why? Have they taken something?'

She doesn't want to say that they deliberately left a glass

on the sink to taunt her. Not only because it sounds like she's imagining things but because possibly someone from his family is involved.

And it's then she realises she doesn't trust him.

She shrugs. 'Probably a teenager on a dare. I must have scared them off before they did any damage.'

'Brats,' he mutters. 'But you're okay?'

'Yeah,' she says.

'Yeah,' he echoes.

For a moment she's thrown back in time to standing by the kitchen bench with Dante's too knowing gaze on her. The kid probably picked up that particular brand of charm from Harry while staying up at the house.

Harry pulls her in close and all thought vanishes under his practised caresses. His hands hold her face. There's desire in his eyes. Eyes that don't seem to completely focus, and show hints of being bloodshot. But here he is, in front of her when she needs him.

'I didn't tell them anything,' she says. 'The police, that is. I didn't get you in trouble.'

'I know.' He leans closer and kisses her mouth. Gently at first and then harder. 'I know you didn't, baby. You wouldn't.'

Relief washes over her. 'I wouldn't,' Lucy agrees. Already some of her fear has drained away. It was silly to get so worried over a glass.

Jake's warning about not knowing the Whitlams vies in her mind with the memory of him trailing Mae into the store. Lucy presses closer to Harry. She lifts her mouth to meet his and lets his expertise distract her further.

Without Hades there, it feels a little like her chaperone is missing. There's nothing to stop her with Harry – well, only herself and good sense. But she's never been much good with either.

Hades... Brian.

She pulls away a little and he moves to kissing her neck. Only days ago, she was kissing Jake. What does doing this with Harry say about her self-respect? The guy was arrested for murder, has left her more than once, and every time she's been with him it's been a mistake.

'This isn't good,' she manages.

He barely lifts mouth from skin. 'You know it is.'

But she's not talking about his skills. God knows if practice makes perfect, he'd have a gold medal.

She's seen the models he usually dates. Would stare at their pictures sometimes on their social sites when she felt especially bloated. She still follows a couple of his more recent consorts on Instagram – visit for curiosity, stay for skincare routine tips. Knowing who he's been with over the years should have frozen her fully clothed. Models, actresses, sportswomen. So much beauty and strength and grace. And she's in leggings and a hoodie – no, somehow he's managed to discard the hoodie without her realising it – but she's sticky and sweaty from a day of cleaning.

She's not in bad shape, she'd probably define herself as average. Thighs without a gap. Upper arms suggesting her next major birthday will be forty. A stomach that wobbles.

But with him, she's beautiful.

He whispers it, and tells her at first with words and then in his kisses, his touches, his appreciative eyes.

'Why are you here?' she murmurs.

'For you.'

She swallows, tries to keep some kind of control. 'Why now?'

He stops. Stares into her eyes. The power of it after all the touching and breathing and frenzied movement freezes the world until it's only her and Harry. Like it's always been.

'I'm here because you believe in me.'

She wavers. 'Are you still a suspect?'

He says nothing.

'Did you kill your mother?'

His eyes close. 'What if I tell you I did?'

She doesn't get a chance to answer because his mouth slams on to hers. So hard her lip slices open and she tastes blood.

'No,' he growls.

Then he's touching her with a rough intensity that removes her ability for rational thought.

Part of her, the sensible part, wants to yell for him to leave her alone, but his hands are on her, sliding across her hips, and she can feel the little noises of assent escaping her throat. Her body is betraying her.

Her hands are already moving with purpose of their own, with the hunger burning inside her and the anticipation of the delights to come. She claws at his T-shirt. Explores the planes of his stomach and the curve of lean biceps. Caresses his chest and feels her power as he sucks in air.

'Please, Harry,' she groans, begging for more. Wanting all of him, wanting him now.

His mouth curves as it presses hard against hers.

If it were up to him, they'd sink to the ground right there on the rug, but she can't help herself. 'Come with me,' she whispers.

They kiss and caress, bite and stagger towards the sunroom, clothes dropping in their wake, left where they land on Nan's linoleum. She hits the light switches as they pass, making it ever more intimate. They fall together on to the bed where she first dreamed of him in a tangle of limbs and, as it squeaks beneath their combined weight, she gives in to sensation and stops thinking at all.

Later, she lies still and sated in the dark, trying to catch her breath. Trying to recover her equilibrium. The heat of him and the thin blanket they pulled over themselves is enough that she doesn't feel any urgent need to retrieve her clothes. The shame is hot too. How can something feel so bad and so good all at once?

Her gaze travels his outline, lit only by the lights they didn't get to in the living area.

Harry Whitlam is lying in the bed where she fantasised about him. And yet, even as his eyes drift closed in happy languor, she can't enjoy it.

'Why?'

His eyes crinkle blearily. Gorgeously. 'Why what, sweetheart?'

'Why were you with her that night?' And she almost adds, *if that is actually where you were*, but the mayor, with her bright, intelligent eyes, does not strike Lucy as the type to lie for him.

Not like Lucy.

Something plays around his mouth. Amusement? Pity? 'Babe, don't go there.'

Babe?

It occurs to her that maybe the affectionate post-coital name is because he doesn't trust himself to remember hers.

'You promised—' Hating the shake in her voice, she clears her throat. 'You promised to meet me at the party.'

For a second, he's looking at her in the low light and he's completely unguarded.

In that moment there's… there's nothing there. Beneath all of it – the charm, the artist, the sex appeal – there is nothing there.

Revulsion shimmers down Lucy's spine at the sight of it.

But then he blinks and he's Harry again and just about the most beautiful man on the planet. She must have imagined it.

And his answer – his non-answer, of course, because that's what Harry does – is, 'I made a mistake, honey, I just had way more to drink than I thought or planned to.' His thumb slides along the inside of her wrist. 'You know I didn't mean to hurt you.'

That, she thinks, is true. But the not meaning to, and the not actually hurting her, are not at all the same thing.

She shakes free, not at all affected by his strokes across her bare skin. She considers telling him how much he hurt her that night. Considers telling him to leave. And almost asks him to explain again how his fingerprints were on the plastic his mother was wrapped in if he really doesn't know what happened.

Could a man who touches Lucy like he has tonight be a killer?

But if not him, who?

Heavy, regular breaths by Lucy's side tell her Harry has drifted off to sleep.

And despite the questions swirling in her brain, she can't help but follow.

JANUARY 2000
THREE DAYS BEFORE THE PARTY

Harry

Harry came to, lying on his back on the ground, with an acrid taste coating his throat. Above was evening sky and trees, and thanks to the lights from the house, the familiar line of the greenhouse. He'd made it home then.

He blinked, then rolled over on to his side, coughing until he vomited underneath a recently pruned bush. He scrambled away from the mess, wiping his mouth with the back of his hand. At least he'd kept the brown puddle off Marcelo's lawn.

It couldn't be too late. Noise drifted from the direction of the main house. He'd likely missed dinner but no one would have come looking for him. It wasn't unusual for him to get lost in his work and growl at anyone who dared disturb him.

But he hadn't been working this evening.

It came back to him in fragments.

Smelling a fire in the old incinerator. Discovering his paintings alight. Reaching into the smoke and flames trying to save them. He stared at his hands, the blisters confirming the memory.

Mother standing there, a smile on her face. 'You were never going to concentrate on what's important with these frivolities hanging around.'

The rage had almost blinded him.

He'd run from her, terrified by what he might do if he heard another word from those poisonous lips.

She'd never listen, he realised now. Unless something happened to her, his future path was set.

She controlled all of them and she'd never stop.

Not willingly.

He heaved again, bringing up more bile, spitting into the bushes. Marcelo would be pissed if he found out Harry had borrowed one of the work vehicles, but the shitty bars where they'd serve him weren't the sort you took his car to. His hands balled into fists and he had to breathe deep not to throw up again. Man, he needed something to take the edge off.

'I'm surprised you made it home in one piece.'

He dragged his heavy head upright. Marcelo stood there.

Harry tried for a smirk. 'You're like one of those demons I can summon just by thinking about him.'

Marcelo crossed his arms, showing the muscle built from working to the bone for the ungrateful bitch that was Harry's mother. 'The scratch on the ute brought me looking for you. As you had to have known it would.'

'Maybe it was Mae,' said Harry half-heartedly. 'And that Anabelle is more trouble than that cute face would have you believe.'

Marcelo dropped to his haunches so he could look Harry in the eye. 'From the look of you, it's lucky you made it back at all.'

Harry blinked, tried his best to look sober. 'I'm fine.' But the shake in his voice gave him away. 'You know what she did?'

Marcelo nodded. 'But only afterwards, otherwise I'd have

stopped her.' He reached out and rested his hand on Harry's shoulder. 'I know it hurts, but you can't keep doing this.'

'Why exactly?'

'You'll end up dead.'

'And?'

Marcelo sighed. 'And I'll have to bring it up with your father.'

This was worse than threatening to tell his mother and they both knew it. More trouble from Mother was one thing, but the thought of Dad knowing just how screwed-up he was… It gave him a different kind of pain in the gut.

'I'll fix the scratch,' Harry said.

'You'll pay me back,' Marcelo corrected. 'The last thing any of us needs is the questions that would come from you taking it into the repair place. And you'll look after yourself?'

Harry shrugged. 'That's not happening any time soon. Unless you have any ideas on how to get rid of bodies.'

'You're nearly eighteen,' Marcelo said, not needing to ask which body. 'Wait her out.'

'It's not that easy. Mae's a fully fledged adult and she's still stuck here playing Mother's games. And you can't talk. You keep taking her shit. The pay can't be that good.'

Marcelo didn't say a word.

Harry sighed. It wasn't the poor gardener's fault. 'Sorry, man.'

Marcelo held out a hand and Harry took it, letting himself be pulled to his feet. He went to move away but Marcelo didn't release his hold.

'I mean what I say,' he said. 'You can do anything. You three kids are amazing, and you must not let that woman stop you growing into the people you were meant to be.'

Harry's throat was tight and he felt like crying. But that wouldn't do. Marcelo might be a good guy, but he was the freaking gardener. And as his mother had drilled into him often enough, he was a Whitlam and it would serve him to act like one.

'Yeah,' he muttered, looking away.

Marcelo let go then, but Harry felt his eyes on him as he walked away.

27

PRESENT DAY

Lucy blinks at the dull light through the blinds. Snatches of dream fragments disappear as fast as she tries to remember them. She was by the fountain at the Whitlam house, in the dark. Music played in the distance as Nan snarled her accusations at a staggering, unusually silent Brooke Whitlam, the words a volley of bullets beating her backwards.

She sits up, heart tripping. But the scene that felt so real is already vanishing, as insubstantial as the fine spray of the sea where it hits the rocks. Impossible to hold.

Harry stirs and stretches, the blanket slipping to reveal a red mark on his chest. Her stomach revolts as memory hits. Her fingernails digging into his flesh.

She clambers out of the bed and makes it to the door without waking Harry. Out in the hall, she catches her breath and pulls on underwear. The air feels thick with the scent of sex and sweat and dust.

The squeak of the front gate stops her heading to the laundry. She grabs her long jacket, shrugs it on and pads to the door, opening it before whoever it is can knock.

Jake jerks back in surprise.

Why did she open the door? She should have let him

hammer on it until his fist bled and pretended she wasn't home. It's not like Harry would have rushed to reveal himself.

Too late. Far too late.

'Jake?'

He takes in her coat, bare calves and hair in disarray. 'I got you out of bed,' he says. And then he looks over her shoulder. He can't possibly see into her room from out there but she feels like he can. His gaze seems to linger on her neck.

Did Harry leave a mark?

'Did you want something?' Her tone is brittle and far too bright.

He shakes his head slowly and then holds out a brown paper bag. 'It's a dog toy. Nothing exciting, really. I saw Tuck... James Tucker, the vet, at the supermarket and he told me Hades had come in. I thought...' His voice trails off and he stares at the floor behind Lucy. There must be something of Harry's left there.

'What did you think?' she probes.

Jake's scowling. 'He's in there, isn't he?'

Lucy doesn't try to deny it. She takes the bag and moves to shut the door. 'I should go.'

'Crawling back to bed, are you? Not worried about where he's been. What he's done.'

'What does it matter to you?' she fires back. 'You're jealous, obviously, but who of? You pined after him yourself, followed him around like an acolyte.'

'Don't tar me with your obsession. I should have known you'd always run to him. You always did.'

The knowledge that she was supposed to be meeting Harry the night of the party burns between them. They shared something tender, but the shadow of Harry was on it. The connection she'd begun to form with Jake nothing compared to the way she lost all thought around Harry. And now, Jake is here and Harry is inside.

'What do you really want?' she asks. 'Why are you really here? Days of not talking and secret meetings with Mae, and now you're on my doorstep as though we're friends.'

'From you, nothing.' He spits the words, disappointment shining from his eyes. 'But I do have a question. Have you ever thought of not coming at that loser's call? How many times has it been?'

She reels back. The taunt hits right in her guilt about Brian. She was with Harry when her husband went to hospital in an ambulance, and she'll never forgive herself for that. As mad as she is at Jake, for herself there's only revulsion.

He folds his arms. 'You reckon he even remembers who he went to bed with?'

It cuts because it's true. Some stupid part of Lucy still can't let go of the belief that there's something special between her and Harry, something that would make all the history between them mean something. An invisible string tying them together. Because if everything that's happened between her and Harry means nothing, then it makes her betrayal of Brian so much worse.

The bag rips as her hand tightens to a fist. The world tinges red. 'Did you come by here on your way to Mae?'

His jaw tightens.

'Just sex between you or business too?' she asks. The words hurt to force out, and his lack of instant denial even more.

Jake's brittle stance hints at the turmoil within. 'Do you remember what I said that night?'

She shrugs.

'I told you how beautiful you looked. And it wasn't a line. You couldn't see it because you were so bloody wrapped up in Harry but I had the biggest crush on you. However you twist things, however much you might not want to admit that I'm telling the truth, you felt something for me too. We'd connected that summer.'

'Connection?' she scoffs. 'We're different, you and I.'

'Thank God for that. But please, by all means, do go on.'

'Big-city girl and small-town cop. Nothing was ever going to come of whatever you think this was.' She pushes away memories of their closeness, their talks. It's not like she was ever planning to stick around Queen's Point. 'Seriously, I just wanted to know if I'm being investigated.'

'That's all this ever was to you?' he asks.

'I have lived, and you have never moved from this tiny town where everyone knows your whole sordid history. You'd think you'd want more out of life than walking past people who must look at you every day for signs you're turning into your dad.'

His jaw tightens. 'Fuck you.'

She makes a show of considering. 'Back to Harry's cast-offs.'

He turns to go and then turns back. 'No, I need to tell you something. It's about that car accident I'm investigating. There's more bad stuff happening than just Brooke Whitlam's body. You're in danger.'

'No shit. My dog was probably baited and I just screwed the lead suspect in a murder investigation.'

'It's more than just Harry. They're all dangerous. The lot of them. And entwined in a way that's not healthy.'

'They're siblings,' she says. 'I wish I had someone looking out for me like that.'

He looks at Lucy like she's failed him again. 'You just don't see it.'

'See what?'

'Please. Keep away from that bloody house. Finish your packing up and go back to your life.'

But that's what he doesn't understand. There's nothing for Lucy in Adelaide. There's no one.

She tilts her head and gives him one of those looks she was famous for in the boardroom before her little indiscretion. One she now knows she modelled on Brooke Whitlam's disdainful expression. 'Don't you have like a parking ticket to give out or something?'

He doesn't flinch but she knows that it lands because he walks away for real this time.

She's gone too far. But it is done now and, in some ways, there is relief in the going. She was always going to fuck this up and now she has. And it's good to have got it over with, not to have drawn out the process. Not let herself think that she could be happy again.

She closes the door with a quiet click, exhaling hard to maintain the self-control that stopped her slamming it. Her eyes close and she leans back against the cool timber, listening to Jake's car disappear into the distance.

How dare he.

How *dare* he!

Her breath hitches on something suspiciously like a sob. Her nails dig into her palm.

She should go to Harry. Face the reality of the morning after. But she doesn't move from the door.

Lucy

The clouds had hidden the moon the night that a scratching on the window by Lucy's bed startled her awake. Her gaze went to the small digital clock. The red numbers flashed back at her: 12:22.

She held still, listening. Bad dream? No, there it came again. A deliberate scratching at the glass. Her heart thudded in her chest even as logic reasoned nothing intending harm would be so polite. Kneeling on the bed, she lifted the blind.

And bit back a cry.

A hooded face stared in. She saw a glimpse of teeth and then the face disappeared, but it had left something behind. A piece of paper stuck against the glass, and on it a message in blood red.

'The witch requires your presence at the fountain. Come if you dare.'

Lucy flashed back to the darkened theatre, the thrills of the movie, and of meeting the Whitlams that first night in Queen's Point.

She grinned. This had to be an Anabelle thing. Mystery and drama and sneaking out; it couldn't be anyone else. *Oh, I dare all right.*

Without making a sound, she pulled on cut-off shorts and

a cropped T-shirt, checked her hair as well as she could in the dark, before padding across to the door, all the while listening for Nan. She eased it open and slowed her breathing, trying to hear over the blood rushing in her ears.

There it was, the faint snuffle and snort of Nan asleep. But it wasn't coming from her bedroom. Poking her head out, Lucy saw Nan on the recliner, head back and mouth open. She'd never get out that way.

Lucy closed the door and returned to the window, her spirits lifting again at the sight of the note. She'd climb out. The old brass lock slid across easily enough, but the actual wooden window wouldn't budge. Knowing the Whitlams were waiting, she heaved. The wood gave with a soft whine then a thud when it hit the frame above.

As an unusually cold breeze stirred the threadbare curtains, she returned to the door and pressed her ear against the crack. Nothing; Nan must still be asleep. Leaving her pillow under her sheet like they did in the movies, she climbed out of the window, falling into one of Nan's prized rose bushes. A branch snapped beneath her weight. Thorns scratched and scraped at her bare skin as she clambered to her feet.

Holy crap.

But she didn't have time to check for damage. Gently, she lowered the window, then she crept across the yard, keeping to the darker shadows beneath the trees. She headed straight for the fence dividing Nan's place from Whitlam land. The wires bowed as she hooked a leg over the top and half fell over the other side. She'd bet Anabelle had managed with more elegance.

Or maybe that had been Harry at her window. Harry looking in at her in bed. The thought sent a thrill through her body. She moved slower, stepping carefully in the long grass. There were gashes in the ground near here, ready traps for a misstep. She skirted towards the driveway, figuring she could move quickly once she reached the Whitlams' garden proper.

Crunch.

She froze. That was a twig snapping, she was sure of it. And there, a rustle. She squinted, trying to stare through low-hanging branches, wild bushes and deep black shadows.

Snap.

Then, a patch of darker inky black in the night. And it was coming right at her. Her stomach dropped even as her brain screamed at immobilised limbs to run.

'Who's there?' she whispered, hating the waver in her voice. 'Anabelle, is that you?'

'It's me.'

The disorientation of the late hour and not expecting him meant she didn't recognise Jake Parker until he was within touching distance.

His face was in shadow but he sounded calmer than she felt. And he'd dressed more for the chill of the night's ocean breeze in an old, faded hoodie with his shorts. He smelled like soap, the kind little kids used in the bath.

'You got a note too,' he said.

'Yeah.' Some of the glow of specialness faded. 'Do you know what's going on?'

'No.'

A scream split the night.

Gone as quickly as it was there but making every shadow blacker, every rustle more sinister. Unable to help herself, she edged close to Jake and was glad when he didn't move away. 'What was that?' she asked.

'I don't know but I think it came from that way.' He pointed towards the depths of the garden, right where the fountain would be, right where they were supposed to go.

He stepped forward but Lucy found herself quite unable to move.

'Come on.' His voice was gentle. 'It was probably laughter.'

'Probably,' Lucy agreed, but she really didn't think she'd ever heard anyone laugh like that. What if this wasn't Anabelle after all? What if it was someone who wanted to lure teenagers out and slash their throats?

Somehow, she kept from sharing her thoughts as they made their way through the garden.

'What's that?'

If not for Jake's arm across her body, she would have walked right into what looked like a pile of wet rags. Wait, not rags, something furry, and was that white thing a bone?

'Oh my God, it's dead.'

The smell hit her then, rotten, and warm. She spun away into the bushes, her stomach protesting. Acid burned her throat and then the cold milk she'd drunk before bed erupted. It dripped from her mouth and even her nose as her eyes watered.

Jake's warm hand patted her back. 'It's probably the remains of a fox or something.'

'Probably,' she agreed, spitting into the shrub before wiping her hand across her mouth. 'Sorry. You must think I'm so lame.'

'Nah, it was gross, I nearly brought up dinner.'

When they moved forward again, her clean hand slipped into his larger one and the warmth of it kept her going.

They reached the clearing around the fountain without

stumbling across any more dead animals. The bubble of water flowing over stone and splashing into the surface below drowned out the wind and rustling noises of the garden.

And was the only sign of movement.

'There's no one here,' Lucy whispered.

Jake nodded, the gesture almost lost in the darkness. She'd noticed no lights at the house but not even the white of the outside of the building was visible from this part of the garden.

The deep thud of her heartbeat filled her ears. No, not her heart, an outside sound. A throbbing bass she could feel as much as hear. Like they stood in the chest of a giant beast. The pulse of it louder and louder until she dropped Jake's hand to cover her ears, and then just as she was about to shout a question—

Silence.

'Nooooo.'

This scream so close as to raise goosebumps on Lucy's arms. Then came another and another, until it became an ear-hurting wail. Lights flashed white in the leaves around them. Then flickered. The strobe effect showed faces appearing and disappearing in the walls of green. The fountain crackled. Lit up. The water flowed red.

She ran, Jake not far behind.

Lights shone out in the branches, drawing her terrified gaze up even as she stumbled. Shock snatched a cry from deep in her lungs. There, above them, bodies swung in the wind, the shapes dangling from straining rope.

And then ahead, at ground level, the hooded figure from earlier. The hood fell back to reveal a painted, rounded face and pretty blonde curls.

'Anabelle,' Lucy breathed, her steps slowing.

Then Harry was there too, and Mae. Arms linked, the three siblings laughed together, until they collapsed on the lawn with the merriment of it.

'Fuckers,' Jake muttered, so only Lucy could hear.

'You should have seen your face,' Anabelle said between hiccupping breaths. 'Wasn't that like the best prank, like ever?'

28

PRESENT DAY

An hour after Jake's surprise visit, following long minutes of standing under the hot water until her skin is raw but still feeling unclean, Lucy puts on her warm clothes and heads for the beach. When she reaches the end of the path, the give of the sand beneath her feet and the taste of the salt in the air provides no comfort.

The bed was empty by the time she returned from talking to Jake, and the back door swung slightly ajar, suggesting Harry's exit that way.

She doesn't know how much Harry heard before he left, but she's past caring. She'd think last night a dream if not for the ache in her muscles and the already fading marks on her skin.

Rather than think of Harry, she keeps replaying the terrible things she said to Jake and the disgust on his face.

She'd tried the vet earlier but there was no answer. She left a message, hoping if there was any bad news overnight that they'd have called. It's strange to walk this way without Hades but soon the numbing sting of the sand on her cheeks and the cold begins to penetrate the fog that has enveloped her since she saw Jake standing on Nan's front porch.

She heads away from town, not slowing when public

beach becomes Whitlam property. No fence means a claim of trespass would be a stretch, but there is the threat of the restraining order.

What does it matter? She's almost done at the cottage and then, if the detectives on the case let her, she can leave Queen's Point and try to put this whole place out of her head. It's the only plan that make sense. That and disposing of the ring somewhere it will never be found.

The wind whips her hair around her face, but her oversized sunglasses offer some protection to her eyes. There's no one around and the trees in the garden hide the house up on the hill, but every cell in her buzzes awareness of the grave site.

The open ground where Brooke Whitlam lay for nineteen years is unremarkable and violently aberrant all at once. Her brain cycles through details she's collected about the case. Like that Brooke Whitlam had a blow to her skull and was wrapped in the special packing plastic Harry used for his canvases. And that she might have lain there forever if not for recent weather.

Turning away from the cliff face, she registers she's no longer alone. There are two figures on the private Whitlam jetty by the renovated boathouse, recognisable despite the distance and her not knowing either man particularly well. Jake's voice in her head tells her to turn the hell around, reminds her there's been a murder and that she shouldn't trust anything to do with the Whitlams, but she lets the wind blow the imaginary warning away.

Mr Whitlam is gesturing wildly, the wind flapping at his light jacket, his hair damp and cheeks ruddy from the cold of the spray off the ocean slamming into the rocks below. The other figure reaches up to him from the wheelchair. It's

Marcelo. His hand finds Mr Whitlam's wrist. Holds it. The touch is that of a magician, stilling the wild movements, until they are both unmoving, staring at each other.

A larger wave crashes below and a stream of water arcs across them, but they don't break eye contact. Lucy imagines she could walk behind them, brush against their bodies, and they wouldn't notice.

Marcelo speaks, what he's saying is impossible to determine from this far away but concern creases his forehead. Maybe the last word is 'Don't'. It's raw and pleading, and Lucy wishes she'd left when she first saw them but it's too late.

Marcelo uses his grip on Mr Whitlam's wrist to drag the other man down to him so they are forehead to forehead. Despite what she'd thought, despite Marcelo's obvious signs of illness, it is the gardener who is the larger of the two. His arms wrap around Mr Whitlam as he cradles him roughly, but with love evident even across the sand.

There's a sheen of water on Marcelo's face. From the sea? Tears? He's shaking his head, begging.

Then Mr Whitlam pulls away, turns his back and lowers his head. His chest rises and falls like he's sucking in great big gulps of salty air.

Marcelo says nothing more but wheels away towards the doors to the boathouse, his head down.

Mr Whitlam sees Lucy then. He wipes a hand across his face and now's the time for her to go, leave them to whatever this is, but she can't seem to make herself move. Not even as he slowly but deliberately walks towards her.

Every line of his body is rigid with frustration, but his face is lined with pain. Pain that hurts to see. That has her stepping back.

This isn't going to be a pleasant conversation.

Like in the hallway, they're basically alone out here. Fear flares in her belly, her breath hitches and suddenly her legs couldn't move even if she tried.

But just as quickly as it appears, the feeling evaporates like mist in the sun. She's sure, completely sure, that this man did not kill his wife. He just doesn't have it in him. Much more likely that someone with Brooke Whitlam's genetics be the one to fight back, much more likely than the man she chose to be in her control.

'It's not an easy thing,' he says, looking back at the boathouse. 'To break someone's heart.' He scratches the grey bristles on his jaw. 'And this is not my first time, of course. Brooke would have preferred it was Vanessa I fell for, that the young, bright woman was the one who gave me the strength to end the charade that was my marriage.' He says his old student's name with an unmistakably platonic fondness. 'When I went to Brooke and asked for a divorce, she told me that the thing with Marcelo was ridiculous. Mostly, she hated that I chose someone else.' He shakes his head.

'She knew?'

'Maybe before I did. I didn't know if Chelo reciprocated my feelings, I just knew I couldn't be with her when I had such desires for someone else. I barely understood what was happening, but she saw right through me. You don't get to be as successful as she was without next-level intuition.'

Lucy can't hide her surprise.

'Yes, successful. Don't let the old money veneer fool you. When her parents died, most of the fortune was gone. She restored her family's wealth with damn hard work.' There's unmistakable admiration in his tone. 'She didn't need anything from me, not really. Except children for her legacy, and she always claimed I was deficient in that area. None of them were what she hoped.' His expression hardens. 'In that, she was wrong.'

'Yes,' Lucy says. 'They've all been successful in their way.'

He nods, clearly pleased with her assessment. 'They're wonderful.' Then he scratches his jaw again and stares out over the ocean. 'You should know that Judy tried to talk to Brooke before the lawyer thing.'

'About my grandfather?'

He nods. 'She didn't want money, not at first. She wanted acknowledgement and for future workers to be safe. I don't blame her for being angry, the way she was ignored. She dropped the whole thing once Brooke... Well, I promised to make sure we'd do the right thing in future. Helped her out.'

That explains the missing financial records from that time. Nan didn't want to keep a record of the sudden influx of money. 'You paid her off.'

He shrugs, more interested in where Marcelo disappeared to. 'First Brooke and now Chelo. I'm not an easy man to be with. Seems I just go around hurting people.'

'Is that a confession?'

He blinks then laughs. 'Not yet.'

Suddenly, she understands with a shudder that there's another reason he's being so open. None of the Whitlams have ever thought of her as anyone but the maid's granddaughter. They simply do not see her as a threat.

Wait a second, he said *Not yet*. That implies... 'Are you going to confess?'

He pretends not to have heard her. 'Life is all about timing. The chance of you being here the night of that party. The bloody shoe washing up now. Chelo's long and draining battle, just like your grandfather's, both of which can be laid at Brooke's door.' His mouth thins. 'She deserved to die. But it's my name on the house and I need to take responsibility. Unless there's a genuine alternative suspect, it will have to be me.'

'What does that mean?'

But he's shaking his head and his hand rests on his stomach as he grimaces momentarily. 'It's almost funny,' he says, his eyes shining with a pain far worse than that brief physical discomfort. 'That Chelo has fought so long, and I can still pass as fit and healthy when I'll be dead before Christmas.'

Then, like he's forgotten Lucy's there, or maybe he just doesn't care, he turns and heads back towards the boathouse and the man he loves, not once looking behind him.

Lucy heads back to the path. What was all that about? He's got something terminal, that much she's sure of from the Christmas comment. She feels a twinge for another life cut short but she doesn't really know him. Maybe if he'll be dead in months, he plans to confess to spare his guilty children?

Lucy's phone buzzes as the cottage comes into view. After last night's prank calls, she can't help flinch at the unrecognised number.

She hesitates. 'Hello?'

'Mrs Ross? It's James Tucker, the vet. I have a dog here who'd like to come home.'

'That's great news. I'll come in right away.'

A few hours later, there's a knock at the cottage door. Hades, home for rest and recovery, slowly lifts his head. He's much better than last night but not quite back to his usual self.

Before getting up, Lucy locks her phone screen. An app that promises to trace calls from private and blocked numbers has just finished downloading. Harry's visit might have been one hell of a distraction but she can't forget the glass and the prank call. If someone tries to mess with her again, she's not going to sit back and let them.

As she crosses to the door, Hades tries to get to his feet. 'It's okay, big fella,' she tells him.

He must be able to hear the lie in her voice, the trace of fear since he was poisoned that means she no longer feels safe. He ambles over on unsteady legs and stands at her side as she edges the door open, leaving the chain on.

It's the detective, Antonio Georgiades, his huge bulk seeming to fill the small porch area. 'Do you by any chance have a moment, Ms Ross?'

Her chest cramps, and blood drums through her ears.

He's here to arrest me.

Heart thudding, she shoves the thought aside. The detective's expression is more 'stoically pleasant' than 'apprehending a danger to society'. But she can practically feel the presence of the ring hidden under the floor only a short distance down the hall as she opens the door fully. 'Detective, hello, how can I help?'

His mouth lifts a fraction at the corners, perhaps his version of a polite smile. 'I understand you've been dealing with your grandmother's estate?'

'Yes?'

'We understand there was a legal issue between your grandmother and the deceased, Mrs Whitlam. Have you by any chance come across any paperwork regarding such a matter? The correspondent would be "MacArthur and Sons, Lawyers".'

Lucy takes a breath and can smell the remnant of the fire from the clump of paper she destroyed, glad that's not the paperwork he's referring to. It's not like the charcoal markings were definitely related to the threats Brooke received, but she's terrified the detective will be able to somehow divine their existence from her guilty expression.

It doesn't prove her grandmother did anything.

'Yes, sorry I didn't get these to you sooner, but there was a problem with my dog.' Having spoken to the lawyers, there's no way she can plead ignorance. She hands them over. 'I didn't know anything about the issue until I spoke with the lawyers.'

'Of course, you were only a teenager and wouldn't have been bothered with such matters.' He skims the first couple of pages then slides them into a bag. 'We'll make copies and return them.'

'Thank you.'

'One more thing,' he says.

She almost had the door closed. Is wanting to get rid of the detective on your doorstep normal or is it the action of someone with something to hide? She jerks the door wide open, and the edge of it hits her forehead. *Ouch*. He's going to think she's crazy at this rate.

'Anything I can do to help,' she manages.

'In those weeks you spent socialising with the Whitlam family, were there any costume parties?'

'Not that I was invited to.'

He nods. 'You're sure? No special dress-up occasions?'

'No.' She must sound as confused as she feels. Not to

mention the stupid shallow part of her that wonders if there was some big party she missed.

She doesn't ask him his reasons. This man isn't going to tell her anything classified.

'If you remember?' he queries.

'I'll let you know. And in the meantime, is there any reason I can't go home? I've given my address at the station interview.'

'It shouldn't be a problem.' He rubs his hands together against the cold. 'It's a nippy one out here. I'll let you get back to your afternoon – after all, there's the big event tonight. The whole town is abuzz. You are going, aren't you? Before you leave?'

'Yes,' she says. But the truth is that she's changed her mind a dozen times about whether to attend the Whitlam-sponsored art show.

He nods like she's confirmed more than her attendance. 'Thank you again for your time.'

This time she waits with the door open and watches him walk down the path and out to the street. But as she's standing there, a sudden memory snatches her breath.

Not a party, but a costume. More accurately, a bunch of them found on an afternoon in Anabelle's secret room. Something clicks. A gorgeous blonde wig among a number Anabelle owned from starring roles in school plays.

Anabelle insisted on trying it on Lucy and when it was finally pinned into place, she remarked that Lucy could have been one of them because she had hair just like Anabelle's mother's.

Just like her mother's.

Blonde, straight and shining locks. With that wig, and given the long coat the woman was wearing on the steps, anyone could have pretended to be Brooke Whitlam that night at the party.

It changes everything.

Everything Lucy's understood about that night relies on Brooke Whitlam having been alive at the end of the party to complete her dramatic exit, but maybe she wasn't.

Lucy almost calls the detective to come back. She's at the steps on the front porch when his vehicle disappears out of sight, heading along the road towards the gates to the Whitlam house. She can't follow him up there with this information. Not when Mae's already shown she'll do anything to protect her family. It might not even be what he was looking for, and it doesn't help narrow down who it might have been.

Lucy's knees are weak with the ramifications of this, but it is certainly possible that the person on the steps storming away from Queen's Point at the end of the party that night was not Brooke Whitlam. Which would mean she was already dead.

Which means she could have died by the fountain with Lucy right there.

If the detective is asking questions about a wig, the police must also believe it's a possibility it wasn't Brooke Whitlam at the end of the party. They'll have asked the family, too.

The carefully constructed cover-up that someone has engineered is falling apart piece by piece.

Mr Whitlam must see all this. It's only a matter of time now before real evidence linking one of the Whitlam children to their mother's death will come out, and he's throwing himself on his sword to stop that happening. He'll take the blame to protect his children because there's only a matter of months before he dies.

He mentioned something about getting the timing right for his confession. Could the art show be it? Get the media to focus on him and back the police into a corner?

Lucy's sinking on to the couch, turning the possibility over in her mind, when her phone vibrates. She's ready to decline any call and let the tracing app do its work when she realises it's a message. The number isn't hidden; however, it's not one she knows. Her stomach drops.

They've found DNA on the death threats.

JANUARY 2000
ONE DAY BEFORE THE PARTY

Judy

'This is embarrassing.'

Judy took her time with deadheading the last few withered flowers from her prized rose bush before turning towards her neighbour. Not least because it gave her a few moments to gather her thoughts and prepare to face her former employer.

She turned slowly, not needing to act up the effort it took to straighten her aching back.

The younger woman stood on the other side of the small fence, her sleek sports car stopped in the middle of the narrow road behind her, and the door left open like she'd flown from it in a rage. Her arms were folded across her white sleeveless shirt, which matched her white linen shorts.

'Good afternoon, Brooke,' Judy said. 'Lovely to see you. Would you like to come in for a cup of tea?'

Brooke's perfectly outlined and painted lip curled. 'I don't want your tea.' She unfolded her arms, allowing Judy to see the balled-up piece of paper she held in her hand. 'I want to know what the hell you think you're doing?' She shook it at Judy to emphasise her outrage.

'I came to you months ago wanting to sort this out between us,' Judy said. 'You turned me away so I went elsewhere. Doug got sick through his workplace, that's your property.

He gave everything to his job and you replaced him the moment he faltered. The treatments cost us every last cent.' She hated how her voice trembled, hated to let this woman, this whippersnapper, see how hard it had been. 'We're owed compensation.'

'I owe you nothing,' Brooke snarled.

Judy lifted her chin, too old and too heartsore to be intimidated by this woman. 'Then it will be a matter for the courts.'

'Darling, my lawyers will stretch this out until Doug isn't the only one dearly departed. You simply cannot win.'

Judy's hands formed frustrated fists. She'd never hit anyone in all her days but how she longed to slap the certainty from Brooke's face. The lawyers said they had a good case, said it was only right that Brooke be made to do the decent thing, for not only Judy's sake but those still working at the property.

But what if Brooke was right?

How long could Judy fight?

She was so damn weary and the bills were already mounting. The weight of it almost bowed her head; only some last semblance of foolish pride stopped her breaking apart right then. At least she could not give Brooke that satisfaction.

'I'm not going to give up,' Judy said, relaxing her hands to prop herself up against the fence.

Brooke reached out, placed her hand on Judy's, let her long nails rest on the dry skin on the back of Judy's hand. 'If we're talking debts, dear, don't forget what my family did for your mother. Without us, she wouldn't have been able to keep you.'

She lifted her hand to the sunshine so the tiny diamonds atop the narrow gold band on her finger glinted. Drawing Judy's attention to the ring was deliberate, of course; this little performance wasn't the first time she'd made such a point. The simple piece of jewellery, so at odds with the rest of her lavish and expensive collection, a mark of her superiority in a way none of the rest could match.

Desperate and widowed, Judy's mother had refused the offered loan at first. Her pride made it impossible to accept such a generous gesture. But then she'd thought of her ring, her one item of value. She'd given it to the Thorne family, to Brooke's grandparents, as a sign of good faith.

They'd not wanted to take it but Judy's mother insisted.

Brooke was the first of their family to wear it, and only then after Judy had gone to her with her saved money and a fair price and requested to buy it back.

'Give me the ring,' Judy blurted.

Her heart was thudding. Where had that come from?

Brooke snatched her hand away. 'Why the hell should I give you my ring?'

'Give it to me and I'll drop the suit. This will all be over. You say you can win and maybe that's true, but I'll go to the press. Play the poor little old lady card.' For Doug's memory, she'd do anything.

Brooke laughed. She leaned in to Judy and lowered her voice. 'Not. On. Your. Life.'

Judy's knees trembled as she watched the younger woman stalk to her car, a car worth fifty times the ring on Brooke's finger. Rage unfurled in her chest.

'Maybe on yours,' she whispered.

JANUARY 2000
ONE DAY BEFORE THE PARTY

Mae

Heart thudding, her palms slick with sweat, Mae stood in the doorway of Dad's study, waiting for him to notice her there. This was her last chance. If she didn't leave before the party, if she stayed and let herself be displayed as the good obedient daughter who'd one day take over her mother's business and role in the community, she might never leave at all.

Dad was dwarfed by the huge dark-wood desk and the floor-to-ceiling bookshelves behind him, and a book of research papers lay open beneath his hand. As she watched him, he neither looked towards her nor turned the page. Rather, he stared out into the garden.

She cleared her throat. 'Dad?'

He shook himself as though from a trance. 'Oh Mae, I didn't see you there. Don't hover in the doorway, come in.'

She entered, choosing her favourite tattered armchair by the window and curling her legs beneath her as she sat. As a child she'd often sat right there while Dad worked on one of his translations. She'd fallen in love with ancient languages as she heard them tumble like music from his lips as he painstakingly laboured on a manuscript. More than once she'd fallen asleep, soothed by murmured Greek or Latin.

The window had caught his attention again.

She glanced outside, unable to see what had him so fascinated. There was nothing but the ever immaculate garden, an empty wheelbarrow the only hint of human habitation.

'Are you working on a translation?' she asked.

His mouth twisted. 'Vanessa wants to submit a paper on Hera, and I need to review it.'

She tried not to flinch at the mention of the Olympian queen of the gods, whose persecution of her own and others' children comprised so much of her mythology. 'Staying here must have been inspiring.'

Dad didn't argue. 'Did you want something in particular?'

Mae nodded, afraid her voice would fail her. If Dad couldn't help her… It didn't bear thinking about.

His features gentled. 'You can talk to me.'

When he spoke like that, she could be nine as much as nineteen, could almost imagine Dad could solve all her problems with the ease of the mythical gods he studied.

'I need your help.'

He listened and didn't interrupt, something she loved about him. And when she was done, she had his promise to send on the relevant paperwork, to take care of the other kids, and to cover for her as long as possible.

There was a deep sadness behind his smile as she left his study, but she refused to think about how her leaving meant he had to stay. She wasn't the parent.

The hours until midnight passed in a blink. She avoided her siblings, knowing a conversation with them would threaten her resolve. At eleven, she heard Mother retire for the night.

Still, she waited.

Just after midnight she was at the petrol station on the edge of town. All she had to do was pay for her full tank of petrol and she'd be gone from Queen's Point forever. A grin spread across her face and it was all she could do not to fist-pump the air.

She was so focused on her task that she didn't notice she wasn't alone in the small store until she almost collided with Lucy Antonello.

'Sorry,' she said, moving to go around the younger girl.

'Hi.' Lucy's eyes widened and her cheeks flushed like she'd bumped into a rock star. 'I didn't expect to see you here. What are you doing out so late?'

Filling up the car before leaving everyone I know and love, oh, and the woman I hate.

'Just hungry,' said Mae. She grabbed the closest packet of crisps to underline her point.

'That's such a coincidence, because I'm starving,' said Lucy. 'But Nan wouldn't have brought me in for that. I got badly sunburnt on my thighs today and couldn't sleep. Nan thought they might have some aloe lotion.' Lucy leaned in and whispered, 'She seems gruff but I think she might actually be a big softie. Mum would have said it was self-inflicted.'

Mae edged towards the counter. 'I think it's over there.' She pointed across the store, thankful when Lucy hurried off in that direction.

Seeing the girl tonight didn't mean anything. Except that it got her thinking of Anabelle, and whether Dad would be able to protect her. She couldn't think of the last time she'd seen her little sister eat properly, and Mother was still at her, constantly sniping.

She shoved the thoughts away. Anabelle would be fine. Mae would call her all the time when she was settled. Before she could delay any further, she paid for the petrol and a packet of salt and vinegar crisps she didn't want, and strode to the door, hoping to avoid any more conversation with Lucy.

Outside, the wind had picked up, sending a piece of rubbish cartwheeling down the deserted road. Her gaze followed it into some shrubbery. Someone should really do something about littering so close to the beach. Not Mae, because she was leaving, but somebody.

'Mae, is that you?'

Fuck.

Mae turned slowly to see Judy Antonello, her kind eyes staring out from the driver's window of her small car. Of course, Lucy would have had to get into town somehow, but Mae wasn't in the mood for polite conversation.

Judy's frown suggested she wasn't either. 'I'm glad I caught you.' She hesitated. 'Harry's been seen out at the Valley Tavern and there are whispers he's been buying stuff from the dealers there.'

'Dealers?'

Judy cleared her throat. 'They've been selling harder stuff out in the back car park since I was a girl.'

Mae blinked back at her. She knew Harry had gone out to bars a couple of times, but Judy was talking about one of the dodgiest bars on the Yorke Peninsula. And drug dealers? What the hell was he playing at?

Seeming to take Mae's shocked silence for annoyance, Judy sighed. 'Look, I didn't want to tell your mother because... Well, anyway, I thought you might want to know. I know kids like to experiment, but the boy could get hurt at a place like that.'

He could. Or worse, he could get killed.

The high Mae had felt only minutes ago vanished just like

that. She should have learned from the classics she studied to keep on walking out of hell, but now she'd looked back, it was too late to wish the mistake undone.

'Thank you,' she said. 'I'll see what I can do.'

As she got in the car, hot tears ran down her cheeks. She started the engine and headed for home. At least she'd made it out of the house this time.

29

PRESENT DAY

'I never thought I'd see valet parking in Queen's Point,' Lucy says to the young man in black trousers and a burgundy shirt as he takes her keys later that evening.

'Parts of the paddocks can get a bit sloshy,' he replies politely. 'Wouldn't want to get anyone's nice car bogged.'

Lucy hurries across the temporary path made by a carpet laid across the dirt, the colour similar to the valet's shirt, sheltered overhead by black canvas to provide some protection if it were to rain later. Ahead is the festival space, a stunning permanent venue dominated by a refurbished barn. Seeing it on the signs and the flyer didn't prepare Lucy for the sheer size of the thing as it rears up over the hill. The ancient wood of the old barn has been restored to a dull gleam and fairy lights trickle through the branches of the towering gum trees that stand on either side of the huge open doors like silvery twin sentries.

She clutches her embossed ticket, given to her at the cocktail party. Mae's enthusiastic 'You must come' so different to the sad look in her eyes when they met outside the Whitlam store.

Her steps slow as the young woman at the door reaches out her hand for the ticket.

Maybe she shouldn't have come.

'Invitation, please,' the young woman says. 'It's protocol. We wouldn't want any uninvited press to sneak in.'

'Of course,' Lucy says.

Lucy hands it over and waits. For the first time she notices a tiny calligraphed number in the bottom right of the invite. They're individual. A chill runs through her. Would Mae be vindictive enough to have put Lucy on a 'no entry' list?

For a second that possibility is so vivid she sees the girl lifting her face, her expression dismayed as she calls for security to haul Lucy away.

Lucy's palms are damp, but she doesn't make the mistake of wiping them on her fancy clothes. Instead, she looks away, as though faintly bored by the whole thing. The weather cleared for a while this afternoon, but now a huge black cloud sits beyond the barn, lurking on the horizon, the dark grey of it a brilliant backdrop against the lights from the event.

Lucy glances behind her. Across the bay, the Whitlam house is lit up by a few shards of light from the setting sun, streaming between the clouds like the bones of an invisible queenly crown. Brooke Whitlam's?

A shiver scuttles down Lucy's spine.

But then the moment passes and the girl on the door is smiling and encouraging her to 'have a wonderful evening'.

She's slowed so much with her dithering there's a small queue of guests waiting behind her, none of whom look familiar. Their outfits suggest her classic black silk dress and cream wrap will be on the discreet end of the spectrum. Perhaps to be expected given the ticket prices – she looked it up – and the arty crowd.

Stepping into the main space, she's hit by the scent of expensive perfumes and a faint underlying farm odour.

Although at odds, the combination is not unpleasant. She scans the half-filled room, her gaze lingering on the clusters of guests, hoping not to see anyone she knows. Doubt licks at her insides. She only made the decision to come after her efforts to trace the phone number of the message she received had failed. Also, she was worried after the visit from Detective Georgiades that staying away might make her look guilty. And she wants to be here in case Mr Whitlam decides to confess.

She'd tried to call Jake about the unidentified message and the DNA discovery, but wasn't surprised he didn't answer. They must have a link to Nan. Otherwise, why would the sender message Lucy? And was the sender friend or foe?

With Hades resting peacefully on Nan's rug and the doors all locked behind her, she'd been sure coming was the right choice. But the reasons for attending that made so much sense half an hour ago now seem flimsy at best. What if it's another mistake? The instincts she once trusted implicitly now have her lurching from one stuff-up to another.

Surely none of the Whitlams would cause a scene in front of all these people? Staff may be checking for members of the media at the door, but these days anyone can make news with their phone and some quick thinking.

A jazz combo plays on a small stage at the far end of the shed. Even with the nod to the location given by the artfully arranged hay bales and rustic hand-carved wooden bar, it's hard to remember that it's in the middle of nowhere. The soulful music intersperses with the clicks of heels on the temporary wooden floor and the clink of glasses.

One whole wall is dedicated to displaying the finalists for the Queen's Point Prize. Each of them has its own spotlight and space to be admired. Guests gather in clumps in front of their favourites, discussing in cultured tones the plays of light and shadow, the evoking of emotion, and the exquisite technique.

Despite the knot of tension in her belly, Lucy engages in a few polite conversations with strangers about the weather – 'terrible' – and the art – 'superb'. Her efforts at circulating take her past the bar for a glass of champagne – yes, it's genuine, from France – and then close enough to the stage to appreciate a skin-tingling, improvised solo from the young woman playing alto sax. Although no expert, Lucy saw Amelie Taylor was headlining a show in London days ago; they must have flown her in especially.

The order of formal events is on a screen that will later be used to show close-ups of the speeches. Lucy skims the times and relaxes a little. With two hours until the official welcome, and then the prize announcements following, it's unlikely that any Whitlam is yet present. By the time anyone from the family arrives, this place will be so full that no one will notice Lucy.

'Honestly, I thought they would cancel.' The voice behind Lucy is less modulated than many she's heard tonight. 'I'm glad for your sake, Barry, that they didn't, but I reckon, like, that showing up and presenting the award is a bit... unseemly. You know, given everything.'

'Innocent until proven guilty, Mama dearest,' drawls the response.

Lucy dares a glance over her shoulder. The woman speaking is maybe fifty and clearly dressed to impress with sequins adorning her turquoise jacket. The young man who called her 'Mama' is wearing a faded Bowie T-shirt and jeans so tight that Lucy hopes his mother isn't hoping for grandchildren.

Barry's hair is lank and greasy, but his eyes are bright, and when he catches her looking their way, he smirks.

She moves away, trying not to look like she's making a run for it.

Bloody artists.

She tries to guess which of the works belongs to Barry-with-the-sequinned-mother as she wanders back along the length of the shed. She's no art critic, but she doesn't know how anyone could choose a winner. Where one piece speaks to her with its blues and greens and thick textured paint, she's just as drawn to one that has actual feathers across one half of the canvas.

Barry's is nearly the last in the line and immediately a favourite. With lines of pink, orange and yellow, it could be a child's drawing of a farm, but the shadows are just off enough to make it jarring and the simply drawn figures tug Lucy closer, the whole thing arousing a melancholy at odds with the warm tones. She looks up from it, feeling a sudden need to talk about the piece with someone, only to find those around her already engaged with others. She lifts her hand to her ear, nervously twisting one of Nan's favourite earrings she picked to wear tonight to have her close. Nan always said the dark blue and purple teardrop stone reminded her of the sea, but Lucy didn't understand until she saw the bay in winter.

It's then she sees him near the door. She grips her empty glass so hard her fingers hurt, and she has to loosen them one by one for fear of it shattering at her feet. This was always going to happen. But reminding herself she was going to see him doesn't help the reality. Composing her features in case he looks her way, she edges deeper into the crowd.

But she can't take her gaze from him. The charcoal trousers

fit nicely around his thighs and butt, and the crisp white shirt adds elegance in knee-weakening contrast to the dark stubble on his jaw. There's tension in the stiff line of his shoulders, and Lucy wonders when it was that she got to know Jake Parker well enough to be able to read his mood from across the room.

'Mae's here.'

The fact of their host's arrival outside ripples across the crowd to where Lucy stands. The buzz in the room, already excited, is dialled up a notch.

Lucy's belly constricts.

Maybe she can't do this after all. Lucy's surer than ever it's Mae who was in the garden arguing when someone killed Brooke Whitlam. And suddenly, as well as hearing it, she can picture the whole thing playing out. Mae lunging at her mother with a heavy stone in a fit of rage and then impersonating her on the steps at the party. It makes sense in a way that takes Lucy's breath and has her staring at the crowd with their artful clothes and artless faces, milling around preparing for worship. She wants to scream at them.

Mae killed her mother.

She'd do anything for her family.

She's strong in a way that Harry and Anabelle are not. Like Brooke Whitlam.

She'd do *anything*.

There's movement by a side door near the bar. Lucy catches a glimpse of tousled honey hair as the crowd are drawn towards Mae, hungry to be in her circle. A tug Lucy feels even now, even knowing what she knows.

But instead of approaching her, Lucy ducks away into a narrow passage. Her breath catches in her chest. There must be another exit. She heads for the bathroom, a place to think. In her rush, Lucy passes a familiar lean figure. Turns back and locks gazes. Dante. In black trousers and an open-necked black shirt, he's handsome as always but his eyes are questioning.

Lucy dare not stop, and she's sure he won't follow her to the ladies' room.

A faint buzzing in her clutch bag distracts her as she enters. Then another. Two women at the mirror look up, assess, and decide she's not interesting. Fine by Lucy. She waits to check the phone until she's in a cubicle with the door locked.

Who needs her so urgently?

'Anabelle.' She breathes the name in surprise before she catches herself, hopeful no one heard. Unlikely, as they're caught up in analysing whether the artists' hotness correlates to ability on the evidence of tonight's display.

'Depends if we include Harry Whitlam in the pool,' one says.

The other laughs, and then responds with a leery, 'I'd like to see Harry Whitlam in a pool, preferably naked.'

Lucy's hands aren't working properly and it takes her two tries to open the message.

Could you come to the house? Please. I am so sorry to bother you, I know the legal people said we shouldn't talk to you but I don't know what else to do. Manan's left me and he's taken the kids. It's all a mess. I have no one else to turn to.

Lucy can hear the begging note underlying the text and feels the tug of their old connection. Anabelle needs Lucy.

Of course she'll go there, that's what friends are for. Things might have been rocky lately, but they have history and bonds that can be relied upon.

Don't they?

Lucy sees again Anabelle's closed expression as she pulled the car door shut, cutting Lucy off as she stood there in the rain. She recalls the messages and the threatening call and what happened with Hades.

Lucy opens the second message more slowly. It too is from Anabelle.

Forget it. I'm sorry, Lucy. I can't ask this of you. Don't worry, I'll be okay.

Lucy's shoulders sag and she slides her phone into her clutch.

That's it then.

JANUARY 2000
THE NIGHT OF THE PARTY

Anabelle

'Don't tell me you're wearing that?'

The question rang from the veranda steps across the yard, audible to all those already gathered for the party. Conversation stopped, heads turned, and Lucy, sweet, gauche, painfully oblivious Lucy, who was standing nearby, actually gasped.

Don't look, Anabelle told herself. But she would eventually. The words were, after all, meant for her. She continued the fumbly task of fixing one of the small paper lanterns that would later illuminate the garden. Or, at least, she tried to, but her hands shook.

'Anabelle, I'm talking to you.'

She lifted her head then. The floral skirt and gorgeous tangerine peasant top that Lucy had gushed over suddenly stuck to her back. Cold sweat made her palms damp.

Please, not tonight.

But Mother was staring straight at Anabelle with the pinch around her lips that said she meant business. The world shrank to her mother's face.

Mae was in town getting the ice after the caterers didn't have enough, and Harry was off somewhere. Dad, of course, had a deadline. No one was coming to save her. Fleeing would only make it worse. She'd be accused of making a scene, overreacting, and being too sensitive. Whatever it was that Mother wanted to share would need to be endured. Hopefully before too many more guests trickled in.

Anabelle composed her features as her mother approached. 'Is there something you'd prefer me to wear?' she asked carefully.

Mother crossed her arms, looked Anabelle slowly up and down and sighed heavily. 'I'm not sure there's much anyone can do. Although there is that dress I brought home for you the other day. The one you didn't have time to try on, remember? I think that dress will be perfect for tonight.'

Anabelle swallowed hard. That was why she'd got away so easily from the clothes battle the other day; Mother was biding her time. 'Where is it?' she ground out.

'On the end of your bed.'

Her skin felt like it was suddenly too small for her body, thinking of the food wrappers she'd stashed days ago. 'You went in my room?'

'There was quite the mess. All kinds of things hidden around the place.' Mother chuckled and shook her head at Lucy. 'Teenagers! I hope you're not like that for your grandmother. From what I've heard, she's under enough stress at the moment with her sudden retirement.'

Lucy bit her lip but didn't answer.

'I'll wear it,' Anabelle said, before Mother could go on about what she'd found in Anabelle's room or say anything else about Lucy's grandmother. 'Lucy, can you come and help me?'

She didn't wait before striding off, knowing the other girl would follow.

'You know I'm only looking out for you,' Mother called after them.

Thankfully, Lucy didn't say a word as she trailed Anabelle inside and they climbed the stairs.

The dress Mother had bought lay on the bed, innocent material of the palest pink with spaghetti straps.

Lucy reached out and touched the edge of the lacy fabric across the bust, her gaze swinging between Anabelle and the dress. 'It's pretty.' She sounded relieved, like maybe she'd misread the tension she'd finally noticed between Anabelle and her mother.

'Yeah.'

Anabelle couldn't bring herself to explain. Lucy would see soon enough. As her friend politely looked away, she wriggled out of her clothes and prepared to slip the dress over her head.

It caught first on the roundness of her upper arms. Skin going clammy, she exhaled. Panicking would only make her hotter and sweatier. Carefully, she edged it down over her chest, feeling it cling to and accentuate every roll. Hips and thighs took a little more coaxing but finally it was on.

She'd faced away from the full-length mirror and now didn't move to look into it.

'Lucy,' she whispered.

Obediently, the other girl opened her eyes. She flinched. Her lips parted in a silent, dismayed *Oh*.

That was all Anabelle needed to see. 'Let's get back to the party.'

'Are you sure?' Lucy asked. 'It doesn't really fit and you looked so pretty before. You're just about the most stylish person I know.'

'It's fine,' she snapped.

There would be no hiding up here and hoping Mother forgot. It didn't matter that everyone else complimented her sense of style, nor that the doctor Mother dragged her to said she was healthy and normal, because she wasn't the daughter Mother wanted.

Her gaze brushed over the mirror as she passed it, just to make sure there was nothing obscene revealed by the far too small and ill-fitting garment.

She winced. No, it was just awful.

Sometimes Anabelle wished her mother hit her, or kept her chained up and working in the attic, something that would let her explain the hate that even now she was trying to push down.

Her legs grew heavy as she made her way down the stairs, towards the noise of the party. Voices were raised in conversation and good cheer. Louder than before, suggesting more people had arrived. Thanks to the warmth of the evening, everyone had been drawn outside, all the better for a single large audience.

Mother does not do this deliberately. She told herself again what so many others had said.

But she knew better.

She stepped outside the huge open doors and the large deck that became like a stage for her reveal.

'Oh no, Anabelly,' Mother called in a sing-song voice. 'That's even worse.' Laughter rang through Mother's tone. Amusement that begged others to look and laugh along.

The tremble in Anabelle's knees should have been dread. The faltering of her steps could have been explained by nerves. Similarly, the tight knot in her stomach as her mother called her name and every face turned her way could have been fear.

But it wasn't. It was rage.

JANUARY 2000
THE NIGHT OF THE PARTY

Lucy

Lucy felt sick inside, torn over the humiliation brought upon Anabelle by her own mother. Revolted by the cruel enjoyment so many of these fancy guests were taking in the younger girl's discomfort. If she were Anabelle, she'd have died of embarrassment.

She took a step towards her friend. What followed seemed to happen in slow motion. Anabelle whirled around and her hand dropped, like a puppet whose strings were cut. The blood-red liquid in her glass sprayed out, spattering the thin, delicate fabric of Lucy's peach and white floral dress. The dress Nan had bought her from the fancy boutique in town for the party.

The cold of it soaked her thighs through the fabric, a faint shock in the warm night air. Each drop of liquid spread wider and wider. The capillary action of science class in evidence before wide eyes.

No, this couldn't be happening.

Anabelle's hand went to her mouth. 'Oh my God. I am so sorry.'

Lucy shook her head, words impossible. Her beautiful dress. Her plans with Harry.

God, Harry.

She lifted her head, eyes darting around the stunned guests, looking for his familiar shape. Maybe if he wasn't here, this would be okay. But no, there he was, across the yard. He was standing with Jake, beneath a string of twinkling fairy lights. Both of them had their mouths open.

'Is that blood?' asked someone loudly.

Lucy shrank inside. Chest aching, she fled towards the closest door. Inside there would be somewhere she could try to clean this up.

A raised hand stopped her in her tracks outside the downstairs bathroom. She lifted her head.

It was Mrs Whitlam. 'Not in here, you little fool. I don't want any of that on my carpet.' She leaned close and murmured, 'And, by the way, stay the hell away from my son. You think you're the only one he's sleeping with?'

Lucy backed up into the hallway wall, her eyes filling with tears as her cheeks burned. 'I'm not… I'm sorry.'

She spun and stumbled away. Brain fuzzy, she didn't know how to find her way out. There were steps behind her when she slowed somewhere in the depths of the Whitlam house. She'd tried to avoid any people and found herself in an unfamiliar hallway.

'Lucy?' It was Anabelle, her face a picture of contrition. 'I am beyond sorry. That is totally my bad.'

Lucy's brain replayed the moment over and over in a nightmare loop. Everyone laughing at Anabelle, and then the liquid spilling. 'It was an accident?'

'Of course. A terrible one.'

Lucy nodded, unable to speak through trying to keep the sobs at bay. Of course it was an accident. Anabelle wouldn't do something so awful. Her cheeks felt wet. So much for not crying.

'Hey,' Anabelle said. 'We can fix this.'

'How?'

'I have so many unworn dresses, tags still on and everything. They're great but not my style. One of them will be perfect. I know it.'

With no other choice, Lucy followed Anabelle up a staircase she'd never seen before, then along a hallway and finally up to Anabelle's room.

She only realised she'd dripped once the first red spot hit Anabelle's rug.

'Don't worry about it,' Anabelle said before Lucy could apologise. 'I'll get someone to clean it.'

Lucy's throat was thick with emotion. She nodded.

At Anabelle's direction, she scurried to the bathroom and removed her dress, leaving it in a pile on the tile floor. She used one of the hand towels to wipe away the red on her legs, wincing where she'd got sunburnt the day before.

For weeks, Lucy had obsessed over the Whitlam siblings, and their mother. Mrs Whitlam in her designer clothes and her designer smile. She had everything and was everything Lucy so desperately wanted to be. But now, instead, she thought of her own mother. Gloriously ordinary in her love for Lucy. Suddenly, she longed for her mum with an intensity that came from somewhere deep inside.

'I don't fit in here,' she whispered.

There came a rap on the bathroom door. It opened a moment later, and Anabelle's hand reached in, holding a dress. 'This one, I think.'

Lucy took it. Anabelle had an eye for style and her taste was much better than Lucy's own. The dress she'd selected was short and summery and the prettiest light purple Lucy had ever seen. It slipped over her head, cooling her flushed skin. She faced the mirror. A different girl looked back. 'I have actual boobs.'

'What did you say?' Anabelle asked.

'Nothing.'

'Show me.'

Lucy didn't hesitate. The tiny straps made it feel like the dress floated around her as she opened the door.

Anabelle whistled. 'That's the one.'

'I think so,' Lucy said, grinning back.

'You look even better than before.'

So happy was she with how she looked in the dress, so excited was she to show it off to Harry – who cares what his mother said? – that she didn't notice until they were back at the party that Anabelle had changed back to her original outfit.

She quickly forgot about it. Tonight she'd be with Harry.

30

PRESENT DAY

The Whitlam house is dark, and light rain sprinkles Lucy's car windscreen as she stops out the front. That heavy cloud she noticed over the barn now fills the sky. Gusts of wind whip the driveway's overhanging tree branches into a frenzy, but she doesn't get out. The white expanse of house fills her vision, blurring as the rain grows heavier.

A look at the screen opens her phone and she reads the message again as the rain grows heavier still. Anabelle sounds desperate. She must be, to miss the art show. And reaching out to Lucy makes sense. Her dad's sick and she wouldn't want to spoil the night for those guests expecting Mae to compère the event and Harry to present the prize.

What would have made her adoring husband walk out? She's going to need a shoulder to cry on and someone to listen. Maybe Lucy will get some answers at last, but not if she doesn't get in there.

The wind catches her car door as she pushes it open, swings it wide with a crunch. Rain – it's pouring now – soaks her lower half, sticking the silk dress to her legs and making goosebumps appear. She makes a run for it. Rain lashes at her, instantly plastering her dress and wrap to her body. She shelters as best she can by the door but thanks to the near horizontal rain, howling in straight off the sea, she might as well be standing out in the open.

Water drips from her hair, twisted into an elegant French knot with so much spray a typhoon wouldn't budge it, and down the side of her face. She wipes it and black appears on her fingers. Excellent, her mascara's run.

Before she can ring the bell, the big white wooden door opens. The wind has its way with that too, crashing it back against the wall. She winces. That'll have left a mark.

The hallway is dark; it's impossible to see much beyond the welcome mat. Lucy steps closer and recognises her friend standing back from the weather, unable to miss the outline of her curvy figure and curly hair.

'Anabelle?'

'Quickly,' she says, her voice catching on what sounds like a sob. 'Before any more of the storm gets in.'

She's right, water is already making tiny streams on the floor, disappearing into the darkness. Lucy crosses the threshold, blinking to adjust to the dark.

Bang.

The door slams closed behind her. For a moment she thinks it's the wind again, but then there's the click of a lock and a low, satisfied chuckle.

'Anabelle?'

A long sigh. 'She said you'd fall for it. For the record, I thought you were smarter than that, but I had plans for encouraging you to come in.' As the woman speaks, she straightens and the emotion clears from her tone.

She's taller than Lucy thought, leaner, and that voice... Lucy's chest cramps.

'Mae.'

A light flicks on overhead, revealing the oldest Whitlam sibling smiling in welcome as though Lucy's arrived for a pre-dinner drink. She's wearing an unusually bulky jumper, explaining the figure. And she's holding a blonde, curly wig in her left hand, seemingly pulled fresh off her head. 'It was the detective asking about such things that gave me the idea,' Mae says, gesturing to the costume item.

But there's something in her other hand. Something black.

Lucy can't drag her gaze from it. Fear surges through her. Hot and sharp, it threatens to loosen her bowels.

Aware of what's caught Lucy's attention, Mae lifts her hand to the light and the sleeve of the jumper falls back, revealing what she's holding. 'I thought I might be able to convince you to come in and have a chat.'

Lucy's shivering again, but the cold is long forgotten. 'A gun?'

'The front door is deadlocked and I'm a decent shot, in case you're considering anything silly. Place your bag on the table.'

Lucy obeys, and then when Mae gestures towards the kitchen with the gun – is she actually holding a gun? – Lucy shuffles ahead on legs suddenly jelly-like. Guns kill people. It's obvious, maybe, but it's all Lucy can think about.

'Is that a gun? Why do you have a gun?'

Mae doesn't answer, just urges Lucy forward, through the hallway to the kitchen and around the bench towards the far steps leading up into the rest of the house. Here is all white marble and clean lines. And, of course, those stunning glass pendant lights.

'Keep moving,' Mae says.

Something hard prods in Lucy's back. The gun barrel?

Her knees weaken further at the thought, and the heel of her shoe snags on something. Lucy stumbles, braces for pain, and clutches at the bench to stay upright. That's when she notices the delicate porcelain teapot they used that day for afternoon tea.

Something triggers in her brain.

Control.

Right now, Mae's completely in control and if it stays that way, this will play out exactly as she has planned, which isn't likely to end well for Lucy. Lucy needs to take back some power.

She grabs at the teapot as she lets herself fall, taking it with her to the ground. It smashes, shards flying across the floor.

'You stupid little bitch.'

Lucy lands on her hands and knees. There's no pain, not yet. Maybe her legs are too numb from the cold. But tiny red spots are blooming where fine fragments have embedded in her skin.

'Get up,' Mae snarls.

Lucy's limbs disobey, but she attempts to comply. Mae didn't shoot. Lucy clings to that fact as, at last, she gets to her feet.

When Lucy's upright again, Mae shakes her head. 'I really liked that teapot.'

'I'm sorry.'

'You will be.'

If it wasn't for the gun in Mae's hand, Lucy would laugh at the predictable retort.

She's still confused. 'You were at the art show.'

'Clearly I wasn't there, but people can get so easily confused.'

Lucy thinks back, realising she didn't actually see Mae, only heard whispers and assumed a woman's hair was Mae.

'What's your plan?'

'It's simple. I'm going to shoot you. In self-defence, obviously. You came here to threaten me that if I tell the police I saw you attack my mother, I'll be next. It all makes sense. The DNA link with the death threats, as tentative as it is, points to you being in on it with your grandmother.'

'You're going to kill me?'

Mae's head tilts in question. 'I thought I made that clear.'

Maybe she did but Lucy can't understand it, not at all. 'I thought we were—' She falters. 'Not friends, maybe, but not this.'

'Oh, it's nothing personal,' she says.

'If Nan did it, then who's been masquerading as your mother online?'

'I'm guessing for a job like yours, you'd need a pretty good knowledge of computers. It ties in nicely with the breakdown at your work when you discovered Mother's body had been found.'

'Breakdown?' Lucy echoes. 'I don't get it.'

She's not shocked Mae could find her. A quick search on Lucy's name would give her the firm and a curated version of her biggest successes. The picture on the company page shows Lucy capable, confident and trustworthy. Stylish and successful. But why bother?

Mae passes the gun from hand to hand. 'It's amazing what someone will reveal about a work colleague after a kind stranger buys them a few drinks and pays off their debts.'

Lucy doesn't ask who talked; that description could apply

to half the board. 'My job is stressful.' She tries not to let shame colour her voice, but fails.

She's done this to herself. So much of her life was balanced on her professional success that some grief and that bloody retirement home and their plan to cut corners had her falling apart.

If Lucy gets out of here... *when* she gets out of here, she will do better. And she'll do her damnedest to help Jasmine learn from her mistakes.

'Stressful?' Mae repeats. 'You abused a key client during a presentation and lost the account for the company, as well as damaged the firm's reputation. They hired some bloke instead of you for senior partner and I've heard they're about to advertise the position you held.'

As Mae speaks, Lucy is back there in that room, her teeth grinding together as she listened to the parent group in charge of Seaview Retirement Lodge discuss the money they could save with fewer staff and cheaper facilities. They'd all smiled and patted each other on the back at their own cleverness in making a few extra dollars at some old people's expense.

Lucy didn't intend to say anything, but once she started, she couldn't stop. She told them in colourful detail just what they could do with their plans. She promised to leak it to the media; she screamed her disgust.

She doesn't know what she's talking about. Her boss, stepping in to interrupt her rant, tried her best to halt her mid-flow but she was too late. At the request of the client – a man who had a foot in height and twenty kilos on Lucy but said he felt threatened – she was escorted out by security, her face red and snotty. She couldn't undo what she'd done, but nor could she bring herself to apologise.

'That doesn't mean anything,' Lucy says.

'Except that the timing fits so well with the discovery of Mother's body.'

Seeing the article did have Lucy on edge. More because it brought up memories of Nan when she'd managed to lock the grief away than anything Mae's implying.

Lucy pulls her damp wrap around her body. 'But I don't own a gun.'

'Don't you?' Mae smiles down at the horrible thing with affection. 'Yet this was sold to someone matching your description in a dodgy part of Adelaide the day you were there.' She smiles. 'At least, that's what the police will hear when they start asking around.'

Mae's thought of everything. Lucy's brain isn't working well enough to get a step ahead. 'And you have some explanation for the messages from Anabelle?'

'Anabelle's phone is with her. The one you've been messaging to try to cover for yourself? That's already in the cottage.'

If Lucy could stop shivering, she might be able to think better, but she has no cause to doubt that Mae's managed to message as Anabelle, plant the phone there somewhere and return to the house. The cottage… Lucy's heart somersaults. 'Tell me you didn't hurt Hades.'

'Of course not. It's in the kitchen, poorly hidden so it can be discovered when the police go looking, and Hades and I are old friends.'

'You baited him.'

It's not a question, but the observation brings a deep,

angry groove across Mae's forehead. 'He's fine. If you'd called him inside quicker, he wouldn't have eaten so much of the stuff. That's on you and your lack of care. Now shut up and move.'

They climb the stairs, but not before Lucy eyes the security camera.

'Not working, alas,' Mae says, seeing the direction of her gaze. 'Been broken for days.'

Lucy's hands are beginning to sting. She picks out small pieces of porcelain and the blood spots become drops. She squeezes as they walk and some drops fall, silent and unseen on the ground. Lucy rests her hand on the dark wood of the banister. If the police go over the place with a UV light, it will at least put Mae's version of events in doubt. Lucy manages to keep her feet, and from being shot, and eventually they arrive in Anabelle's secret room. It has a new lock on the outside of the door.

'So, what happens next?'

'You wait in here. Later, we'll argue downstairs. Then, this goes bang.' Mae makes a motion with the gun that has Lucy flinching.

'Why wait?'

'I need to delay so that Dad, Harry and Anabelle can get to the art show. They're on their way now. No point in any of this if they could be under suspicion.'

'Do they know?'

Lucy means Harry, specifically, and Mae smiles pityingly even as she's shaking her head. 'Of all the questions? God, Lucy, what do you think they are? Monsters? This is my family you're talking about.'

'But you are one?'

Mae's jaw tightens. 'Of course I'm not. But family is the most important thing. And although you seem like a lovely woman, you simply are not family. I can't have Dad going away for this, I can't.'

'So, they don't know?'

'I didn't say that. We have always been close. First living with that tyrant, then it was all hands on deck for burial after she died. Some things can't be trusted to others. And of course, Harry went down to the cottage last night to make sure I'd be able to get in. Those old locks are easy enough to mess with.'

Lucy doesn't show any reaction when Mae mentions Harry's part. Not so much because she's that good an actress, more that she's not as shocked as she would have hoped.

'You know who did it, and you're covering for them. If I'm going to die anyway…' Lucy's voice shakes but she finishes the sentence. 'You might as well tell me.'

But maybe she's guessed. It's not Harry, the police proved that much with their bungled arrest. He had an alibi, although he certainly helped with the clean-up. And Mr Whitlam doesn't have it in him. It could be Mae, possibly, but she's been all about doing this for family. 'It's Anabelle,' Lucy blurts before Mae can answer.

Mae says nothing.

'I know it is. I was there close by that night at the fountain when she did it.' Lucy's gut feeling is that Mae is more likely to do all this in protection of her sister than herself. Anabelle always was entirely, delightfully, self-centred and she had a temper. 'She argued with your mother, understandably after how awful she was earlier, then lashed out with one of those decorative rocks in her hand.' Something in Mae's face tells

Lucy she's missing something. 'Or did she push her and her head struck the fountain?'

She can almost, almost see it. Brooke Whitlam in the shallow water. Could she have drowned? The skull fracture found on the body doesn't mean that is all that happened.

The gun is suddenly pointing straight at Lucy. 'All the more reason to get rid of you.'

It's an admission of sorts, but there's no joy in the validation. Turns out being right isn't much consolation.

'But not yet,' Lucy reminds Mae quickly.

She smiles. 'Not yet,' she agrees. 'We need to wait until everyone arrives and then I'll let them know that I've been delayed by a message from you. Then, I'll call the police.' She glances down. 'Oh, and since I'm rushing to the show, I probably need a change of outfit.'

Mae stops at the door.

It would be irrational to hope she's changed her mind. Then again, hope is hardly a rational thing.

'You should know the truth,' she says.

'About your mother? I already do.'

'No, about that summer.' Her tone is pitying but her eyes are cruel. 'Anabelle only hung out with you because she owed your grandmother.'

It's ridiculous after nineteen years that Lucy should even care, but the jab lands deep.

'She damaged Judy's car the day before you came,' Mae continues. 'Being nice to you was the condition of her not blabbing to Mother.'

Part of Lucy wants to hit back, to tell Mae the disdain is mutual and she didn't like any of them back then. But she'd be lying.

'I liked her,' Lucy replies, slowly and deliberately. It fits with the way Nan always said not to get too caught up with the Whitlams, like she'd started something she didn't mean to. 'I liked all of you. Maybe that makes me naive, but I was sixteen and I believed in people. I can live with that.'

Mae's lips press together. 'Or not,' she says, leaving and slamming the small door closed.

Lucy lunges for it, but not in time. There's the rattle of the lock sliding into place on the other side.

She's trapped.

31

PRESENT DAY

Lucy sits on the window seat in the tower in Anabelle's secret room, anticipating pain. She must end this somehow before Mae, with her polite smile and deliberate hands, can return.

But there's no way out.

No way to overpower her, no one wondering where Lucy is, as the rain and wind lash the windows and somewhere, far away, the ocean pounds the sand. It's the knowledge of what's coming that makes her skin slick with sweat.

She'd rather ten violent blows than this waiting. This knowing.

She should be using this time to think, plan, attempt to escape, but her initial search of the room for an exit yields nothing. The smell of her own damp and sweaty fear overrides the musty odour of old teenage things left forgotten for years. Forgotten like Lucy will be if she doesn't do something. She forces herself to move again, closely examining every window, but even if she could smash the glass and lever off the designer metal grille, it's a long way down to the ground. The window maintenance Mae had Dante doing the day Lucy came for tea was time well spent.

Frustrated, she kicks off her heels, satisfied when they thunk into the wall. Less so when they leave no damage.

As she returns to the seat, her dress clings to her cold skin. Suddenly alive with something to do, she diverts instead to a box of old clothes next to a bookshelf. At least she can thaw out before she's killed. And her body dressed in Whitlam clothes adds an extra layer of difficulty to Mae's story. Lucy's under no illusion Mae won't think of an explanation, but she's making it harder.

Old tracksuit bottoms and a hoodie lie beneath some dress-ups. Once she longed for these labels. Swapping the dress for the warmer clothes, she leaves it draped across the top of the box to be found. However, she places Nan's earrings less obviously by the window in the hope they'll be a clue to what really happened here.

The tiny wounds on her hands have dried, but any blood she leaves will be difficult to explain to the police. When she fell earlier, she grabbed the largest piece of teapot she could, hiding it from Mae's sight. Now, gritting her teeth, Lucy pretends this is happening to someone else, and slices the sharpest edge of the porcelain shard across her palm. The skin parts, red appears, and a moment later pain wobbles her vision.

Eyes closed, she sucks in air until the world steadies, then spreads the blood as far as she can. Under the seat cushions, beneath the pink and purple rug, in the pages of childhood books.

Too soon, she's sitting again on the window seat with nothing but her dread for company. The last few days replay in her head. From wishing she'd never come at Anabelle's message, to the deep regret of hurting Jake. Fucking up again, and sleeping with Harry.

Because sex with Harry is safe.

It hits Lucy like the teapot shattering across her head.

She didn't sleep with Harry because he's hot and charming and radiates charisma. She didn't sleep with him because she's clinging to some teenage fantasy. Nor because she thought he might tell her who really killed his mother.

Harry is safe. Safe in a way that Jake Parker – decent local cop who watches *Great British Bake Off* and tells Lucy to be careful – isn't. Turns out that the most thrilling and dangerous man she's ever met appeals so much because she's so damn scared of losing someone again.

Jake was right about that summer. They'd become friends. And she trusted him in a way she never trusted Harry. That was why she stayed with him that night. Not because she was drunk or overflowing with teenage hormones, although that's true too, but because she liked Jake. Really liked him.

She really likes him now.

Pity she didn't work this out without being imprisoned in a tower, her death approaching.

Tears threaten again and Lucy struggles to swallow past the lump in her throat. She's always had a knack for timing. She presses her nose to the glass and stares out into the darkness where the town lies somewhere beyond.

The town below.

She jumps to her feet, slips the shard into the hoodie pocket and grabs the biggest blanket she can find. It's threadbare and moth-eaten but mostly intact. Surely a flashing light will catch the attention of someone out there.

Too late. There's the thud of steps and then the door is opening. Still, Lucy grips the blanket and lifts one foot on to the window seat.

'I will shoot you,' Mae says calmly.

'Shooting me in the back up here doesn't fit your story. No one is going to believe it.'

Mae chuckles. 'That's the problem with new money, you can never understand. If I pay enough, people will believe whatever I want.'

Lucy lets the blanket fall.

Mae's gaze flickers over her outfit. 'Nice try, but I'll say you must have stolen them days ago. Come to think of it, we did have a disturbance.'

'Did you always plan to frame me?' It's something Lucy can't get her head around.

'I've thought about how this would play out and made a number of plans but I have to admit, when you opened the door of Judy's house it was quite the gift. Judy was already a candidate, retiring at the right time and that silly vendetta. It was just my luck that you couldn't stay away. Like on Mother's social media – well, let's just say those messages you sent her were quite touching. Did you never think it strange that she didn't reply?'

Heat floods Lucy's body, embarrassment at what she wrote to Brooke Whitlam being read by Mae still affecting her, despite the threat.

'Back to the kitchen,' Mae says.

Lucy takes her time, rewarded with a nudge of the barrel more than once.

'So, you stayed here out of guilt?' Lucy asks at the top of the stairs. 'Is that it? You turned down Oxford as some kind of penance?' It's as much to occupy Mae as because Lucy wants to know.

'I am not going to change my mind, Lucy.'

She is so calm. So in control. And Lucy needs to find some

of that, but every time she speaks her voice breaks. The fear. The panic clawing at her chest. The sight of that fucking gun.

But Mae doesn't seem to notice the blood on the banister.

'Why not change your mind?' Lucy asks, when they reach the kitchen. 'Someone as successful as you must be able to admit the possibility of change. To ignore it is to close off paths, paths that may well be optimal.' Her voice wobbling at the end takes away from her little speech.

'Because there's no better plan,' Mae says. 'Not for me, anyway. And regarding your question, Anabelle needed me here. They all did.'

The shard of porcelain bites into Lucy's waist where she tucked it into the pocket of the hoodie. It's not a lot against a gun, but its presence takes the edge off the panic. Only this morning she was sure she didn't have a life to go back to; now she's not going to give it up without a fight.

Keep Mae talking. Time gives Lucy hope, gives her a chance to think of something. She must believe she's smarter than Mae realises. Must believe the other woman will crack if pushed.

Lucy scrambles for something to say. 'The police are close to working it out.' It's a guess but as the words come out, they feel right. Jake repeatedly telling her that she's in danger. His mention of the car. Combined with Mae's comment on how hard Nan has been to replace. She said at the dinner party that the waiting staff were new.

The Whitlams would have to have been talking about the discovery of the body around the house, easy to be overheard by the help, which none of them even really consider as people. With all the security cameras, Mae would know if the housekeeper had been nearby when they were talking about their mother.

How would Mae handle a housekeeper who knew too much? A faked car crash and a fire to get rid of the evidence? Disposing of some hired help would mean nothing to the woman in front of Lucy when it's to save her family.

'Who?' Mae frowns. 'What?'

'Jake. He's going to identify the woman in the car. He's going to link the supposed accident to you and then everything will come undone.'

Mae doesn't flinch, and despite herself, Lucy's impressed.

'A staged accident killing off your hired help and me dead, too. You're building quite the body count. The police will be suspicious.' She thinks of how Jake trailed Mae into the store, that strange connection between them, and how suspiciously he's been acting. Maybe Jake isn't much of a threat. 'You might be able to fool the locals, but you've met Georgiades.'

'Everyone has a price,' Mae says. 'Even your boy.'

'He's not mine.' Lucy doesn't try to hide the sadness in her tone.

One side of Mae's mouth kicks up in a twisted smile. 'I'll be sure to pass on any farewells you have to Jakey-boy. Of the physical variety, anyway. He's certainly had a... what do the kids say these days? Glow up? Not bad at all.'

It seems Lucy's reached some kind of fear maximum because the taunt doesn't do anything but give her an idea to keep Mae talking. 'If you're fulfilling last wishes and all, tell me this – how did you manage to set up that whole fake exit, and then get rid of the body with no witnesses? The place must have been crawling with people. I know we went home just after your mother supposedly left, but others stayed for the drinks and the food. Nice touch with the wig and the dramatic exit, but Georgiades is on to you. So, Anabelle killed her, you wrapped her up and then waited for the coast to clear?' Lucy shakes her head. 'That's an almost impossible feat.'

Lucy holds her breath. Has she pushed too far? Been too obvious in her attempt to goad Mae into telling more? Some of the dread has gone, replaced by a whole lot of nothing. Like Lucy's an observer rather than a participant. A numb distance that lets her think.

Mae sighs. 'Not really. Just took a bit of timing. Had to beat the dawn swimmers. And avoid the drunks on the beach.'

'Drunks?'

Her lip curls. 'Public beaches aren't for sleeping, and that goes double for private property.'

'Someone saw you.' Lucy tucks the nugget away. If she can get out of there, she'll be able to tell the police there was a witness.

'We did Jake a favour,' Mae says. 'If his dad hadn't stuck his nose in, I wouldn't have had to deal with him. Still, turned out well for young Parker, I reckon. Put him on the right track.'

Is she actually claiming responsibility for Jake's career... and before that for his father's death? Lucy's witness hope vanishes as fast as it appeared.

'What has any of that got to do with you?' she asks. 'Teddy Parker shot himself in their wool shed.'

Mae's eyebrows arch. 'So they say.'

'What does that mean?'

She'd been leaning against the bench but now she straightens. 'Enough talking.'

Lucy's lost her attention. And she's no nearer to getting close enough to use the porcelain shard, nor far enough to run. 'But what about the ring?'

Mae shrugs, but the show of indifference doesn't matter. Her eyes tell a different story.

'You want to know about it, I know you do. What is it? Some kind of memento?'

'It's nothing.'

Again, the flash of pain on her face says otherwise.

'Maybe it's something you remember on your mother's hand from a time before she poisoned you all against her. Maybe it's the trophy that will allow you to believe she really is gone, after you've spent so many years pretending to the world that she's still alive. It must be hard to tell fantasy from reality after so long.'

Is the barrel of the gun drooping a little towards the ground?

Mae's listening.

Lucy pushes on. 'I think you want your mother's ring back more than anyone knows.'

'I don't.'

'It must be so hard,' Lucy continues. 'In all of this, I bet no one stops to think how hard it's been on you. Staying here. Being the one to hold everything together. You lost your mother long before that night. Who looks after you?'

The gun straightens. 'My family.'

'I know,' Lucy agrees quickly. 'You are all so close. Except, well, they're not here, are they?'

'What's that supposed to mean?'

'It means, they're at a party and they've left the dirty work to you. Again.'

Mae's face changes as the words land. She lifts a hand to drag it across her eyes. Tears?

Whatever. It's Lucy's chance. She hurls the porcelain as hard as she can. But not at Mae. Above her head, the spun-glass pendant light shatters. Glass rains.

Mae ducks.

Lucy runs.

32

PRESENT DAY

Bang.

Heat flares in Lucy's left arm, a red poker scraping across her flesh.

Don't stop.

Don't look down.

She's in the hallway, slamming doors behind her, but Mae's following.

Lucy makes it out to the porch, trips and fall down the steps, landing on the perfectly manicured lawn. Tasting the rain, and enveloped by the scent of wet earth. She risks a glance behind her and her gaze locks with Mae's, distant though she is through the open door.

Bang.

No heat this time.

She scrambles back to her feet and veers into the trees. She can't give Mae another clear shot. Ducking and weaving, she ignores the scrape of branches and sting of stones beneath her feet. The rasp of her breath drowns everything else.

Taking cover behind the trunk of a tree, she tries to listen for Mae.

Big mistake.

Stopping allows enough of the shock and adrenaline to

fade so that pain flares. It's like fireworks of agony, set off from her arm, searing through her body to explode behind her eyes. A yelp escapes her throat. She looks down at what she's been avoiding since that first bang and sees red seeping through the thick material. Acid burns her throat as her brain tries to make sense of the evidence before her.

Mae shot her.

She's been shot.

Somewhere, there's the snap of a branch beneath a foot, but it's impossible to tell how close it is because of the gusts of wind, and Lucy's flailing brain. Knowing her confusion is probably shock doesn't help her think straight.

She pushes off the trunk, forces her legs to move faster. Away from Mae and her gun. From the house and the pain. Away. Must get away.

In her head, the bang of the gun is the slow-motion, echoing soundtrack to the memory of Mae's face when she fired that second time. Teeth bared in fury, eyes blazing with intent. Skin flushed with rage. Nobody thwarts a Whitlam.

She will not miss again.

The knowledge beats through Lucy like a whip. Drives wobbly legs to move, despite the flare of her ankle from the fall on the first day. Somehow she stays upright, dodging low branches and jutting, hungry roots. Her breath snags and hisses in her throat.

She will not miss again.

Moving with the ease of familiarity with the garden, Mae follows. Soundless, but for the crunch of sticks underfoot. The faint slap of her steps across wet lawn. She wastes no energy on threats. They both know her plan.

She will not miss again.

Hot fire spreads from Lucy's arm. There's red soaked through the hoodie but she can't let herself think of what that might mean. Can't bring to mind arteries and bleed-out times. She can only hope it's all bark and no bite. She fights for oxygen in agonised gasps as her chest protests the rapid thud of her heart. There are no more trees ahead.

'No further.'

Lucy stops. Not only because Mae's command is accompanied by her raising the gun, but the edge of the cliff must be close. Maybe the path is past the silver birch around to Lucy's left but in other places it's only sheer rock face and a very long way down. The growl of the sea striking stone suggests the tide is in somewhere far below, but the water won't be deep enough to break Lucy's fall.

Each gasp for breath sends pain shooting through her arm. The tree branches high above and behind Mae begin to spin again and Lucy blinks hard to make them stay still.

She's all out of ideas, but she can't give up. 'You should know that whatever story you've concocted won't work. The police won't buy it.'

'Really?'

Lucy holds up her palms, ignoring the stab of pain, hoping Mae can see the marks despite the low light. 'I bled all over the place after I fell.' There's the wail of sirens in the distance and Mae's hand tightens on the gun. 'Through the hallways, on the stairs, and Anabelle's secret room is basically a bloodbath.'

The gun wavers. 'I'll think of something.'

'You're running out of time.'

It was the wrong thing to say. Mae moves closer, each foot placement deliberate and sure. Unlike Lucy, she knows every inch of this garden. 'I am, aren't I?'

Lucy edges backwards. The ground gives beneath her heel. She lurches a little and hopes Mae didn't notice. The dirt and gravel Lucy freed with her movement tumbles down and down. The tiny sounds of pebbles bouncing off rock fade, rather than stop.

Her mouth dries. It seems she's found the cliff.

Mae approaches in a slow saunter. 'We need to be a bit closer for this self-defence thing to work, and of course I need your prints on the gun. But that part can wait until afterwards.'

Lucy chances her luck and takes a step sideways, away from the cliff. Maybe she can confuse Mae about exactly where the edge lies. 'I looked up to you,' Lucy says, trying to keep Mae's focus. 'I should have realised what kind of person you are.'

'We Whitlams can be a persuasive bunch.'

With every step, the chance Mae will miss Lucy decreases. Some vain part of Lucy hopes the other woman can't see her hands shaking. Fear? Shock? It probably doesn't matter.

A shaft of moonlight brightens the small clearing, but it's gone again a moment later as clouds scurry overhead with the wind. Not even the weather is on Lucy's side. The heavy rain of earlier might have given her a chance.

'Any last words?' Mae asks.

The intent in her tone turns Lucy's insides to liquid. The jagged pant of her breath is loud and the end of the gun fills her vision. Everything else disappears.

There's a rustle in the bushes.

They turn as one. But Mae doesn't react in time. The shape launches at her. A monster from the dark.

Thud. Paws hit her chest. She flies backwards.

Crack. Her head hits a branch. She lands hard, the gun sailing from her hand into the darkness.

Forcing her feet to move at last, Lucy stumbles towards where Hades stands over Mae's unmoving body, teeth bared. Every part of Lucy wants to run, but she can't be sure where the cliff lies and she can't leave Hades.

Lucy holds her breath, both hoping and not that Mae will move. Exhaling only when Mae stirs and tries to roll over on to her hands and knees. Lucy can't let her. If she gets up, she'll find the gun. Ignoring Mae's efforts to rise and the weak blows to her face and body, Lucy collapses on to the other woman's chest. She tangles a hand in her hair, pulls back her head and plants a knee on her throat to pin her to the dark, wet earth.

'Good dog,' Lucy says to the panting hulk close by. And then to Mae, 'Seems you didn't shut Nan's cottage door properly.'

Mae blinks rapidly, her pupils dilated. Clearly, she's disoriented from the blow to her head, but she could regain her senses at any moment. Lucy grits her teeth and manages to move to pin her arms as well. Mae's nails dig into Lucy's flesh but the pain is distant.

Lucy chokes in a breath filled with the expensive, oriental notes of Mae's perfume. The smell tugs at her memories of wanting so badly to be part of the Whitlams' expensive world.

'You don't have to do this,' Lucy says.

She just needs to hold Mae for a couple of minutes. The sirens are close now, stopped in the drive. There's the distant flash of red and blue through the trees. The police will come.

'They'll go to the house first,' Mae says, as if she can read

Lucy's thoughts. She strains, edges Lucy back. 'You won't hold on.'

If she gets away, she'll go for the gun. Lucy might find it first... but she might not. Tears blur her vision as the pain in her shoulder ramps up another notch.

Hades growls, reminding Lucy of what's at stake.

She can't risk it.

'We're here,' she cries, the effort making the garden spin. 'Help!'

'You won't hold me,' Mae says. 'And then I'll kill you.'

'You have that night all wrong,' Lucy blurts out. This close, with Mae's face exposed by the dull light from a moon trying to break through the thinning clouds, Lucy can't miss her eyes widening. 'Anabelle didn't kill your mother.'

'Bullshit.' Mae squirms with renewed effort. 'You'll say anything.'

That's true, but through all of tonight, as the last pieces have fallen into place, another truth has formed in Lucy's head. One that fits what happened just as well. Maybe better. Lucy presses her knee harder into Mae's throat and she stills.

'Yes, your baby-faced sister slammed a rock into her mother's skull in a fit of rage, something the woman probably had coming. But I don't think she fell into the fountain.'

'I don't care,' Mae grinds out. But again, Mae's eyes give her away. She can hear the sincerity in Lucy's voice. She's interested.

Or she figures the energy Lucy's wasting talking will help her. She's powerful and brilliant and has experience spinning the facts to suit her story. Lucy shifts and more of her weight is on Mae's neck. Her eyes bulge.

Could Lucy hold her long enough to truly end this? Does she have it in her?

Mae smirks.

No.

Lucy eases away and nearly loses her grip as Mae arches her back with a snarl.

'Listen,' Lucy begs. 'My nan was there that night. She argued about what working here had done to my grandfather, threatened her with a lawsuit. Your mother taunted her that she'd be tied up in legal battles until she was dead like my grandfather. Nan lost her temper.' The words slur a little, but Lucy can see it so clearly. Mae has relaxed a fraction, giving Lucy's screaming muscles a reprieve. 'Nan pushed, with all the rage of her beloved husband's agonising death, and your mother, dazed from Anabelle's blow, fell into the water. Effectively, Nan drowned her.'

'The ring?'

'Picked up afterwards in panic, hidden for nineteen years when she didn't know what to do with it. I have it, you saw it on my hand. For a while I thought it was my great-grandmother's, but it must be your mother's. What about it is so important?'

'You don't know?'

'Clearly.'

'It was given to my grandparents in exchange for a loan that allowed Judy's mother to keep her child. Mother took a shine to it, had the rose and thorn engraved.'

Lucy suddenly understands the ring was a symbol of Brooke's power. Lucy can imagine what it must have felt like for her grandmother to see her boss wearing the family heirloom, flaunting it. 'That's even more motive.'

Mae snorts her disdain. 'Even if that's true. So what?'

'I'll tell the police everything. Nan is dead, it won't hurt her. No one else needs to die.'

Mae's head tilts.

'Think about it.' Lucy's begging now. 'We can work together.'

A door slams up at the house. There's a faint buzz, then the garden is lit up like a football field. Lucy reels back, squinting to adjust.

Mae jerks her head, lifts and twists, and then she's out from under Lucy.

Lucy scrabbles to hold on but her limbs don't obey. Too stiff and sore from holding so tight. She falls back into some bushes.

Lit up in terrible silhouette, Mae dives across the ground and rolls up on to her feet a little distance away. Gun in hand, but right by the edge of the cliff.

Hades growls and lumbers to stand in front of Lucy, his hackles raised in warning.

'The marks from that first night didn't come out,' she says conversationally, gun pointing straight at Lucy and Hades. 'And I really liked that jacket.'

'Away,' Lucy screams. She kicks out at Hades' rump, her toe barely grazing fur. 'Stupid, stupid dog. Get away from me. Go home.'

Mae's lifting the gun.

Maybe she's a good enough shot to hit Lucy and miss Hades. But his muscles are bunching, ready to leap. He'll get in the way.

'No.' The cry rips from Lucy's throat. Of all the times to decide he's hers. 'I never even wanted a dog. Hades! Go! Go home. Get away.' But sobs have choked her voice and he's not listening. He never listens.

Lucy drags herself forward, trying to push him away, bringing herself close enough to see the glitter of glass from the light she smashed, twinkling in Mae's hair.

'Put down the gun.'

Is it the police? Lucy turns towards the command.

It's Jake. He's approaching from the deep shadows beneath one of the giant golden elm trees. His white shirt is stuck to his skin, showing muscles ready to spring into action. 'Ms Whitlam, I asked you to put down the weapon. The police are coming. They know it's an active armed offender.'

'I'll put it down once my attacker is dead,' Mae sneers, and lifts her chin without sparing him a glance.

'I don't want to have to fire,' he says, but Lucy can't see a weapon.

Mae hesitates then takes a few steps and swings the gun around towards him. 'Bit too late to play the good guy, isn't it?'

33

PRESENT DAY

'What does she mean?' Lucy cries. 'Tell me, Jake.'

'Yes,' Mae adds. 'Why don't you explain? The years of deals and looking the other way that benefited both of us, the long nights keeping each other warm. Thanks, by the way, for keeping an eye on her for me the last few days. Trailing her and telling me about the lawyers.' Mae smirks. 'There's no bonus for whatever else you did with her.'

Even though Lucy suspected he was hiding something, she never really thought... 'Please, Jake, tell me she's lying.'

Jake's eyes are hollow and his shoulders slumped, the usual proud line of his back missing. 'I just wanted to be something in this town. I didn't know what she was hiding or I'd never...' He swallows hard. 'It was just small things at first, and yeah, there was sex, it's not like I ever said I was a monk. But I spent time with you because I wanted to. Like getting here tonight, that was because I saw the light flash in the tower and I remembered what you said. I came here for you. We had something real, Lucy, you know that.'

There's something in his voice that makes Lucy believe him, but she believes Mae, too. This town, this family, it's impossible for it to be any other way, not for someone like Jake, someone like Lucy.

'I know,' Lucy whispers, but she can't tell if he hears.

He moves towards Mae. 'Drop the gun.'

She shakes her head. 'It will be terrible when I have to explain that the two of you were in this together. Nobody likes a bad cop.'

Lucy can see the certainty in her profile, outlined by the garden lights with the blackness of the distant ocean meeting sky. She's going to do it. So bloody confident in her privilege and her power. She'll kill them both.

Her shoulders shift. Brace to fire.

Lucy launches without thinking. Fuelled by rage. She can't let this happen.

Bang.

She feels the recoil of it a moment after her good shoulder hits the soft expanse of Mae's exposed side. The jolt of it rips a scream from her throat.

'Lucy,' Jake cries.

Then Mae and Lucy are landing, and black expands in a void beyond Mae's snarling face. It's the edge of the cliff. Lucy scrambles back, pain making pinpricks of light around everything. 'Look out.'

But Lucy isn't sure who she's warning.

Mae's eyes are fixed on Lucy. There's no gun in her hand now; maybe it went over. Blood trickles from where she's scraped her temple on the rock. She's as gorgeous as the first day they met. Murderer chic.

There's the faint clatter of pebbles tumbling down the cliff, almost drowned by the sounds of people approaching through the garden.

Mae's mouth lifts at one side. 'Didn't think you had it in you.' The ground shifts beneath her and she reaches out towards Lucy.

Automatically, Lucy reaches too.

Derision flares in Mae's eyes as she snatches her hand away. Then she's gone, over the edge. Lucy crawls towards it, her brain refusing to believe Mae's really fallen.

'Jake?' Lucy calls.

But there's no answer.

Afraid to turn her back on the threat of Mae, Lucy leans over the edge of the cliff. She half expects to see Mae miraculously unscathed in the water, but her body is crumpled unnaturally on an outcrop about halfway down. The angle of her head makes the acid claw again at Lucy's throat.

As she shuffles back to safer ground, a damp nose nudges her good side, then a rough tongue slides along her cheek. Hades. 'Thanks, big fella. If you hadn't…' Her throat closes over. She's going to be…

She vomits on to the grass. Heaving and heaving, until she's whimpering with what the whole-body convulsions are doing to her arm. The world goes wavy at the edges but she fights it; she needs to know what happened to Jake.

'Steady there.' It's a stranger, a paramedic whose arm comes around Lucy to support her. 'We're here to help.'

'What about Jake?' Lucy says. 'Mae fired and I don't know if he…'

Her voice trails off as she sees the paramedic's face.

No, no, no.

'He can't be dead, he can't be.'

But before the paramedic can answer, the black closes in.

Lucy wakes in the ambulance to a different paramedic

explaining to her how she'll be taken to the nearest hospital, and there she tries her best to answer all their questions, grading her pain out of ten and describing what happened. The officer gives her a green tube to suck on, and its effects make the ambulance ride into the hospital, and all the check overs that follow in emergency, a blur. Oblivion beckons but no one can tell her what happened to Jake beyond that there was another patient taken to hospital in another ambulance.

Despite the fuzziness, she can't forget that Mae's dead.

Lucy retches more than once over a green bowl someone hands her, but there's nothing much left inside her to bring up. Her eyes sting but no tears come. Not for Mae, not for herself. And as for Jake, there are only questions that no one seems to be willing to answer.

In emergency, the doctor explains that Lucy's gunshot is only a flesh wound and that she should be fine. The ambulance officer cut away the sleeve of the hoodie back at the house to examine where she was hit, but a nurse eases her into a gown and cleans her up a bit before theatre. The same doctor returns to stitch up the gash that Lucy's shocked and drugged-up brain keeps confusing with the open grave site on the beach.

After she's returned to her room, she's able to wash herself a little more and cleanse the horrible taste from her mouth before nibbling at some red jelly the nurse finds in the children's ward for her when she can't stomach the prospect of anything else.

When she's left alone in the curtained-off room, she turns on the small, grainy screen to try to drown her thoughts.

The same journalist from Jan's café that night with Anabelle stands outside the Whitlams' gates.

'Police aren't commenting but sources suggest that without the brave actions of a local off-duty policeman at the scene tonight, more than one life would have been tragically lost. Sergeant Jake Parker is recovering in hospital, along with another victim who has not yet been named.'

The screen shows Jake being carried into an ambulance and Lucy feels some of the tightness in her chest relax. The journalist keeps talking about Jake's decorated career and service to the community. The details are like a mosquito buzzing right inside Lucy's brain, and she soon switches it off.

He's being painted as a hero and she's not sure how that fits with all that Mae said. Her memories of Mae's accusations and Jake's response shift in her head like the softest sand on the beach.

How much of it was real?

Police officers she doesn't recognise come by and Lucy tells them all she can remember. Mae luring her to the house with the messages and wig. The gun and the threats. Jake trying to reason with her. That Lucy reached out to stop Mae falling. She describes where she left blood and how Mae admitted the whole family were covering for Anabelle.

Lucy doesn't mention Nan.

The Whitlams don't deserve it, and anyway there's no proof. Neither does she mention what Mae said about Jake, but it doesn't mean she can forget. Where's the line between hero who saved her life and dirty cop?

A nurse comes and fusses pointedly over Lucy's chart and the police take the hint and promise to return with more questions when she's feeling better. Finally, to the soft hum of the hospital activities and the regular beep of the machines, Lucy sleeps.

34

PRESENT DAY

Lucy wakes to near darkness and a figure sitting on the side of her bed. A man close enough that he could have already smothered her with a pillow, and she'd have never woken.

Reflexively, she tugs the blanket up to cover herself like an old nana, aghast at a man in her room.

Dante smiles a slow, knowing grin. 'I'm not here for your virtue.'

She looks for the emergency bell and discovers it's out of reach. 'What do you want?'

'To give you an opportunity to thank me,' he says. He's passing something small from hand to hand in the rhythmic way of someone deep in thought.

'What should I thank you for?' Lucy asks. But it's only to buy time to calculate whether to run or scream. It might be the middle of the night and this a private room, but someone will come.

'Stop it,' he says, still overtly relaxed, but there's a new edge to his voice.

'Stop what?'

'The panicked estimating that's so obvious on your face. The whole fight or flight thing, like you're under attack. I am not going to hurt you.'

The assurance gives Lucy little comfort, but not wanting to antagonise him, she makes sure he sees her settling back into the pillow. 'So I'm thanking you?'

'Yes. Men, I have found, are so predictable. Women too, to be fair. But men in particular. I only had to see how he looked at you to know how he'd react to a simple suggestion. I'm just sorry it took so long.'

He reaches out and Lucy flinches, but his touch on her shoulder is gentle. 'I didn't want you to get hurt,' he says. 'You were never a target in all of this.'

It's like she's arrived in the middle of the conversation. 'Is it Jake?'

'At last you understand. It's so easy to make a suggestion, in this case a simple mention of your name. Hint at having a special interest in you and wondering where you'd gone so suddenly.' He raises his eyebrows suggestively. 'It doesn't take much to bring out the primate in a guy. Triggered like that, I knew he'd go looking for you. He had to.'

'You made it so Jake would come looking for me?'

An apologetic wince. 'I didn't think it would take him so long. You must have done a number on the guy. Oh well, he got there in the end.'

Lucy suddenly gets it. She somehow has Dante to thank for Jake coming to the house to find her. Or at least, that's what the boy thinks. It probably is more likely than the story Jake shared about seeing the light in Anabelle's tower.

Dante's gaze is expectant. It seems that in his head he's controlled the evening and just him getting into her room at this hour shows he's resourceful, if not dangerous.

Lucy pushes the required words out of her cramped throat. 'Thank you.'

'You're welcome,' he says, clearly pleased. 'You must have guessed by now that's not the only reason I'm here.'

He's possibly giving Lucy more credit than she deserves. With everything that's happened, she's not exactly at her best.

But he's orchestrating this thing, and he takes her silence as agreement.

He holds out his hand, now curled into a fist, turns it palm up and slowly, theatrically opens it, finger by finger. Until, despite the low light, she can see what he's holding. A fine, golden circle with three small diamonds and a distinctive engraving.

'The ring.'

'Brooke Whitlam's ring,' he says. 'It was all about this, really. Who had it? Who took it? Why?'

She waits for his explanation, but her brain is working. *Dante. The ring.* It's like she's staring at a picture on the ocean floor but the waves are moving and the sand churning and she can't make it clear.

'Your great-grandparents were the first to own the cottage outright,' he says. 'Before that, it was part of the property on the hill. There are copies of all the keys to every building up there if you know where to look. Including your grandparents' home.'

'But Mae had Harry break in.'

He shrugs. 'Not exactly slumming it with the help, was she? Wouldn't know half of what was in different sheds and cupboards away from the main house. I had a copy made weeks ago. It was easy enough to get in and leave a little something for Judy's granddaughter to find once the property manager who works – sorry, past tense, of course – worked for Mae, let us know you were coming. Like in a set of old drawers.'

'Why?' she asks, because he has to be telling the truth. Otherwise, how would he know where she found it?

'To get you thinking, to stir up the past. I thought you'd take it to Mae and she'd be worried who knew their little secret.' Amusement plays around his mouth. 'Her panic when she learned I'd reported a strange plastic-wrapped object unearthed on their land was delicious. It only took a suggestion that they'd left other evidence behind for Mae to drop any idea of hurrying me out of the picture. She kept me close to keep me under control, but that was exactly what I wanted.' He shrugs. 'It was time for Brooke Whitlam to be found. Took a bit of digging to help the weather so the body could be discovered but cleaning up the property is part of my role.'

Mae's protectiveness of Dante makes sense to Lucy now. She needed him to behave. But the rest of it is still puzzling.

'Are you saying you planted the ring? But it's been missing since that night. Mae said so. How could you possibly have it after all these years?'

'How?' he says. 'My mother took it from the bitch's dead body.' Then his brows lower and his mouth twists. 'That woman wanted her to have an abortion. She thought that I was simply a problem she could remove with an envelope filled with cash, and a private doctor's appointment in the city. Got a maid to drive Mama there like it was just another errand.'

'What woman?' But this Lucy can guess and she says it before he can respond. 'Brooke Whitlam.'

He sighs. 'They argued about keeping me, that night by the fountain. Mama pushed her. Funny though, she was ripe for a lot of arguments that night. Someone was going to do it properly. And the rest of that family certainly deserve to be punished for it. Particularly Mae, disposing of a housekeeper who learned about their involvement like she was taking out trash.' He's been staring off a little but now he looks at Lucy. 'That was clever. I might not have worked that out if not for you and your boyfriend. Anyway, my mother saw them deal with Brooke Whitlam's body and it was easy enough from her description to find it and help nature deliver the shoe below the jetty where someone could find it. It was quite the thing to tangle it to keep the bones attached. It needed to get them looking for the rest of the body.'

He seems to expect her to say something but she's still trying to put everything together. Who is his mother?

'As for the other Whitlams, well, money buys a lot and I can't see any of them really suffering from this for too long, not with those lawyers. Other than Grant. He's got a short, miserable road ahead.'

'Vanessa!' she says as it clicks. Her two girls that Lucy found on her social media must have been with a new partner. 'Mr Whitlam's graduate student is your mother.' She'd thought they had a strong connection, but dismissed it because of Mr Whitlam and Marcelo. 'How though? Isn't Mr Whitlam gay?'

Dante shakes his head, disappointed. And there's something in his expression, something painfully familiar right here in this bed, in the half-light.

And then Lucy really gets it.

At last.

The charm, looks, charisma. The attraction she struggled to ignore, despite feeling simultaneously repulsed. Combined with her memory of the time nineteen years ago she saw Vanessa walking away from the pool house just before being seduced herself in the pool. 'You're Harry's. Of course, you are Harry's son.'

Dante smiles. 'Before you get any ideas about blowing this open or telling someone, Harry already knows. About our relationship anyway.' He adopts a suitably earnest expression. 'I went to my father tonight, obviously worried about revealing our real relationship. He welcomed me with open arms. He's looking forward to getting to know me better, and absolutely understands why I was afraid to come forward sooner. Really, if you think about it, it's fortunate that he and Aunty Anabelle will have someone up at the house who knows how it's all run. Someone who's family.'

Part of Lucy wonders if she should warn Harry about Dante, but not for long. If he was dumb enough to screw around at seventeen without protection, then he needs to take responsibility. She suspects Dante will have control over everything soon enough and maybe he deserves it as much as any one of them.

More importantly: 'Does that mean Nan wasn't involved?'

'She wasn't, but you can be sure she wanted Brooke Whitlam dead. So many did, but only my mother had the strength to hold that woman under the water, to ignore her pitiful struggles and make sure she was dead. And they thought it was Anabelle? One blow and she ran for big sister, horrified by what she'd done to their mother. They might have saved her, if Mama hadn't got there first.'

The guilty weight Lucy's been carrying on her chest lifts. Not that she didn't understand Nan's rage at what they did to her husband, but it's nice to know she's not a killer.

He flips the ring in the air and catches it. Then stands. 'I will let you rest. You'll work out soon enough that you have no proof about any of what I've told you. I just thought you'd want to know what really happened.'

With him about to walk out, she can't resist asking. 'You knew that Jake was in her pocket, didn't you?'

He shrugs. 'I saw through the good guy cop persona. He didn't like it.'

There's an ache in Lucy's chest every time she thinks of Jake. She's dreading seeing him again, but glad it's possible when she feared him dead along with Mae.

Dante crosses to the door, pauses and smiles. 'You're acting all surprised but you're not. Not really. Because you walked right past the fountain that night and didn't do anything to try to save her. Mama was there in the shadows and she says there's no way you didn't see Brooke Whitlam in the water.'

Her stomach lurches. 'I didn't.'

But is she trying to convince him or herself? She closes her eyes and Brooke Whitlam is there, pale beneath the surface of the water like she's been waiting all this time for Lucy to remember.

But before she can work out if it's memory or imagination, the exhaustion and medication take over, lulling her back to sleep. This sleep is filled with snatches from that night, conversations she couldn't possibly have heard and Brooke Whitlam's face under the water.

When Lucy wakes again, there's a different slumped figure, lightly snoring, in the chair beside the bed. Her long legs are stretched out, her bushy brown hair is up in a messy bun and her face is all squished on the side of the chair, drool shining on her chin.

Lucy blinks, but Dr Jasmine Ross, Brian's daughter, is still there.

There's no sign of Dante.

Jasmine startles awake, perhaps sensing the change in Lucy's breathing, and catches her glasses just before they slip off her nose. 'Lucy?'

'I'm okay,' Lucy says quickly.

A smile spreads across Jasmine's features and she straightens, wiping her face with the back of her hand. 'How is the arm?' she asks in a doctor voice.

'Fine.' Lucy shifts her arm to prove it and winces. The morphine coming in via a drip isn't good enough for silly demonstrations.

Jasmine raises her eyebrows meaningfully. 'Careful, you. I came as soon as they called me, but I made sure Hades was safe at the cottage before I came in. Figured you'd be out for a bit.'

'They called you?'

She shrugs. 'Probably found me through Dad's information.'

'And you came?'

Her expression softens; she reaches out and touches Lucy's good arm gently. 'And I came.'

Lucy closes her eyes, the prickling threat of tears hard to control. Having Jasmine there after all that's happened is more than her emotions can handle.

Jasmine doesn't press, giving Lucy time to pull herself together.

'I tried to save her,' Lucy says when she can talk.

Jasmine listens then, as Lucy tells her as much as she can about the night and everything leading up to it. She skims over details about Harry and Jake, not wanting to go there with Brian's daughter. And she doesn't share her theory about Nan.

She shares what she told the police.

What is truth anyway? Guessing and fearing that Nan

might be involved? Lucy told them what they should be able to prove. She's not going to sully her nan's name for the sake of speculation.

'Jake sounds like one of the good guys,' Jasmine says when Lucy finishes. 'They reported how he came to your rescue, took a bullet in the chest.'

Tears threaten again for Lucy, hearing it put into words. 'Have you heard anything about how he's doing?'

'Stable for now but he's got a big night ahead of him.'

Lucy can't help but think about what he admitted with Mae. 'If he hadn't come looking for me... Well, I'll always be grateful. I just hope I get a chance to tell him so.'

'The doctors here aren't as bad as I thought they would be. He's in good hands.'

Quiet settles between them.

Distant sounds of the hospital filter through, despite what must be the late hour. Lucy's mind veers away from her memories of earlier, self-protection from the pain of it. She remembers the art show and wonders who won the prize. Or whether the police stormed the fancy barn and arrested the Whitlams before it could be announced.

'As soon as I clear everything, I'm selling the cottage,' Lucy blurts.

Jasmine probably doesn't care but Lucy needs to say it aloud for herself. She's done with the Whitlams. All of them. Every time she thinks of Harry she thinks of the dead, vacant look in his eyes when they were in bed, and the fact that he knew at least something of Mae's plan. There's no desire for him left.

But she knows at some point she'll need to talk to Jake. If he survives.

35

PRESENT DAY

With Jasmine's help, it doesn't take long for Lucy to finish packing up Nan's place.

A week to the day after the confrontation with Mae, Lucy walks through the small cottage for the last time. She glances into each room, ostensibly to check for anything left behind, but really she's saying goodbye. To the peeling paint, the rattling window over the sink and the view of the Whitlam house, but she'll take the precious memories of her grandmother with her. Finally, she's at the front door; the one 'only for visitors', as Nan always said. It's right that Lucy leaves this way; she's only ever been passing through Queen's Point.

Her arm aches a little as she pulls the door closed, the wound hidden under her warm jacket well on its way to being healed. If only the memory of Mae's sneering face as she went over the edge rather than accept Lucy's help could be banished so easily.

Lucy spoke in more depth to the detectives on her second day in hospital. She explained again about Mae's plan to lure her to the house and frame her to cover for her sister, as well as her memory of the wig in Anabelle's room and possibly overhearing Anabelle by the fountain.

Her warning to Mae that the police were close to working everything out anyway wasn't unfounded. As Lucy guessed, Jake had linked the burned-out car and then the woman in the accident to Mae.

After speaking to Lucy, the police questioned Anabelle again. Reeling from the shock of her sister's death, Anabelle admitted to striking her mother with a stone from the garden that night with enough force to explain the skull fracture, but insisted she had no knowledge of Mae's plan to frame Lucy.

With Mae having been handed the business reins, it was Brooke Whitlam's social media that interested the public. How could they maintain it for that long?

But once it became clear the whole family knew Brooke was dead, and that they'd dropped Brooke Whitlam's few friends before emails were a thing, the media moved on to the collapse of the carefully constructed cover story. Lucy read online that unnamed sources working on the case revealed that each of the remaining Whitlams declared Mae responsible for the years of cover-up. They cited her as the one who came up with the plan to pretend Brooke Whitlam was still alive. According to her family, they wanted to go to the police the night it happened, but she insisted they unite for Anabelle's sake and hide the body.

All of that might even be true.

Lucy doesn't have any real proof that anyone other than Mae knew about her being lured to the house, but she's sure they were all involved. Simply because they've always protected each other.

They've closed ranks tighter than ever before. Anabelle and Harry supporting each other with Mr Whitlam in the background.

Nan didn't come up in any of it. Whoever sent Lucy the message before the art show was lying, they hadn't found DNA on the hate mail so she'll never know for sure if Nan sent them or not. Her connection to any of it is weak without Brooke Whitlam's ring. And Dante has that. Lucy wondered if their conversation in hospital was a dream but the ring was missing when she'd looked for it at the cottage.

A nudge from Hades' damp nose breaks Lucy from her thoughts. She locks the door and heads down to where Jasmine is waiting next to her car.

'Ready?' Jasmine asks.

Lucy nods. 'Do you mind taking Hades? There's one stop I need to make on the way back to Adelaide.'

'Sure.' Jasmine is heading to Lucy's place anyway. She doesn't ask for details but she can probably guess where Lucy's going.

Once, Lucy would have taken the younger woman's silence as disinterest but she's learning more about her step-daughter and understands that if she needs to talk, Jasmine will listen. Otherwise, she's not one for prying.

No one questions Lucy's right to be there as she makes her way to Jake's private room at the hospital. The location is given to her immediately when she says who she is; her spiel about wanting to thank him for saving her life isn't required.

He's alone, his eyes closed, and she lingers in the doorway to study him.

He looks better than she'd feared after hearing Jasmine's blunt descriptions of lung collapse and drowning in his own blood. He's still attached to monitors after his most recent surgery but when his eyes open, they're clear.

He blinks and registers her standing by the door. His mouth curves and she feels a tug of the old attraction. 'Come in.'

She edges into the room but doesn't risk hurting him with a kiss to the cheek. The pulled-up blanket can't hide the tubes and bandages around his torso.

'How are you?' she asks when she can't think of a single other thing to say.

His mouth kicks up on one side. 'I'll live.' His gaze searches her face, then runs over her body as if to make sure she's in one piece 'You?'

'Fine.'

He must read something in her expression. 'You're leaving town?'

'It's time.' Her boss seemed keen for her to return in her most recent email, but Lucy's thinking that she'll take another couple of weeks and make sure going back is what she really wants to do. There's a whole world she hasn't seen yet.

She doesn't extend an offer for Jake to come and visit and he doesn't suggest it. Whatever was between them died with Mae in the garden of the Whitlam house.

She wants to believe he was one of the good guys who went a bit off track. He wouldn't be the only one led astray by a Whitlam. But maybe she didn't know him as well as she thought. She kept thinking he reminded her of Brian but it could be she just wanted to see her husband in someone, giving Jake credit that he didn't deserve.

She swallows hard. 'Thank you.' Her voice catches and she has to start again. 'Thank you for coming that night. If you hadn't, I don't know what would have happened.'

He lifts his hand off the bed as though to brush off her

thanks. 'I think we both saved each other. She would have finished me off.'

Lucy nods because she has no doubt that Mae wouldn't have left any loose ends. She gestures to the sea of flowers on every surface around the room. 'Seems you've got some admirers.'

'The media haven't hurt in that regard. I'll not want for meals when I get out of here, nor company.'

She understands that he's letting her off the hook. Telling her she doesn't need to hang around out of some sort of guilt. 'If there's anything I can do,' she says half-heartedly.

'I'll be sure to let you know.'

But he won't. They both know it.

'I just need to know if it was all on her orders?' Lucy can't help the question.

He shakes his head, wincing as the movement shifts his body. 'No.'

It's simple, but maybe it's enough. 'I won't be adding to my official police statement,' she says, hoping he understands, aware that they're not truly alone in the busy hospital. What Mae said that night about Jake and that he admitted about bending rules won't be repeated by her.

She asks for no guarantees about him cleaning up his act. Looking at him in the bed, she figures he'll have enough on his plate getting back to the job at all.

'Thank you,' he murmurs. 'You know, I've done good things for this town.' His eyes plead with Lucy to understand.

She looks away. He's probably talking about the petty criminals he's kept off the street but her thoughts go to her grandmother and the visit he made to the nursing home before she died. From what she's seen of him looking out for the elderly swimmers, that's typical of his role in the town as much as anything else he's done.

It's not up to her to judge someone for being seduced by a Whitlam into making a few poor decisions.

Lucy takes a step to the door and then turns back to him and sets herself. 'Mae said something else that night that I think you need to hear.'

His brow creases in question.

The words to change someone's past don't come easily for Lucy. 'It was about your dad. I think he knew something about what they did with Brooke Whitlam.'

'My dad,' he repeats, obviously trying to make sense of it.

'You said yourself he's unaccounted for that night after the fight. What if he went down to the point after the fight to sleep it off and caught them with the body? They would have tried to distract him with some cover story, but he was drunk, not stupid.'

'He would have gone to the police.'

'Not if he wasn't sure. Not if he needed some time to find proof.' Lucy bites her lip. 'I don't think he killed himself.'

Jake's eyes close but not fast enough to disguise the warring hope and devastation. 'Mae couldn't have—'

'She could, with help. And they were all in on Brooke Whitlam's death. They couldn't start feeling squeamish just because your dad didn't deserve to die.'

Lucy sees in her head Harry's early paintings. Violence and pain. A mind not resting easy.

Jake drags a hand over his eyes. 'There's no way to be certain.'

'That's why I didn't know if I should tell you.'

When he takes his hand away from his face, it's damp with unshed tears. 'I'm glad you did. Or at least, I think I am.'

She nods. 'Goodbye, Jake.'

'Goodbye, Lucy Antonello.'

'It's Ross,' she corrects him.

Then she heads out of the hospital into the gloomy afternoon and hits the road back to Adelaide. As her car climbs the hill from the town, she doesn't slow for one last glimpse back, so she doesn't notice the break in the clouds over the huge white house at Queen's Point.

There's a hint of sunshine.

ACKNOWLEDGEMENTS

It takes the combined efforts of many to produce a published book and I offer my heartfelt thanks to anyone not explicitly mentioned below.

Thank you to the amazing team at Head of Zeus Publishing. You have been wonderful to work with at every stage. Special thanks to Martina Arzu who took a chance and then brought out the best in me and this story. Thanks to Jenni Davis for the copyedits and Emma Rogers for the incredible cover. Thanks also to the Australian Bloomsbury team for all your support.

Special thanks to Hattie Grünewald for her incredible insight and support and for appreciating the 10-minute version of 'All Too Well'. Thanks too, to all the team at The Blair Partnership for always being in my corner.

Much thanks to Sergeant Sean Patton, SA Police, for your help answering my questions on country policing in SA. All mistakes are my own and your advice is much appreciated. Thanks also to Nat for putting us in touch.

Merci beaucoup to the music teachers at my daughter's school who inspired the French exchange student, Andre. Hope they don't mind that she brought home this story. Teachers can have such an impact on people's lives and

I've had some wonderful teachers including my high school English teacher Mrs Dowd, thank you.

My writing friends keep me showing up to work at the computer every day. Sharing the ups and downs of creating a story with people who understand makes everything a little easier. I've met so many wonderful writers and readers at events and online, and it's inspiring to be around you all.

To the Monday Murder Group who meet online to talk all things crime book related. Bev, Cat, Con, Elle, Gayle, Liam and Louise, thanks for the feedback and the friendship and support.

Thanks to the Writers Camp girls for the Voxes that help to keep me sane. Lisa Ireland and Emily Madden you're so appreciated. Thanks to Amanda Knight for reading an early draft of this and helping with brainstorming and general panicked questions on a daily basis. And, of course, to Rach Johns for all of the above and the steadfast insistence that this would happen. I couldn't have done this without you all.

Thanks to my family and friends for your love and support. Especially to Caroline, Rowan, Susan, Amy, Alison and Julie.

This book wouldn't have been written without the holidays I spent as a child at one of my favourite places in the world. Thanks so much to all of the Tuckers for having us stay.

Although Queen's Point is a fictional town, it's located in a real part of South Australia, the Yorke Peninsula. I would like to acknowledge the Narungga people as the custodians of this land and pay my respects to their elders past and present.

Thanks to Aunty Anne for the interview that helped begin this new journey. And remembering Uncle Ron who'll always hold a special place in my heart.

Also, many thanks to Dick and Shirley.

To Wendy, for our messages back when this book was just an idea. I wish you could be here to read it.

My Dad passed away as this book was going to print after a long battle with Parkinson's, supported the whole time at home by Lyn – thank you. Wishing you peace now, Dad, and I'd like to think you heard me telling you about this one and I believe you would have loved it.

Thank you to my sisters and their families, especially to Mitch and Chloe – you both are always happy to answer my questions when various characters end up your age. Fi and Kirst, this book is dedicated to you both, and I hope you know how much I adore and appreciate you. No one understands like a sister. As always, thanks Mum. I miss you every day – your belief in me is something I'll always treasure. Reading at your side shaped so much of who I am.

Thanks to my kids. Amelie, James and Claire. You three are growing into such amazing humans and I marvel at you every day. I am so very lucky to know you and so much prouder of you than you can imagine.

To Dave. It's been hard these last couple of years but there's no one else I'd rather go through each day alongside (with Harriet there too, of course). I love you. Thanks for everything. Always.